DATE DUE

BEFORE

THE

DAWN

KAPCO

OTHER BOOKS AND BOOKS ON CASSETTE
BY CAROL WARBURTON:

Edge of Night

BEFORE THE DAWN

A Novel

Carol Warburton

Covenant Communications, Inc.

To my mother,
Evalina Whipple Payne—
my angel on the other side.

My special thanks to Nancy Hopkins of Tillamook, Oregon, who introduced me to the beautiful Tillamook Valley and the grandeur of the rugged Oregon coast. Also to Dorothy Keddington, Ka Hancock, and Charlene Raddon, who discovered Oregon with me. Without your encouragement and helpful insights, this novel would never have come to be.

Cover painting *Next Day* © William Whitaker.

Cover design copyrighted 2003 by Covenant Communications, Inc.

Published by Covenant Communications, Inc.
American Fork, Utah

This is a work of fiction. The characters, names, incidents, places, and dialogue are products of the author's imagination and are not to be construed as real.

Printed in the United States of America
First Printing: February 2003

10 09 08 07 06 05 04 03   10 9 8 7 6 5 4 3 2 1

ISBN 1-59156-173-6

Library of Congress Cataloging-in-Publication Data

Warburton, Carol, 1937-
    Before the dawn : a novel / Carol Warburton.
        p.   cm.
    ISBN 1-59156-173-6 (alk. paper)
    1. Willamette River Valley (Or.)--Fiction. 2. Runaway husbands--Fiction. 3. Single mothers--Fiction. 4. Pregnant women--Fiction. 5. Women pioneers--Fiction. I. Title
    PS3623.A69 B4 2003
    813'.6--dc21   2002041212

PROLOGUE

Missouri—1858

The slap of a hand against flesh echoed throughout the tiny kitchen. My fingers flew to my cheek, my eyes staring in disbelief at the man who stood with his hand still raised.

Jacob's angry brown eyes glared back at me, his mouth pulled into an ugly grimace. "That'll teach you to keep your trap shut. I'm tired of your yammering . . . always tellin' me what to do." His words were slurred, and spittle sprayed onto his unshaven chin.

"Don't you ever hit me again," I hissed. Anger and fear trembled through my words. I took a deep breath and fought to hide my fear. "Not ever," I repeated.

For a second I glimpsed Jacob's shame—shame quickly replaced with a sneer. "Then learn to keep your mouth shut. How I spend money is my business . . . not yours."

Jacob turned and stalked across the room, his steps unsteady as he reached for the door. I was glad to see him go, wishing with all my heart I'd never see him again.

"What have I done?" I whispered. It was a question I frequently asked myself, regret at having married Jacob Mueller a daily presence at my table. Then the determination that had helped me weather my three-year marriage to him set in. Sighing, I poured water into a basin to cool my throbbing cheek. I tried not to think of the near-empty flour barrel and the past-due payment on the farm while my lips formed the question again. "What have you done, Clarissa?"

* * *

Tillamook, Oregon—2003

Jessica Taylor followed the old man up the steep stairs to the half-attic, the boards creaking and the musty, closed-up smell of the stairwell filling her nostrils.

"Like I told you when you phoned . . . there's just this old trunk." He opened the door into the cramped room at the top of the stairs. "Think it belonged to my wife's grandmother . . . or maybe it was her great-grandmother." He paused and scratched his grizzled head. "I never paid much attention to things like that. Effie mentioned it a time or two when we were younger, but since we never had any children to pass it on to, the trunk kind of got forgotten." There was another pause and a regretful shake of the head. "Since Effie's passed on, I guess you've got as much right to the trunk as anyone."

The man's name was Bob Whiting, a name that hadn't meant anything to Jessica until three years of research had led her to the yellow-frame home in Tillamook. After the sweet experience in the temple with her ancestor Tamsin Yeager, Jessica had hoped to discover something about Tamsin's elusive sister Clarissa. She'd almost given up hope, but persistence and bits of information gleaned in genealogical libraries and from the Internet had finally borne fruit.

"Thank you so much, Mr. Whiting," Jessica said.

"Just call me Bob," he responded. "Though you'd probably thank me more if I was to give you some light so you can see better." His blue-veined hand reached for the switch. "There," he said as light turned shadows into a hodgepodge of boxes and cast-off furniture. "The trunk's over by the window."

Jessica's gaze followed his pointing finger to the rounded lid of a brown leather trunk.

"If you need me, I'll be downstairs," Bob said. "There's a couple of old chairs you can sit on, quilts too, if you get cold. Make yourself at home."

Jessica smiled at Bob's attempts at hospitality, but she scarcely heard him when he started down the stairs. By then she'd dropped to her knees by the trunk, not minding the cold of the dusty floor, her fingers exploring the short buckle that fastened into an ornate metal clasp. Was it locked?

She pushed at the fastening. Her impatient fingers found resistance, so she tried a second time with more force. She was rewarded by the click and release of the buckle, rewarded again when the heavy lid lifted and she leaned it back against the attic wall.

An array of items met her eager gaze as she looked into the musty trunk, mementos she hoped would reveal something about Clarissa Yeager, born in Massachusetts in 1839.

Jessica pulled a quilt off a stack of boxes and spread it on the floor next to the trunk. She felt a stirring of excitement when she reached for a pair of gold spectacles, then a cameo locket with an auburn curl tied with a blue ribbon tucked inside. Who had they belonged to, and why had Clarissa kept them?

More questions followed when Jessica took out a worn dog collar with the name "SAM" etched into the old leather. Then a china baby rattle decorated with tiny pink flowers and engraved with the name "Tamsin" and the year 1866 caught her eye. She stared at the name and date. Had Clarissa named one of her children after her sister Tamsin?

Jessica moved her jean-clad legs into a more comfortable position on the quilt, glad she'd worn the thick green sweater to ward off the attic's chill. When she turned back to the trunk, she closed her eyes and invited the past to gather itself around her, the past that had been the present to Clarissa, the time when she had sung or played from the yellowed sheet music lying next to the dog collar, the time when Clarissa had eagerly opened and read the bundled letters before tying them with pink ribbon.

She also found, carefully folded between sheets of tissue paper, a blue dress with sprigs of darker blue flowers covering the full skirt. Her first impulse was to take it out of the paper and hold it up, but caution whispered that something that old should be handled with care.

Laying the tissue-wrapped dress on the quilt with the rest of Clarissa's treasures, Jessica pushed back a lock of her blunt-cut, dark hair and looked at the three remaining items—an old daguerreotype of a man and woman and baby, a Bible, and a large leather-bound book that looked like a journal.

She took out the picture first. Through the wavy glass in the gold frame she saw a tall, good-looking man standing with his hand on the shoulder of a pretty woman who, though she did not smile, gave the impression of suppressed laughter, as did the child sitting on the woman's lap, her babyish head covered with thick curls.

"What a little angel," Jessica breathed. "And they're so happy. I can see it, feel it." When she looked more closely at the picture, she was able to make out the dark, sprigged flowers on the woman's skirt and realized it was the same dress that had been stored away in the trunk.

Her gaze returned to the daguerreotype, certain the woman must be Clarissa, the man her husband, and the child theirs. If only she could discover the husband's name, and the name of the baby too. Had there been other children?

Something told Jessica that the answers to her questions were in the brown leather book lying in the bottom of the trunk. She picked it up, feeling the smoothness of the leather as she settled it onto her lap. As she opened the cover she saw the swirl of old-fashioned writing. Beginning to read, she forgot about the chill of the attic and the hardness of the wood floor as the flowing script transported her back through the years and into the life of Clarissa Yeager, her great-grandmother's youngest sister.

CHAPTER 1

Oregon Territory—1861

I did not come to love a man, needing him like sun and air and the soft Oregon rain, until I'd been married six years—and the man I loved was not my husband. Lest one might think me wanton, I'd best explain. Wantonness was never in my nature, though I confess there were times in my youth when I was inclined to flirt, knowing others thought me more than comely. I must also confess I was not above studying myself in the mirror to confirm the fact.

Although I was sometimes vain, I was never one who could be untrue to my marriage vows. Yet to understand how I came to love and be loved by another man, I must first explain why I married Jacob Mueller.

When I was thirteen years of age, I moved with my widowed mother and elder sister to a farm near the village of Mickelboro, Massachusetts. Deacon Mickelson and his wife, Hester, took us in following the death of my father, letting us live in a cottage on their property. The deacon was inclined to spoil my sister Tamsin and me, his overbearing goodness putting him at odds with his wife, whose resentment of us was but barely concealed. Even so, we were happy. Tamsin and I spent many hours exploring a wooded headland towering over the Atlantic, its protecting height forming a little cove which we came to think of as our own. Our delight in tide pools, shells, and gulls skimming white-capped breakers vied with our enjoyment of evenings in the cottage. I can see us still, the two of us curled up close to Mother—Tamsin dark and angular, me fair and more rounded—listening while she read to us from Shakespeare or sometimes Tennyson. Often we would end the evening with music, me playing the pianoforte and singing while Mother and Tamsin listened, pleasure evident on their faces.

All went well until I approached my sixteenth birthday. Although Tamsin was a year and a half my senior, she was slower to mature, her slender frame still that of a girl, while mine took on the curves of womanhood. More than that, Tamsin was inclined to shyness, while my nature was more open. I dared while Tamsin hung back. I often took the lead, my confidence such that I never doubted I knew best. Perhaps it was my pertness and confidence that first attracted Deacon Mickelson, though my looks were a factor too. It was then that I first noticed him watching me in a manner that made me uncomfortable. For some months it was only looks and knowing glances. I tried without success to explain them away. Amos Mickelson was like a jovial, benevolent uncle. Surely I was mistaken in what I read in his eyes. But deep down I feared I was not.

Some months later, in fulfillment of a terrible premonition, Deacon Mickelson's looks progressed to a touch. A more timid girl might have looked away and pretended it hadn't happened. But I was not timid. To the deacon's surprise, I lifted my head and glared at him, taking satisfaction in the smear of red that came to his fleshy jowls, watching his gaze slide from me to Mother, who was in conversation with his wife.

That glare and my subsequent aloofness bought me time, months actually. Once again the deacon became a paragon of propriety when he came to call, which was frequent, for Mother's health wasn't good and he made it a practice to check on her almost daily. In time I relaxed my guard, laughing with Tamsin and Mother when he made a joke, convincing myself the deacon had learned his lesson and would not try his sly advances with me again. In this I erred.

The day it happened is still vivid in my mind. I had spent the afternoon with my friend Pru Steadman, the two of us giggling about boys and at the antics of her baby sister. My heart was light as I made my way home. I remember the song I hummed, the softness of the evening air, the smell of lilacs. Having stayed longer than planned, I entered the cottage with an apology on my lips. The spicy smell of brown Betty told me Tamsin had spent the afternoon baking. I hung my cloak on a peg by the back door and turned, expecting to see Mother and Tamsin lingering over supper. Instead, I found Amos Mickelson sitting at the kitchen table, his bulky legs stretching the fabric of his trousers, his arms folded across his barrel chest.

"Oh," I gasped, surprise making my voice breathless. "Where are Mother and Tamsin?"

"Gone to Wednesday prayer meeting with my wife and the servants."

"Why aren't you . . . ?" I began.

"I told them I had other business to attend to." The deacon smiled and patted his leg while his eyes traveled over me in a hungry manner. "Come sit on my knee like you used to and I'll explain."

I tried to quell my nervousness with a smile. "I'm not a little girl anymore, Deacon Mickelson. Nor do I think it proper for you to be here when my mother and sister aren't present." As I spoke, I reached for the door and jerked it open.

"Close the door," Amos commanded.

Heart pounding, my mind searched for escape. Could I outrun the bulky man? If only we lived closer to neighbors. If only . . .

The deacon's fist hit the table. "Close the door!" he shouted. He seemed to have read my thoughts, for before I could act, Amos was on his feet, the chair toppled, and the door slammed shut.

"There," he said. His features had lost their genial expression, his heavy jowls and face tightening, his blue eyes narrowing. "Lest you think to play any more tricks, let me inform you there's no one close enough to hear you if you scream." He paused and took a deep, satisfied breath. "I've planned this for days . . . though it took some talking to convince your mother that this evening's prayer meeting was the very thing to make her feel better."

Amos had hold of my arm, his fingers pressing into the tender flesh. "I don't want to hurt you," he went on, his voice softening. "Indeed, I hope this can be pleasurable for us both."

"*This?*" I demanded, striving to make my voice cold and steady. "Just what do you mean by *this?*"

"I think you know," Amos chuckled. "I've seen the way you look at the young men . . . how you smile and flirt. I want no more than what you've probably given to them. Only your company and a sweet kiss or two."

I won't attempt to describe what happened next, the fumbling and attempts to kiss me as he pulled me onto his knee. Instead of fighting off his advances, I sat stiff as a tree with my eyes closed, hoping that just as my glare had stopped his hungry looks before, so would my coldness stop him now. After several unsuccessful attempts to loosen my tight-pressed lips and force my stiff frame to curve against his neck and chest, he swore and pushed me off his lap. Rising to his feet, he glared down at me, his face tight and angry.

"Let me tell you, Miss High and Mighty—"

"Just what are you going to tell me?" Though I pretended bravado, my legs were shaking so hard I feared they'd collapse. *Please, help me . . . oh, please,* I prayed, for to faint or give way to tears would undo any advantage I held over the deacon.

"If you don't do just as I say, I'll stand up in church and denounce both you and your mother as harlots."

"That's a lie!" I cried. "No one will believe you."

"Ah, but they will." Amos waited, the satisfied smirk on his face telling me this had been long planned. "More than one of my friends has joked about the little house I keep right under my wife's nose . . . of my three doxies."

"You . . ." My control vanished and I flew at him, anger overriding fear, blind rage stilling good sense. For an instant my fingers found his face and raked the fleshy skin. Then he pinned me tight against him, his arms pressing so hard I feared he'd break my ribs. I couldn't breathe . . . couldn't think.

Just when I thought I would faint, the deacon's hold on me relaxed slightly. With my arms still pinned to my sides, he forced up my face, his fingers bruising and harsh like his voice when he spoke, "Do exactly as I say."

I closed my eyes and let his greedy mouth cover mine, but when his pudgy fingers began to work at the fastening of my bodice, I tried to twist away. *Please . . . oh, please.*

The barking of a dog broke through the wall of my fear. Amos stiffened and his head jerked up when a male voice called from the direction of his house. "Ho, there, Amos. Where are you?"

There was a moment of startled silence, the heavy pounding of the deacon's heart the only movement until his eyes flitted toward the door. "Meet me at the apple cellar on Friday afternoon. If you don't do exactly as I say, or if you breathe one word of what happened today, I swear I'll talk to the reverend and the two of us will denounce both you and your mother as harlots. Tamsin too."

Amos paused, his breathing ragged as if he'd been running, the scratch on the side of his face oozing blood. My breathing was as ragged as his, my starved lungs acting with a mind of their own. As he forced me to look into his narrowed eyes, I thought only of how much I loathed the man. *Pig eyes,* I thought. And he, like a huge boar who'd gone mad, could wipe out my life as I'd known it—Mother's and Tamsin's too. Unless I did as he said.

"Do you hear me, Clarissa? Do you understand?"

All of the fight had gone out of me. Even so, I had to force the word through my lips. "Yes," I whispered.

"Let me hear you say it again. This time louder."

"Yes."

"Good."Amos released me so suddenly I almost fell. I grabbed onto the table, only dimly aware he had gone to the door, wiping his bleeding face with the palm of his hand.

"I'll make you pay for this," he snarled. Then he closed the door and left.

* * *

It was several minutes before I could collect myself. My mind jerked in a dozen different directions, unable to stop long enough to consider any one thing. Thankfully by the time Tamsin and Mother returned from prayer meeting, I had fixed the fastenings on my dress and gotten my shattered thoughts into a semblance of order. I have no memory of what we talked about, only of the seemingly endless night as I lay staring up at the shadowy ceiling, forcing myself to lie still so Tamsin wouldn't wake and ask what was wrong.

What am I going to do? The question arose again and again, alternating with prayer and tears and the desire to throw myself on Tamsin and Mother and tell them what had transpired. Then I remembered the cold glint in the deacon's narrowed eyes, his hurtful hands on my face, his threats. I did not doubt he'd carry it out. Everyone in Mickelboro courted Amos Mickelson's goodwill. Didn't he own the largest farm and the only store? Even the town bore his grandfather's name.

My mind jumped and twisted throughout the long night, flailing against the clever trap the deacon had set for me. *What should I do? How can I escape?* Just before dawn the answer came. I grasped at it like a starving dog lunges at a fresh bone. The solution was not perfect, but it offered escape from the deacon's fumbling hands and hungry mouth.

Even so, I was loath to do it, for my escape could come only if I betrayed my sweet sister. Each time I think of what I did, I wish I could go back and change it. Although Tamsin was older than I was, in many ways it was as if she were younger. Even so, she had begun to blossom and catch the notice of some of the young men—in particular that of Jacob Mueller, the son of a neighboring farmer.

I think it was Tamsin's lack of confidence that made her think she had developed a liking for him. Jacob was not what you would call handsome, though if he wanted to he could be charming. Auburn hair and a quick wit made him stand out in a crowd. But he possessed a wandering eye, and it was well known that he was not overly fond of work.

More than once I'd warned Tamsin about Jacob's unsteadiness, and I felt heartened when she turned down his proposal to marry him and move to the West. Although my sister's no had been more against moving away than against his proposal, I was hopeful in time she would see him for what he was.

But time was a commodity I no longer had. If I didn't want to be caught in Amos's trap, I had to find a way to leave Mickelboro before Friday. *Tamsin doesn't really love him,* I rationalized. *And if I leave, it will protect her reputation . . . Mother's too.* I tried not to think of my sister's hurt and the shattering of her fragile confidence.

My plan came off so easily that my respect for Jacob fell even further. I only had to flirt and let him know I was not averse to moving out West and the deed was done. Early on Friday morning I met Jacob at the crossroads north of town. He came with his father's best team and wagon, the back loaded with tools and supplies he said his father had given to him, though I found out later he lied.

The smile and kiss I gave Jacob after he helped me onto the seat beside him was a sham. Inside I felt sick—for what I was doing to Tamsin, for my pretense of liking Jacob, and for myself. But I was desperate. Anything was better than suffering any more of the deacon's kisses, or worse. Anything.

I slept in the back of the wagon and Jacob on the ground for the first two nights. I would not let him do more than kiss me on the cheek until we found a justice of the peace to marry us in a sleepy town west of Holyoke.

I knew as soon as I married Jacob I had made a terrible mistake, but I was determined to make the best of it. I tried to make a success of our small farm in Illinois, then the one in Missouri. Jacob's restlessness and ne'er-do-well ways cost us dearly. When he heard of Oregon, a heaven on earth where land could be ours just for the taking, he determined we should go there. But as was Jacob's habit, he failed to realize it would require a commitment to hard work and dedication, qualities he did not possess.

I went with him, holding tight to the dream of free land with rich soil and trees and water aplenty, trees so big a man could build both a house and barn and use only one tree. Oregon was locked in my thoughts as we bounced and walked and fought our way across endless plains and treacherous rivers, over rugged mountains, through dust and heat and the threat of Indians.

My joy was full when we finally arrived in the Willamette Valley. The trees and lush vegetation lifted my heart in a way I'd never experienced before. But Jacob's enthusiasm for Oregon did not last even a year. Once our claim was registered on land farther west along the coast and a house and small barn built, his mind turned to something new. Such was Jacob—always scheming and planning, but never wanting to work and settle down.

This time California called him. He said there was still easy money to be found in the gold mines and plenty of ways to make a living in San Francisco or Sacramento, ways that didn't require a man to work himself to death at farming.

"What about our home and land here?" I cried. Before Jacob could answer, I went on, my face upturned and determined. "I won't leave, Jacob. I'm through chasing after you and your dreams. I'm staying here."

"What do you mean stay here? A wife's place is with her husband. Besides I need someone to do my cookin'."

Not wanting to escalate the situation, I made an effort to keep my voice calm. "And I need you to stay here. For once, try to make a go of things."

We measured each other—Jacob with color high in his cheeks, me with my hands on my hips and my chin lifted.

"Why must you always look for something easy?" I asked.

"You callin' me lazy or somethin'?" Not waiting for an answer, he went on. "I haven't done so bad. Look at the stove you have . . . your cupboard. Not many women in these parts have such." Satisfaction sounded in Jacob's voice and his lips lifted in a smirk. "You didn't want me to go to Oregon City last fall, neither. But look how good that turned out. A new stove and cupboard. Extra cash to see us through the winter."

"Where did it come from?"

"What do you mean?" A closed look slid over his face, one that came each time I asked him about the money.

"You barely had enough cash for passage on the boat to Oregon City when you left. Then suddenly you had enough to buy a stove and cupboard . . . a fancy new suit and hat for yourself. Where did it come from, Jacob? Did you steal it?"

It was the wrong thing for me to say. I saw it in his narrowed eyes, felt it when his fingers closed hard on my arm. "Where I got the money is my concern, not yours. And it's none of your business what I did while I was in Oregon City." He gave a humorless snort that passed for a laugh and pulled me hard against him. "Just so you know, you ain't the only woman in Oregon with a pretty face."

With that, he pushed me away from him, laughing when I lost my balance and fell against the wall. "We'll see who wears the pants in this marriage," he said, the smirk still stretching his lips as he turned to leave. "For sure, it ain't goin' to be you."

Tension filled the next week while I waited, expecting Jacob to say more about leaving. When he didn't, I began to take heart. Was it just a whim? Maybe he'd reconsidered.

Then after being away one morning, Jacob cantered the sorrel gelding into the yard, his movements quick and angry as he dismounted and walked to the house. I stepped away from the window, sensing trouble.

"We're leavin'," he said as soon as he entered the kitchen. "I mean to be away from these parts within the week. So start packin'."

When I didn't move, his eyes turned hard. "I said start packin'." His voice was nasty, and the tightness around his mouth told me to take care.

Determination kept me in my place. This was my home and I wasn't going to leave. "If you *let* me stay, I think it will work to your advantage." I smiled in an attempt to be ingratiating, and my voice lingered on *stay*. But inside, my mind raced for an argument that would appeal to Jacob's reasoning. "That way, if things don't work out for you in California, you'll still have our claim to come back to here."

A half-smile found its way past the tightness of his mouth. "You spect to run this place by yerself?"

"I do. You left me to milk the cow and look after things when you went to Oregon City. I can do it again."

Something flickered through Jacob's brown eyes—something that gave me hope. "I'll have to think about it," was all he said. Which was quickly followed by, "But you're to stay far away from the Odd Brit's property. Do you hear me? The man's plum crazy." With that he turned and went back outside. Later when I heard him start to whistle, I knew I'd won.

So it was decided. While Jacob tried his hand in California, I would stay in Oregon and keep our land. I knew his dream of riches was foolish. But my scheme was just as foolhardy. How could a lone woman manage an unimproved farm by herself? How would I survive?

This is where my real story begins—the story of how I discovered the depth of my heart and soul, the story of how I came to love and be loved by a man who was bigger and more wonderful than the wild Oregon coast.

CHAPTER 2

Less than a week later I stood outside our little house and waved good-bye to Jacob as he set out for California. In my mind I can see myself holding my red shawl close against the March chill. My blond hair was still in its bedtime plait, the loosened tendrils blowing around my face. He was gone. Thank heaven, Jacob was gone.

Although I had been married almost six years, my figure was still that of a young woman, though if God and all the sweet angels would continue to bless me, the tiny entity growing within me would shortly change that. "A baby," I whispered, unwilling to let myself think or say more. There had been other disappointments, and I had learned not to hope and dream too soon. Instead I turned to look at my home. It had only two rooms, but it was built of planks instead of logs, with a steep-sloped roof to shed the rain, four windows, and rhododendrons growing close to the house.

I felt pleased at having so much, not only a house, but a barn and woodshed and a little coop and fenced run for the chickens. Even so I experienced a twinge of fear as I turned to watch Jacob and the sorrel gelding disappear into the trees. Although I was glad to see him go, he was nonetheless a man whose arms and hands were stronger than mine, one who knew how to use a gun. My fear swelled to momentary panic as I realized my vulnerability—a woman alone on an isolated farm with bears and wolves sometimes spotted on the higher slopes of the mountains. What would I do if Indians or wild animals came? How would I manage to do all the work myself?

Determined not to let fear spoil the day, I looked up at the tree-covered mountains. I had loved the farm we had in Illinois, the one in

Missouri too. But when we finally got to Oregon I felt as if I had truly found my home. It's hard to explain the hold this country had on me. The towering Sitka spruce and lush ferns and rhododendrons seemed to call a welcome to me. When, on a whim, Jacob decided to push on to the coast instead of staying in the Willamette Valley, I knew as I looked out from the misty rainforest to the creamy breakers of the Pacific Ocean that somehow God had heard my prayers and reached down and handed me my own little spot of Eden.

My home was part of that Eden. I thought of this as I returned to it, pausing to wipe my damp shoes on the piece of toweling I kept by the door. The warmth from the stove was welcome, for the damp chill of the Oregon coast was quick to penetrate the bones. After adding wood to the fire, I sat down at the table to finish my breakfast.

The queasiness of the past weeks had lessened and I ate with relish, my gaze traveling around the cozy room with satisfaction. There was much to make me thankful that morning—a comfortable bed, enough staples to get me through until harvest, the brindled milk cow that had just calved, and my little flock of hens. With hard work and God's help, I was confident I could survive.

The first few days after Jacob left passed quickly. The nights were a different story. Extinguishing the lamp also extinguished my confidence, letting half-formed fears and the reality of my situation crowd into the bed with me. The patter of a squirrel across the rooftop could bring me upright out of the covers as could the sudden cry of a nighthawk. Although I tried hard to reassure myself, fear and unease replaced Jacob in the bedroom.

A week after Jacob left, I awoke to the steady drumming of rain on the shingles. I sighed and pushed myself out of bed, not liking the idea of sloshing through puddles to milk the cow and feed the chickens. After I finished my chores and checked on the horse in the fenced pasture, I hurried back to the house, my shawl draped over my head, trying not to slosh milk onto my skirt.

By noon I was thoroughly sick of having to stay in the house, tired of my own company and the absence of another voice. In an effort to break the oppressive silence, I commenced to sing, my mind harkening back to the sweet days in Mickelboro when I had sung and played for Mother and Tamsin.

Instead of buoying me up, the songs filled me with melancholy, making me miss my mother and sister with pain so intense I wanted to cry. Had Tamsin forgiven me? Why, oh why, hadn't she answered the letter I'd left and the ones I'd written later? Although I realized the letters might have been lost, deep down I feared a more terrible reason—that Tamsin and Mother were still angry with me for running away with Jacob.

"I'm sorry, Tamsin. Won't you please forgive me?" I spoke the words to the empty room. If only I could see her and explain about Deacon Mickelson. But I had explained—in the note I'd left, in letters I'd written since then. *Surely she must know I am sorry. Unless . . .*

Before I could carry the thought any further, a male voice called from the yard. My heart jumped and for a second I thought Jacob had returned. The voice came again. "Hello, Mrs. Mueller. Are you home?"

I was on my feet, my curiosity such that I opened the door without thinking. A tall, bearded man clad in a wide-brimmed hat and slicker stood in the muddy dooryard.

"Afternoon, Mrs. Mueller." When he took off his hat, I recognized Ben Tomkins, one of the men who'd helped Jacob put up our house and barn. Since he and his family had settled over by the bay, I hadn't seen much of them since the previous summer.

"Mr. Tomkins." I smiled and moved out onto the step. The rain had let up and slanted shafts of sunlight pierced through the clouds. "Jacob isn't home," I went on, "but . . ."

"I know." Ben swung down from his horse and looked toward the barn and pasture. "I've come to pick up the horse and wagon Jake sold me last week. He said the horse would be in the pasture and the wagon in the barn."

"Horse?" Surprise made my voice quaver. "You must be mistaken. Jacob left the horse for me."

Ben shook his head and his homely features tightened. "Ain't no mistake, Mrs. Mueller. Jake came by last week after hearin' I was lookin' for another horse. Said he needed the money to get to California. I paid him the last of my cash for it."

"But . . ." I stopped and studied Ben's rugged face. He'd come to Oregon with his wife and four children, determined to make a success of the land he'd claimed through the Donation Act. His lean, muscular frame spoke of hours of hard labor, and his face showed determination and ambition. He was also known as a man of his word.

I stared at him, my mind still reeling from shock. "That . . . that can't be."

"I've got the bill of sale." Ben replaced his hat and reached inside his slicker. Leaving his horse, he walked across the yard, his wet boots slogging in the damp grass and mud.

I took the piece of paper he handed me, read it once, then twice, my mind having difficulty assimilating the few words scribbled across the paper.

> *Received of me on this 24th day of March*
> *from Benjamin Tomkins the sum of ten dollars*
> *in exchange for my bay mare and wagon and harness.*
> *Jacob Mueller*

The shock of these words was such that it made me light-headed. *How could Jacob do such a thing? How could he betray me this way?*

Sensing my distress, Ben reached out to steady me. "Are you all right?"

"Yes." My voice was a whisper, and inside I was still reeling.

"I'm sorry, Mrs. Mueller. I thought this was somethin' you and Jake had decided between you. I didn't know . . ." The compassion in his gray eyes told me the rest—that he'd thought I was planning to go back East. He'd had no idea I was staying, just as determined as he was to hang onto the land. "I'm sorry," he repeated.

"It's not your fault." My voice sounded as weak and trembling as my legs felt.

Ben rubbed the side of his bearded face. "If it was just me, I'd say keep the horse and wagon, but I got Naomi and the young 'uns to think about. My horse died, and I need this one to pair up with Nick here so I can get in my crop." He swallowed and looked down at his muddy boots. " 'Sides, I gave your husband the last of my cash."

Ben's remorseful face made my throat tighten. Now wasn't the time for crying. I took a deep breath and attempted a smile. "Let me help you get the horse." I started toward the pasture. "She's a good mare, but it's been awhile since she's been ridden."

Few words passed between us while the mare was caught and hitched with Mr. Tomkins's horse to the wagon. Had I been myself, I would have asked about Naomi and the children, asked how the rainy winter had treated them, and if any more had been done about starting a school.

But I was not myself and neither was Mr. Tomkins. His thoughts seemed to be somewhere other than on the team and wagon. Once I saw him shake his head and mutter something that sounded like, "oughta be shot."

The fear I had experienced when Jacob left was nothing compared to what I felt when Ben Tomkins drove away with my mare and wagon. There went my means to improve the homestead and fulfill the land agreement—there went my means of getting supplies and visiting with my neighbors. How was I going to survive?

I turned with a heavy heart and entered the house. How could Jacob do this to me? Anger and hurt warred for position. I slammed the door shut. Only then, with the door closed and no one to hear me except the terrible silence, did I give way to tears. I threw myself onto the bed, my sobs shuddering and wild like those of a frightened child. *What am I going to do? Dear God, what am I to do?*

* * *

It was never my nature to give in to despair. So it was that day. After my sobs were spent, I got up and made my way to the basin on the table next to the window. Steeling myself against the shock of the cold water, I plunged my hands into the basin and brought them to my throbbing face and eyes, letting the coolness penetrate my skin, welcoming the relief that came.

"It's not the end of the world, Clarissa," I told myself, needing the sound of a human voice for some semblance of comfort. "You still have your home and the cow. Chickens, too, so you won't starve. And the baby." This last thought came in a whisper, as if by saying it aloud, life would hear and snatch it away like before. Unwilling to follow the thought, I added in a stronger voice, "You must think of the baby . . . eat right . . . make sure you get plenty of rest."

Following my advice, I soon found myself in the kitchen, an egg cracked and frying in the pan, milk and slices of cheese and bread cut to complete the meal. My stomach almost rebelled, but determination got me through, though I had to stop and rest my head on the table before I was finished.

Only then did I remember the money I'd insisted Jacob leave with me. I went to the cupboard where I'd put the coins. Why hadn't I remembered them when Ben was here? If I had, I could have bought back the horse and wagon. I lifted the cup where I'd put the money, frowned at its lightness, stared in disbelief. They were gone. The two gold eagles that had been my nest egg were gone.

In their place was a folded piece of paper. I slid it out of the cup, thinking at first that Jacob had left me an IOU. The reality of Jacob's character was quickly revealed when I unfolded the paper and read the words scrawled across it.

> *Surprise, Clarrie. I got to the money first.*
> *I'm not comin' back neither. Maybe Flora and*
> *Sven will take you in. If not, a woman as purty*
> *as you can find someone to take care of her.*
> *　　Jacob*

Boiling anger sent me to the door. Flinging it open, I shouted my rage. "I hate you, Jacob Mueller. Do you hear me? I hate you!" My voice was shrill, my hands clenched, wishing they could pummel Jacob's chest and let him feel my rage.

"Coward!" I screamed, hoping the wind would carry my voice over the mountains to confront him. I'd known he was a ne'er-do-well, but I'd trusted that he had enough character not to desert me and leave me penniless.

"I should have known," I whispered. Shock put a quaver in my voice. Not liking the sound, I squared my shoulders and took a deep breath. "Even though Jacob took the money, you're better off without him you know." Hearing my own voice helped; so did the lift that came to my lips when I realized the irony of my situation.

For years I'd wanted Jacob gone. Now, thankfully, he was. Gone for good!

Some women might have crept back into the house to lick their wounds, but the part of me that had always been able to find sunlight hiding in the midst of raindrops reached and took my blue cloak from the peg by the door. Shrugging my arms into its folds, I set off across the yard, not minding that it and the grass were still wet from the rain, not minding that thick clouds half obscured the sun. For now it was enough to walk across my own yard, look at my own meadow, gaze up at the tree-shrouded mountain that was mine too. Mine, if I could hold onto them, because my name was entered on the claim with that of Jacob Mueller.

Today I would walk over my domain, speak to it with my heart, gain strength from its wild beauty. Then when I was calm, I would begin my plans to make it truly mine—a home for Clarissa Yeager Mueller and her unborn child.

* * *

Spring's approach was still tentative; the leaf buds on the alders and blackberries were swollen and rounded in preparation for its coming. Only a few scattered buttercups were fully in bloom.

I took a path that angled along the side of one of the hills and into the forest. The man who'd surveyed the claim said it was likely a game trail or maybe even a path used by Indians. I followed its winding course through mottled gray-and-white trunk alders and thick-branched fir and hemlock, my breathing growing labored as the incline increased. I loved it there, the forest's stillness and the lush growth of fern and bracken, the trailing tendrils of green-gray moss. It was like going back in time, to a time and place where pixies and fairies flitted through gossamer strands of moss and ferns to play tag with unicorns.

Jacob had scowled when I'd shared my fancies, calling me daft and quickening his stride until he reached the openness of the meadow. I think Jacob was a little afraid in the forest. He said the moss reminded him of witches and claimed there were snakes and "who knows what other kind of varmints" hiding in the ferns and undergrowth. The trees were another story. He couldn't get over their size or the idea of the wealth that would be ours when he set up a mill and turned to lumbering. This had been before he caught the fever of California—before he realized lumbering required hard work and long hours.

I was pleased, however, when Jacob stopped his talk of lumbering. The thought of cutting down the mighty trees and denuding the mountain made me sad. "I'm glad he's gone for good," I said aloud. "Now I won't ever have to worry about his temper again."

It took me awhile to reach my destination—a craggy ledge on the side of the mountain surrounded on three sides with trees, the other side an open vista of earth and sea and sky. From there I could see the house and barn and meadow, the rolling, thick-treed hills that made up the bulk of our claim, and in the distance the shining water of the Pacific. Today the melding of the gray pewter ocean and low-hanging clouds was almost indiscernible.

If I'd had my way, we'd have built our home there. Jacob was quick to point out its impracticality, but he could not take away my delight in the spot. Just being there brought a lift to my spirits, something I sorely needed.

Thoroughly warmed from the steep climb, I removed my cloak and used it to pillow a rock for a chair. I looked out at the land, following the course of the Tillamook River running westward to empty into Tillamook Bay.

The other settlers had chosen land over by the bay, but Jacob with his eye on easy wealth from lumbering, and me with an eye on beauty, had chosen land less suited for farming. Only one other person had settled so close to the mountains. He'd been here longer than anyone else—a good four years, so rumor said. Rumor had also labeled him the "Odd Brit" though his true name was Quinton Reynolds. Little else was known about my neighbor. Only that he was from England, that he was rich, and that he spent most of his time digging for Indian relics.

"He's plumb crazy!" I remembered Jacob had declared the day he'd come home and told me to start packing. I could tell he was upset, but no amount of questioning could make him tell what had happened. I knew only that he'd had some kind of run-in with Quinton Reynolds.

"The man's plumb crazy," he'd repeated for emphasis. "He walks around with a big cane and acts like the whole country belongs to him." Jacob had looked at me with eyes still filled with anger. "Make sure you stay away from his property."

Such wasn't difficult, since Mr. Reynolds's property sat some distance from ours and was shielded by the forest. The only sign of his presence was the occasional barking of his dog and the thin spirals of smoke that came from his chimneys—three if rumor were to be believed.

That day I wished most fervently that my neighbor were someone other than the Odd Brit. If only it could have been a young family with children, a wife for my close friend, her husband one who wouldn't be averse to helping should the need arise.

The fact was, I was thoroughly lonesome. One week of being entirely alone had proven how much I needed others. But without a horse, I was stranded. At least until the rains let up. Until summer.

My heart lowered at the thought. That could be another two months. I realized then just how much I had come to look forward to the twice-monthly religious meetings held over in the valley. Although they were but loosely organized without favoring any specific religious belief, it was comforting to meet, to sing hymns, and to read from the Bible. Although Jacob was not of a religious nature, he enjoyed the food served following the meetings. Both of us had enjoyed the chance to visit and exchange news with the other settlers.

The past winter had been extremely rainy, the five rivers converging on the Tillamook Valley flooding their banks. As a result, I hadn't been to a meeting for several weeks. Now it looked like it would be several more.

Not liking that gloomy thought, I walked to the edge of the ledge to look down on my land stretching like a carpet of green.

"The grass over Tillamook way stays green year round," the man at the land-claim office had told us. His words had sent Sven Larsen and his wife from the Willamette Valley to Tillamook Bay, and we had followed. Sven knew cows, and he was already building a small herd, figuring to make his living that way rather than farming.

"What if I were to do the same?" I spoke the question aloud and laughed when I answered, "Why not?" even as I looked at the enclosed meadow where the brindled cow and her calf were pastured. Maybe Sven would let me have one of his cows on a trade, though what I had to trade, I didn't know. But it was a thought, perhaps a plan that might one day lead to fruition.

On this thought I looked out to the ocean. The sun had broken through the clouds to gild the pewter water with streaks of iridescent gold. The sight reminded me of the carefree hours Tamsin and I had spent at the cove below our cottage. Unlike me, Jacob had not cared for the ocean, balking whenever I'd suggested an outing. As a result, my visits there had been few and far between.

"But Jacob isn't here anymore." My face lifted in a satisfied smile as I picked up my cloak and set out for home. On good days I could walk to the ocean on my own, spend a whole afternoon there if I took the notion. Although I might have been penniless, God's treasures were still free.

CHAPTER 3

Although the walk did much to lift my spirits, I had only to enter the house and glance at the cupboard to be reminded of my predicament. Other reminders were there, too, pricking like a thorn each time I went to the flour bin and remembered Jacob's magnanimous air when he'd returned from across the river with extra flour.

"So you won't be going hungry while I'm gone," he'd said with a quick smile. I'd been surprised by his generosity, surprised even more when without me asking, he'd spent a day dragging logs down from the hills, and another day chopping and stacking them into the woodshed. He'd pulled me close when I'd thanked him, quirking his auburn brows and shrugging his shoulders in a way that let me know he was inordinately pleased with himself.

All the time he'd been planning to desert me, perhaps having sold the horse and wagon on the very day he went for flour, pilfering the half eagles from the cupboard when he came in from chopping wood.

"Hypocrite!" I cried, angrily pulling the door open and throwing a stick of wood across the yard. "You're nothing but a hypocrite and a coward." The act did little to help my anger, especially when I had only to walk the few steps to the barn and see the empty space where the wagon had been.

I tried not to think of the mare when I made my way to the pasture, endeavoring instead to keep my mind on the cow and calf. What would it take to make a profit from cows? How many pounds of butter and rounds of cheese?

My mind was still occupied with my plans two days later when I heard the sound of voices. Hurrying out of the house, I saw a team and wagon.

Who? I asked myself, as I started toward the man and woman and two children who rode in the wagon. My steps quickened when I recognized the multicolored shawl on the woman, and heard one of the children call my name.

"Flora!" Now it was me who called, my feet wanting to break into a run toward Flora Larsen and her husband, Sven. We'd been through much together—the long trek from Missouri to Oregon, then the journey by boat from Portland to Tillamook Bay. Flora was my best friend, her husband a tall, broad-shouldered man I both liked and respected.

I blinked back tears when Sven helped Flora down from the wagon, clinging to her longer than was my habit when we embraced. I savored the feel of her short, compact body, drank in the sound of the children's happy voices. Though I'd been alone less than two weeks, it seemed much longer.

Everyone began talking at once. My, "So good to see you," was drowned out by Flora's, "Why didn't you let us know Jacob had left?" and Sven's, "We'd have come sooner if we'd known."

It wasn't until I'd admired each of the children—Hans, a sturdy boy of five with blond hair like his father, and Little Sarah, a dimpled three-year-old named after her Grandma Sarah who lived with them—that Sven took the children for a walk so Flora and I could talk.

"What happened?" Flora asked as soon as they were out of earshot. The two of us still stood next to the wagon. "Ben Tomkins said Jacob had gone to California. Why?" Her brow furrowed as her gaze traveled from the house to the barn. "Why?" she repeated. "How could he leave you and all of this?"

My friend continued to frown and shake her head while I told her of Jacob's restlessness and ne'er-do-well ways, of his yearning for easy riches.

"But to go off and leave you . . ." Indignation hardened Flora's voice. "To desert you."

"It was by mutual consent. I told Jacob I was through chasing after him and his dreams. I love it here, Flora. I'm not leaving." I paused and looked up at the mist-shrouded mountain. "I intend to stay and make a home for me and my baby."

"Baby?" Flora stared for a moment before she pulled me into a hug, the two of us laughing. Flora had been with me after the difficult crossing of the Snake River where I'd miscarried the last baby, and she also knew of the two other disappointments. She was the first to pull away, wiping her tears with her hand, her full mouth stretched into a smile. "When?"

"In the fall . . . probably the last of September."

"I'm so happy." There was another quick hug, followed by sudden stiffening. "How could Jacob leave with a baby on the way?"

"He didn't know."

"Didn't . . . ?" Flora's pretty face was a study in consternation.

"At first I didn't tell him for fear of another disappointment. But later . . ." I paused to choose my words. "I wanted Jacob to leave, Flora. Although I didn't know then it would be for good, I've wanted him gone since the day I married him."

Even though Flora was my best friend, I think she was a little shocked by my disclosure. I watched the play of emotions on her round face, saw her mouth open, then close.

I reached and took Flora's hand. "Let's go inside where we can sit down and be more comfortable."

Flora smiled and squeezed my hand. "Are you afraid I'm going to faint from shock? I promise I won't, though after the long ride I could use a drink of water."

"You'll have more than a drink of water. Tea it will be, and drunk from the very cup from which Jacob stole my nest egg and left me the cowardly note—freshly washed to get rid of the bad memory."

Flora's eyes grew large, her surprise alternating with indignation when I related what had happened with the money and showed her the note, the two of us sitting at the table, Flora in Jacob's chair, while we waited for the kettle to boil.

"I'm so glad you didn't love him," Flora put in when I paused for breath. "I can't tell you how many times I wondered how you could ever love such a man . . . all the times Sven and I lay in bed at night speculating as to why you married him." Her eyes searched mine as if she hoped to find answers to a dozen questions. "Why, Clarissa? How did you ever come to marry Jacob?"

While the tea steeped, I told her about Amos Mickelson's threat and of my fear of what he would do if I stayed. The only thing I left out was how I'd betrayed Tamsin. This was something I still held close. Something I only shared with God.

By the time I finished, tea was poured and cream added to our cups. "There you have it," I concluded. "It's not a pleasant story, but perhaps it helps you understand why I married Jacob Mueller."

"It does, and it answers many other questions. Why two such opposite people ever came to be together. Why someone so obviously educated and used to better things would choose to come all the way out here." She paused and took my hand. "I'm so sorry, Clarissa."

"Don't be." Then in a stronger voice, "Don't ever be. I love it here. The land. All the trees. This is where I want to be and why I mean to stay and keep the home and claim."

"But how?"

I shook my head. "I don't know yet, though I have given some thought to joining you and Sven in dairying."

Flora's chestnut head was shaking, her mouth firming into a straight line. "It will never do. All the work . . . the milking. It will be too much. Not to mention the money to build up a herd. No." She came around the table to my chair. "Sven and I want you to come with us. That's why we're here. To invite you to live with us."

I tilted my head so I could look up at her. "No." My answer came without hesitation. "Thank you for your good heart. Sven's too. It means much to me . . . more than I can put into words. But it doesn't change my answer."

"Please, Clarissa."

Shaking my head, I got to my feet, needing the advantage of my height. "My place is here. I've known it from the moment I saw these mountains . . . the ocean—everything. For some reason God led me to this spot. Now it's up to me to find out why."

* * *

Flora and Sven and the children stayed the afternoon. They agreed to join me for dinner only if Sven could milk the cow and bring in several loads of wood. Sven shook his head and muttered something in Swedish when he found I couldn't be persuaded to leave with them. I ignored his muttering while Flora and I gossiped and laughed as we cooked and prepared the food. For a while it was like we were back on the trail, the two of us more like sisters than friends, knowing beforehand what the other was going to say. Our conversation didn't turn serious until they were preparing to leave.

"We'll try to get over every week or two . . . if not us then Ben and Naomi or some of the others. We talked about it at worship meeting yesterday. We all want to help, though it would be better if you changed your mind and came with us."

"No." I met Sven's gaze and let him read my determination. "I'll be fine, though I would appreciate some help getting in a garden. But after that . . ." I smiled, as if my problems had all been taken care of, as if a cow and chickens and a garden could feed me and my child indefinitely. I cleared my throat and went on. "I'm serious about wanting to get another cow. I want to make my own way, not be a burden."

"You won't be a burden," Flora argued.

"I will be when I run out of flour and beans and sugar. The only way for me to replace them is by earning money. So far the best solution seems to be learning how to make good cheese and butter."

I could tell Sven thought I had my head in the clouds, but he was too considerate to say so. "We'll talk about it the next time we come," he said.

After he loaded Flora and the children into the wagon, he paused and looked up at the mountains. "I'd feel a lot better if you had someone besides that Brit for a neighbor."

I felt a twinge of unease. "Why?"

"No reason exactly, except that Jacob said the Brit threatened him and ordered him off his property." Sven shrugged and climbed up into the wagon. "He doesn't sound like he's very neighborly."

"Since I never see him, it shouldn't matter one way or the other."

"I suppose not." He picked up the reins. "Did Jacob leave a gun with you?"

The unease came back. "No."

Sven gave a mirthless chuckle. "I didn't expect he did." But the look on his face was saying, *What kind of man would desert his wife and leave her without the means to protect herself? What kind of husband would leave without asking friends to look after her?* Then his expression softened, and he became the Sven I'd come to know and appreciate, the one who always made me feel like things would turn out all right.

"I should have known I could expect Clarissa Mueller to take good care of herself," Sven said. "Right?" The smile he gave me was almost pleading, like he could see the unease in my eyes and was regretting what he'd said to put it there.

"Right," I said, my answering smile as bright as I could make it.

Sven flicked the reins and the wagon rolled away. "Someone will be over to check on you in a couple of weeks."

"There's no need. I'll be fine." Inside I felt anything but fine.

Flora and Hans and Little Sarah turned to wave. Tears stung my eyes and for a second I wanted to run after them and say I'd changed my mind. Determination kept me there. But it could not stop the dreadful loneliness. How was I ever going to survive the long solitary weeks and months until the baby came?

* * *

Over the next few days I began to establish a routine, rising early to slosh through the rain to milk the cow and see to the chickens, eating a leisurely breakfast, then turning to little tasks to keep me occupied. Sometimes in the afternoon, if the weather permitted, I would explore the wooded hills and mountain, watching as the fragile green leaves of the alder unfurled, listening to the cheerful songs of the black crown sparrows and juncos. I also found myself listening and watching for signs of the Odd Brit. Perhaps it was loneliness that caused it, though more likely it was my lively curiosity. I'd always liked to speculate about others, letting my imagination run wild as I conjured up ideas for their behavior and wondered about the secrets they might be hiding.

So it was each time I heard the distant bark of my neighbor's dog. Instead of filling me with unease, I wondered about its size and coloring and if it were a pet or a watchdog. Other than the dog, the only other sound was the sharp crack of ax biting into wood. I heard the ax more often than I heard the dog and decided that it must take a great deal of wood to keep fires in three chimneys burning.

The following week on a particularly fine day, I decided to venture across the mountain to the ocean. I set out before noon, bread and cheese wrapped in a cloth, my red shawl around my shoulders. I took the trail that led to the craggy ledge, my footsteps but whispers on the thick carpet of needles, and hummed softly between breaths as I climbed.

I stopped to rest when I reached the ledge and looked westward to the ocean. The view was breathtaking, the sea reflecting the cerulean-blue sky in ripples of satin. *Home,* it whispered, turning me into a girl again, one who had often looked down in awe at the churning Atlantic, feeling Tamsin's hand tighten with excitement upon mine. If only she could be with me today, the two of us exploring another vast ocean a continent away.

I continued on the trail, knowing it would eventually take me down to the sea. Conscious of the precious burden that thickened my waist, I chose my steps with care and picked up a stick to aid me on the steep descent. Soon I could hear the sound of breakers punctuated by the raucous mewing of gulls. Then I was there, the trees thinning into a sloping meadow that dropped steeply to the shore.

For a time I was content to stay in the meadow, to drink in the sight and sound and smell of the sea. I hadn't realized how much I'd missed it—gulls and pelicans skimming the waves, the rattle of rocks on pebbles as the waves receded. Some distance from shore, like gray bastions, two craggy monoliths rose out of the water. Sea stacks, the sea captain had called them on our trip down from Astoria— remnants of the mountain hewn away by the restless Pacific.

Spreading my shawl on the grass, I sat down and opened the bundle of bread and cheese, ate, then drowsed in the sun, not minding that my hair had loosened from its pins, not minding that the wind played tag with straying blond tendrils. Jacob's betrayal and my worry about the future dissipated. For now it was enough to soak up the sun and to feel at one with the sea.

* * *

By the time I overcame my lethargy the tide was ebbing, leaving a curving apron of rocks and sand and silver-gray logs. I looked for a way to navigate the steep drop to the shore and eventually found a path angling down the side, its outer perimeter shored up with slabs of rock and wood, the descent graduating into a series of steps. I wondered at this, wondered even more when I reached the sand and discovered a set of footprints. For a moment, fear overrode curiosity. My eyes skimmed the shoreline and the line of trees to the south, the peace I'd felt shattered by awareness of my vulnerability. Although I couldn't see anyone, unease would not let me enjoy the beach or search in the tide pools. Someone had been here recently—someone whose footprints were much larger than mine.

Stubbornness kept me on the sand and set me on the same course as the footprints. As I followed them, I watched for signs of anyone approaching, my eyes darting from the sand to the trees and finally up to the shrouded headland jutting into the ocean. Nothing. No one.

As the minutes slipped by I began to relax—after all, the prints had been made by boots, not moccasins. Perhaps it was a settler from the other side of the mountain, one who looked for clams and oysters along the coast instead of in the bay. Such reasoning might explain the path, but it didn't explain the curious round hole that punctuated the sand to the side of each left footprint. Was it a tool for clamming, or a man's walking stick?

I recalled Jacob's words about our neighbor. *He carries a walking stick and acts like he owns the whole country.* The answer came with a rush of certainty. It had to be Quinton Reynolds, the Odd Brit. I bent over and traced the indentation of the hole left by the cane. Why would a man cling to the trappings of fashion in a place as rugged as the Oregon coast? And why all the work to build a path down to the beach? Was it part of his search for Indian antiquities, or was my neighbor truly an odd Brit?

Strangely, the unanswered questions quieted my fear. Curiosity played a part in the change, but so did perversity. Since Jacob had warned me about Quinton Reynolds, I would judge him to be safe. By the same token, if Jacob declared him odd or crazy, then I would consider him sane. Such was my reasoning that afternoon, a reasoning so intense that I turned my back on the trees and forested mountain and drank in the beauty of the charging columns of waves, the froth of breakers calming me with their rhythm as they washed across the sand.

I sat down on a sun-bleached log and removed my shoes and stockings. Recalling the times Tamsin and I had played tag with the waves, I lifted my skirt to challenge them, walking boldly into the foaming residue. My toes flinched and curled against the coldness, and my breath caught as I walked in farther, the blue-green water clear as a forest pool as it covered my calves, the sand giving firm footing as I braced myself for the next wave.

In my mind I heard Tamsin call a warning, heard her excited squeal and my laughter as I ran to safety. This day I did not turn and run, but stood waiting for the onslaught, my knees almost buckling when the wave hit me, the edge of my lifted dress sopped by the brunt of water. I laughed, my satisfaction muffling the chattering of my teeth and lessening the effect of the bone-chilling water.

Not wanting to risk harm to my baby, I wrung out the wet portion of my blue skirt and went to retrieve my shoes and stockings. I wasn't sure what alerted me to the fact I was being watched—the sudden need to hurry, the prick of something closely akin to fear. I quickly searched the way I had taken, then turned to look southward to the headland.

Then I saw him—the figure of a man silhouetted between the dark trunks of the rainforest. I sensed the scrutiny of his gaze despite the distance, feeling unwelcome heat rise to my cheeks.

The Clarissa of my youth would have jumped to her feet and shouted a challenge, but the Clarissa of that day felt a mixture of curiosity and caution. I returned his gaze, noting that he was a man of more than average stature, his head covered by a hat so I could not judge the color of his hair. Then as quickly as I saw him, he was gone, his dark coat and trousers melding into the shadows of the trees. Distance prevented me from seeing his features. But I was certain of one thing; the man didn't use a walking stick for fashion—he moved with a slight limp.

* * *

I did not say anything about the sighting of my neighbor when Sven and Flora arrived the next week. I was too surprised to do more than gape when they presented me with a half-grown pup. He was short haired and brindled like the cow, and at an awkward stage that tugged at my heart even as I wondered what I was going to do with him.

"For company," Flora explained.

"And protection," Sven added. "I got him from the Sidaways. He should be good for helping you bring in the cows . . . that is if you're still set on wanting to earn money from cows."

"I am." I met his gaze with determination and a smile.

Sven reached into the wagon and took out a cheese press he'd made for me. It was fashioned out of wood, even the screws, and I knew it had taken hours of his time.

"You shouldn't have," I protested. "Not when you're so busy."

Sven brushed aside my protest, claiming that working with wood was his play and that they had taken on the neighbor's son to help with the milking now that two more cows had freshened. "Extra help is what I must have until Hans gets bigger."

"I'm already big," Hans declared.

"You are, indeed. So big your papa is going to let you help him dig Aunt Clarissa's garden," Flora put in.

While Sven and the children worked outside, Flora showed me the ins and outs of making cheese. With pen and ink I wrote down many directions that day, knowing I would need them. As I listened and wrote, my mind harkened back to my mother, remembering how she'd spent her time doing needlework, reading, and playing the pianoforte. She had no interest in the workings of my father's farm and had cheerfully turned over the cooking and house chores to the hired help. Although I was grateful for having learned the wonders of the written word and an appreciation for music, still I regretted my ignorance of things most women had been taught from childhood. Would this lack work against me when it came to making good butter and cheese?

"Just follow the recipe and directions," Flora said. "With time and practice you'll be surprised how well it will turn out."

Then our conversation turned to other matters—how Naomi Tomkins was thought to be increasing again. "She has not said so, but her waist is growing, just as yours is."

My hand rose to my middle, something it was wont to do of late. I smiled and patted the slight rounding. "I'm almost four months." I swallowed and pushed aside a twinge of fear. "Everything is going so well this time. I hope . . ."

Flora slipped her arm around me. "It will," she promised. "Sven and I are keeping you in our prayers. Everyone at worship meeting is doing the same."

"You told them?"

Flora nodded. "I hope you don't mind. I thought the extra prayers would bring you peace of mind."

I remembered Flora's words as I watched her and Sven plant the sliced potato tubers. They wouldn't let me do any of the heavy work.

"Just watch," Sven insisted. With a wink he added, "Watch and tell us how we ought to do this . . . that's what women do best."

Flora threw a clod of dirt at him, the rich loam breaking into granules as it hit Sven's broad back. I felt a prick of envy when Sven turned and grabbed her, saw the love shining in his laughing blue eyes, heard Flora's answering laughter when he planted a playful swat on her behind. There had never been playful banter between Jacob and me—never any love. I closed my eyes and looked away, wishing for the hundredth time that things had been different, that I'd married out of love instead of desperation.

It was late by the time my friends left, so late I feared it would be dark before they reached their farm.

"It will be all right," Sven assured me. "The horses know their way home once we ford the river."

I stood in the dooryard until the wagon was hidden in the trees. I tried not to think of the lonely days ahead, that it might be two or three weeks before I saw a human face again. The dog nudged me and looked up with mournful eyes. I bent down and put my arms around him, enjoying the feel of his warm, gangly body. "You're lonely too, poor thing."

He yipped and licked my face. Laughing, I dodged his kisses and realized that as I did, I no longer felt so alone.

CHAPTER 4

For the next few days the dog took up most of my waking hours—the nights too—for he set up a howl for his brothers and sisters the moment I left him. On the second night, instead of leaving him tied outside, I let him come in. I told myself it was only so I could get some sleep. The fact was, I was hungry for company too, and the pup's loud yawns and little snuffles were oddly comforting.

"But you must sleep on the floor, not my bed," I told him. He studied me with solemn brown eyes as his tail beat a steady tattoo on the floor. "And I think you need to have a name."

I considered several—Oregon, Eureka, even Goliath. In the end I settled on Sam, for no better reason than that the dog cocked his head and almost grinned when I tried it out on him.

By the fourth day Sam had pretty much learned my routine, following me out to the barn while I milked the cow, nipping at her heels to help me herd her back in the pasture. By the end of the next week, I'd taught him to understand "stay" and to guard the cow when I left her with him. Since Sam had a name, I decided the cow and calf must be named too—Brownie for the cow and Star for the little calf. For the first time I understood why spinsters often keep a menagerie of cats. If there were a lack of humans to talk to, animals could be a satisfying substitute.

I was thinking about this a few evenings later as I milked Brownie, my forehead resting against her warm flank, milk coming in two steady streams into the bucket. What would Mother and Tamsin think if they could see me now, hands that had known little of work except to play the pianoforte now milking a cow, a woman who turned to animals for company instead of Tennyson and Shakespeare?

Sam's low growl jerked me out of my reverie, his tone deep and menacing. The hair on the back of my neck rose, and my heart jumped hard against my chest when I lifted my head and saw the dusky form of an Indian filling the opening of the barn door.

Only the tiniest sound escaped my lips, though inside I was screaming. *Help, oh, help me God!* Sam's growl had progressed to a rumbling bark. Brownie kicked her hobbled legs, and I scrambled to my feet just as the stool and bucket tipped over.

The Indian and I stared at each other, his dark eyes but glints in his brown features, the evening light coming from behind him. Though Brownie was tied to a post, she continued to kick, lowing softly while Sam barked and growled, his hackles raised and his hind legs ready to spring.

While on the Oregon trail and later in the Willamette Valley, I'd heard tales about Indians walking into people's homes without invitation and taking what they pleased—food, clothing, cooking utensils, sometimes even molesting the women. My frightened eyes darted around the barn. There was no way out except through the door.

"What do you want?" I managed to get out, my voice trembling like my knees.

The Indian swayed to one side and grabbed the doorframe as a helpless look slid over his face.

"What do you want?" I repeated. Inside, I thought, *He's drunk!*

As the Indian opened his mouth to speak, his leather-clad legs buckled and he collapsed to the floor. Sam was on top of him before I could blink, biting and growling like a full-grown dog.

"No, Sam!" My command was almost a scream, the force of my fear compressing the air from my lungs. Then I was in the thick of it, trying to pull Sam away from the man without being bitten even as I wondered why I intervened. "No, Sam!" I repeated. "Stay! Sit!" The commands came without thought. Sam obeyed when he felt me yank on his collar. Still growling, he stood stiff-legged at my side while we looked down at the unconscious figure sprawled by the door.

The intruder's eyes were closed, his mouth opened slightly, his breathing uneven. My eyes noted this in a thrice, saw his long dark hair and rounded face, and that his upper torso was unclothed except for a vest.

I jumped back when the Indian groaned and turned on his side and retched. I gave Sam's collar another jerk. "Stay," I told him and ran for the pitchfork. Holding the handle with shaking hands, I snatched the intruder's knife out of its leather holder.

Feeling less vulnerable, I studied the savage more closely, checking for signs of sickness or injury. Thankfully, there wasn't any blood. No odor of liquor either. I had to force myself to bend over and lay my hand on his forehead. I snatched it away as soon as I determined his skin was cool and normal.

"No fever," I whispered. "And no sign of injury."

Sam barked when I spoke. The Indian's eyes jerked opened and his head turned. For a second I read fear in the black, unfocused eyes. Only then did I see the dark, ugly welt over his left temple and congealed blood matted in the hair above his ear.

My first instinct was to take the pitchfork and run, although there was no one close enough to run to. And why flee from an unconscious and unarmed man?

My presence of mind surprised me as I remembered to untie Brownie and lead her out to the pasture, as did my calmness as I left Sam to guard the intruder. Carrying the knife in one hand and the pitchfork in the other, I hurried into the house to heat water for his wound. While I waited for the water to heat, I examined the Indian's weapon and shuddered at the bloodstains on the hilt of the handle, shuddering again when my mind conjured up images of how it had gotten there. Shivering, I dropped it onto the piece of toweling by the door, wrapped it tightly, and stuffed it behind the wood box. *There.* It was gone.

Night was coming on, so I was hindered by lack of light as I ministered to my patient. Strange that the simple act of heating water and finding rags to clean his wound had changed him, in my mind, from savage to patient. But that was how it was. Fear left me when I knelt on the dirt by his side. I flinched when he flinched, and despite my reluctance to touch him, my heart was calm and filled with compassion.

I didn't know if the intruder spoke English, but I talked to him anyway, needing the sound of my voice to bring a sense of normalcy to the scene. "I'll try not to hurt you."

He jerked when the warm cloth touched the welt and groaned softly as I bathed the cut by his ear, the muscles in his jaw tightening against the pain. I saw a deep scrape on his arm and another across the knuckles of one hand.

"How did you get hurt? Did you fall?"

Thinking I was talking to him, Sam laid his head against my arm and looked at me with a quizzical expression.

"Yes, you're a good dog, Sam. So brave." But my mind was on the Indian. Although I wasn't eager to take care of him, I didn't feel right about leaving him to lie in the dirt. He needed to be moved to a more comfortable place. Although the intruder wasn't tall, he was muscular, his weight such that I knew I couldn't lift him. Even to drag him would be difficult. He would have to stay in the barn.

I gathered what was left of the winter fodder and mounded it into a bed. Then I went into the house for a quilt. After I spread it over the hay, I grasped the Indian under his arms and pulled him to the hay. Lifting him was hard, his dead weight like that of a heavy log, his head slumped against my knees as I pulled him. "I'm sorry," I whispered.

My patient made no response to my voice or the jarring. When I finally got him onto the quilt, I bent to peer at him. His eyes closed, he lay without moving. For a moment I feared he had died, that moving him had killed him. I placed my hand on his chest and felt it rise and fall. "Thank God," I said, even as I wondered what I would have done if he'd stopped breathing. *How would I dig a grave?*

What to do with him if he lived was just as perplexing. I knew nothing about head wounds and only a smattering about caring for the sick. Should I try to feed him, or would it be better to just cover him with the quilt and leave him to sleep? After deciding on the latter, I took part of the quilt and pulled it over the inert form. Then calling softly to Sam, I closed and latched the barn door.

Guilt followed me as I went back to the house. But it did not slow my steps. Since I didn't know what else to do, I had to wait and see what the morning brought.

* * *

Even though Sam slept on the rug beside my bed, I did not have a restful night. Dreams came between intermittent sleep, fragmented and making no sense. One was of an Indian stalking me through the forest. This last was so vivid it brought me struggling out of sleep, my heart pounding at the memory of a face half obscured by a tree, a raised hand holding a hatchet, a swarthy face mottled by a large bruise across the temple.

I lay for several minutes trying to wipe the scene from my mind. *The Indian is unconscious and locked in the barn,* I reassured myself. Even so, I was unable to return to sleep. I tossed restlessly until the cheerful chirping of birds told me it was time to get up.

I did not wait to fix breakfast, but went at once to the barn, my head covered against a light drizzle by my red shawl. The dog's presence quelled some of my unease, as did the sight of the barn door, closed and latched just as I'd left it.

As I swung the door open, my gaze flew to the hay in the corner, to the quilted form lying still as a corpse. Was he dead? *Oh, please, God, don't let him have died.*

Sam was already by the Indian, sniffing tentatively at the blanket before looking at me. He was little more than a pup, and I, at the moment, didn't feel much older than he.

"Are you awake?" My eyes searched for signs of life. I found them when the Indian stirred, heard them when he groaned. Whatever had caused the injury had left him in pain.

Reassured, I hurried back to the house for water. He had to have been thirsty, and a cool compress on the welt and forehead would be soothing. My attempts to get the Indian to drink did not meet with success. Each time I lifted his head he moaned, his pupils large and unfocused, his tightly closed mouth refusing to drink. When I eased his head back on the pallet, he turned and retched.

I left him while I cared for the cows and fed the chickens. But the intruder was never far from my mind, like a tooth that wouldn't stop aching. Throughout the day I checked on him. Finally in the afternoon I got him to take a few awkward sips of water. His eyes looked at me without expression as he drank, but he sighed with relief when I placed a cool compress on his forehead.

By now I'd had ample time to study the Indian, his well-worn moccasins and leather breeches examined with curiosity. How had they been sewn without needle and thread, not to mention the strange fabric of grass and bark and wool woven to make his vest? I found much to wonder about that day and on the days that followed while he lay barely conscious, refusing food and only accepting an occasional drink of water. The lines in the leathery skin above his black, heavy brows made me think he was probably near forty. His black hair was cut short just above the shoulders, and his muscled arms and legs spoke of strength. What had caused the blow to his head? And what had brought him from the forest to me?

I voiced some of my questions to the Indian when he roused enough to drink, but he met them with silence, even when I asked his name. I began to call him Hawkeye, the name of my favorite character in the book Mother had read to us by Mr. James Fenimore Cooper. Perhaps in a forest setting he would be a tall and stately warrior, though that day he was nothing more than a sick man.

On the fourth morning when Sam and I unlocked the door and entered the barn, Hawkeye was sitting up, his head resting against the wall of the barn, his eyes half open. I knew as soon as he roused that he had turned a corner on the road to recovery. His pupils were less dilated and for the first time I saw interest.

Reminding myself that untamed animals often bit the hand that fed them, I remained a healthy distance from the Indian. "Good morning. How are you feeling?"

Instead of answering, my patient squeezed his eyes shut, then opened them, blinking rapidly as if trying to clear his vision.

"Can you see me?" I spoke slowly and watched for any change of expression.

There was no reaction except for another blink as he pushed with a moccasined foot to sit up better. The movement made Sam bark, his tone deepening as he darted in a half-circle just outside the Indian's reach. Like me, Sam was unsure of our uninvited guest.

"Stay, Sam!"

The dog gave one last growl before he sat down at my side.

We continued to study each other—me standing in my blue gingham dress holding the pitchfork, and the Indian stolid and watchful, as if he didn't trust me any more than I trusted him.

"Would you like something to eat?" I cupped my hand and pantomimed eating.

Hawkeye slowly nodded, but his dark, rounded features remained as expressionless as they'd been in sleep. Did he ever show emotion?

Glad to have something to do besides stare at my silent patient, I hurried to the house, mentally trying to decide what to fix for him. *Do Indians eat eggs? What about bread? Or would it be best to begin with a thin gruel like the one I'd offered him the day before?*

I decided on a gruel made from leftover mush sweetened with a little sugar. What the Indian thought of the concoction, he didn't say. Nor would he let me feed him, shaking his head and reaching for the bowl when he realized my intent.

"Very well," I said, not knowing whether I liked his refusal. But at least he ate it, awkwardly slurping the gruel from the spoon before lifting the bowl to his mouth to drink the last.

Instead of watching every awkward bite, I gathered stray pieces of hay with the pitchfork. All was done with only half a mind, the other half on Hawkeye. I watched him out of the corner of my eye and wondered what he was thinking.

When the bowl was empty, instead of setting it down, he held it out to me, his expression like a child asking for more.

I shook my head. "You shouldn't eat too much at first. You've been hurt. Sick."

Hawkeye's brows lifted and a slight frown creased his stolid features.

"Hurt," I said, pointing to the welt on his temple. "How did you get hurt?"

His only reply was a scowl.

Not one to give up easily, I tried again. "What is your name?"

He looked at me as if I hadn't spoken.

"Name?" I repeated. "What is your name?"

Again no answer. Still I persisted. Part of it came from the need to talk, but part of me didn't want the Indian to think he was winning. "My name is Clarissa Mueller. Since you won't tell me your name, you'll have to go by the one I've chosen for you. It's Hawkeye, and whether you like it or not, that's what I'm going to call you."

I waited, still hoping he'd say something, even if it were in his language. When no reply came, I went on. "I have to leave and do my chores. My husband has gone . . . deserted me and taken off for California to get rich, which is all right with me, since I never cared for him, much less loved him. But it does leave me with a lot to do."

Holding the empty bowl and the pitchfork, I left Sam to guard my patient. When I came back to the barn, I spied Sam circling the prone form of the Indian lying several feet from the pallet. I dropped Brownie's rope and held the pitchfork ready with both hands.

"Hawkeye?" For a second, concern for my patient warred with caution. Had the Indian fallen as he'd tried out his legs or was it a ruse to make me drop the pitchfork and go to his aid?

The Indian groaned and rolled from his stomach onto his side. After a moment, he eased himself into a sitting position and crawled back to the pallet, the look he shot me holding neither apology nor embarrassment.

Part of me wanted to scold him for trying to walk too soon. Instead, I decided to ignore the incident and get on with the milking.

Later, I went out to check on the garden. Although it was too soon to expect anything to be up yet, such hadn't stopped the weeds. Yet even without crops, the rich loam of the soil was beauty in and of itself. As I pulled weeds, I thought about Tamsin. At home, she'd been the one to spade and work the soil while I'd picked and arranged glorious heads of peonies and foxglove in jars and vases throughout the cottage.

"You can never have too many flowers," I'd told Tamsin. The years hadn't changed my opinion. Next summer, with the baby safely here, I would plant a whole yard full of flowers.

When a catch in my back ended my gardening, I went to check on Hawkeye in the barn. The first time I looked in he was sleeping, but the second time he had roused and was sitting up again.

"Would you like to eat?" I asked, pantomiming with my hands.

When Hawkeye nodded I went to the house for another bowl of thinned mush. The Indian ate it all and took a few swallows of water. I took inordinate pleasure in the return of his appetite and the fact that his dark eyes were no longer dilated. Such meant he was healing and that in my own small way I'd had a part in the process. *You and*

God, something whispered. In those days I was only on casual speaking terms with God, seldom remembering to call upon him except in times of crisis or danger. That day I felt safe enough to put God out of my mind, though caution kept the pitchfork within easy reach. All in all I was pleased with myself. And because I was pleased, I started talking again.

"Where is your family?" I asked him. "Where do you live?"

When Hawkeye made no reply, I went on just as if he had. "My husband and I moved here more than a year ago. We'd been in Missouri, places you've likely never heard about. They were nice, but not as beautiful as here. I've never been in such a lovely place . . . all the trees, the streams, the ocean." I paused and met his steady gaze, wondering briefly what he thought about all my talking.

I think I told Hawkeye my entire life story—about my parents and sisters, why I ran off with Jacob, of his abusive nature, the loss of the babies, and of my hopes and dreams for the little one I carried. When the warmth of the sun got too much, I moved to lean against the shady door, and when my legs and back tired of standing, I got the milking stool and sat down. Now that I had a captive audience, I didn't seem to be able to stop. Flies lazily buzzed in circles through slanted sun rays, chickens clucked and scratched in the hen yard. All meshed with the words that flowed unchecked from my lips. Lonely words. Healing words.

It wasn't until my stomach reminded me it was well past mealtime that I paused. "You're probably hungry again . . . probably tired of listening to all my yammering too." I gave the Indian a sideways glance as I hung the milking stool back on the wall. "Do Indian women talk this much?"

I could have sworn I saw a slight shake of his odd, flattened head. Even though his mouth remained stern, there was laughter in his dark eyes. On my walk back to the house, I decided Hawkeye was a lot like Sam. He knew what I said without understanding the words.

* * *

I killed one of my laying hens and cooked it for dinner. I came close to shedding tears as I did it, for my chickens were almost as dear to me as Brownie and Sam. But after listening to me so patiently, I decided Hawkeye deserved a treat. The only treat I could think to make that would also build up his strength was stewed chicken.

It was late afternoon by the time the chicken was ready. I ladled the broth and a few pieces of meat into a bowl and carried it out to the barn. The Indian was upright and leaning against the doorframe for support. Sam stood beside him, his stance telling me he couldn't decide whether to attack or wag his tail.

I felt the same as I scolded Hawkeye for getting up, my fear of him all but forgotten. I beamed with pride when he smacked his lips and rubbed his stomach to show appreciation for my cooking. Jacob had never been one to show appreciation. I lapped it up like a kitten being offered a saucer of cream.

That day I was so carried away with feelings of goodwill that I didn't remember until the following morning that I'd forgotten and left the pitchfork in the barn with the Indian.

Fear sat on my shoulder as I pulled the door open, then it jumped to my heart when I couldn't see the pitchfork where I'd left it. It must have shown in my face, for just as if he could read my thoughts, Hawkeye pointed to the wall where I kept the milking stool. The pitchfork hung next to the stool, the tines and handle cleaned of debris and looking as if someone had taken special pains with it.

I glanced over my shoulder at Hawkeye, saw his nod of acknowledgment and, unbelievably, a smile. I found my mouth doing the same as I asked how his night had been, if he was feeling stronger, and what sounded good for breakfast.

Although he didn't answer, his lack of conversation didn't deter me. It was as if during the night my mind had filled with a hundred new things to say.

Sam took it all in, looking first at the Indian, then at me, his mouth opened in what could pass for a grin, his short tail wagging. He continued to watch both of us—me chattering about my plans for keeping the farm, Hawkeye sitting on his pallet and listening.

"I'm going to hang onto this place," I concluded. "It doesn't matter whether the baby is a boy or a girl, we're going to have a home."

I thought Hawkeye nodded, but I couldn't be sure. Then he snapped his fingers and spoke to the dog.

Sam cocked his head and looked from me to Hawkeye.

I nodded. "It's all right, Sam."

The dog moved forward and cautiously sniffed Hawkeye's large hand and fingers, his tail a tentative wag. Then with a happy yip, he moved closer and let the Indian rub his head and neck.

Hawkeye glanced at me and smiled. I grinned right back. "I guess this means we're friends," I said. "Friends." I lifted my hand in a sign of peace.

More strange words came from his lips.

Figuring they must have meant *friend*, I smiled and nodded again, gladly exchanging friendship for my earlier fear.

After I'd milked Brownie and strained the milk into containers for butter and cream, I took a large bowl of chicken broth and a slice of bread out to the barn for the Indian. As a sealing token of our friendship, I took the knife I'd hidden behind the wood box and hooked it onto the band of my apron.

Hawkeye was testing his legs inside the barn when I got there, his steps those of a healthy man, not lopsided and staggering like they'd been when he first came. His dark brows lifted and his gaze flew to my face when he saw the long knife. He studied me intently, his eyes searching and probing.

"I took it from you when you were sick," I said as I set down the bowl of broth. "I was afraid you might use it on me."

I held out the knife to him, averting my eyes from the blood-stained handle.

Hawkeye began to speak, the strange sounds and syllables of his language rolling effortlessly from his tongue. What they meant, I didn't know, but I understood the gratitude on his face, the warmth of his black eyes as they looked down at me. "Thank you" and "friend" were there as clearly as if he'd spoken in English.

"You're quite welcome," I replied when he'd finished. For once I couldn't think of anything else to say. I felt a little uncomfortable when he slipped the weapon into the leather thong by his waist.

The uncomfortable feeling stayed with me while he ate. Conversely, the return of the knife seemed to have an opposite effect on Hawkeye. He vigorously rubbed his stomach in appreciation when he finished the bread and broth, though he kept back the last crust and offered it to Sam.

The dog swallowed it in one gulp and looked expectantly for more. I snapped my fingers. "Come on, Sam."

Sam gamboled at my side as we returned to the house. After the dog had been fed, I spent the remainder of the morning closeted in the house. Since the Indian's arrival, I'd neglected my indoor chores, preferring to be outside where I could keep a better eye on my patient. After washing and drying an accumulation of dirty dishes, I turned my attention to churning butter and seeing to the cheese.

Noon was approaching and I was about to go out to the barn to check on Hawkeye when I heard someone call, "Hello?"

I looked out the door and saw a team and wagon pulling into the yard. My first thought was Sven and Flora, my second thought the Indian. Dear as my friends were, I was unsure of what they would think when they learned I'd taken in an injured Indian. It was too late to run and close the barn door—too late to tell Hawkeye to stay inside so he wouldn't be seen. I would just have to explain to Flora.

A feeling of dread washed over me when, instead of Sven and Flora, I recognized Virgil and Grace Petty, a couple I'd met at worship meeting.

"Hello, Mrs. Mueller," Virgil called. He was a big man, both in height and breadth, his voice seeming to come from somewhere deep inside of him.

"Good day," I answered. I brushed nervously at a strand of hair that had escaped from its pins, and I forced my mouth into a smile of welcome. *Why couldn't it be Flora and Sven?*

I watched as Virgil helped his wife down from the wagon. Like her husband, Grace was big, her voice almost as deep as his as she asked how I was feeling.

"Quite well, thank you."

Her close-set blue eyes were busy looking me over. They paused when they reached my middle. "I understand you're increasing."

I nodded, expecting to be congratulated or at least hear about one of her numerous pregnancies. I received neither.

"All the more reason for you to leave this place and come where it'll be easier for folks to look after you," she boomed. "I told Flora I was gonna see what I could do to make you change your mind—see the sense to it."

"But I don't want to change my mind."

That earned me a sharp look from Grace and one no more pleased from her husband, who'd taken an ax and sharpening tools out of the wagon.

"Thought I'd get some wood chopped," Virgil said, but his look implied that I ought to pay more heed to what his wife was saying.

I cast a quick look at the barn. What was Hawkeye thinking? I prayed that he'd found a place to hide. And where was Sam?

Just as if he'd heard me wondering, the dog sauntered around the side of the barn, his tail wagging as he barked to let me know we had company.

"I told Sven that mutt wasn't cut out to be a watchdog," Virgil remarked with a shake of his head.

"Actually, he's doing very well," I said and wished I could tell them how Sam had torn into Hawkeye.

"A half-growed dog won't be no help should wolves or Indians decide to pay you a call," Grace pointed out.

"He'll grow." My argument sounded as weak and distracted as my thoughts were. How could I get Grace to stop lecturing me without being rude? And what if Virgil decided to go out to the barn?

"Could I fix you and Mr. Petty a cup of tea?" I asked in desperation.

"No, thank you. Me and Mr. Petty got too much to do to be sitting around drinkin' tea." She plunged a large hand into the pocket of her brown apron. "I have a little seed left over from my garden. Thought I'd plant it for you, though we can't stay but just long enough for Mr. Petty to get some wood chopped and see what else you need him to do."

"The wood is all I need."

"Good." She was already on her way to the garden, me trailing a step behind.

"I'll get the hoe," I told her, glad for a reason to go to the barn to see for myself that Hawkeye was well hidden, though where I didn't know. One thing I did know—I was going to make sure the door to the barn was closed this time.

My step was quick, my eyes busy as I entered the barn, searching for the Indian and not the hoe. There were no sacks of grain or humps of fodder to offer a hiding place. Not even a hayloft. Just the walls and the horse stall.

"Hawkeye?" My voice was a whisper, my pulse making queer jumps and starts as I searched the dim interior. It took only a few seconds to realize the quilt was no longer part of a pallet, but was folded over the side of the stall. The fodder was scattered too; everything looked innocent and normal. No one would suspect the barn had recently housed an Indian.

"Thank heaven," I whispered, glad Hawkeye had gotten away without being seen. But where had he gone? Would he be all right?

These questions followed me as I carried the hoe to the garden. Grace wouldn't let me wonder about Hawkeye for long. Before she had the row of peas half planted she set in again.

"It's a shame what your husband done," she began. "How he hoodwinked our men into helping him build your house and barn. Mr. Petty said he never met such a sweet-talker. Got everyone to help build his house and barn first with the promise to return the favor when it was their turn." She shot me an unfriendly look, like I was Jacob, not Clarissa, and gave a mirthless chuckle. " 'Course, your man seldom showed up to help anyone. There was always some excuse—a hurt back, or his horse gone lame."

"Excuse?" I stared at her, remembering the times Jacob had ridden off in the wagon to help Sven or Virgil or the Tomkins—the times too, when I'd gone with him, fixing food and gossiping with the other women while the men worked on someone's house or barn. "I was with him. I saw Jacob help."

"Only when you came with him, just often enough to keep the neighbors from running him back to Missouri or wherever you came from."

Fresh anger at Jacob rushed through me—shame and embarrassment too. Tight control was all that kept the tears in check. "I never knew. I thought . . ."

Grace was immediately contrite, the indignation that had filled her voice and tightened her broad features slipping into something that resembled compassion. "It's me that should apologize. I promised myself—Flora too—that I wouldn't say nothin'. But when I saw your barn all done and shingled . . . your house too." She paused and dropped a few more seeds into the moist soil. "Sometimes I don't know when to keep my mouth shut."

Grace was more kind after that, letting me know she'd had considerable experience at delivering babies and that she hoped I'd call on her when it got to be my time. "That's another reason we want you to move back across the river. So you'll have women to help when the little one comes."

I thanked her for the offer and thanked her again a few minutes later when she insisted on helping her husband carry in extra loads of wood. I was sure the Pettys meant well. Even so, an hour later, it was with a sigh of relief that I waved them on their way.

As soon as they'd disappeared into the trees, I hurried out to the barn. "Hawkeye." I called, half hoping the Indian would materialize out of the horse stall or one of the deep shadows. When I received no response, I called louder, listening as my voice echoed and bounced against the rafters, feeling glad and sad all at the same time. Glad Hawkeye was well enough to leave and that he'd done so without the Pettys knowing. Sad because once again I was alone.

CHAPTER 5

The next morning as I left the house, I found a mound of damp leaves and fern fronds lying on the doorstep. Pricks of unease skittered across my shoulders as I stared down at the green mass. What was it? How had it gotten there?

Sam was already investigating, his nose sniffing excitedly around the edges. I realized it was a cache of fish just seconds before the dog did.

"No, Sam!" I grabbed the fish, wet leaves still clinging to gray scales, the fishy smell bringing memories of Mickelboro and fresh-caught cod fried up in batter. The leaves held two large fish, cleaned and ready for me to cook for breakfast if I took the notion.

I knew who had brought them—knew with a rush of gladness. "Hawkeye!" I called his name and looked toward the barn, the trees, then finally the mountains, hoping to see his brown image materialize out of the forest even as something told me this was not the Indian way. A jay's raucous scolding was the only answer. Undaunted, I lifted my arm and waved. "Thank you, Hawkeye." A pause while I watched and listened. "Thank you!"

My heart was happy as I fried up the fish—my mouth watering, Sam drooling as he expectantly watched the frying pan. It had been months since I'd eaten fish, for Jacob wasn't much of a fisherman. Thankfully there was no trace of queasiness from my stomach that morning, and the dog and I both ate with appreciation and gusto. Of late my appetite had grown just like my waistline, the baby but four months from being born.

Two mornings later I found a skinned rabbit hanging from a leather thong above the barn door. Recognizing its source, I smiled and called my gratitude into the quiet of the overcast morning.

After breakfast a steady drizzle set in, one that lasted the day. Since Jacob's departure, I'd come to dread such days, not liking to be cooped up in the house with no one but myself and my thoughts for company. Sam was little help on rainy days, for he either slept or prowled the house as restlessly as I did. The storm lasted three days with only brief intervals of sunshine, ones just long enough for me to splash out to the barn or woodshed.

It was a relief to finally wake up to sunshine, to hear the merry song of finches, to feel warmth instead of rain as I ventured outside. Although it was too wet to work the soil in the garden, the damp didn't prevent me from inspecting it and pulling up a few weeds. The potatoes and cabbages were up now, droplets of moisture beaded and sparkling on the green leaves. The row of peas Grace Petty had planted showed only mounds of dark earth.

"Too soon," I told Sam who'd joined me. Although I didn't care much for Mrs. Petty, I knew in July I'd bless her as I ate tender new peas.

Around noon as I was closing the door to the chicken pen, the dog started barking. Not the happy yips he emitted when chasing a squirrel, but a deep bark filled with unease. I watched Sam hurry across the yard, his brindled head and tail lifted, the deepness in his bark increasing as he looked up at the mountains.

My first thought was a bear—my second how to get Brownie and Star into the barn. Then, mingled through the incessant barking, I heard the distant sound of singing. "Quiet, Sam!" I said, mistrusting my ears.

The dog looked over his shoulder, his expression quizzical.

The singing increased in volume, lilting and happy, coming from the mountain, not the river. *Who on earth could it be?* The answer came a moment later as two women and a boy emerged from the trees. I lifted my hand to shade my eyes, the words to the song they sang preceding them down the hill.

"Land of Song, said the warrior bard, Tho' all the world betray thee . . ."

I joined Sam at the edge of the yard, the eggs I'd put in the basket of my blue apron all but forgotten. Were they weary settlers who'd come by foot across the mountains? I dismissed the idea when I noted that the women only carried a small basket between them, and the boy carried nothing.

As they came closer, I studied their features. I decided the women were likely mother and daughter, the eldest in her early forties with delicate, pleasant features, the younger one pretty and perhaps sixteen. All had red hair, the daughter's long unbound hair a bright flame to her mother's subdued russet, the shaggy locks under the boy's cap more sandy. The boy, who looked to be about ten, grinned and waved.

"Good day to you," the older woman called when the song ended. A happy lilt still sounded in her voice.

"Good day," I called back, my mind swarming like a beehive with questions. Where had they come from? And why had they come to my home?

"Hi there, Sam," the gangly boy called.

Sam barked and wagged his tail, looking up at me as he did. How did the boy know Sam's name? I thought of Hawkeye and immediately shook my head. *Surely not.*

The woman's lilting voice intruded into my thoughts. "Have you ever seen a more glorious mornin'?" she asked. "Since likely you're wonderin', we're the O'Connors. I'm Maggie and these are my children, Bridget and Shamus." The young woman dropped a quick curtsy and smiled while the boy took off his cap and nodded. "We're from up the mountain and heard you're alone and might could use some help and company."

"Who told you?" I asked, and before she could reply, "I thought Quinton Reynolds was the only one who lived up the mountain."

"Aye 'tis so," the woman answered, "but there's those that live with him . . . me and my husband, Mick, and our children being the main ones, though there are others from time to time."

"Others?" I asked while my mind strove to assimilate it all.

Eagerness danced across the daughter's fine-boned features as her eyes took in the sight of the house and barn—Bridget, her mother had called her. "Indians," she put in. "They're peaceful as lambs, so there's naught for you to be worryin' your pretty head about."

Maggie nodded as she set down the basket and rubbed her arm. "Tillamook Indians . . . and them so few you hardly know they're here. They help Lieutenant Reynolds with his research."

Questions continued to tumble through my head. Even so, I remembered my manners. "You must be tired after your long walk. Won't you come inside and I'll put the kettle on for tea?"

Shamus's freckled nose crinkled as he grinned his acceptance while his mother nodded. "'Tis a lovely idea, though just a drink of water would be fine."

Shamus and Bridget picked up the basket. "I brought a few things I thought you might be needin'. Some ham and tins of beef." Maggie nodded when I opened the door and motioned her inside. "I tucked in a wee tin of tea, too, some the Lieutenant himself had sent on the last ship from England. 'Tis sure to be the very thing for you in your condition."

I looked after Maggie and her children in bewilderment, watched the determined set of Shamus's chin as he hefted the basket up onto the table. "How did you learn about me?"

Maggie sighed and pulled out Jacob's chair to sit down. "'Twas Nastachee who told us about you . . . but the Lieutenant who said we must help."

"Nastachee?" I stared at the Irish woman.

"The hurt Indian you nursed, though I'm thinkin' he said 'twas Hawkeye you were callin' him."

Understanding flooded through me, quickly followed by embarrassment, especially when I recalled all the things I'd told the Indian. "Not . . . ?"

"Aye." Laughter brimmed in Maggie's blue eyes. "He said you and me ought to get on well together since we both take such pleasure in talkin'." Her laughter bubbled out, kind and wholehearted, inviting me to join in.

Which I did, even as heat rose to my cheeks. "If only I'd known," I laughed. "I'd like to box that man's ears."

Bridget and Shamus joined in the merriment, clearly delighted at Hawkeye's joke. Sam joined us too, making dog noises and wagging his tail.

"All I got out of Hawkeye were some strange Indian words . . . that and rubbing his stomach to tell me he liked my cooking," I said when our laughter quieted. Into the stillness I added, "In some ways I'm glad I didn't know. I've been terribly lonely. I think all that talking did me good."

Maggie nodded. "I'm thinkin' Nastachee knew that. 'Twas why he pretended not to understand you."

"How is he?" I asked.

"Oh, all recovered he is, thanks to your good care. He had naught but praise for your nursin'. Your bravery too." Maggie nodded when I started to protest. "Aye, brave you were with only the pup to protect you." She shot a disapproving look at Bridget, who was peering into my bedroom. "Nastachee is wise about people. I put great stock in his opinions."

* * *

I learned much that day about the O'Connors and the life they lived in the big house up the mountain. Much, too, about Mr. Quinton Reynolds, whom Maggie affectionately referred to as "the Lieutenant"—all learned while we sipped tea and Shamus chopped and brought in loads of wood, his arms stronger than his slight frame suggested. The O'Connors and the Lieutenant had been together for almost thirteen years, Mick serving as aide for the lieutenant, who was the youngest son of a wealthy Englishman that had bought Quinton a commission in the English army. Quinn— as the lieutenant was also called—was young, barely eighteen, when he was sent with his regiment to the vast reaches of western Canada.

" 'Twas then he fell in love with this country," Maggie explained, "though in those days the English were as determined as the Americans to claim Oregon." She shot me a quick look. "'Twas a big decision for us . . . to let Mick go off to parts unknown and me stay behind in Ireland with three little ones. 'Tisn't a time I like rememberin', for we were always hungry . . . always strugglin' to keep ourselves together. The army was Mick's only hope for work and a shilling or two. But he promised to come back for us. And he did."

I tried to picture this woman as she had been then—young like her daughter, with fiery red hair, in love with her young husband, and left with three children and trying to keep them from starving. I looked at her with compassion and felt a blossoming kinship. Maggie knew firsthand what it was like to be left—how it felt to be lonely.

After the Lieutenant returned from Oregon, the O'Connors were able to stay together, billeting being provided for the soldiers and their families during the years Mick had been posted with Lieutenant Reynolds in England.

" 'Twasn't the case during the Crimean War, though." Maggie's voice grew somber. She and I still sat at the table, tea cups empty, Bridget having gone outside to help Shamus with the wood.

I knew very little about the Crimean War, for Mother's illness had occupied my thoughts during the years it had lasted. But I learned of it now, of the terrible carnage the English army had suffered in Sevastopol and Balaklava—how Lieutenant Reynolds had been badly wounded and left for dead amid the tangle of twisted, lifeless bodies he'd led into battle.

"When the Lieutenant didn't come back, Mick went out to look for him." Maggie shifted her weight on the chair, her blue eyes sorrowful. " 'Twas in the dead of night, with Russian snipers still shooting into the blackness each time they were for hearin' or seein' movement. Mick don't talk of it . . . the moaning and terrible cries from them that was wounded . . . of his fear of bein' shot himself. 'Tis still somethin' he has nightmares about."

She paused, the pop and crackle of the fire in the stove the only sound to fill the silence. In my mind I was there, watching her husband furtively make his way among the dead and wounded, stopping to offer a drink from his canteen to one, a word of sympathy and encouragement to another. Although I hadn't met Mick, I came to know him as his wife related their story, came to like and respect him during the time she talked. Maggie and Mick O'Connor were the kind of neighbors I'd longed to have.

"When did Mick find the Lieutenant?" I asked.

" 'Twasn't 'til almost dawn. Mick had about given up . . . was goin' to turn back. Then he saw the glint of the silver medallion the Lieutenant always wore 'round his neck. His good luck piece he called it, one given to him by his sister when he first got his commission."

I watched the play of emotions on Maggie's fine-chiseled features, saw the pursing of her full lips, the lift of her light-colored eyebrows. While we'd talked, I'd come to know her features well, the sprinkle of freckles across her narrow nose, the habit she had of running her tongue across her front teeth just before she spoke.

She did this now as she made the sign of the cross. " 'Twas the Holy Father himself and his sweet angels that brought Mick and the Lieutenant back. Mick could only half carry Mr. Reynold's, not bein' able to stand, for men still be firin' their unholy guns into the battlefield."

A tiny smile lifted Maggie's lips. " 'Tisn't my way to brag, but you should be knowin' that my Mick is not a big man . . . not but a bit taller than meself. Had you but seen the Lieutenant, you'd be knowin' that he, on the other hand, is right up next to the trees—tall and broad through the shoulders. 'Twas quite a feat for my Mick. But he did it. Saved them both, though God had a part in it too."

"Was the Lieutenant badly wounded?" I asked.

"Aye." Maggie's answer was a sigh. "The poor man's leg was shattered by a cannon ball and him out of his head with pain and loss of blood. When he rallied enough to speak, he begged Mick not to let the doctors amputate."

Maggie's lips tightened and she looked down at the table. "All this came to me but secondhand, me and the children left behind again. I know naught of the terrible suffering the poor man went through, or of what my Mick did to get him away from the doctors. I know only that when I saw them three months later, the Lieutenant looked like he belonged in a coffin and my Mick not much better."

Neither of us spoke for a moment, the sound of Shamus's ax taking the place of conversation.

Bridget's young voice intruded into the silence. "Mam be leavin' out some o' the bad parts . . . all those poor soldiers dyin' from cholera and fever."

I glanced at Bridget who stood in the doorway with an armload of wood, her unbound hair catching the light of the sun, her voice thick with emotion. "Paddy Mulvey said sickness killed more of our soldiers than Russian bullets did." She paused and crossed herself. "Every day I thank the Blessed Virgin for bringing our da and the Lieutenant home to us."

Maggie crossed herself and nodded. "Aye, 'twas a miracle."

As she spoke, my mind harkened back to the tall figure I'd seen standing at the edge of the rainforest, his walking stick, the slight limp. I wanted to hear the details of Quinn Reynold's recovery, learn the hows and whys of their coming to Oregon. Before I could ask, Shamus put his head in the doorway.

"Unless you be wantin' a wetting, I think we'd best be headin' for home. Dark clouds are coming over the mountains and rain can't be far behind."

In no time we were standing in the yard, the gathering clouds as ominous as Shamus had warned.

"You'd better hurry," I told Maggie after thanking her again for the gifts. The best gift, though, was their company—the sound of their voices, the welcome clutter of extra legs and bodies around the table as we sipped tea.

The dog and I followed them across the grassy yard. "I just met you and already I miss you," I said. "Please, come again."

"Aye, we shall." Maggie paused and leaned close. "I liked you a'fore I came just from the things Nastachee told us. After meeting you, I like you even more."

Bridget nodded. "We'll come again soon," she promised. "I'm in need of the sound of fresh voices." The look in her eyes told me how badly she wanted to have a friend.

"Better yet, the next good weather I'll send Shamus down the mountain for you." Maggie laughed at my puzzled expression. "'Tis your turn to visit us, and Shamus can be your guide. 'Tisn't far . . . not much more than a little stroll. 'Twill do you good to get away from here for a few hours. Too much of yourself and the sameness of the cottage can be very wearing."

Then the three of them set off up the sloping pasture to the first hill, turning to wave from time to time while Shamus kept a wary eye on the clouds.

I smiled and waved back, the prospect of an outing to Quinn Reynold's home up the mountain beckoning like a lively Irish pixie.

* * *

More than a week passed before I was able to visit the O'Connors. It was as if nature and God had decided to teach me lessons in patience, the two of them conspiring to bring about a long spate of rain. Each time I thought it was about to clear up, another army of gray clouds marched over the mountains, their bellies dark and laden with more moisture.

Then one morning in early June I wakened to bright sun and a sky so blue it hurt my eyes when I looked out the door. Sam was as eager as I was to be outside. There was much to do; my first destination after milking Brownie was an inspection of the garden. The potatoes and squash seemed to have grown a foot and the weeds not far behind. By now the peas had sprouted, the green plants marching in neat ranks down the row Grace had planted. I was enormously pleased at the garden's progress, envisioning summer meals with the table piled high with fresh peas and carrots. Of late my increasing waist and appetite made any prospect of food tantalizing.

Two sunny days passed before I heard Shamus's merry whistle and saw his gangly form emerge from the wooded hill above the house. I think the dog was almost as glad to see him as I was, streaking off across the yard as soon as Shamus called his name. Unfortunately, a few minutes later, Sam was put in the barn and the door locked.

"Our hounds don't take kindly to strange dogs. It will be better if we leave Sam at home," Shamus explained.

I wore my blue dress for the occasion, one that brought out the blue of my eyes. I had already determined not to climb the mountain empty handed. Snatching up my red shawl, I reached for a basket, the inside lined with cloth and feathers to cushion the eggs I'd been hoarding for the O'Connors. With so many to cook and bake for, I figured Maggie must often wish for more fresh eggs.

The path Shamus and I took was the same one I'd used to reach the craggy ledge. I hadn't ventured that way for several weeks, and I took delight in the changes nature had wrought. The white trillium and yellow globes of the skunk cabbage had given way to the pink blossoms of bleeding heart and wild roses. The tangle of salmon berries and fern was now so dense and thick we were forced to keep right to the path.

Until that day the changes wrought on my body had been but minor inconveniences, the need to loosen the fastenings on my clothes the most obvious. But I hadn't gone far before I realized I could no longer climb the trail like a carefree girl, but must step carefully to maintain my balance and rest more frequently to catch my breath.

Shamus, bless his soul, kept looking back to check on me. I'm not sure what Maggie had told him, but he treated me as if I were a princess and he the knight sent to see me safely over the mountain.

Just past the craggy ledge, before the trail plunged downward to the ocean, Shamus took a lesser trail that veered to the left and continued climbing. Along the way he found a sturdy walking stick to help me climb. The forest was all around us, our feet making little noise on the needle-carpeted path, the distant sound of a rushing stream melding with the sigh of wind in the tops of the hemlocks—a world scarcely disturbed by human touch.

Shamus began to sing, his voice clear and true despite the steepness of the climb. "Oh, did you hear of the Galway boy who went to sea a singing?"

His brogue grew thicker as the song progressed, which made it difficult to follow the words of the story. In the end I gave up and lost myself in the tune and lilt of the music.

"You have a beautiful voice," I said when the song ended.

"Oh, aye," he replied as if he received compliments a dozen times a day. "You should be hearing me da and me brother Liam, though. They've voices to set the fairies dancin'."

I smiled, liking Shamus's colorful speech as much as I liked his ready smile.

"You'll have to join us an evening . . . me da playin' the pipes and the rest of us singin'. We make some grand music. Sometimes the Lieutenant himself joins us . . . sometimes even the Indians."

"Does the Lieutenant sing too?"

"No, but he likes a cheerful tune as well as the next man. 'Tis not uncommon to see his toes tappin'." Shamus stopped to catch his breath, brushing his sleeve across his forehead.

I welcomed the chance to rest and looked back along the path as it twisted between thick columns of hemlock and Sitka spruce, to watch the flash of silver water from the stream as it tumbled and plunged toward the sea.

" 'Twas the Lieutenant who suggested we sing so you wouldn't be nervous when we came to visit you." Shamus nodded at my look of surprise. "Aye, he did, though 'twas Mam who thought to bring the tea, and Bridget who was for seein' that you got the ham."

"What about you?" I asked.

Shamus shrugged and gave a rueful grin. "I came for choppin' wood."

"Something I've been thankful for every morning since you left."

Shamus flushed and looked away. " 'Twas nothin'." But I could tell he was pleased, as well as being proud of his burgeoning muscles.

I smiled to myself as we resumed our climb, watched how he self-consciously straightened his shoulders and stepped out with a bolder stride. We climbed in silence for several minutes, the cry of a jay and the sound of rushing water taking the place of our voices. I wondered how much farther we had to go, what the Englishman's house looked like, and if by chance I would see Hawkeye. I was about to ask when Shamus stopped and pointed.

"There 'tis," he said. "Graystone, as Bridget likes to be namin' it, though the Lieutenant just calls it the lodge."

I looked through the trees to a clearing, staring in amazement at the sprawling log structure with a high, multigabled roof and three gray-stone chimneys rubbing shoulders with the gables. My eyes were too busy noticing how the numerous windows broke the symmetry of the logs to pay much heed to Shamus, but I suspected he grinned, pleased that I was properly impressed. "Oh," was all I could think to say.

" 'Tis grand," Shamus agreed, "though not as grand as where the Lieutenant used to live. Least that's what my da says, and he should know since he helped the Lieutenant get home when his leg was hurt so bad."

Shamus put his fingers to his lips and let out a long, piercing whistle. Immediately, two of the largest dogs I'd ever seen came running toward us—gray and square-muzzled with long floppy ears.

My fingers tightened on the walking stick and I moved closer to Shamus, though he was smaller than I. No wonder he'd told me to leave Sam behind.

"They'll not harm you," Shamus assured me. "Not when I'm with you. Once they get to know you, they'll be friendly even when I'm not around." He paused and grinned at me. "Hold out your hand."

I transferred the basket of eggs to my other hand and did as he instructed, reminding myself that dogs had always liked me.

"This be Balor," Shamus told me as the first dog sniffed my fingers. "We named him after one of our famous Irish warriors."

"Hello, Balor."

The dog wagged its dark gray tail and licked my hand, his companion but a step behind him, head erect and ears pricked forward.

"This one we call Finn," Shamus went on. "He's not as quick to make friends, but once he does you can't find a better dog." He patted the second dog's head, which came well past his waist.

"I've never seen such big dogs," I said when Finn finally licked my hand.

"Irish wolfhounds." Pride sounded in the boy's voice. "You'll not be findin' a grander dog anywhere. Loyal they are and so strong they can take down a wolf. In the old days Irish kings took them into battle."

I looked at the dogs with growing respect, pictured them loping beside a mounted rider—Finn, shaggy haired and silvery-gray like a ghost, and Balor gray like his brother with shadings of black on his face and tail. "Are the dogs yours or the Lieutenant's?"

"The Lieutenant's." I heard the regret in his voice, one quickly replaced by a cocky grin. "But next to him they like me best."

A movement from the house took my attention from Shamus and the dogs. Bridget's bright curls and excited voice came simultaneously. "They're here," she called over her shoulder. And in the next breath, "What took you so long? We thought you'd never get here." She hurried toward us.

"I'm afraid it was my fault," I explained. "I don't walk as fast as I used to."

Bridget took hold of my arm and drew me across the grassy yard to the house. "Mam has tea waiting with fresh-baked scones and the first strawberries." Her hand tightened with excitement as she added, "You're the first company we've had in ages."

I looked at Bridget with new eyes, realizing that despite being surrounded by family, she too was lonely for new faces, new voices.

Maggie waited at the door to enfold me in a quick hug followed by a kiss on the cheek, exclaiming how good it was to see me. "How did your poor legs do on the climb? Did Shamus take proper care of you?" Not giving me time to answer, she hurried on. "For sure you'll be needing a rest. Come inside and sit. I've already put the kettle on."

The kitchen was large with a long table running the length of the room. I looked around with interest, noting the cast-iron sink next to a worktable, two multishelved cupboards filled with crockery and cooking utensils, and a large freshly blackened cooking stove.

"Is it not the grandest kitchen you've ever set eyes on?" Maggie asked. "'Twas the Lieutenant's doing. He insisted I have the very best."

"To be sure Mam's the best cook in all of Ireland . . . Oregon too," Shamus put in. His gray eyes had found the plate of scones and the green bowl sitting beside it brimming with strawberries.

"It's lovely," I agreed, though I was referring as much to the warmth and color and shine of the room as I was to its size and furnishings. All were nice—"grand" in the O'Connor vernacular— but it was the glow of polished brass and silver pewter, the reflection of sunlight on the well-scrubbed puncheon floor that made me feel welcome; such was warm as Maggie's hug, as heartfelt as Bridget's handclasp.

"I brought you something." I handed the basket to Maggie. "It's not much."

"Aye, it is. I'm always sending Shamus out to hunt for more eggs." Maggie peered more closely into the basket. "Can you believe? Not a single one broken."

In no time the four of us were seated at one end of the long oak table, drinking steaming tea served in green flowered cups. A large pitcher of cream for the tea and strawberries filled our view. I'd hoped to meet the rest of the O'Connors, perhaps even Mick. Instead I learned that Liam, their eldest son, had accepted the Lieutenant's help to get land of his own and was homesteading in the Willamette Valley. Fiona, the eldest daughter, had gone with him to keep house.

"Everything is working out grand," Maggie told me. "Liam was able to claim good land, build a house, and find himself a wife all in the same year."

"A good Catholic girl," Bridget put in. "Fiona found someone too. Pure daft for him she was. The Lieutenant hired a boat for us to go to their double wedding." She paused to savor the taste of a strawberry and glanced significantly at her mother. "Soon 'twill be my turn. That is if Mam will be letting me go."

"You're forgetting how young you are. Still not old enough to be going off to live with Fiona."

"But, Mam . . ." Bridget gave an impatient shake of her head.

"Will I be able to meet your husband while I'm here?" I asked Maggie, thinking it wise to change the subject.

"Perhaps later. He and the Lieutenant are cleaning Indian relics. Artifacts, Mr. Reynolds calls them, and right rare so he believes. He has a great room for them in the far wing. That's where he and my Mick are now."

Maggie drained her cup and looked over at Shamus. "Speaking of your da, are you remembering he told you to check on the animals? We don't want to risk the cows wandering off." She gave me a quick glance. "Living so close to the forest we take thought of bears and wolves and such things, though we've not had any unwelcome visitors for more than a year. Finn and Balor are grand at keeping the creatures away."

As Shamus stood up he reached for another scone.

"Only one," Maggie said. "And no more strawberries. Your da and the Lieutenant will want some too."

When Shamus had gone, Maggie pushed back her chair. "Would you like to see the lodge while you're here?"

I nodded, curious to discover the living arrangements. Did the O'Connors live in one of the smaller structures outside, or in the lodge with the Lieutenant?

Bridget led the way, smiling back over her shoulder as we left the kitchen, bright curls a frame for her pretty face. "This is our part of the lodge," she said, pointing with pride through the door at a large comfortably furnished room with a gray-stone fireplace. "Our very own parlor and three sleeping rooms just beyond."

My surprise must have shown, for Maggie added, "The Lieutenant said his home would be our home if we'd but come with him to this grand new country." A nod of her head followed. "Said the children would be looked after too. Land of his own for Liam, Shamus, too, should he want it, and grand dowries for Fiona and Bridget. We'd have been daft not to come." Another nod. "As you can see, Mr. Reynolds is a man of his word. That and even better, for he looks after us like we're for being his family."

My eyes traveled around the room, noting the green sofa, matching overstuffed chairs on either side of the fireplace and the flowered carpet covering the center of the polished pine floor. "Doesn't Mr. Reynolds have a family?"

"Oh, a mam and da the same as you and me . . . two older brothers and a sister too."

"But no wife and children?"

Maggie sadly crossed herself and shook her head. "A young wife who died in childbed . . . and a wee baby daughter who followed her mam just a day later. Both are with the Holy Mother and the sweet angels now."

I experienced a wave of sympathy, realizing that for all his wealth, Quinton Reynolds had not had an easy life. I then learned more of this intriguing man—a man who'd left the luxury of privileged England to build a home in the wilds of Oregon—as I followed Bridget and Maggie back to the kitchen and through a side door to the wing of the lodge that made up the front of the structure.

When I entered the first room, I felt as if I'd walked into the home of my childhood, one of velvet-upholstered sofas and chairs with scrolled cherry-wood legs, shelf after shelf of books rising to the ceiling, thick carpet, and, most amazingly, a pianoforte.

I smiled my pleasure, thinking that except for the varnished log walls, I might as well have been standing in an English drawing room with windows stretching floor to ceiling, draped in rich burgundy curtains held back by gold-braided tassels to let in the light. "How lovely," I breathed.

"'Tis that," Maggie agreed. "The Lieutenant did not stint on windows. He likes plenty of light—not to mention his view of the forest in the back and the grand view of the ocean from here in front."

Bridget ran fingers over the covered keys of the pianoforte. "'Tis my favorite room. I'd be dusting and polishing it every day if Mam would let me."

"She would that," her mother agreed, pride sounding in her voice. "Always sitting in here and reading books. She can even pick out a tune or two on the pianoforte."

I almost told them I'd often played a similar instrument, but decided that today I wanted to learn of the O'Connors and the Englishman's home rather than talk about my own life.

"How did Mr. Reynolds bring all of this to Oregon?" I asked, knowing that winter storms often made navigation into Tillamook Bay impossible—how mail and supplies sometimes took weeks to get in.

"His da has made a fortune in trade . . . big ships and the likes. 'Twas one of his ships that brought us here, all the way 'round the cape. Took us weeks to get here. Brought other Irishmen too, for helping him fell the grand trees and build the lodge. We were like a wee village for a time. Men chopping and sawing and building."

Questions bobbed through my mind. What had become of the other Irishmen? Where had the ship landed?

"The ship put in at the cove you can see from the window." Bridget pointed outside.

I'd been so engrossed in the drawing room I hadn't paid any attention to the view. I followed Bridget to the window where the wide expanse of the Pacific was visible—shimmering blue with white breakers—and the cove where I'd glimpsed the Englishman. I recalled the steps hewn into the steep drop to the beach, steps that must have been used innumerable times to bring Quinton Reynolds and the O'Connors ashore along with their furniture and supplies.

" 'Twas no small task," Maggie said. "We lived rough the first year while the men built the house. 'Tisn't a time I like remembering . . . all the rain and no proper roof to shed it. When the second ship finally came with the furniture, we had a grand celebration with singing and dancing and more drinking than was wise. The Lieutenant saw how it was with the men, understood their need, though he's not a drinking man."

I shook my head in wonderment. "Instead of calling Mr. Reynolds the Odd Brit, the settlers should call him a miracle man."

Maggie laughed. "We've heard of the name they call him. I suppose, to some, a man so interested in old Indian things might seem odd." She and Bridget shared a smile. "But to us, he's our friend the Lieutenant."

* * *

We were standing at the window looking out at the restless Pacific framed by hemlocks when I heard the outer door to the kitchen open. We turned as one and retraced our steps to the kitchen. I immediately recognized Mick from his wife's description—bandy-legged and short of stature with curly brown hair growing well past his ears. His gait was almost a swagger as he entered the room.

"You must be Mrs. Mueller," he said, extending his hand. "I'm Mick O'Connor and glad I am to meet you." His calloused hand closed around mine as his gray eyes took me in. "Aye," he said after a tiny pause, "When Maggie said you were fair as the fairies, she was not stretching the truth."

I felt the color come to my cheeks as I shot a quick look at Maggie. "Thank you."

"'Tis true," she declared. "Still and all, we don't want to be makin' Mrs. Mueller blush."

"Please call me Clarissa."

"Clarissa." Maggie smiled as if the sound of it pleased her. "What a lovely name, one I'm likin' better than Mrs. Mueller."

She bustled around the kitchen, urging Mick to wash up so he could have a bite to eat, heating water for fresh tea.

"And how is life down the mountain?" Mick asked as he dried his hands on a towel.

"Good. Better now that the sun is shining again."

"Oh, aye, but without the lovely rain we'd not be havin' all the lovely trees and flowers, now would we?" He paused and hung up the towel. "Maggie tells me you have a snug little home . . . a right nice barn too, according to Nastachee, though I guess 'twas Hawkeye you called him."

"It was. I hoped to see him today so I could give him a piece of my mind for tricking me like he did."

This brought a chuckle from Mick, his bushy brows lifting over merry gray eyes. "I'm afraid your dressing down will have to wait. Nastachee's gone home to his wife and family or perhaps off hunting. We never know with the Indians. They come and go as they please."

"Do they live close?"

"Just over the next mountain, what few there are of them. 'Tis sad to think there used to be hundreds of Tillamook Indians."

I looked from Mick to Maggie. "What happened?"

Maggie sighed and took down clean cups and plates from the cupboard. "Small pox took most of them. That and measles. The white man's curse. Diseases they never had before the white man came."

"How awful."

"Aye." Maggie moved back to the stove to measure fresh tea. "Is it any wonder they're not over trustful of us? Not trusting was likely one of the reasons Nastachee pretended not to understand you."

Bridget busied herself straightening the table—spills and crumbs wiped up, fresh scones added to the half-empty plate. I picked up clean cups to help her. As I did, the outside door opened and a tall broad-shouldered man entered the room. I knew who it was, of course, but knowing didn't help me. The truth was, Quinton Reynold's appearance was not what I had expected—the open friendly smile, his rugged features. Taken aback, I found myself staring, and for the first time in my life I couldn't think of a single thing to say.

CHAPTER 6

Although I'd been raised on Shakespeare and Tennyson, I was well acquainted with the works of other English authors, my favorite work being Charlotte Bronte's *Jane Eyre*. I'd read it so often that Jane's Mr. Rochester had, for me, become the embodiment of all English gentlemen. Whenever Maggie mentioned the Lieutenant, instead of picturing him in the red uniform of an English officer, I saw a man with finely chiseled features and brooding eyes—someone dark and aloof like Mr. Rochester.

Quinton Reynolds was none of these. It was his eyes I first noted—an arresting shade of hazel with little flecks of gold. Instead of brooding, they were bright with interest and his rugged features were pleasantly framed by thick, light brown hair and a squared-off chin. But it was his smile that held me—one slightly lopsided, but so open and friendly I found myself responding in kind.

Leaving his walking stick by the door, the Lieutenant advanced into the kitchen, his limp scarcely noticeable as he approached me. Instead of wearing a dark waistcoat with a snowy cravat, he was dressed in coarse, woven brown trousers and a loose-fitting white shirt. The vest he wore with it was similar to Hawkeye's—woven of grass, cedar bark, and wool, and trimmed with small clamshells—but his feet were shod with sturdy boots instead of moccasins.

"I'm Quinton Reynolds." He extended his hand.

I managed to set down the cups and offer him mine, aware of the warmth of his fingers as they closed around mine. I was also aware of the directness of his gaze, which made me conscious of the faded but still serviceable blue dress I wore, of the straying locks of curly hair that were forever pulling loose from their pins.

"I'm pleased that you could come to visit," he went on, raising my hand to his lips.

My mouth remained motionless and the part of my brain that usually furnished it with things to say was occupied with disjointed impressions—that he had actually kissed my hand, that his tall stature made me feel small and vulnerable, that a tiny scar creased his right eyebrow, and that his hazel eyes brimmed with pleasure and curiosity. The fact was, I was completely taken aback—a woman who was already spoken for, one married almost six years.

Maggie shot me a quick glance and came to my rescue. "As you know, this is our neighbor, Clarissa Mueller."

"It's a pleasure to meet you." His tone was clipped and brimmed with a British accent, though his eyes still smiled.

Thoroughly discomfited, I said the first thing that came to my mind. "You're not at all what I expected."

The Lieutenant chuckled. "If the truth be told, you're not what I was expecting either." Laughter threaded through his words as he asked, "Just what were you expecting?"

His laughter broke the ice and unlocked my tongue. "A proper English gentleman . . . rather like *Jane Eyre's* Mr. Rochester."

"Not the Odd Brit?" Amusement danced in his hazel eyes.

"Perhaps a little."

Mr. Reynolds walked over to the washstand and poured fresh water into the basin. "If preferring to study the ways of Indians instead of farming makes me seem odd, then I'm content with the title." He lathered soap onto his hands and plunged them into the water. "I left 'the English gentleman' behind when I came to Oregon, though I do like a few comforts." He glanced at me as he dried his hands. "Has Maggie shown you anything of the lodge?"

"She and Bridget."

Quinton's eyes shifted to Bridget, who was busy setting the table. "Wanting Bridget and Shamus to have a proper education is another reason for having my comforts. I brought plenty of books so they could read and keep learning."

"Did ya know he has plans to start a school for Indians?" Bridget said.

The Lieutenant shrugged. "Now do you see why the settlers think me odd? Not only do I educate the Irish, but heathen Indians as well."

Before I could answer, the Englishman pulled out a chair and invited me to join him for tea. I glanced at Maggie and saw her nod. When I sat down, I was aware of the lieutenant's long, sun-bronzed fingers resting on the arms of the chair, of his tall frame standing above me. "Giving people opportunity to learn is admirable, not odd," I said after I was seated.

"'Tis a fact, for sure," Mick agreed. He self-consciously pulled out chairs for Maggie and Bridget, a polite gesture I gathered he'd learned from the Lieutenant.

In a short time, fresh tea was poured and the five of us were sitting at the table. Conversation flowed easily with everyone joining in. Although Quinton Reynolds might have been the O'Connors' employer, the easy laughter and banter that passed between them was more like that of family. I welcomed the sound of voices, the sight of so many pleasant faces sitting around me.

Although I hadn't expected to be hungry again, one bite of Maggie's light scone convinced me otherwise, as did the wild strawberries, sweet and no bigger than the end of my finger, and the expensive English tea liberally laced with cream and sugar. I was content to listen more than talk, observing each detail as if I were an artist painting a picture. I hoarded it away to be taken out later when there was only me sitting at my solitary table—Mick's affection as he looked across the table at his wife, Bridget's delighted giggle when the Lieutenant teased her, how Mr. Reynold's smile and glance made me feel a welcome part of it, a rich, vivid portrait of warmth and sound to ward off my loneliness.

* * *

I had hoped to have a look at the Lieutenant's Indian relics, but we talked so long I ran out of time. Shamus and Bridget came to see me safely down the mountain. I turned for one last look before we entered the forest and saw Mick and Maggie waving from the door. I purposely refrained from looking at the Lieutenant. Even so, I was aware of where he stood, of the gray wolfhounds on either side of him, one of his hands resting on Balor's head.

Shamus led the way, while Bridget followed and carried my basket filled with the remaining strawberries. "What did you think of the lodge?" Shamus asked before we had gone many steps. "Did I not tell you it was grand?"

"When Mr. Reynolds decides to do something, he doesn't do it by halves," I answered.

"We never thought to live in anything so grand, though it does get lonely," Bridget added. "Now that you know the way, will you come again soon?" she asked.

"Oh, aye," Shamus put in, "though if Mam has her way, you'll be comin' to live with us before long."

I stopped so quickly I almost lost my footing. "Why would your mother want me to do that?"

"Why . . . so yourself would not be livin' all alone," Shamus answered, stopping too.

"Especially with the baby soon to come," Bridget added.

I looked into their faces, Bridget eager and wanting a friend, Shamus rueful as if he feared he'd spoken out of turn. "I appreciate your kind thoughts, but since I intend to keep the homestead for me and the baby, I have to stay there."

My voice bespoke determination and neither of them attempted to argue the point. Instead we talked of Shamus's hope to one day go to a university.

"My da would sooner I stay and take up farmin' with Liam," he concluded.

"What about your mother?"

"She wants me to get more schooling, to stick to my books so one day I can go to a university."

I thought about this as we covered the last few twists of the trail and about Bridget and her lack of opportunity for friends and marriage. Although following Quinton Reynolds to Oregon had opened the way for an easier life for the Irish family, it was not without drawbacks.

I left them at the edge of the forest and made my way across the meadow and to the barn. When I opened the barn door, Sam shot out like a bullet, forgetting his manners as he jumped and tried to cover my face and hands with kisses.

It wasn't until after the milking was finished and supper cooked that I had a chance to sit down. Instead of thinking about Jacob's empty chair, I filled my mind with the memory of me sitting at the long table with the O'Connors. As I did I realized it wasn't just Bridget who longed for a friend. Maggie was lonely too, no doubt missing the friends and family she'd left behind, the chance to talk and gossip with other women over a cup of tea, the stimulation of learning about lives and interests different from her own.

As I readied myself for bed, my long flannel nightgown tucked under my knees as I brushed my hair, I let my thoughts turn to the Lieutenant. In my mind I saw him smiling down at me, felt the warmth of his gaze, sensed his curiosity. He had not been what I had expected, and I didn't know whether to be disappointed or glad.

* * *

The next two days kept me close to home. In addition to the garden's weeding, cream needed to be churned into butter and two yellowing cheeses waited to be turned.

By Wednesday I'd had enough of staying inside. The weather remained fair with only occasional puffy clouds to mar the blue sky, and a soft Oregon breeze blowing inland. The happy song of blackbirds and the warmth of the sun urged me not to waste such a glorious day. Like the clarion call of a trumpet, the mountains and sea beckoned. I answered without hesitation, wrapping hard-boiled eggs, cheese, and bread into a towel. Then I tied them into my red shawl and looped it over my shoulder. Not wanting to leave poor Sam locked in the barn again, I whistled for him to come, laughing as he gamboled across the dandelion-strewn meadow, his nose sniffing excitedly.

I found my walking stick at the base of the hill. With its help, I entered the forest with Sam. The dark green hemlock intertwined with pink clustered rhododendron, and delicate gray-green mosses laid patterns on the mottled trunks of alders. I welcomed the chance to stop and rest when I reached the ledge. Although my advancing

pregnancy made climbing difficult, the rippled blue of the sea urged
me on. Something inside me, bright and expectant, whispered its own
heady excitement. I responded as I'd done as a girl, reaching out to
embrace it even as I wondered what it might be. Caught up in the
magic I began to sing—melodies I used to sing to Mother, ending
with a rollicking sailors' ditty with Sam adding a happy yip each time
I came to the chorus.

The next thing I knew, I was thinking of Quinton Reynolds,
recalling the amusement in his hazel eyes when I'd mentioned Mr.
Rochester, the way I'd responded to his lopsided grin. His face was
neither handsome nor plain, but one I found attractive and appealing
just the same.

In no time we reached the last of the trees and stood on the
stretch of grass and rocks that bordered the drop to the beach. Sam
raced ahead, glad to be out of the close confines of the forest. He
stopped on the edge of the embankment, tail and head held high, ears
pricked as he took in the endless expanse of water.

"Isn't it glorious?" I called.

Sam trotted along the ledge until he found the steps and scrambled down. I followed at a more decorous pace, breathing in the salty
smell of the sea and watching gulls skim across the rolling waves. By
the time I reached the bottom step, Sam was running after the gulls,
barking a happy challenge.

The tide-tumbled black rocks at the bottom of the steps were a
challenge to cross, and I was grateful for my walking stick to give me
balance. When I reached the sand, I looked up and saw Sam coming
at a desperate run with two Irish wolfhounds in hot pursuit.

"Sam!" My voice was a scream. I lifted my walking stick and
hurried toward them. The wolfhounds' long legs gobbled the
distance. I could see the fear in Sam's eyes, read the hounds' purpose.

"Balor! Finn! Stay!" a male voice shouted.

The wolfhounds slowed to a lesser pace.

"Stay!"

The two dogs stopped and looked back at the man advancing on
them. My mind registered this in the blink of an eye as Sam rushed
past me, ears laid back, his tongue lolling.

"Sam!"

Sam circled to face the dogs, his rough-haired sides heaving. I grabbed his collar, my heart pounding a quick accompaniment to Sam's heavy panting as I watched Quinton Reynolds approach.

"It's all right. They won't hurt your dog now."

Despite his reassurance, I felt mistrust. What if Balor and Finn chose to ignore their master? What if they changed their minds? Nervousness kept my eyes pinned to the wolfhounds while some part of me noted that the Englishman's limp was more pronounced when he walked on the sand.

Sam edged closer as the hounds neared, a low growl rumbling from his throat. I patted his head. "It's all right."

The Lieutenant and his dogs stopped before they reached us. "I'm sorry." His voice was contrite. "I didn't know anyone was here until I heard you scream."

"They could have killed my dog," I accused.

"I don't think so." That's all he said, but his gaze told me of his concern. "If you'll let your dog go, Balor and Finn are ready to make friends with him."

I gave him a long, measured stare. "Are you sure?"

Quinn nodded and snapped his finger. "Come, Sam. They won't hurt you."

Sam whined and looked up at me.

I gave him a little shove and held out my hand to Balor. "He wants to be friends," I said when Balor sniffed and licked my hand.

Sam advanced on stiff legs, tail lowered, his ears laid back.

Balor cautiously sniffed at Sam. Then, as if speaking a silent language, they touched noses and their tails began to wag. I felt the tension drain out of me, saw Quinn smile.

"They'll be all right now."

There were a few more tentative sniffs before Quinn picked up a piece of driftwood and flung it toward the surf. All three dogs raced after it and were soon involved in a dog version of tag.

"There," the Lieutenant said, but his expression was questioning as a tiny silence stretched between us.

A dozen questions raced through my mind. "Do you come here often?" was what came out.

"Several times a week, weather permitting. The dogs like the water." A small pause followed. "And so do I."

"I saw you here one day."

Quinn nodded. He was wearing a hat, brown like his vest in color, the brim pushed back to show a lock of light brown hair. He looked down at me and smiled his lopsided grin. Its appeal was even stronger than I'd remembered. Recalling how I'd just been thinking of him, I looked away, surprised to feel heat come to my cheeks—Clarissa Yeager who rarely felt embarrassment. I was suddenly conscious of the faded color of my pink dress. Thank heaven my apron hid the places where the seams had been let out.

"If you look close, you can see an eagle flying above the headland," Quinn said in a soft voice.

I followed his pointing finger and realized that while I'd been lamenting the shabbiness of my dress, the Lieutenant had been searching the sky for the eagle. It took me a moment to find it, the white of its neck and head visible under the broad spread of black wings as it rode an air current in a graceful circle.

"I've never seen one before," I whispered.

Quinn grinned. "Eagles may have keen eyesight, but I doubt it can hear you." I laughed, my embarrassment forgotten as he went on. "That's the male. He and his mate have a nest in one of the old growth cedars up on the headland. I've been watching them since spring."

We continued to watch the eagle's lazy circle. The magic that had lured me to the sea seemed to be wrapped in that moment of sunlight and sky and the graceful spread of dark wings.

Without speaking, we made our way to a driftwood log and sat down. I untied my shawl and unwrapped its contents. "I brought some boiled eggs and cheese. Would you care to join me?" When he hesitated, I added, "There's plenty."

"If you're sure."

I nodded and spread the red shawl on the log between us, the towel unwrapped like a napkin with the food lying in the middle. I was aware of Quinn's long, deft fingers as they cracked and peeled the eggs and found myself comparing them with Jacob's broad, blunt ones. There was an underlying tension as we ate, Quinn as aware of me as I was of him. Twice I looked up and found him studying me, saw admiration before he quickly looked away. Though I strove for nonchalance, excitement threaded its way through the tension. I didn't remember food ever tasting so good, the boiled eggs eaten without salt, wedges of cheese broken off and sandwiched between thick slices of bread.

When we'd finished, Quinn unhooked a leather-lined canteen from around his waist and offered it to me. "Spring water, fresh just this morning."

I drank long, the water chilling my teeth. Then I watched Quinn's muscled neck as he followed suit. By now the dogs had tired of their game and had joined us. Sam lay contentedly by my feet and the wolfhounds stretched in the sun at the end of the log.

Quinn rose and looked out at the sea. Something in his stance tugged at my heart. There was much about him that spoke of loneliness.

"Why did you leave England?" I asked.

He shrugged and didn't answer at first. "There was little to keep me there," he finally said.

"Doesn't your family mind that you've left?"

"My sister does." He continued to watch the tumbling surf, his thumbs hooked in the pockets of his brown trousers. "My father is a difficult man with little interest in anything or anyone that doesn't concern his business. My oldest brothers are very like him, so they get on well. My mother . . ." Quinn took a breath that came out as a sigh. "I think my mother loves me in her own way . . . loves all of us, but the main focus of her life has always been friends, the latest fashions, and which social events to attend." He turned to face me. "Please don't misunderstand. There was love of a sort and many good memories. I was not unhappy as a lad."

I sat on the sun-bleached log and nibbled the last of the cheese. Mother had often chastised me for my frank questions, saying they were impolite and none of my business. But something whispered that this was my business; that in some unknown but exciting way, the Lieutenant would play a vital part in my life.

"Why Oregon? Why so far?"

Again Quinn was slow to answer. His eyes met mine for a long moment, and I sensed that he was not the kind of man who enjoyed talking about himself. "Knowing Maggie, she probably told you I've spent a good many years in the British army . . . that I was wounded in the Crimean War."

I nodded and brushed crumbs from my rounded lap, felt the kick of the baby and Quinn's eyes taking me in—a woman well gone in pregnancy, with tendrils of blond curls blowing around my face.

There was a tiny silence before he went on. "For a time they didn't know whether I would live or die—or if I would have two legs if I did survive. During the long weeks of convalescence, I had plenty of time to think . . . a good thing really, for until then I'd spent little time doing that." He paused and gazed down at his booted feet. "I decided that since God had given me a second chance, I wanted to do something with my life. Make it count for something."

He paused and his brows rose. "You're probably wondering what this has to do with Oregon." That lopsided grin came again, one that caused a curious warmth to gather around my heart. "I decided I wanted to help Mick and Maggie. Mick saved my life, and Maggie is like a second mother. But it was more than that."

He rejoined me on the log, a soft breeze blowing off the water, the three dogs napping in the sun. "I've only been to Ireland once. I found beauty there, much to remind me of Oregon. But there was ugliness too. So much poverty." He shook his head. "This was all Mick and Maggie had to go back to. More than that, my great-grandfather was one of Cromwell's officers, and I knew he was responsible for bringing some of the misery to the Irish."

I was mesmerized by the deepness of his voice, his British accent like a song of its own. I watched Quinn scratch Balor's gray head, anxious for him to go on.

"What I have in mind will take a few years." He shot me a sideways glance. "I'd like to bring families over from Ireland. Perhaps one a year. Help them get established so they can homestead here in Oregon. It will be in the form of a loan, something they'll need to pay back so they will appreciate it more. Then I'll use the returned loan to help another family come over, then another."

The sibilant sound of the waves followed his words. I thought how my perception of the Odd Brit had changed now that I viewed him through new and appreciative eyes. Small wonder Maggie and

Bridget came well nigh to worshiping their Lieutenant. "What a wonderful plan. Revolutionary too."

"Oh, aye, as Mick would say. Unfortunately, my father isn't over fond of the idea. He has no great love for the Irish. No love for what I want to do for the Indians either. He thinks me a radical, a real rebel." His lopsided grin resurfaced. "If I'd been alive in 1776, no doubt I'd have fought with the colonists."

I laughed for no other reason than that I was happy, liking Quinn Reynolds better each time he opened his mouth. Sam heard me and rose to his feet, sniffing my hands and the empty shawl and looking up with disappointed eyes when he realized the food was gone.

"I'm sorry, Sam." I glanced up and saw Quinn frowning, his thick brows furrowed and a fierce look in his eyes.

"What kind of man would go off and leave a woman like you?" he questioned.

"I . . ." I meant to say, "I don't know," but something in his eyes stopped me—admiration tinged with tenderness. I'd never seen such a look, one that made it difficult for me to breathe, the sound of the surf an accompaniment to the rapid beat of my heart. *Dear heaven, what is happening?*

Then Sam nuzzled against me and reminded me of who I was— Clarissa Mueller, a married woman, though since Jacob had deserted me that was now just a formality. The dog seemed to have reminded Quinn too, for his face slipped back into its customary expression as he said, "It looks like I've eaten your dog's lunch."

"Not really, though Sam believes all I have should be shared. He's good company though. I've given thanks many times that I have him."

"Even with Sam, you shouldn't be living alone."

"I know." I made a point of meeting his hazel eyes. "But for right now, it's what I have to do."

"Has Maggie told you her plan?"

"No, but Shamus has. My friends across the river want me to live with them too. I've told them no, and I'll do the same with Maggie." As I got to my feet, Quinn's hand shot out to steady me, my pregnancy making the act of rising awkward. "I want my own home."

Quinn's hand cupped my elbow. "Then we must do all we can to help you." He paused and repositioned himself with his cane. I was struck by his total lack of embarrassment at his limp. "What would you say to having Shamus stay with you? He could keep your wood chopped and do the chores."

"And who would do yours?"

"Mick and I."

"That will interfere with your work with the Indian relics."

"Only a little."

I thought for a moment. "If you wouldn't mind letting Shamus come once a week to chop wood, I would greatly appreciate it. But there's no need for him to stay." I smiled my gratitude. "I'll be all right."

So it was settled. Shamus would come once a week, and I would pay him with extra eggs from my laying hens.

I don't remember what else we talked about that day, but I do remember the feelings I had as I folded my shawl and Quinn called the wolfhounds. The feelings followed me as we made our way up from the beach and climbed the mountain, the Lieutenant's hand always ready to steady me if I needed it, the wolfhounds and Sam following behind. The feeling was one I hadn't felt for a long time— the security of being with someone strong and capable, someone who wanted to take care of me.

* * *

The next two weeks passed quickly, golden days interspersed with rain. I felt pleasure each time I looked at the garden, saw the growth of the squash and tiny white blossoms on the pea vines. I went after the weeds with a vengeance, the ugly slugs too, my mind intent on a bountiful harvest and food put by for the winter. Two of the hens were setting, which meant there would be baby chicks before long too. I wanted all to be ready for the baby.

Although I tried to keep my mind firmly fixed on the baby, there were times my thoughts took off on little trips of their own. Fanciful trips a woman in my circumstances shouldn't have been taking, ones that wandered along trails that led to the Lieutenant. Without meaning to, I'd find myself smiling at the memory of his grin, or trying to recall the cadence of his British accent. When I realized what

I was doing, I'd push the thoughts away and set my mind on something else, even as I reminded myself that with Jacob gone for good, now would be a good time to see what needed to be done to officially end our marriage. Even so, my eyes kept glancing up at the mountain when they ought to have been counting eggs, staring across the meadow in hopes of seeing Quinn's tall shape emerge out of the trees.

It was Shamus who came, not the Lieutenant. Although I enjoyed the boy, there was a tiny prick of disappointment. Maggie and Bridget took turns accompanying Shamus. Their happy chatter did much to put my thoughts back where they should have been.

The day after Shamus's second wood-chopping venture, Flora and Sven arrived.

"I'm so glad to see you," I said as Sven helped Flora down from the wagon.

"And I you." She hugged me, then stepped back to look me over, smiling as she did. "Just look at you, Clarissa Mueller, heavy with child."

I laughed, happy to have someone else as thrilled as I was at my condition. I placed a hand on my rounded stomach. "It's growing by leaps and bounds. And it's strong too."

"How much longer?"

"A good two months yet. Probably sometime in September." Sven, bless his soul, had moved away to give us privacy.

"Where are the children?" I asked when Flora reached into the back of the wagon for a bundle.

"Home with their Grandma Sarah. Little Sarah has a touch of summer complaint, so I thought she'd be better off there."

I proudly showed off the garden to Flora while Sven unhitched the team. When he was finished we went inside for a cup of tea.

"I've brought you something." Flora set the bundle on the table— a yellow shawl by the looks of it. "Things for the baby from the women at worship service."

I lifted the shawl, felt its softness. Tears moistened my eyes. "Thank you."

"There's more inside."

I unfolded the shawl and found two tiny white gowns and some squares of flannel. Although they showed evidence of wear, they were still in good condition.

"The dresses are from Hannah Mayfield. She wants them back should she have another baby. Otherwise, they're yours to keep. Mrs. Petty put in the flannel. The shawl is from me and Grandma Sarah."

I put my arms around Flora. "You are a dear. All of you are." A happy giggle escaped me. "Even Mrs. Petty."

I didn't mention my meeting with the O'Connors and Quinton Reynolds until after Sven had finished the chores and we were sitting over a second cup of tea. "They're really very nice people," I concluded.

"I'm glad," Flora said. "It will ease my mind to know you have good people living so close."

Sven said nothing to this. In fact, he'd been strangely quiet during my recital about my neighbors.

"What's wrong?" I asked.

His answer was long in coming, and a frown creased his usually pleasant features when he finally spoke. "I don't know that anything's wrong. It's just . . ." He paused and his frown deepened. "The Irish family is probably all right. But the Brit—"

"What about the Brit?" I interrupted.

Flora shot me a quick look, my sharp tone seeming to hang in the air.

"I've never met the man, but some have . . . Mr. Petty being one, your own hus . . . Jacob being another." Sven's mouth tightened. "Neither man had anything good to say about him."

Threads of worry knotted in my stomach. "What did they say?"

"That he has some strange notions about wanting to educate Indians and that he spends most of his time digging for relics around the old villages."

"What's so wrong about that?"

"Nothing I suppose, but you'll have to admit it's a strange way for a man to live . . . cutting himself off from people and making no attempt to farm. Besides, there are mission schools for the Indians."

"That's true."

Silence settled around us. The expression on Sven's face told me there was more. "What else did they say?" I prodded.

"This is only an opinion, mind, but Mr. Petty thinks the Brit keeps an Indian woman."

"Sven!" Flora protested.

Sickness settled in my stomach while threads of worry tightened around the thought. "Surely not," I said.

Flora sensed my distress. "That's just Mr. Petty's opinion," she said. "And you know what little stock we should put in that."

I wanted to bless her even as part of me wanted to know more. *Better to know the worst,* I reasoned. *Then there's no room for surprise.* "What did Jacob say about him?"

Sven scratched his forehead and glanced at Flora.

"Since you've told her this much, you might as well tell her the rest." She sighed.

Sven pursed his lips. "Jacob wasn't too clear about it, so I'm not certain how it happened. I think he accidentally wandered onto the Brit's property and saw him with an Indian woman."

In my mind I pictured the lodge and the spreading trees of the forest.

"Jacob must have said something to the Brit about the squaw. You know how Jacob could be sometimes, mouthy and belligerent. The Brit didn't care for Jacob's tongue and set his dogs on him. Jacob said they were the biggest dogs he'd ever seen and that he barely escaped."

I thought on Sven's words long after he and Flora left. They sat with me at supper and followed me when I climbed into bed. I kept seeing the Lieutenant smiling down at a dusky-skinned woman, perhaps the one who'd made his vest, and wished with all my heart I'd never mentioned my meeting with the O'Connors and Quinton Reynolds.

CHAPTER 7

I had difficulty putting what Sven told me out of my mind. Just when I started to think about something else, it would pop back in— Quinn Reynolds and an Indian woman, the Lieutenant with his squaw. Back and forth I went, believing, not believing, even as I recalled the worshipful way Maggie and Bridget talked about Quinn, and Mick's affection for his employer. If the Lieutenant had a squaw, wouldn't it lessen their admiration?

I decided the only way to solve my unrest was to ask Maggie. She, of all people, knew the man. She would tell me the truth.

I waited impatiently for Wednesday to come, my ears attuned to Shamus's cheery whistle, looking up at the mountains more often than usual. Sam's welcoming bark took me to the door. Disappointment cut through anticipation when I saw that Shamus was alone.

"Where's your mother?" I asked when he'd finished greeting the dog.

"Da and the Lieutenant are needing her today. They've broken one of the cleaning tools, and Mam's the only one who knows how to fix it." He paused and gave me a quick smile. "But she said to tell you she'll be comin' next week and should you be in need of a gossip, you're more than welcome at the lodge." Another pause followed. "That is, if you're feelin' up to it."

I thought on this while Shamus chopped wood and dug the first of the new potatoes. When he'd finished, I invited him to stay to eat, the tiny potatoes boiled and garnished with salt and melted butter. We ate in silence, savoring each bite while I searched for a tactful way to ferret out information about Quinn and the Indian woman. Hadn't Mick said there was an Indian village over the next mountain?

"Is your father the only one who helps Mr. Reynolds search for relics, or does he hire Indians?"

Shamus swallowed a bite of potatoes. "Both."

"Do many Indians help?"

"Mostly just Nastachee and his brother, though once in a while his father-in-law comes."

In spite of frustration, I persisted. "How about the Indian women? Do they come as well?"

Shamus shook his head. "They mostly stay in the village." He leaned back in his chair and rubbed his full stomach. "What's that?" he asked, noticing the shawl I'd left out on the table.

"Some things for the baby." Thrilled to have someone to share them with, I held up the items for Shamus to admire.

"They're nice," he said, but I could tell he wasn't impressed.

I planned to visit Maggie the next day, but each time I thought about it a strange reluctance bade me stay home. Restless and not understanding my emotions, I thought to make a few things for the baby.

Not having access to any stuff goods, I cut up my best petticoat for a baby gown. The white cotton fabric was soft from numerous washings and the ruffle of lace at the bottom could be used for trim. Using one of the dresses Flora had brought for a pattern, it took me only two days to complete a tiny gown and bonnet. Mother's careful training had made me an accomplished seamstress. My stitches were tiny and even, and when the miniature garments were finally finished, I viewed them with both anticipation and pride.

While I stitched, I allowed myself the luxury of dreams, holding up the tiny gown and picturing my baby wearing it. So small. So fragile. If it were a boy, I wanted to name him Robert. If it were a girl, I'd call her Amelia. Being baby hungry, I had no preference. Even so, a thought niggled at the edge of my mind. What if the baby looked like Jacob? What if every time I looked at the baby I saw its father— the man who had abused me and then abandoned me like a coward?

Not liking the disquieting thoughts, I decided to leave the house and go for a walk. I chose the meadow instead of the forest, the flatland instead of a climb. Although it had been fair most of the day, thick herringbone clouds had rolled in to block the sun—a portent of a storm. I welcomed the coolness and took off my bonnet. Using it for a basket, I picked tall stems of blue and purple larkspur that grew wild amid the grasses. When I returned, I would put them in a jar on the table and invite them and the new baby dress to be my company for supper.

Remembering how delicious the new potatoes had tasted, I paused at the garden on my way back to the house. Shamus had left the spade leaning against the wheelbarrow. Surely it wouldn't take much to dig a few potatoes for supper.

I picked up the shovel and set it next to a potato vine. In no time three potatoes were dug. As I bent to pick them up, an aching sensation spread across my back and stomach. It was only a twinge, but it gave me pause. The three potatoes would have to do.

That evening a bouquet of larkspurs shared a spot on the table with the potatoes. I ate with relish until the second pain came. I'd taken the first as a signal to be careful, but when the second one came, it brought on worry. Seven-month babies did not often survive. I must take care.

I went to bed early. When I blew out the lamp, I was grateful for the darkness to absorb my concern. I was able to sleep for a while, the quilt pulled up around my shoulders, my legs drawn up as I curled on one side. Even so my slumber was light. Something didn't feel right. What was wrong? Sometime in the night I was wakened by a third pain, and later a fourth.

"Please, God . . . oh, please," I whispered my prayer into the predawn darkness, whispered it later to the pale gray square of the window when dawn and the next cramp came. *It's too soon. Too soon.*

Worry jerked at my nerves and I started to shiver, trembling so hard it made my teeth chatter. Hating the unnerving sensation, I got up to walk around the room. I hadn't taken more than a few steps when I felt a gush of warm fluid run down my legs. I knew what it was. Knew, too, that when the birth sack broke, delivery was imminent.

My fingers flew to my trembling mouth. "What am I going to do?" I whispered. "Oh, Sam, I need help."

Sam, who was sniffing the wet floor, looked up. The nearest help was Maggie. Could I make it there in time?

Not waiting to think, I searched for shoes and stockings. As I did, another cramping ache spread across my back. I leaned on the bed for support and let out a sigh when it ended. My hands were shaking so hard I had difficulty tying my shoes, difficulty thinking. All my instincts clamored to hurry. I didn't wait to dress, did not wait to do anything except grab my blue cloak from the peg and call for Sam.

It wasn't until I opened the door that I discovered it was raining, not a soft, misty rain, but a steady drizzle. I threw the hood of my cloak over my head and set out.

Head down, I hurried across the meadow, my hand clutching the front of my cloak, my breathing ragged and uneven. Rain and the lowered clouds obscured the mountain. But I knew the way, just as I knew the spot where I'd left the walking stick.

Another wrenching pain began to build just after I found the stick and began the steep climb. I stopped and leaned on the stick for support, my head bowed and droplets of rain running down my cheeks. When it passed, I pressed on with renewed vigor. I had to make every second count. *Hurry!*

Doing so was difficult, for rain had slicked the needle-carpeted path and my sodden nightgown and cloak clung to my legs. Each step became more awkward and burdensome. Sam climbed ahead of me, stopping from time to time to wait, whining plaintively. I drew in a quivering breath as another pain came, more wrenching than the last and lingering longer.

"Oh, Sam." My whisper was frantic as I wondered how I would endure the next and then the one after that. Inwardly I cried for my poor, helpless baby. Too small. How could it live?

My teeth began to chatter again, my nerves and pain and the cold drizzle seeming to take over my body. "Please, God, help me." The prayer became a litany that meshed with my ragged breathing. "Please . . . oh, please."

I was dimly aware of when I reached the craggy knoll, though recognition was quickly supplanted by a pain that struck, building until I thought I would burst. *Dear heaven, did Mother endure this five times? What terrible agony!*

Only instinct helped me find the place where the paths separated, for rain and the gray light of the cloud-shrouded morning made it difficult to see the trail leading on to the lodge. After that everything became a blur, my flagging steps and harsh breathing, the dripping foliage and dark trunks of the wet trees. Cold seeped deep into my bones to join the pain. As my strength waned, my footing became less steady. The walking stick saved me from falling the first time, but I landed hard on my hands and knees the next time I slipped.

I lay on the trail, panting and moaning with barely enough will to whisper, "Get up, Clarissa." Somehow I did, staggering and leaning heavily on the stick. *How much farther? Merciful heaven, how much farther?*

The next contraction made me double with pain, my gritted teeth all that kept me from crying out. I forced more awkward steps. Each one brought me closer to the lodge. *Oh, please . . .* Then I slipped on the wet path and fell hard, gasping and hurt from the jarring, my cheek cradled on my hand.

For a moment, all I could do was lie on the wet path and let the damp leaves and twigs pillow my tortured body, my legs drawn up against the pain and cold. My thoughts were fuzzy and almost past caring. I don't know how long I lay there—perhaps minutes, maybe only a few seconds. Then something warm and moist touched my cheeks, and I heard Sam's plaintive, puzzled whine.

"Sam." My voice was no more than a croak.

Sam started up the path, his wet body a sodden silhouette in the stormy light. He looked back when he realized I hadn't followed him, yipping and waiting.

As I tried to get up, another pain built, its grip like a cruel vice around my middle. I felt Sam's rough tongue on my cheek, heard him whine again. I knew then what I must do, although it took great effort to raise my head.

"Go." I tried to summon strength to my voice. "Go find Shamus."

The dog's short ears moved, but he remained where he was.

I pointed up the path. "Go Sam. Go."

Sam whined, then after a moment he slowly started up the path.

"Find Shamus," I called after him. Then I was caught in the familiar wracking pain. When it finally subsided, there was no rough tongue to warm my cold cheek—only silence and the steady drip of rain.

* * *

The barking of dogs roused me from stupor, the sound echoing and seeming to come from the tall branches of the trees. I tried to put reason back into my mind, but nonsensical images were all that came: Sam bristling and ready to spring at Hawkeye, the wolfhounds gamboling with Sam in the shallow water of the surf. Then masculine voices penetrated the images, and I felt Sam's rough tongue lick my hand.

"Good dog," I attempted, but a hoarse whimper was all that came out.

It was Hawkeye's dusky features that peered down at me, his strong arms that carried me up the trail. I tried to smile my gratitude, dimly aware that the wolfhounds were there, along with Mick and the Lieutenant.

"Blast this leg," Quinn said, his deep voice rasping with frustration. "I'm strong and should be carrying her."

Then another pain gripped me, shoving past the cold and the men and the dogs until there was only me and the terrible pressure of my sweet baby trying to be born. *Too soon. Too soon.*

The warmth of the kitchen roused me enough to hear someone gasp when I was carried through the door.

"Sweet Mary," Maggie whispered.

Bridget crowded close and took my cold hand and kissed it. "Clarissa, what's wrong?" she cried.

"The baby . . . it's coming."

"Dear heaven," Maggie whispered. And in the next breath. "You'll be fine. We're here to help you. But first, we've got to get you out of these wet clothes."

Quinn took me out of Hawkeye's arms and headed for the room off the kitchen. His gait was firm and surprisingly steady, his arms strong. I closed my eyes and for a moment I felt safe.

Bridget hurried ahead and opened the door to another room. Then I was laid on Bridget's bed, and Maggie's capable hands shrugged my arms out of the sodden cloak while Bridget tugged at my wet shoes. I heard the Lieutenant tell Shamus to bring more wood and heard the sound of someone building up the fire. I stifled a gasp and held my breath as a hard pain again tightened my abdomen.

"How long have they been coming?" Maggie asked. The cloak was removed, but she waited until the contraction passed before she took off my nightgown.

"Last night," I managed to get out. My teeth were chattering so hard my entire body shook.

"Take a quilt and hold it up to the fire," Maggie said to Bridget. She rubbed me with a towel, the vigorous movement softened by her concern. "Dear child," she crooned. "You'll be fine. You'll be just fine."

I wasn't sure whether she spoke to me or the baby, but her voice brought comfort. So did Bridget. The sight of her bright curls and the warmth of the quilt she and Maggie wrapped around me gave me a moment of respite and the feeling that somehow everything would be all right.

After that I only remember pain, the contractions following one after the other like bursts of thunder in an advancing storm. I was vaguely aware when Bridget placed warm rocks wrapped in towels close to my feet, and of Quinn's hovering presence. Maggie's voice broke through the torture as she told Mick to start some water boiling and for him and the Lieutenant to leave the bedroom. "This is no time for a room full of people. The poor girl needs to be left alone." One of her capable hands took hold of mine, and when her voice came again, it was soft and reassuring. "You're doing fine, sweet girl. It won't be long now."

I wanted to be brave, but each new pain stretched my endurance as moans threatened to burst into agonized cries. "Help . . . oh, help!" I held my breath and arched my body against a new contraction.

"Don't fight them," Maggie instructed. "Just let them come. That's the way, darlin'. That's the way."

I tried to relax against the unrelenting pressure—tried not to fight.

"Bite on this." Maggie thrust a piece of toweling into my hand. "I need you to push. The baby's almost here."

I followed Maggie's instructions the best I could, bit down on the toweling, and pushed.

"That's the way, sweet darlin'." Her voice was a mother's croon. "You're doing grand, Clarissa. Just one more."

With a final agonized thrust, my baby was born. My eyes were squeezed shut, and a shrill cry tore from my lips despite the cloth. It took me a second to catch my breath. "Is it alive?"

"Yes . . . yes. A sweet girl."

Too weak for further speech, I watched Maggie cut the cord with a pair of scissors, heard a tiny cough as she wrapped a doll-size figure in a towel. "You're sure she's all right?" I managed to whisper.

She was doing things with the baby. Things I couldn't see. Then I heard a tiny cry, one that sounded like the mew of a newborn kitten.

"A wee one, she is, no bigger than a pixie." Maggie handed the baby to Bridget who hovered at her mother's shoulder. "She's got to be kept warm. Take her in by the stove."

Maggie bent and placed a warm hand on my stomach.

"Please, I want to see my daughter."

Bridget hesitated and glanced at her mother. Seeing her nod, she brought the baby close, pulling the lip of the towel back so I could see the baby's face.

"Amelia." I looked at the tiny face, one no bigger than a large apple, her miniature features so perfect and complete I could only marvel. I did not mind that her closed eyes were without lashes or brows, or that her head was covered with golden fuzz.

When I reached for her, Bridget laid the baby on my shoulder. My heart constricted with tenderness as I nuzzled her soft little head with my cheek. "Let her live," I prayed. "Please, God, let my baby live."

* * *

I dreamed I was back in Mickelboro, a winter storm blowing inland from the sea, snow heaped in the meadow and sleet stinging my face. The wind howled and tore at my blue cloak, whipped it away from my body to expose it to the arctic chill. I could see the cottage just ahead. Mother and Tamsin looked worriedly out the window, lamplight silhouetting their figures against the glass. I tried to hurry, but my feet were buried in the drifts. Cold seeped into my toes while the biting wind numbed my face and arms. A violent shiver shook my limbs, and my teeth began to chatter.

I tried to call and alert Mother and Tamsin to my plight. But the wind's icy threads snatched the words and blew them away. I was cold—so very cold. I moaned, but perhaps it was the wind. Then someone's warm hand touched my cheek, and warm stones were placed next to my feet.

"Drink, Clarissa. It will warm you." I thought it was Mother who spoke, Mother with an Irish brogue and hands roughened from scrubbing and cleaning.

I opened my lips and felt hot tea trickle into my mouth and down my throat. My teeth chattered against the cup.

"Sure and we've got to do something to warm the girl," a male voice said.

I tried to open my eyes, to remember where I was. Something important had happened. Someone needed me. Before I could remember who, the swirling snow returned and covered me with a soft, warm quilt.

* * *

"Clarissa." An incessant voice called my name, tugging at my brain and refusing to leave me alone. At first I thought it was Jacob—Jacob, who'd come back to take care of me. His touch was strangely gentle—firm too as he lifted my aching head to help me drink warm liquid from a cup.

I tried to comply, though swallowing was difficult. My throat felt swollen, and it ached as badly as my head.

"Another swallow," the resonant voice coaxed.

I lifted leaden eyelids and saw a face framed by light brown hair and a lopsided smile. "That's my girl," he said when I swallowed. "Now another."

The hazel eyes looked tired, and I could see the growth of day-old whiskers beginning on his chin. *So odd. So very odd.* And then I remembered.

"My baby," I whispered.

"She's alive. Miracle of miracles, she still lives."

I smiled, or tried to, for my aching head spun dizzily. The Lieutenant's face receded and grew dim, as did the light of the lamp. I closed my eyes and welcomed back the darkness.

Days meshed with nights and nights with days. My mind swirled and drifted like a silent gray mist hovering over the ocean. Sometimes I thought I held my baby, feeling the tug of a tiny mouth. But where before everything had been icy, now all was hot—throbbing and suffocating—pressing in on my chest so I could hardly breathe. Each breath was torture and all was heaviness. My eyelids were as heavy and unwieldy as the covers someone tucked back around me each time I whimpered and tried to move.

Through it all I was aware of voices, sometimes whispering and anxious, other times pleading. Most of the time it was Maggie I heard, gentle as she coaxed me to drink more hot liquid.

"Just a swallow is all." She lifted my head and held the cup to my lips. "I know it smells like the devil himself brewed it, but Bright Star says it can cure the fever and help you breathe."

I choked when I tried to swallow, the warm liquid spewing out as my aching lungs convulsed in a hard, wracking cough. For a second I fought for breath and felt as if I were drowning. Strong arms snatched me upright—Quinn's, not Maggie's—and I was able to gulp in air.

"Holy Father," Maggie whispered. In the background I heard a soft, trembling voice praying.

I was dimly aware that the Lieutenant was sitting behind me on the bed and holding me upright against him. "Breathe, Clarissa. That's the way, my girl. That's the way."

I fought to pull air into my lungs, the act taking concentration and labor.

"Does it help when I hold you up?"

A nod was all I could manage, followed by a hoarse croak that was meant to say, "Baby?"

"Alive." My head lay against Quinn's chest where his voice came as a rumble against my ear. "She's a scrapper just like her mother."

Alive. I held the thought in my mind like a bright talisman of hope, clung to it as I was caught in another frightening fit of coughing. I dimly heard Quinn command me to breathe and I did—once, twice, and then the third, my heart beating rapidly against my chest. I thought of my baby fighting for life, of my daughter who needed a mother. *Please, Father, heal us.*

Prayers brought a change and pulled me away from the edge of death's precipice. At first it was no more than the realization that my breathing was less labored, that the suffocating heat and heaviness was not quite so oppressive. The Lieutenant stayed with me—his arms and chest supporting me in a sitting position, his presence lending me strength through the frightening paroxysms of coughing. Maggie and Bridget were there too. The warm, smelly poultices they put on my chest were changed at regular intervals and the bitter tea coaxed down my throat. Through it all I was aware of the rhythmic click of beads as the two women counted the rosary. Their fervent Catholic prayers blended with my hesitant Protestant ones and God heard and answered.

Mother played a role in my healing too, and in my faltering walk toward God. Although I shared this with few, she was there by my bed during the crisis. At the time I couldn't understand how Ellen Yeager could be transported from the Massachusetts shore to a mountainside on the Oregon coast. Later, when it was confirmed that Mother had died two years previous to my illness, I knew without doubt that her presence had been real and not the imaginings of a fevered brain. For are not mothers always mothers? And after they die, do not angel mothers still watch over their children?

At first she was only a quiet, angel-like presence standing at the side of my bed. Her smile radiated a love so overwhelming I felt enfolded in its peaceful warmth. Then when my cough would not let me catch my breath or rest, Mother reached out to me, and warmth and comfort flowed around me.

Rest, sweet Clarissa. The words didn't come from her lips, but the thoughts poured into me along with the healing power of God.

I'm so sorry about what I did to Tamsin . . . about running away with Jacob. Like her, I communicated through the same electrifying yet peaceful process. *I wouldn't have done it if it hadn't been for the deacon.*

I know. The smile she gave me overflowed with the same love her touch conveyed. She was clothed in white, and her face was young and beautiful. *I've done things that need to be forgiven too. We'll talk of them another time. Now you must concentrate on healing. Give yourself over to God.* She smiled sweetly and moved her hand to my forehead. *I must leave you now. Your baby needs me too.*

Tears of awe and gratitude trickled down my cheeks. I was aware that the Lieutenant slept, of the rhythmic movement of his chest as he supported me. I felt his goodness, felt God's goodness, and from that moment I began to heal.

CHAPTER 8

The days became clearer after that, no longer meshing with the nights, standing distinct. Each brought greater strength—awareness too, and an unrelenting desire and need to see my daughter, to hold her and touch her tiny hands and feet.

"Tomorrow," Maggie said on the day the terrible deep cough relented. "As wee as she is, we want to make sure what you have isn't catchin'."

"She's got to eat." I frowned and looked up at Maggie, the vague memory of someone putting my baby to my bosom returning. "How many days has it been?"

"Since she was born?"

I nodded.

"Today marks the tenth."

"Ten . . . ?" Fear clutched at my insides and my trembling faith faltered. "Where is she? Have you lied to me? Is she dead?" Fear and my questions collided with Maggie's calmness.

"The babe is alive . . . that she breathes and moves is a daily gift from the Holy Virgin herself."

"How?"

Maggie drew a chair close to the bed and sat down. "Hawkeye's wife has been nursin' the baby. Her milk keeps your Amelia alive."

"Ellen. I'm naming her Ellen after my mother." Just speaking my mother's name tore at my heart and filled me with emptiness, this gentle woman who had imbued me with a love of books and music. *She must have died but how?* If only I could have touched her one more time. Sighing, I turned my thoughts to those who were still living. "How did Hawkeye's wife come to be here?" I asked.

"Are you rememberin' that Nastachee was here the morning it happened, the day when your dog led the men down the mountain to find you?"

I nodded, though my memory of the day was hazy. "Wasn't it Hawkeye who carried me?"

"It was." She paused as if she were unsure of how to go on. "In all the confusion no one noticed when he left. It must have been after the baby was born, when he saw the need . . . for need there was with you sick and none of us knowin' whether you were about to be joinin' the angels."

"I almost did."

Maggie's hand closed around mine. "That you did, love. Except for when the Lieutenant looked to be dyin', I never prayed so hard." She smiled before she went on. "Just so you be knowin', the Lieutenant made a wee bed for the mite to lie in, and Bridget has lined it with soft towels. It sits by the stove so she can stay nice and warm."

I thought of the tiny, wizened face I'd glimpsed.

"But that first day when Bridget was holdin' your baby close to the stove, and all of us wonderin' how to feed and keep her alive, Nastachee walked in with his wife and their baby." Maggie paused before she went on. "When Hawkeye said he'd brought his wife to feed the baby, none of us knew what to say. Sure and Bright Star was like an answer from the holy angels, but still . . ."

I pictured the scene, the O'Connors and Quinn Reynolds in the kitchen, Hawkeye and his wife standing a little apart with their baby. "I don't mind," I said, sensing her unease.

There was a visible relaxing in Maggie's features. "I'll be thankin' the Holy Mother then, though I've already been thankin' her every time I see the wee mite take to the nursing—strong like she was nine months instead of early."

"Ellen's growing then?"

"Oh, aye, though not so you can tell unless you be lookin' close. Bright Star has enough milk for both babes. She's been sleepin' in the kitchen, her baby too. Won't hear of a bed, though if you be lookin' for the truth, I don't know where I would put her."

I squeezed Maggie's hand. "I'll never be able to repay you and

Bright Star." Tears came to my eyes. "Thank you, Maggie. You're the best of friends."

"'Tis nothing." Answering tears came to her blue eyes. "Though 'twas nip and tuck for a while. But we made it . . . all of us helpin'—Bridget and Mick, even Shamus." A pause. "The Lieutenant did not sleep for three nights when your cough was so bad."

"I know," I whispered. I thought of Quinn's steadying presence, how he'd battled the cough as if it had been his own, his voice willing me to take another breath—and then another. But so much thought and talk made my eyes grow heavy.

"You'd best sleep now." Maggie got up from the chair. "And I'd best be fixin' something to eat." She paused and winked. "We can both be thankin' our stars we don't have to be boilin' or drinkin' that vile devil's brew anymore."

* * *

When I woke, Bridget was sitting by my bed, a book in the lap of her green calico dress and her brows furrowed in concentration.

"What are you reading?"

Bridget's eyes lifted from the page, and she gave me a bright smile. "*Jane Eyre*. Since I kept pesterin' the Lieutenant to tell me about Mr. Rochester . . ." She paused and her smile broadened. "Do you remember how you were tellin' him you expected him to look like the man?"

At my nod she hurried on. "I suppose he was tired of me askin' so many questions, for the very next day he gave me the book and said I should be readin' it for myself."

"What do you think of it?"

Bridget hugged the red-bound book to her chest. "I'm lovin' it. I've never read anything so romantic, though I'd like Jane better if she'd speak her mind." She gave a self-conscious giggle. "This is my second time through it. And you were right. The Lieutenant doesn't look the least little bit like Mr. Rochester."

"No, he doesn't." I took her hand as I'd done with her mother. "Thank you for taking such good care of me . . . for all you've done for my little Ellen."

At the mention of the baby, her green eyes took on a glow. "Sure and I've never seen anything so small, so sweet. Like one of the fairies, she is." Her slender hand made the sign of the cross. "I've said dozens of prayers for her . . . for yourself." Bridget dropped to her knees, and her eyes filled with tears. "I thought we was losin' you," she said with a quaver in her voice. "I thought you was goin' to be gone to heaven before I'd had a chance to get my fill of you."

My tears joined with hers, spilling freely, emotion and weakness eroding my usual control. "Sweet Bridget."

She gave a sniff and wiped at her tears. "There . . . I'm makin' a regular fool of myself. If Mam finds out I've set you cryin', she'll not let me sit with you again."

"Then we won't tell her." Which we didn't. Instead our talk turned to the baby.

"No bigger than a wee kitten she is, and sounds like one too when she cries, which isn't often. Next time she wakes, I'll bring her to the door so you can have a look-see."

It was late afternoon by the time I got my second look at Ellen. Bridget carried her to the door. "Isn't she a dear?" she asked.

I nodded, although all I could see was the little head, the distance making her features indistinct and hiding the light fuzz of her hair. I saw movement behind Bridget and thought at first it was Maggie. When the person stepped more fully into the doorway, I saw the brown face and twin plaits of Bright Star's hair, the loose-fitting jerkin made of the same curious material as Hawkeye's vest.

I felt her black eyes on me, saw the broad features of her face, a face that was neither pretty nor plain, but carved with gentle lines of character. There was no change of expression, no hint of a smile, only a quiet assessing that made me conscious of my uncombed hair.

"Thank you." My voice was weak when I spoke. Thinking perhaps she couldn't hear me, I smiled.

Bright Star continued to stare at me, then with a slight nod of her head, she turned and left. Bridget gave a quick smile and followed her, closing the sitting-room door behind her.

I thought of Bright Star as I drowsed away the rest of the afternoon. To leave her village and stay in the strange and unfamiliar trappings of a white man's kitchen was no small sacrifice. What had prompted her goodness, and how could I ever repay her?

"You already have," Maggie said when I expressed my concern the next day. She'd finished feeding me my breakfast—a thin gruel made from porridge, much like the one I'd given to Hawkeye. She'd had to spoon it into my mouth since I was still too weak to feed myself.

"How?"

"Wasn't it you who was nursin' her husband back to health two months ago? I don't want to belittle the good Bright Star's done, but I'm sure gratitude was at the bottom of it."

"I never thought of that." But I thought of it often afterward, the strange twist of circumstances that had sent Hawkeye to my home instead of the lodge—the same twist of fate that had placed him at the lodge on the fateful morning I'd given birth to Ellen. Had it been fate? Or was it God? The month before I would have said the former. Now I was not so certain. Hadn't Mother told me to put myself in God's hands?

* * *

I did not get to hold and nurse Ellen until that evening. In the meantime Maggie fed me tempting gruels and urged me to drink frequent sips of water. This last took little urging, for since the fever had broken, I seemed always to be thirsty.

"The water will help bring back your milk . . . God willing that it can still happen."

I looked at Maggie through worried eyes. "Can it? Will it?" I asked, for there'd hardly been any sign.

"Oh, aye," Maggie replied, but I could tell she wasn't totally convinced. "'Tis true you've been terrible sick. But we've seen miracles already. What's to stop there from being more?"

I clung to her words and looked with eyes filled with hope when Bridget and Maggie finally brought Ellen, wrapped in the yellow shawl, to me.

"Shamus told us about the baby clothes you had. Bridget went down for them when Shamus brought your animals up so he could be milking and taking care of the chickens," Maggie explained.

I listened to her with only half a mind. The rest was on the tiny yellow bundle Bridget held out to me. I was propped up with pillows, and weak though I still was, Ellen felt light as air when I took her. Cradling her against me, I gazed with awe at the delicate porcelain-like face peeping out of the yellow shawl. Her eyes were closed, but when I spoke her name her face screwed up and she let out a tiny cry.

"She's hungry," Maggie said. "Would you like to be tryin' to feed her?" Before I could answer, she went on. "Bridget has things to do in the kitchen. If you'd like, I can be showin' you the ins and outs of it."

And she did, though much of it came natural. After the first awkward moment, I began to relax, and felt a joy and fulfillment that was difficult to describe. Tears misted my eyes. *So small. So very small. Yet strong too.* I could feel strength in the tug of her little mouth, read determination in deep blue eyes that opened briefly. A *scrapper,* the Lieutenant had called her. "A scrapper just like her mother," I whispered.

* * *

Just before noon the next day I heard the dogs bark and Quinn calling them off, accompanied by the sound of male voices. One of them sounded like Sven Larsen. A few minutes later a knock came to the kitchen door followed by the same deep voice. It was Sven, of that I was sure, but Maggie didn't look too sure when she ushered Sven and Ben Tomkins into the bedroom.

"Sven," I whispered and held out my hand.

Sven awkwardly made his way to the bed and took it, his hold conveying relief. "We've been worried," he said. "Me and Flora came to check on you yesterday—found the place empty, the dog and cows gone."

"Oh, Sven," I replied, concern at my having worried them in my voice.

"Flora couldn't sleep last night, she was so worried. So me and Ben said we'd come back and see if we could find you." He paused and his voice took on more purpose. "I remembered you'd met your neighbors." He glanced at Maggie, who'd come to stand by the bed. "We was glad to learn you're safe, though we was sorry to hear about what happened."

"I'm doing much better now," I assured him. "Have you seen the baby? Isn't she a miracle?"

"She is." I could tell something was bothering Sven—Sven who'd always tried to look out for me. Suddenly I realized what it was. Not only had he seen Ellen, he'd also seen Bright Star.

I wanted to tell Sven it wasn't what he thought—that Bright Star was Hawkeye's wife and that her willingness to nurse Ellen had saved my baby's life. Then I realized I'd never told Flora and Sven about Hawkeye and that to try to explain about him now would probably make things worse, not better. I also remembered the rumors about the Lieutenant and his Indian woman, rumors of which Sven and Ben were aware.

"As soon as it's safe for you to be moved, I'll be back to take you down to our place. Flora will want to look after you." A quick glance toward the kitchen. "Your baby too."

"Thank you, Sven, though as you can see, we're well taken care of here."

Ben Tomkins cleared his throat when I said that.

I wanted to say more, to reassure them, but my slender reserve of strength was ebbing. "Maggie and her daughter have been angels." I paused for breath. "We'll both be fine."

"Still and all—" Sven began.

"I'm thinkin' you'll not be able to get your team and wagon up the mountain," Maggie interrupted. "And Clarissa is in no shape to be goin' down on her own. We'll look after her and the baby as if they were our own." Maggie smiled to add warmth to her words. "Sure and there's no need for you to be worryin' your head about her now, Mr. Larsen. We'll see that she and Ellen are kept well and safe."

I sensed that Sven wasn't convinced and that he wanted to argue with her, but a long look at me made him change his mind.

"Thank you for coming, Sven. Thank you for caring."

Sven nodded and gave my hand another squeeze. "Knowing Flora, she'll want to see you and the baby for herself. Are you sure you'll be all right?"

It was my turn to nod.

"Then me and Ben will be leaving."

I watched Sven leave with mixed feelings. As friends, he and Flora had always held first place in my heart. Now I was finding that position crowded. Couldn't Sven see that the O'Connors were good people? Didn't he realize they'd saved my life?

* * *

Later that evening the Lieutenant knocked on the door and asked if he could come in.

"Of course." I'd come to look forward to his visits, to the smell of the outdoors that clung to his clothes and the interesting things he shared with me—how Sam and the wolfhounds were settling in, or an idea he had for preserving his Indian relics. This particular evening he carried a book. After pulling up a chair and turning up the wick of the lamp, he opened it.

"If you're in the mood, I thought I'd read to you."

"I'd like it very much. The days are beginning to drag."

"I know how that goes. I was two months in bed with my leg— thought at times I'd go mad from boredom. That's when my sister Anne started to read to me. Books and the sound of her voice became my salvation." A pause and a shy grin. "The poor girl got hoarse from so much reading. We must have gone through five or six books before I regained my strength."

"What did you bring to read?"

"Jane Austen's *Sense and Sensibility.* Do you like her?"

"Very much. The book too. It's been several years since I've read it."

Quinn took a pair of spectacles out of his shirt pocket and put them on. "The family of Dashwood had been long settled in Sussex. Their estate was large, and their residence was at Norland Park," he began. I reveled in the cadence of his voice, in his fascinating accent that gave reality to the British dialogue he read. I watched his face and thought that the gold spectacles lent character to the high planes of his cheekbones. Soon, instead of being in Oregon, I was in the English countryside. Such was the talent of Jane Austen, the magic of the Lieutenant's diction and voice.

As Quinn finished the first chapter, Maggie came in with a glass of milk and a slice of bread spread with freshly churned butter. "To fatten you and the baby."

My appetite had returned and I welcomed the snack, though I didn't welcome the interruption.

"Sure and what a lovely idea to read to her. I'm surprised Bridget didn't think of it." Maggie pulled up a chair on the other side of the bed and sat down, looking at the Lieutenant as if she hoped he'd go on with the reading.

We were both disappointed when Quinn placed a marker in the book and removed his spectacles. Leaning back in his chair he gave me a long, steady look. "The men who came today . . . Mr. Larsen and Mr. Tomkins, are they?"

I nodded. "Sven and Ben."

Quinn frowned and pursed his lips. "I know the settlers think me odd because of the work I do, but . . ." A pause and another frown. "I felt something more than that today. Though we'd never met, the men acted as if they didn't like me, as if I'd done something to offend them." Quinn's eyes never wavered from mine. "Do you know what it is? What they hold against me?"

I knew, of course, but how to tell Quinn? I nervously moved my feet under the sheet and looked at Maggie instead of Quinn. She'd picked up yarn and needles from the table, her eyes suddenly intent on the sweater she was knitting for Ellen.

"I know," I finally said. "But I . . . you . . ."

"Just say it," Quinn prompted. "I have thick skin. You won't hurt my feelings."

"That may be, but . . ."

Maggie was no longer looking at the white yarn on her needles.

"They believe you keep an Indian woman," I said.

"Indian woman?" It was Maggie, not Quinn, who spoke.

"That's what they say."

"Well, they're sayin' a pack of lies." Maggie's voice was loud and indignant. "The very idea."

My embarrassment was such that I hadn't been able to look at the Lieutenant. The quiet control in his voice when he finally spoke drew my gaze to his face. "Who says this?"

"Mr. Petty. And Jacob," I hurried on. "Jacob never told me, but he told Sven he saw you with one and that when he said something to you about it, you set your dogs on him."

"Jacob is a liar." The calm control was still there.

Such was not the case with Maggie. Her voice was angry. " 'Twas your husband with the Indian woman. Bright Star it was. My Mick and the Lieutenant heard her screams and got there in time to save her."

Sickness settled in the pit of my stomach. "Oh, no," I whispered.

I was dimly aware that Quinn had gotten to his feet and that Maggie was patting my arm.

"I'm sorry," she said, her anger gone as quickly as it came. "I never meant to tell you, but I couldn't let you be thinking such things about the Lieutenant. 'Twas lucky Hawkeye had gone up the coast to visit relatives or your husband would not have lived to spread such lies. Most likely that's why he left in such a hurry and is not comin' back. He knows Indians have long, unforgiving memories."

"Dear heaven." I remembered how upset Jacob had been when he warned me about the Odd Brit, and of his hurry to leave for California. I shot a glance at Quinn who was absently playing with the bookmark, saw the intent look on his face. Had he realized how Bright Star's presence in the kitchen today had added to the men's mistaken belief?

"I'm sorry," he said. His eyes held mine for a moment, soft and filled with concern. "I didn't want you to know, didn't want you to be hurt by knowing the truth about your husband."

"There's no need to apologize. I'm glad I found out." I attempted a smile. "Even before I married Jacob, I knew he was a man I could neither love nor admire. If Hawkeye told you even half of what I said, you know how bad Jacob was."

"Aye." Maggie sighed and patted my arm again.

"The man should be shot," Quinn growled. The fierce look on his face said more—that he wished he had the power to change things, that he wished he could fill my life with only good.

* * *

My strength continued to return, and by the end of the week I was strong enough to leave my bed and spend time sitting in a chair by the window. The Lieutenant continued to read to me. Once or twice a day he'd knock on the door that separated my bedroom—Bridget's actually—from the O'Connor's sitting room and ask if he could come in. Sometimes he'd leave as soon as he finished a chapter, saying he didn't want to tire me, but more often he stayed to visit.

Next to holding Ellen, Quinn's visits became the high point of my day. I quickly recognized his voice floating from the kitchen and found myself smiling when Maggie and Bridget laughed at something he said. The awkwardness that had marked the afternoon when we'd eaten lunch on the beach had passed. In its place was friendship and the quiet sharing of thoughts and ideas. Sometimes after we'd discussed a recent chapter of *Sense and Sensibility*, I'd ask Quinn to tell me about England. Other times he regaled me with amusing things that had happened to him in the army.

"What a life you've had," I said one day. "You've been to so many interesting places."

"I have." He pulled out a handkerchief to polish his spectacles. "But life and travel lose much of their pleasure when you have no one of import to share them with."

The note of sadness in Quinn's voice reminded me of the loss he'd experienced. "Maggie told me about your wife—that she and your baby died."

"They did." His clipped tone told me not to tread further. After a tiny silence, I asked him about the time he'd spent in Scotland, while inside I wondered about his poor wife. What had she looked like? How long ago had she died?

* * *

On a day when I was finally strong enough to venture into the kitchen, I asked Shamus to bring Sam to the back door. I don't know which of us was happiest—me or the dog. My laughter mingled with Sam's excited yips as I petted and hugged him.

"Yes, Sam, I love you too. You're such a good dog."

The happy staccato of his tail on the floor told me of his pleasure.

When I stepped back to look at him, I could see that he'd grown some while I'd been sick, his gangly, brindled body filled out and more muscular.

"I guess you know you're a wonder," I went on. "Going for help like you did."

Sam's answer was to prick up his ears and move closer. He was not going to be easy to get back outside. Rather than try, I sat down on one of the straight-backed chairs. Sam, alert and watchful, sat down next to it. His eyes followed Bridget and Maggie as they washed and dried the breakfast dishes. Ellen slept through it all, her box near the back of the stove, the constant heat keeping her small body warm, the flannel wrapped snuggly around her.

I felt greatly blessed on that sunny August morning—Sam dozing by my feet, good friends to help and keep me company, and God's sweet gift from heaven sleeping and growing more healthy and beautiful every day.

Good as the O'Connors were to me, it did not take many days out of bed for me to realize that all was not perfect with the Irish family. Threads of discord were woven just under the surface, putting a bite to Mick's tongue and setting him and Maggie at odds. I caught my first glimpse of it one afternoon when Mick walked into the kitchen and found Shamus reading a book by the stove.

The boy jumped to his feet, a guilty look on his face as he shoved the book under the chair.

"What are you doing inside? Didn't I tell you to clean out the woodshed?"

"Aye."

"Then why are you not doing it?"

"I . . . I did. 'Tis done already."

Mick paused with his hand on the door. "Such doesn't give you the excuse to be sitting with your nose in a book. There's to be no readin' until night, especially when there's work to be done outside. Now off with you."

"But, Da . . ."

"Off with you." Mick held the door wide. "And don't let me be seein' you with a book in your hand during the day unless the Lieutenant's teaching you."

From my place on the other side of the stove, I watched Shamus's mouth tighten, saw the slump that came to his thin shoulders.

"Do as your da says," Maggie told him. I sensed her concern—sensed, too, that she didn't agree with her husband.

No one spoke until Shamus was outside and the door closed, though tension spoke with a voice of its own, one that told me this was not the first time such a scene had taken place. Although I did not doubt that Mick loved his wife and she him, the look that passed between them was lacking in warmth.

"Will you never stop encouragin' the boy to shirk his duty?"

"He wasn't shirkin'," Maggie retorted. "His work was done, so what's the harm in him readin'?"

" 'Tisn't normal, that's what. He should be wantin' to be outside, or with me or the Lieutenant."

"He was, earlier." She took a step toward her husband, her voice thick with emotion. "You're too hard on him, Mick."

"And you're for bein' too soft."

A long look passed between them, one of entreaty conditioned from years of living together.

Mick's broad shoulders lifted as he let out a sigh. "I worry for him, Maggie, small like he is for his age, preferring books to runnin' and playin'. You saw how he was in England, how the bigger boys picked on him. He needs to learn to take care of himself!"

"And the outside chores you keep findin' for him will teach him that?"

"They will at least give him some backbone and put some muscle on him. 'Twas what my da did for me." Mick gave her another long look, his mouth firm and determined. "I'm sorry, Maggie, but 'tis what's best for the boy." His gray eyes flicked to me, then he turned and walked out of the house.

I was glad Bridget hadn't been present to witness the scene. If she had, I felt certain she wouldn't have been shy about adding her opinion on the matter. *Poor Shamus*, I thought, remembering how his shoulders had straightened when I'd praised him for chopping my wood, the swagger, so much like Mick's, that had followed my compliment. Couldn't his father see that his son needed praise?

Maggie's sigh intruded into my thoughts. "I'm sorry you had to be around when the O'Connors aired their dirty laundry. 'Twasn't pleasant for you, I'm sure."

"For you either," I answered, feeling sorry for both Maggie and Mick.

She pulled out a chair and sat down at the table. "That Mick. Sometimes I'd like to be shakin' him . . . or yellin'. Anything to make him see that harshness is not the way with someone like Shamus." She shook her head, the high color that had come to her cheeks when she'd been arguing with Mick slowly receding. "'Tis not that his da doesn't love him," she added. "It's just that Mick has only one picture of what a true man is for lookin' like—someone strong and exactly like himself."

* * *

When Ellen was six weeks old we bathed and dressed her in the little gown I'd made for her, the first clothes she'd worn other than the flannel diapers. By now I was feeling almost like my old self, though I still tired easily. But I'd insisted on being a part of the bathing and dressing, slipping Ellen's little arms through the sleeves that came several inches past her hands. Although her sticklike arms and legs were filling out—turkey legs, Shamus liked to call them—she was still very tiny. But from the three pairs of female eyes looking down at her, there was only admiration.

"Is she not grand?" Maggie asked.

"She's beautiful," Bridget sighed. "Just like her mother."

"She is that." This from Mick, who'd joined us at the kitchen table where we had her on display. "Fair as a summer's morn, she is."

I beamed with pride, delighting in the fact that Ellen's tiny face had begun to assume a look that was entirely her own—one I, too, thought beautiful. If only she didn't have that golden hair, hair that would probably one day turn to russet. Why couldn't she just be mine? All mine?

Since the O'Connors didn't know the color of Jacob's hair, they considered Ellen's bit of golden fuzz as but another reason to love her. "'Tis just like our Fiona's hair when she was first born—gold that turned redder with each birthday," Maggie said.

Quinn had come into the kitchen in time to hear Maggie's remarks. I felt his steady gaze on me. Did he remember the color of Jacob's hair? Did he sense how much the idea of red hair bothered me?

Before I could think about it, Quinn had washed his hands and scooped Ellen up off the table to cradle her in his arms. I saw the tenderness in his expression as he smiled down at her, heard the same tenderness in his voice when he spoke to her. "How's my girl today?"

I could have sworn Ellen smiled at him, even as I knew it was too soon. At least that's what Maggie claimed, maintaining that since the baby wasn't supposed to be born until September, it was only wishful thinking that made me announce that she had smiled at me the day before. But it didn't diminish my pleasure in watching Quinn and Ellen.

That my baby was everyone's favorite was evident. Now that she was gaining in both weight and strength and didn't need to be kept so isolated, everyone vied for the chance to hold her. More and more the Lieutenant won out. He was as taken with Ellen as Maggie and Bridget were.

I wasn't the only one who noticed. Maggie, too, watched them together, smiling like the rest of us did. But there was something threaded through her smile—something that spoke of worry.

* * *

Now that my strength was returning, I began to go farther afield. First it had been the O'Connor's sitting room, then the kitchen. Soon it was the Lieutenant's sitting room filled with shelves of books that stretched from floor to ceiling and comfortable upholstered chairs and couches. Most times I only went there to read, for Maggie and Bridget still insisted on babying me, and I had little except the care of my daughter to keep me occupied.

But one afternoon I walked to the pianoforte and lifted the lid from the keyboard. My friendship with the Lieutenant was such that I didn't think he would mind if I played it. I sat down on the round stool and after only the slightest hesitation began to execute a few scales. From there I went to Beethoven's "Für Elise," a piece I'd played so often I could do it with my eyes closed. Lack of practice marred my first two attempts, but by the third time I found myself playing as easily as I'd done at home, my fingers welcoming the familiar feel and placement of the keys, my mind remembering the notes. My concentration was so complete, I was unaware that anyone had come into the room until I heard soft applause when I reached the end.

I turned and saw Quinn standing at the door. Pleasure showed on his face as he leaned against the doorframe, his walking stick in his left hand, his broad shoulders outlined by the linen fabric of his white shirt.

"I didn't know you could play."

"I'm sadly out of practice." I flexed my fingers. "It's been almost six years since I touched a keyboard."

"No one would suspect that from hearing you play."

I suddenly felt self-conscious, for I could read more than approval for my playing in Quinn's eyes. Over the years I'd been aware of the way men's eyes followed me, both before and after I married Jacob. Comely was what they said of me, beautiful some even claimed. But what I saw in the Lieutenant's eye was more that that. Instead of the callow admiration I'd grown used to, his expression showed a depth I'd never encountered before.

Friendship. It's only friendship, I told myself. And that was what I felt in return. Friendship and admiration and respect. Emotions I'd never experienced with Jacob.

Quinn walked over to the desk and opened a drawer. "I have some books of music someplace." He closed a drawer and tried the second. "Here they are." He turned and handed them to me.

"Do you play?" I asked.

"No, but my sister did. Quite well, I might add. I grew up often hearing music in my home. It was something I wanted to be a part of my home here as well." He laughed when he read the questions on my face. "I imagine you're wondering who I had in mind to play, and the answer is I didn't know. I thought only of wanting to bring the things I love with me. Music and good books—my dogs too."

"Did you have Finn and Balor before you came to Oregon?"

"Actually they were just pups when we came, but I'd had their mother for eight years. It was her last litter, and I knew she was too old to do well on a long sea voyage." He paused and leaned against the pianoforte, his cane left by the desk. This was something Quinn often did when he was in the house, the even surface of the floors making the cane unnecessary.

"My family has owned wolfhounds for almost two hundred years."

"That long?"

Quinn nodded. "My ancestor who fought with Cromwell was the first to own them. As a reward for bravery, he was awarded a home and an estate in Ireland. The land and dogs have been in our family ever since."

He ran long fingers through his brown hair that didn't look to have been trimmed for several weeks. "Unfortunately, the estate wasn't always well looked after, but the dogs were. In fact, my grandfather liked them so well he brought a pair of them over to England with him. I grew up with wolfhounds, played with them from the time I could walk. Naturally, I wanted to bring wolfhounds with me to Oregon."

"Naturally." I smiled up at him from the piano stool as I pictured a younger Quinn romping with the wolfhounds. His smile was warm in reply.

"I wrote my brother last winter and asked him to send a female wolfhound on the next ship that comes this way. One is supposed to sail to San Francisco this fall. With the new dog here, I shouldn't be running out of wolfhounds."

Bridget and Maggie had already mentioned the ship's anticipated arrival. Not only was it bringing Quinn's dog, but also Mick's nephew and his young wife—the first of the struggling Irish that Quinn planned to help. Our conversation turned to Mick's nephew, then back to music.

"How did you learn to play?" Quinn asked.

"My mother taught me." My mind flew back to the times I'd struggled with scales, my pride when I'd succeeded in playing "The Spinning Song" for the first time. "My mother loved music and books, so my sisters and I were exposed to both."

Quinn still leaned against the pianoforte, his head tilted in interest toward me. "How many sisters?"

"Four. The first three are several years older. Tamsin and I close together at the end."

"And no brothers?

I shook my head, remembering the tall, fair-haired man who spoke with an accent—Pennsylvania German to the core. "Father must have been disappointed, but he never let on. Growing up, I think each of us felt we were his favorite. He was a good father for girls."

"Was?"

"He died when I was thirteen."

"And your mother?"

I thought of the woman I'd seen when I'd been so ill—recalled the love and power radiating from her. Her love for me had been strong and unshakable.

"She and my sister Tamsin still live in Massachusetts," I said, but inside I knew Mother was dead. How else had she come to me?

"Was it in Massachusetts that you married Jacob?"

I nodded and looked down at the music books in my lap.

"Nastachee told us why you married him." There was a momentary awkward pause. "Please . . . will you play for me?"

So I did, my fingers stumbling from lack of practice as I tried something from Schumann, and then an étude by Chopin, both found in the music books. My mistakes didn't seem to interfere with Quinn's pleasure in the music. An occasional glance showed him sitting in a chair smiling as he listened with his eyes half closed, a booted foot crossed over his knee.

"'Tis fair glorious," a soft voice said when I finished. "Like I was in heaven listenin' to the angels playin' at their harps."

I turned to find Bridget and Maggie standing at the door.

" 'Twas grand," Maggie agreed. "And not once did you tell us you knew how to play."

"It's been many years."

"Too many years," Quinn put in. "While you're here, please feel free to treat us to it often."

Thereafter I slipped off to the drawing room at least once a day. I played for my own pleasure, but always ended up with an audience. If it wasn't Bridget or Maggie, it was Mick or Shamus. But most frequently, it was the Lieutenant.

CHAPTER 9

A few days after we dressed the baby for the first time, Sven and Flora came to visit. As before it was the dogs who alerted us to their presence, the wolfhounds' voices deep and menacing, but Sam's more like a greeting.

Still not fully recovered, I waited in the kitchen while Maggie went out to invite them inside. Sven stood awkwardly inside the doorframe while Flora and I embraced and exchanged kisses.

"I'm so glad you came," I said. "I've missed you."

"And I you. We've been very worried."

"As you can see, I'm doing very well."

"We were afraid she would die," Bridget put in.

Realizing my friends hadn't met, I made the introductions. Although smiles and hands were extended, constraint was painfully evident. Mistrust too. I could sense it on both sides, though why I didn't fully understand.

"The O'Connors have been goodness itself to me. Mr. Reynolds too. You'll have to meet the rest of them before you go," I told them.

Flora glanced around the kitchen. "Can we see the baby?"

I led them to the bed behind the stove. "She's so sweet. You won't believe how tiny she is."

Their admiration of Ellen was all that I had hoped for. Flora exclaimed in awe when I pulled back the flannel, her eyes taking in the little face and tiny, perfect hands and fingers, the even rhythm of her breathing.

"What did you name her?"

"Ellen." To me it was a beautiful name and my daughter the most beautiful of babies. Such were my thoughts, and dear friends that Flora and Sven were, they seemed to concur with me.

Once the baby had been properly admired, Maggie told me we were welcome to use their sitting room and that she'd ready some tea for us while we visited. In no time Flora and I were gossiping. I asked about Hans and Little Sarah who'd been left with their grandma again, asked for the latest news about friends from worship service. Through it all Sven sat straight on his chair, his eyes taking in the room's comfortable furnishings, a slight frown on his rugged features.

"What's wrong, Sven," I finally asked. "You're strangely quiet today."

Sven shrugged and looked down at the floor, something that was out of character for the big Swede.

"Out with it, Sven. We've been friends too long not to be able to say what's on our minds."

"I hope that's true." There was an uncomfortable pause before he went on. "It's the Englishman that bothers me . . . him and his Indian woman. I don't like it that you've been exposed to it. Them living together in the same house as you and your baby."

I shook my head. "The Indian woman you saw is married to an Indian who helps Mr. Reynolds. The only reason she came was to nurse my baby. Without her, Ellen would have died."

Sven didn't say anything for a moment, his blue eyes going from me to Flora. Knowing what they were thinking, I went on. "Mr. Reynolds is a good and honorable man. What Jacob told you about him is a lie."

Sven's skepticism dissipated as I explained about Bright Star's screams and how Mick and the Lieutenant went to her rescue. By the time I finished, there was a visible relaxing in Sven's posture and acceptance in his face.

"This takes a great weight from my shoulders," Sven admitted. "You'd think I'd have learned by now not to trust what Jacob says."

"What will you do if Jacob comes back, Clarissa?" Flora asked.

I shook my head, not even considering the possibility. "After all that Jacob has done, he's too much of a coward to come back."

Now that Sven's mind about the Lieutenant had been put to rest, he took an active part in the remainder of our conversation. Maggie's light scones were the hit of the afternoon and helped to break the ice between Flora and Maggie. By the time Sven said they must go, Maggie had shared her recipe with Flora.

"We'd be counting ourselves fortunate to have you come again," Maggie said to them.

As I watched Flora and Sven make their way across the grass to the forest, I became aware of the Lieutenant's quiet presence by the barn, watching with interest to see what he would do. I wondered if he'd speak or make himself known, and felt a twinge of disappointment when he turned and walked back into the barn.

* * *

Although I was getting stronger, Quinn continued to come every day to read to me. After he finished, we would talk—sometimes of what he had just read, sometimes of other things. The day after Sven and Flora came, I broached the subject of their visit.

A wary look slipped over Quinn's features. "What did Mr. Larsen say?"

"That a great weight had been taken off his shoulders."

"He didn't disbelieve you?"

"No, he knows Jacob. They both do."

Quinn's features relaxed, and the corners of his mouth curved up. I could tell he was pleased. Relieved too.

"How is your work coming? Have you been able to find any new Indian relics?"

"Not lately." His tone was evasive. "Would you like to come and see what I have?"

"Yes, I would."

Quinn took me through his sitting room and past a series of rooms on the other side of the lodge, his hand cupped on my elbow. He stopped at a room at the end of the corridor, opened the door, and let me precede him into the room.

"Most of what I have is in here."

Since I'd had but little contact with Indians, I was uncertain of what I would see. Afternoon sun shone through three large windows onto tables and cabinets covered with tools and baskets.

"Some of the things I've found are very old, others newer," Quinn explained.

Most of what he showed and told me that afternoon is forgotten, but I remember my feelings as he spoke, the deep timbre of his voice, his excitement when he held up a wooden utensil and explained its use to me. I saw baskets woven from grasses, whalebone clubs, and several bone needles. Quinn's pride was evident. So was his pleasure in having me as his audience.

"What do you plan to do with them?" I asked when he paused.

"Give or sell them to a museum or university. There's a growing interest in Indian relics. Not as great as in Egyptian artifacts, but growing just the same."

Perhaps I stood more closely to Quinn than I had intended, or maybe it was just that sunshine pouring through the glass highlighted the blue of my dress so that it more closely matched my eyes. Whatever the case, he seemed to lose his train of thought, and instead of talking seemed content just to look at me.

The moment was long and neither of us knew what to say. Then Quinn cleared his throat and quickly stepped to the next table, his mind seeming to grasp at something safe to talk about. "When Lewis and Clark reached Oregon there were over two thousand Tillamook Indians. Today there are less than two hundred." Both his voice and expression were distracted.

"Maggie told me how disease has almost wiped them out," I said, but my mind was taking in the flush that had come to his cheeks.

Even so, his voice when he spoke was solemn. "Before we know it, all the Indians will be gone. I want to preserve their ways and history through their artifacts."

The Indian relics were still on my mind the next day when I nursed Ellen. "I had no idea the Indians had their own kind of needles and could weave such beautiful baskets."

Maggie was mixing bread, her hand kneading the dough. "Aye, their women are right clever with their fingers. Their way of life is old." She paused to form the dough into a loaf. "The Lieutenant thinks some of the tools he found by the Wilson River are over five hundred years old."

I was properly impressed, and Maggie was pleased she had done the impressing. I lifted Ellen to be burped, her soft warm head snuggled next to my cheek. I could think of nothing more wonderful than holding and rocking my very own baby.

"Of course, the Lieutenant hasn't done much searchin' the last little while," Maggie went on. "Keeps himself right close to home, nowadays, he does."

"Why is that?"

"'Tis the baby, I'm thinking. The man's pure daft over her. He's always stoppin' by the kitchen in hopes of holdin' the wee mite." There was another pause while she formed a second loaf. "Before Ellen was born, we mostly only saw the Lieutenant at meals. Nowadays, he seems to be here most of the time."

After I succeeded in getting a burp out of Ellen, I laid her on my lap to admire her—the way she stretched her little arms, the bubble of milk on her pink lips. I was aware that Maggie watched us with a quiet expression on her face.

"Of course, there could well be another reason."

Although I was wrapped up in admiring my daughter, I heard what she said and sensed the implication. My heart quickened, and despite myself, I smiled.

* * *

September was half gone, but the days, whether rainy or fair, were tranquil. Part of it was the return of my health, and part Ellen. During those days I came to recognize a much-missed dimension to my life—that of friendship and being pampered, and knowing that for now at least, my life was secure.

Until I came to the lodge, I hadn't realized how fraught with uncertainty my life had become. During the months I stayed there, I didn't once worry about where my next meal would come from, how I would milk the cow, or what danger lurked outside when the sun went down. More than that, Jacob and the tension of our unhappy marriage was gone. In our cabin there had been curses and endless talk of becoming rich; in the lodge there was laughter and caring and always someone with intelligence to converse with and share ideas.

A few evenings later as I sat rocking Ellen and listening to the pleasant banter of my friends, my mind turned with reluctance to thoughts of my own home. Now that I was stronger and Ellen was thriving, I needed to be thinking of going back.

Back home—a thought that should have filled me with happiness. Instead, I felt a stab of dread followed by the memory of the terrible loneliness. Even with Ellen, it would be lonely. Especially after the bustle and conversation I'd grown accustomed to with the O'Connors. And Quinn. The thought of not seeing him every day, not hearing his voice as he read and talked to me, made me feel as if part of me were dying.

Something of my thoughts must have shown, for after clearing his throat, Quinn spoke, "You're looking very solemn, Clarissa."

I looked at him and attempted a smile.

"Is something wrong?" Maggie asked. She and Mick and Bridget were sitting on the sofa, Shamus on the floor, the Lieutenant in the chair opposite mine next to the table.

"No, nothing." I attempted another smile. "I was thinking how good you have all been to me. Your love and caring." Shamus had stopped reading and watched me, his finger marking his place in the book. "But it's time to be thinking of going back home," I finished.

"Please don't, " Bridget protested.

"I'm better now, and Ellen grows stronger and bigger every day."

Everyone spoke at once—Maggie to say it was still much too soon and Mick agreeing, Bridget declaring that she wanted Ellen and me to stay forever. But it was Quinn that I was most aware of—how closely he watched me, his brows slightly furrowed, one brown-booted foot crossed over the other. Much as I would miss the O'Connors, I knew I would miss the Lieutenant more—miss watching the quirk of his brows just before he asked me a question, the careful way he had of polishing his spectacles. The realization of how much his friendship had come to mean to me made my throat tighten. *What have I done? Dear heaven, what have I allowed myself to do?* Although Jacob had deserted me, I wasn't free from my marital vows yet. And though meaningless now, I still intended to keep them.

The sound of Quinn's voice drew me away from my revealing thoughts. "Do you think it is the wise thing to do?" he asked. "Remember you have someone besides yourself to think about."

There was concern in his eyes, and I knew he was wondering how I would cope if Ellen became ill, how I would get help.

Even more frightened of what might happen if I stayed, I answered with more force than I was usually wont to show. "It's what I have to do."

Something in my expression kept the Lieutenant from saying more, but I could tell that his mind was busy and that I hadn't heard the last of the subject.

* * *

Two days later the Lieutenant sought me out in the drawing room where I'd gone to return a book.

"Clarissa."

I turned, one hand still resting on the bookcase, my heart quickening at the sound of his voice.

"Do you have a moment to talk?"

I nodded, wondering what he was going to say, even as I resolved to keep my expression neutral.

Quinn indicated one of the burgundy chairs for me to sit in. He continued to stand, his booted feet planted firmly on the flowered rug, the thumbs of his hands hooked in the pockets of his brown trousers. He smiled as if he weren't entirely sure of the best way to begin, but his voice when he spoke was purposeful.

"It's about you returning home that I'd like to talk to you. I can understand why you feel you need to go, your reasons for being there, but may I make a suggestion?"

Even as I gave my consent, I rallied arguments, my hands folded in the lap of my blue-flowered dress.

"For you to want to hold onto your homestead is admirable, but to try to do it alone causes us all concern."

"I must—"

Quinn held up his hand. "Will you hear me out before you give your answer?" He smiled when I nodded. "What I propose is that you take Shamus and Bridget to live with you. That way you'll have someone to do the heavy work and a woman to keep you company."

I stared at him. "What about you? And how will Maggie make out?"

"We'll make out very well. As you know, Mick's nephew, Patrick, and his wife are on their way from Ireland. They're due to arrive anytime." He looked down at me with a smile. "If you'd stay with us until they get here, we'd all rest easier."

I got to my feet, uncertain of what to do. "I don't know what to say." But inside my heart rejoiced.

Quinn placed his large hands on my shoulders, his touch seeming to sear itself into my bones. "Say yes," he said. "Say yes, and make everyone happy."

* * *

Over the next few days, I tried to convince myself that Quinn and I could be no more than friends, the only right and noble way to be until I was free of my marriage. And even that was enough—to keep me satisfied—the sweet anticipation of knowing he would be coming to look in on me or read to me, mingled with the joy of motherhood and the warmth of the O'Connors' friendship. Although I was still determined to make my own way, I welcomed the wonderful extension of my stay at the lodge with wide-stretched arms.

Then on a cloudy, overcast day toward the end of September, Shamus ran into the kitchen. "Come quick," he panted. "There's a ship makin' its way into the cove. I'm thinkin' our cousin Patrick and the dog are here."

We followed Shamus outside and around to the front of the house. Quinn and Mick were already there, Quinn with a long, round tube held to his eye.

"It's the *Merryweather*, all right," Quinn said. "They're putting a boat over the side." He slipped the instrument into the leather case and handed it to Bridget. "Would you put this on my desk in the study?" He looked at Mick and Shamus. "We'd best hurry down."

Bridget wanted to go too, but was told she was needed to put the finishing touches on the little house by the barn that was waiting for Patrick and his wife.

"We'll be needing to start a fire to take off the chill," Maggie said. "Besides, the Lieutenant asked you to take his telescope into the study."

Although Bridget's mouth looked rebellious, she did as she was told. I asked Maggie what I could do to help and was set to work plucking a chicken. "Roast chicken we'll be havin' to welcome Patrick and Eileen to their new home."

The party from the ship arrived just before sunset. Finn and Balor, who'd gone down to the cove with the men, bounded into the yard first. Shamus was right behind them with Sam and a black wolfhound on a leash.

"Is she not grand?" Shamus asked, his young face flushed with excitement and exertion. "Finn and Balor are thinkin' she's grand too. And the Lieutenant said I can be namin' her."

Before I could think of a comment, Patrick and Eileen arrived. Other than his sandy hair, Patrick O'Connor bore no resemblance to his uncle. Tall and sturdy of build, he set down the heavy bundle he carried and wrapped Maggie in an affectionate embrace.

"Aye, but it's good to be here. Would you be believin' we've been at sea for more than two months?" He paused and gave Maggie a hearty kiss. "Sure and 'tis good to see you again, Aunt Maggie."

"And you, Patrick, though the last time I saw you, you were no bigger than one of the dogs. If I'm for remembering correctly, you were a right cocky lad too."

"And still is," Patrick's wife put in cheerfully. Eileen was of medium height, dark where Patrick was fair. Though she was no more than average in looks, her wide smile and the mischievous twinkle in her blue eyes made her appealing.

The rest of the party came into the yard—four burly sailors, who carried the supplies brought on the ship from England, followed by Quinn and a pretty dark-haired woman who looked to be about my age, slender of build, with delicate features and blue eyes fringed with thick, dark lashes.

I stared at the woman, feeling a sense of unease. No mention had been made of another passenger. Who was she? Seeing us, she smiled and came forward.

"This is Deirdre, Eileen's sister," Patrick explained. "She asked to come with us. I hope you don't mind."

"Now, how could you be thinkin' that," Maggie said, though I could tell she was as surprised as I was. "Anyone from home is always welcome."

"Thank you," Deirdre said. The smile left her face, and her expression turned solemn. "I promised Patrick and Eileen they'd not be sorry they brought me. I mean to earn my keep."

"For sure, she'll be doin' that," Eileen put in. "There's no one can bake scones as light as she can. And you should hear her sing. 'Tis like listenin' to one of the angels."

Deirdre blushed. "My sister's always makin' more of me than is polite. I want only the chance to better myself and will be doin' all I can to make you glad I've come." She glanced at the Lieutenant when she said this, the smile back on her face. "What a lovely place this is. And the house . . ." She paused as if at a loss for words, while a calculating expression crossed her face. "I never thought to find anything so grand."

"Oh, 'tis that," Maggie agreed. She turned to introduce Bridget and me.

Deirdre's expression was open and friendly as she reached and took my hands. "Clarissa . . . what a beautiful name. I can hardly wait to get to know you."

I couldn't help but be drawn to the woman, her charm such that she made me feel I was already her friend. Yet part of me held back—the part that acknowledged her loveliness and wondered if, as comparisons were made, I would be the one who came up lacking. More than that, I had seen the way she'd looked at Quinn.

I glanced at him and wondered what he was thinking. Instead of watching, he was busy helping the sailors take the supplies into the house—foodstuffs and boxes of books and bolts of fabric.

After the sailors had gone back to the boat, nine of us sat down for supper at the long oak table. It was a merry group with the O'Connors having much to catch up on in news from Ireland and talk of mutual friends. Quinn and I sat more quietly than usual while happy voices chattered around us, Mick's and Maggie's brogue growing thicker by the moment. More than once Deirdre made an effort to include Quinn in the conversation. Her enthusiasm was contagious, and I thought he was drawn to her just as I was, as most people seemed to be. Then I felt Quinn's hazel eyes on me from the other end of the table, their expression somber instead of merry. I wondered if my feelings showed, if the wrench that came to my heart each time I thought of leaving was evident. When I raised my head and met his gaze, I knew we were both thinking that soon little Ellen and I would be gone, the two of us returning to my house at the bottom of the mountain.

* * *

Although Patrick and Eileen and Deirdre lived in the little house across from the lodge, they soon became an integral part of life there, coming in and out of the lodge at will to help Maggie with the cooking and cleaning. Both Eileen and Deirdre were enamored with Ellen.

"What a wee beauty she is," Deirdre crooned the day after they arrived. She had asked if she could hold the baby and sat in Maggie's rocking chair, humming softly as she rocked. Though plainly attired in a dark blue dress, the red shawl she wore around her shoulders accented the porcelain-like quality of her skin and the sheen of her black hair. I had heard of the Black Irish and thought Deirdre must embody the phrase.

"How lucky you are to be having such a sweet angel," she said.

"I thank God for her every day."

"Mick was tellin' me how you almost lost her, how you was almost for dyin' yourself."

" 'Twas our prayers and Bright Star's tea that saved her," Bridget said, looking up from ironing her father's shirt. "Though the Lieutenant played a part in it too. 'Twas him that sat up with Clarissa during the nights and kept her breathing."

Deirdre gave me a quick look, but said nothing, though I felt she wanted to, full of questions as she was. This was something I discovered over those first few days—her curiosity about others, but her reluctance to talk about herself.

"'Tis her way," Eileen said when Maggie commented on the fact when Deirdre left the room. "She's one who's for keeping herself to herself."

"As pretty as your sister is, I'm surprised she's not married," Maggie went on.

"Oh, aye, you and half of Ireland are wonderin' the same. Every man from miles around has tried his hand at winnin' her. Except for

Patrick, that is. He says she's too flighty by half and not one he'd ever want to be marryin' up with." This was said with satisfaction, one that made me think that although Eileen might adore her younger sister, she took pleasure in knowing she was of consequence as well.

"Was there no one she could feel a likin' for?" Bridget asked.

"There was one." Eileen's mouth tightened. "A Protestant he was. One with money, but not with any intention of marryin'." Eileen was rocking Ellen while I helped Maggie peel potatoes, the kitchen clock's soft rhythm filling the silence left by her words. "For all her beauty, Deirdre also has a brain for thinkin'. She soon saw that the road he was wantin' to lead her on would only come to grief. 'Twas then she asked if she could come with us . . . and lovin' her like I do, how could I be for sayin' no, or Patrick either, though I had to do some talkin' to convince him of it." She looked up from Ellen and smiled. "Knowin' my sister, 'twill all be coming out right. She has an uncanny way of landin' on her feet."

I thought of this later when Quinn came into the kitchen. Deirdre was rocking Ellen again, the baby fast asleep with her head nestled against Deirdre's shoulder. I watched his face soften as he took in the sight, saw color leap to Deirdre's cheeks when she looked up and saw him watching them.

"I see our Ellie has found someone else to spoil her," he said. His voice was soft like his face, and I wondered if it was the baby or Deirdre who had prompted the softness.

His eyes were still warm when he turned to me, smiling down as I sat at the kitchen table with Maggie, a knife in my hand and the peels falling into the pan on my lap. "When you're through, I have something I'd like to show you."

"All right." I smiled large, the tightness around my heart easing. Quinn had come to see me, not Deirdre.

"I can finish these," Maggie said, while her eyes told me to go with him.

So I did, wiping my hands on my apron while Quinn held the drawing room door open for me. One of the wooden crates from the ship sat in the middle of the floor, the lid off and stacks of books set on the rug beside it. I looked from the books to Quinn and smiled.

"I thought you'd be pleased. Come see what they brought." He reached and took a green-bound book from the top of a stack. "This one especially. It's one of Charles Dickens's newest novels, *A Tale of Two Cities*. My sister Anne says it's about the French Revolution and most enjoyable."

Before I knew it, we were sitting on the floor with the books, Quinn's long, gray-clad legs folded Indian fashion, the folds of my pink skirt tucked modestly round mine while the afternoon sun shone through the west window and wrapped us in its warmth. There were dozens of titles, some dealing with science and antiquities, others with mathematics and astronomy.

"These are for Shamus and me," Quinn said, pointing to the farthest stacks, "but these . . ." He paused, his eyes warm with pleasure. "These are meant to be savored on long evenings by the fire." He handed another book to me, then another, ones by Brontë and Austen and Dickens, sonnets and poetry too.

I leafed through them, the books new and crisp, while Quinn read one of the poems aloud, the rich timbre of his voice and his accent adding to my pleasure.

"I wish . . ." Quinn's voice broke off and his lips tightened in frustration, as if the words he sought weren't coming out the way he wanted, or were perhaps words best left unspoken. He cleared his throat and his expression was earnest. "I greatly enjoyed reading to you . . . our time together. I shall miss it when you're gone."

"So will I." My voice came softly as I met his gaze, the two of us looking deep as we sought to know the other's thoughts. I've wondered since if it was wrong, but at the time it seemed proper, the two of us sitting on the floor like good friends with soft autumn-afternoon sun streaming in on us. Deirdre's soft knock on the drawing room door, to say Ellen had wakened, broke the spell.

Quinn quickly got to his feet and reached to offer me his hand, its warm clasp one I'd feel for days. With a shake of the head, I remembered that for now I was a married woman, one with a child who needed her, one who would be wise to put her mind on other things.

Even so, I was slow to leave the room, my reluctance prompted by Deirdre's next words.

"Oh, would you be lookin' at all the lovely books. Did they come on the boat with us?" Not waiting for an answer, she picked up a green-bound volume. "Glory," she whispered, holding it to her as her eyes took in the stacks of books. "To own but one book in Ireland is counted a fortune, but to have so many . . ." Her voice held reverence and the look she fastened on Quinn was filled with awe.

"I count myself fortunate," Quinn said.

Deirdre smiled before looking down at the book. "The Cow . . . unt of Mon . . ." She shook her head in frustration.

"*The Count of Monte Cristo*," Quinn read for her.

"Oh, aye, though I'll have to be takin' your word for it." Another smile at Quinn. "Times were such that I only had a few days a year at the hedge school. Just enough to whet my hunger for more."

"You're free to read any of my books," he said.

I saw that he watched her closely, whether to admire her looks or because he saw an opportunity to help, I couldn't be sure. I only knew I was forgotten and that Deirdre was now the focus of his attention.

She colored becomingly as she realized this. "'Tis ashamed I am to be tellin' you I can't read enough to tell front from back of one of these lovely books." She paused and gave him a sideways glance, the afternoon sun painting blue-black glints in her hair. "Shamus was sayin' you taught him to cipher."

"I did."

One of her slender fingers traced the gold lettering on the book's cover. "'Tis my dearest wish to learn to cipher better . . . to read from books like these." There was a pause, and I saw hunger in her deep blue eyes. "Could you be findin' it in you heart to teach me like you did Shamus?"

I thought wariness flickered across Quinn's strong features, though perhaps that was only my wishful thinking. "Of course," he said. "When would you like to start?"

I slipped from the room before I heard Deirdre's answer. But I'd seen the satisfied look in her long-lashed eyes—satisfaction that came from more than the possibility of learning to read.

* * *

Two days later we had more company. Hearing the dogs, I went to the kitchen window. "Look who's here," I said. "It's Hawkeye."

"You mean Nastachee?" Maggie winked, for since I'd come to the lodge, the O'Connors had started calling him Hawkeye at times as well.

"I've got to remember," I laughed. Eager to greet him, I put Ellen into her bed and went outside. Maggie was close on my heels.

Hawkeye touched his wife's shoulder when he saw us. He wore the familiar leather breeches and moccasins, but he'd exchanged his woven vest for a blue cambric shirt similar to the ones worn by Mick.

"Hawkeye." My resolve to call him by his correct name vanished when his stolid brown face broke into a smile.

When he reached us he began to speak, the Indian words rolling off his lips in a steady cadence.

"Thank you," I said, laughing up at him, "but I know you speak English."

Hawkeye threw back his head and chuckled, the sound coming deep and full from his chest—this Indian who I'd wondered if he knew how to smile. "Was better keep silent," he said.

"For sure I wasn't silent." I felt no embarrassment for the things I'd told him. Quinn and the O'Connors were now my friends. In time I would have told them myself. Still smiling, I added in a more serious tone, "Thank you for the fish and the rabbit—and for carrying me up to the lodge."

I looked at Bright Star and the chubby-cheeked baby strapped to her back. "Thank you for feeding my baby." My eyes misted over as I reached for her arm. "You saved Ellen's life."

Bright Star nodded, her solemn expression unchanged. I took heart when she didn't pull her arm away from me, however.

"Do you speak English?"

She glanced at Hawkeye, who nodded. "Little . . . little." As Bright Star spoke, she held out an object made from fabric similar to Hawkeye's vest. It took me a second to realize it was a cradleboard. "For baby," she said.

I took the cradleboard from her, noting the beadwork that decorated the brown fabric woven from grass, the narrow rawhide thong that lashed the fabric to the padded board. "Thank you, Bright Star." I looked at Hawkeye. "Thank you."

Both of them nodded. "Thank you . . . for save him," Bright Star said.

I nodded and turned back to Hawkeye, eager to learn how he'd been hurt. When I asked him, he shrugged sheepishly.

Bright Star was not so silent. "Bear," she said. "Run from bear. Fall down mountain."

The look Hawkeye shot his wife indicated he was not pleased. Sensing this was not the time to tease him, I changed the subject. "Come inside and see the baby. You won't believe how much she's grown."

By now Quinn and Maggie had joined us. I held out the cradle-board so they could have a better look. "Isn't it beautiful?"

After it had been admired, we went inside where the baby became the object of attention. Bright Star smiled and touched one of Ellen's dimpled fingers. I took great pride in the fact that her legs and arms no longer looked like sticks and that her little cheeks were now round and filled out.

Later, Bright Star showed me how to fasten Ellen into the cradle-board. Small as she was, she was lost in the soft cedar-bark lining. But she would grow. Ellen was like a tiny seedling stretching toward the golden sun. Each day brought delightful changes.

Before they left, Hawkeye and Bright Star invited me to come to their village. "You are friend. You are all time welcome," Hawkeye said.

I thanked him and stood at the door to wave as they left.

That night after supper I lingered at the O'Connors' sitting-room door, watching those I loved gathered in their usual places. Quinn held Ellen, smiling down at her and trying to coax an answering smile from her. When one finally came, he looked up in triumph.

"Did you see that? She smiled at me." He lifted Ellen and rubbed her cheek with his cleanly shaven jaw. "Oh, what a smart one you are, sweet Ellie. Beautiful, too, like your mother." His voice was a caress, his brown head tucked close to the baby's gold one as he looked across the room at me.

For a second I couldn't breathe, and I wanted nothing more than to forever clasp in my heart the picture of Quinn holding my daughter close.

"That she is," Maggie said. I realized with a jerk that we were not alone.

With a twist to my heart, I looked from Maggie to Quinn and spoke. "Now that Patrick and Eileen have arrived, I really need to get back home." I watched Quinn frown, but it was Maggie who spoke.

"I was afraid you'd be saying that. Is there no way we can persuade you to stay?"

I shook my head. "You've all been wonderful . . . grand." I smiled at my slip into the Irish vernacular. "But it's time."

Except for the crackle of the fire, the room fell still. Quinn was not the only one to greet my announcement with a frown. Mick joined him and even Shamus looked glum. I realized that the loss of Bridget and Shamus would be a sacrifice to the O'Connors—not only their help, but the hole it would leave in their family.

"The baby and I are doing so well, it's not necessary for Bridget and Shamus to come with me."

"Yes it is." This from Quinn while Maggie and Mick nodded.

Bridget left the sofa and came to my side. "I want to come with you, Clarissa. You're the best friend I have, and besides helpin' you with Ellen, I'm sure we'll be havin' our share of fun."

I looked at Shamus who sat in his usual place on the floor in front of the fire. "I'll not be for mindin' it," he said, meeting my gaze head on. "Except for the dogs, that it. But there will still be Sam."

So it was decided. On Wednesday, weather permitting, the four of us would leave the lodge and make our way down the mountain.

* * *

Mist hung low over the mountain on the morning we left, swirling among the treetops and dripping from hanging mosses and leaves. But patches of blue sky could be seen out over the ocean, a promising sign for the day.

Such wasn't the case for my heart. Only my strong will pushed my feet out of the house and kept my tears in check when Quinn helped me mount his black horse, appropriately named Midnight.

Bridget led the way with a bundle of clothes on her back. Ellen and I followed with Quinn leading the horse. Shamus, Sam, and the cows brought up the rear. I turned for one last look, and saw Mick and Maggie waving from the yard. The sight of them tore at my fragile hold on control and sent silent tears down my cheeks. I was going home, but why did it feel as if I were leaving it?

There was a strange quiet among the towering trees. A mulch of leaves hushed our footsteps, and the sound of the stream came like a distant sigh. I tried not to think of Deirdre, that Quinn would be seeing her several times a day, the two of them sitting close as he taught her to read. Why did she have to be so pretty? Why did her quick movements and speech make me feel drab and uninteresting? Wiping furtively at my tears, I noticed the tiny white mushrooms and fungus that grew on mossy logs, a sight that would ordinarily have brought pleasure, but on that day they were scarcely seen. Even my appreciation of slanted sun rays on serrated pine tips was diminished.

Twice Quinn looked back at me, his features shadowed by the broad brim of his dark hat. Even with the shadows, I sensed his concern. "Are you all right?" he asked each time.

"Yes." I tried to keep the quaver out of my voice and hoped he couldn't see the traces of tears on my face. Fearing I might lose what remained of my control, I grasped at something to say. "Have you ever seen anything more beautiful?"

Quinn turned his head to look at me, his heavy, black, worsted jacket covering his white shirt. "Only the ocean, though I have a hard time deciding which one I like best. When I'm on the beach, it's the ocean. On a day like this, it's the forest." Although he strove for enthusiasm, I sensed that like me, he was using conversation to cover emotion. "Of course, you're talking to the man who lost his heart to this wild country more than thirteen years ago."

"How old were you when you first saw it?"

"Only eighteen, fresh out of school and scarcely dry behind the ears. The army and this country made me grow up fast."

Now that we were talking, I began to feel better, so much so that I mentally added eighteen to thirteen and decided his thirty-one years was a nice age for a man. Then I was trying to picture Quinn as he had been then, dressed in the red uniform of the British army, unproven and probably a little brash. He had that power, even though I still wanted to cry, to fill my heart with wondering. What had his thoughts been? Had he had an immediate affinity for the Indians?

When I asked him, he shook his head. "I was posted to Astoria to protect the Hudson Bay Company. The trappers and men were a pretty rough lot and a real eye-opener after my proper English upbringing." He shot me a quick glance. "A lot of the Indians around the post had been corrupted by liquor. It saddened me even then to see what it had done to them, especially after I visited some of their villages and saw how they lived before the white man came."

He paused to steady his footing on the steep trail with his walking stick, his other hand holding the horse's reins. I said nothing to Quinn, thinking instead of how strange he must have looked sitting among the Indians in his red uniform.

"Have you ever seen an Indian village?" Quinn asked in the silence.

"Only a few tepees when we were crossing the plains."

"The Indians out here don't live in tepees. They live in lodges—long wooden structures big enough to hold four or five families."

"Is that how Hawkeye and Bright Star live? In a lodge?"

Quinn laughed. "I'm afraid poor Nastachee has lost his name. Since he met you everyone has started to call him Hawkeye."

"It's his own fault."

By now we were on the final descent to the house. I sat up straighter in the saddle with my pink dress bunched up around my stocking-clad legs, trying to peer through the trees. How would I find my home? Would anything be changed?

The place looked much as I had left it, the doors to both the house and barn closed, the garden a neat plot of ground between the two structures.

"I wonder who's been looking after the garden?"

Quinn looked at Shamus, who was herding the cow and her half-grown calf into the pasture. "I sent Shamus down a couple of times. Likely your friends from across the river had a hand in it too."

Then Quinn helped me down from the horse, and I had no room in my mind for anything except for his hands on my waist and his head bent close to mine when he set me on the grass. For a moment, neither of us spoke or moved, our gazes holding, longing trembling in the air around us. The muscles in his jaw tightened. "There," he said with effort, and we both stepped apart.

The house greeted us with a closed-up, unlived-in smell when Quinn opened the door. I wrinkled my nose and followed him in, Bridget just behind us.

"We'd better leave the door open," I said.

Bridget nodded as we looked around at the dank, cold room and at the dead larkspurs in the moldy jar. The first thing we needed was a fire. Luckily, there was dry wood and kindling left in the wood box and matches on the cupboard shelf. In no time Quinn had a fire going in the stove, and Shamus's bedding had been brought inside. After seeing to the cow and calf, Shamus joined us.

When the room began to warm, I asked Bridget to help me lift the cradleboard over my head and set it and Ellen on the table. She was still sound asleep, the long jolting ride having lulled her into a deep slumber.

"Just look at the sweet angel," Bridget breathed. "I'm thinking the cradleboard is a gift you'll be thankful for."

Quinn did not leave until after the house was warm and had been put back to rights. Even then, he seemed reluctant to go. Twice I heard him admonish Shamus to keep plenty of wood chopped and not to let the fire go out, and he stopped several times to look down at Ellen and gently touch her cheek.

There was an awkward yet heart-lifting moment when he said good-bye to me at the door.

"You take care." Simple words really. But his smile was gentle, and his gold-flecked hazel eyes said more. Against my will, my eyes filled with tears, and I wanted to reach up and cling to him. *Please don't forget me,* I wanted to say. *Don't lose your heart to Deirdre.* Deirdre, who openly showed her interest and who, unlike me, was not married.

CHAPTER 10

The next morning I awoke to the soft patter of rain on the shingle roof. I stretched my back and shoulders, glad it was Shamus not me, who must venture out in the damp to milk the cow. I immediately felt guilty. Poor Shamus, who'd given up his bed to sleep on my hard kitchen floor, who'd left the beloved wolfhounds to chop my wood and do my chores. All had been done with a smile and his merry whistle. *What a fine boy he is, and Bridget just as good.* I turned my head to look at her snuggled into her pillow next to me, the thick plait of her red hair barely visible. How fortunate I was to have such good friends to help me, and how very blessed to have Ellen thriving and growing more beautiful each day. *If only.* I wouldn't let my mind carry the thought further, wouldn't let it fill with thoughts of the one I wished were here too.

Instead it was filled with thoughts of divorce. *What steps must a woman take to win freedom from a husband who has abused and deserted her? Surely with the note Jacob left for me, it shouldn't be too difficult. And once that happens, how things change between Quinn and me?* I held the thought close, like a warm flame on a cold night. It was something I would take out and examine at another time—a time when I would be free to explore my feelings for Quinn. A soft sigh from Bridget reminded me of my friends and set my mind on a different path. I wanted to enlarge Shamus's and Bridget's world. Shamus needed to claim friends among boys of a similar age. So did Bridget—young girls to giggle and whisper with as Tamsin and I had done, young men to cast longing eyes at her and make her sigh. Although a home with the Lieutenant afforded the O'Connors security and ample food for their table, their isolation had created a famine of another kind. Friends were what Shamus and Bridget needed, and I set my mind to do something to help them.

That morning set the precedent for the days to follow. While I fed and saw to Ellen's needs, Bridget started breakfast and had it ready by the time Shamus came in with the milk. This became our time to visit, the three of us lingering over the meal with Sam waiting expectantly from his place by my chair for Shamus or me to slip him a scrap. As yet, the dog didn't quite know what to make of the baby. He chose to watch her from a distance, ears pricked to baby noises.

On the following day, Shamus set out for the lodge to bring back my chickens. After Ellen's birth, Shamus had put the chickens into burlap sacks and lugged them up the mountain where they'd been kept with the O'Connors' hens. This day he repeated the process in reverse. Eight unhappy hens and a rooster were glad to escape from the sacks into the familiar chicken pen.

I watched them for a moment before I wandered over to the garden. Some of the carrots had gone to seed, but the squash was thriving. The row of potatoes was ready to be dug. I felt a rush of gratitude when I saw them, remembering the first labor pain that had struck me there, of how close I'd come to losing my baby.

That afternoon I sat down and wrote a letter to tell my sister Tamsin about the birth of my baby. It was filled with proud and loving descriptions of Ellen and ended with the request that she write to me. Mail came and went from Tillamook Bay several times a year. Maybe by spring, if Tamsin relented, I would hear from her.

As the days passed I found myself looking up at the mountain. Would Quinn come to visit, or had I misjudged the depth of our friendship? This thought was quickly followed by the knowledge of Deirdre's close proximity and the fear that any feeling he might have for me would be swallowed up in the excitement of someone new.

We had been home four days when the Lieutenant rode into the yard on Midnight. The wolfhounds followed close on his heels. Sam was in seventh heaven to see his friends, and I wasn't far behind in my happiness. Strange how just seeing the familiar dark coat and hat brought a lift to my heart—what the sight of his smile and his rumpled brown hair when he took off that hat did to my insides. By then I'd given up trying to explain the happiness I felt when I was with Quinton Reynolds. It was enough that he came.

Quinn's excuse for visiting was to make a bed for Shamus so he wouldn't have to sleep on the floor. As it turned out, Quinn spent so much time holding and playing with Ellen or talking to me that he ended up staying the night and the bed didn't get finished until the next day.

"I told Mick it might take more than a day," Quinn explained when it became evident he wasn't going to finish. He and I had walked out to look at the garden and from there had wandered to lean against the pasture fence and look at Brownie and Star.

It was the soft time of day with the sun pale and slanting from the west, a flock of red-wing blackbirds singing out their triple cadenced song from the alders. The day was cool enough for me to be glad for my red shawl, but warm enough not to mind lingering at the edge of the meadow. Signs of fall were evident—in the browning leaves of the alder and the yellowing of the taller grasses.

"What a fine place you picked for your home," Quinn commented. He was looking back at the house silhouetted by the dark green of the trees and the mountain, a thin spiral of smoke coming from the chimney. "Did you know I seriously considered it myself four years ago, the mountains at the back and the valley to the front?"

"What made you change your mind?"

"The ocean. It didn't take much scouting around to realize that if I wanted to be able to have a view of both the ocean and the forest, I'd need to go up higher."

"Maggie told me how hard it was to pack everything up the mountain."

"It wasn't easy," Quinn conceded. We were leaning with our backs against the rail fence, our elbows almost touching. "The men from the ship and those that helped build the lodge thought I was a little crazy, so the settlers aren't so different." A quirk of his thick brows. "It's my nature that once I make up my mind to do something, I don't give up easily, no matter what people think."

He looked hard at me when he said that, and for a moment I thought he was going to say more. Then something frustrated and almost desperate passed through his hazel eyes, and I thought for a moment he would take me in his arms and hold me. I wanted him to. Heaven forgive me, but I did. Thank goodness neither of us moved, though for a moment I forgot to breathe. Then all too quickly reality snatched me back and reminded me I was still a married woman, one not free to give my heart to another man. At least not yet.

Quinn was the first to move away. He muttered something about needing to help Shamus with the milking, though how the two of them would milk one cow at the same time, I didn't know. I only knew I was disappointed and worried, the two emotions wrapped into something that sat uncomfortably around my heart. Even though I didn't want anything to happen that would spoil my friendship with Quinn, part of me longed for more.

* * *

I didn't sleep well that night. I don't think Quinn did either, for there were smudges of gray under his eyes the next morning and he didn't look rested, something he blamed on the hardness of the floor when Bridget commented on his appearance at breakfast.

Quinn treated Ellen and me with his usual friendliness. The baby was held and admired, and he teased me about the bouquet of autumn leaves I'd picked and arranged. But I could tell he'd stepped back. There was a distance between us that hadn't been there on the previous day. I wanted to call the nearness back, even as I knew it was for the best.

While Quinn and Shamus worked on the bed, I looked for things to keep me busy outside, knowing I needed physical as well as emotional distance from the Lieutenant.

Then all too soon he was gone, calling Finn and Balor and the new dog Shamus had named Belle. We stood in the yard to see him off, Ellen in her cradleboard and Sam looking after the hounds with a mournful expression.

I bent and scratched Sam behind his ears. "They'll be back," I promised.

"Maybe not," Shamus put in. "The Lieutenant was sayin' this morning he was thinkin' of having Nastachee take him in his canoe up the coast. There's a place up there—Neahkahnie, I think he called it—where an old Indian village used to be."

I tried not to let my disappointment show, but it stayed with me through most of the next week. It wasn't that I was exactly unhappy. How could I be unhappy with Ellen and her smiles to fill my hours? Nor was I lonely. Bridget's and Shamus's pleasant company prevented that. Yet in a strange way I was both unhappy and lonely. My heart wanted something more—the voice and smile and presence of a man I couldn't have.

* * *

I did not see the Lieutenant for almost three weeks. During that time, I alternated between happiness and despair—happiness when I recalled the way he'd looked at me that afternoon by the meadow, despair that he'd changed his mind and no longer wanted to see me, especially now that he had Deirdre to warm him with her smiles and ready laughter. I'd never felt the threat of competition before. It was something I tried not to dwell upon—the fact that Quinn might think Deirdre more comely than me. Hovering just at the edge of this shadowed thought was the reminder that she was also not married as I was at present. The need for finding out how to legally free myself from Jacob pressed upon my mind again. Would the evidence of his note be enough? The fact that we now had a child worried me for the first time.

We were well into October, the days growing shorter, the potatoes and carrots dug. It had been misting all day, not wet enough to drip from the trees, but moist enough to dampen my face when I crossed the yard to check on my hens and collect their eggs.

Before I could reach the pen, Sam took off at a run, his happy bark making me turn to watch. I saw the wolfhounds first, gray like the fog with their fur damp from the mist as they came to greet me. My attention was more on the rider who followed them. Maybe it was only Mick or Patrick. But maybe . . . My eyes took in the familiar dark coat and hat, saw the walking stick Quinn carried next to the rifle in his scabbard.

I told myself to act as if he were one of the O'Connors—glad to see him without being carried away by excitement. That was what I planned to do. Instead, I walked eagerly toward him, the dogs ignored and a smile lighting my face.

Quinn reined in the horse and looked down at me without speaking, his eyes welcoming as I stood in the mist in my blue woolen cloak with the hood pulled back and lying across my shoulders. A smile slowly lifted the corners of his mouth. "I thought for a moment I'd ridden out of the mist and found Jane Eyre."

A happy giggle bubbled from my throat. "You are neither dark nor brooding enough to be Mr. Rochester."

The happiness I felt continued to build as Quinn dismounted from the horse. "How have you been?" he said, but his hazel eyes asked, *Did you miss me?*

"Very well," is what I said, while I nodded an answer to the question in his eyes.

"How is Ellie?"

"Growing like a puppy." Forgetting myself, I took his arm and urged him toward the house. "You won't believe how big she is . . . or what she can do. Would you believe she laughs out loud?"

As we entered the house, I called to Shamus and Bridget. "Come see who's here."

Their welcome showed their affection. As I went to get the baby, I listened as Shamus went on about his duties to Quinn, and how Star had cut her front leg, but that it was healing.

Ellen was asleep in her little bed by the stove. I picked her up anyway, as eager to show her as Quinn was to see her. After he'd hung up his coat and hat and washed his hands, he took her from me, grinning down at her when she favored him with a sleepy smile.

I drank in the sight of Quinn and Ellen and stored it in my heart to keep forever—father and daughter as I wished it could be. Was it wrong of me? Perhaps. But I hoped God would understand my longing and trust me not to do anything improper with Quinn. It was a line I'd drawn in my mind, the line between friendship and doing that which wasn't proper for a married woman—a line between honor and guilt.

Shamus's arrival disrupted my solemn thinking. "Did you go up north with Hawkeye? Did you find any relics?"

"Yes to both questions," Quinn replied. He sat in a chair with the baby, her hair like auburn fluff against his white shirt.

"What kind? How many?" Shamus asked.

"Several tools made of whalebone and some mats and baskets. I want to go back with a bigger canoe in the spring when storms are less likely."

"Can I go with you?"

The Lieutenant gave him an indulgent smile. "We'll see."

Talk turned to other things—that Shamus had gone fishing in the Tillamook River and come home with several large salmon, and how he was digging a pit for the potatoes and carrots.

I wanted to ask questions of my own. Had Quinn spent the entire three weeks with Nastachee or had part of it been passed at the lodge with Deirdre? Instead I said, "Shamus has done more in the four weeks he's been with me than Jacob did in a year."

Shamus grinned his pleasure, the scattering of freckles across his nose matching the color of his hair. "Since I'll soon be turnin' eleven—almost a man—I thought I should be practicin'."

Unwilling to let Shamus have more than his share of attention, Bridget asked questions too—about her mother and if Quinn had thought to bring any books.

"I did. They're in my saddlebag by the door."

While the two of them looked at the books, Quinn gave me a long, searching look. A hint of his lopsided smile played at the corners of his mouth. "The lodge is not the same without you. The pianoforte sits silent, and no one uses the rocking chair anymore."

"Why is that?" I tried not to look at Quinn's mouth and the curve of the almost-smile that lingered there.

"Maggie hasn't the heart to use it. She says it makes her miss you and the baby too much."

"I miss her, too. Miss all of you." I lifted my eyes to his, read the tenderness there, and quickly looked away even as I worried at what Quinn might have seen in mine. *It can't be, Clarissa,* a tiny voice warned. It was a voice I intended to heed, but not before I said part of what was in my heart. "The weeks I spent at the lodge were some of the happiest I've known. Your friendship and caring is something I'll always remember."

"'Tis something we'd do again without thinking twice," Bridget put in.

I'd forgotten about her and Shamus, forgotten about Ellen too. For a moment there'd only been Quinn and me, our eyes adding meaning to ordinary words, turning them into feelings that couldn't be spoken.

"Thank you for bringing the lovely books," Bridget went on. "Next to *Jane Eyre*, *Ivanhoe* is my favorite."

"And I've always liked *Swiss Family Robinson*," Shamus added.

From there the conversation turned to ordinary things—that Mick had seen a bear the week before and that Patrick was proving to be a good, steady worker.

"In the spring, he and Eileen and Deirdre want to have a look at the Willamette Valley—see if it's there or here they want to settle," Quinn concluded.

Bridget's face brightened at this. "Please, can I go with them? Fiona says there are ever so many people there. Boys. Friends."

"Your parents will have to be the ones to decide that." He gave her a long steady look. "Are you forgetting Clarissa's need for you?"

"No." She dropped her eyes, but not before I saw her disappointment.

Even so I took hope at the thought of Deirdre moving inland to the Willamette Valley. Before I could take pleasure in the thought, the baby began to fuss, her little face screwed up and turning red as she let out a cry. Instead of panicking, Quinn gently bounced her. "What's wrong with my girl? Don't you like being ignored?"

"I think she's hungry. It's been awhile since she ate."

Quinn took his cue, handing Ellen to me and suggesting that Shamus show him the pit he'd dug for the vegetables. By the time she had been changed and fed and settled, Quinn and Shamus had gone to look for deadfall trees to drag in for firewood.

" 'Twill make it easier with Midnight to do most of the draggin'," Bridget pointed out.

Since this was a task that would take several hours, Bridget and I decided to cook up a special meal; ham and potatoes and carrots topped off with blackberry cobbler and sweet cream—cobbler being one of the Lieutenant's favorites, this last imparted to me by Bridget.

"He's for likin' fresh-caught salmon too, but since Shamus hasn't been fishin' today, we'll have to make do with the ham," Bridget went on. " 'Twas him taught Shamus to fish. They were forever takin' off to try their luck."

While I mixed dough for the cobbler, I pictured Quinn casting for fish on the edge of a rushing stream and thought of this English gentleman dragging in logs, a man more at home in the tangled rain-forest than on a busy London street. With my mind still caught up in these pictures, I studied Quinn with new eyes when he and Shamus came in to eat, noting his trousers tucked into sturdy boots, his muscled shoulders stretching the fabric of his blue shirt, his wavy brown hair—instead of being freshly barbered—brushing the collar of his shirt. All signs that the English gentleman had vanished, replaced by a man of the outdoors—one at peace with himself and nature.

Quinn cocked his dark brows when he saw my close scrutiny. "Have I dirt on my face?" he asked, his tone light and teasing.

"No."

"You're sure? The way you're looking at me I have the feeling something's wrong."

Aware that Bridget and Shamus were watching us, I strove to match his teasing tone. "Well, perhaps there's a little dirt there, but actually I was thinking that no one would ever guess you were once an English gentleman."

Quinn glanced down at his heavy boots. "That's all in the past . . . something I seldom think about, though I hope always to treat others with courtesy."

"Which you do."

Quinn's hazel eyes were on me, not his boots. "I pass muster then?"

I nodded and smiled. "You do."

His answering grin wound itself around my heart and stayed there, making me laugh at small unimportant things and think there had never been a finer day, though in truth it was dreary and overcast. But such are the ways of the heart—a heart that needed to be watched closely lest it did something foolish.

Supper was a happy meal with everyone full of things to say. Ellen cooperated by sleeping through the whole of it.

When Quinn finished a large helping of blackberry cobbler, he leaned back in his chair and sighed. "A meal worthy of a king. My compliments to both of you. Maggie is not the only one with a gift for cooking."

Bridget dimpled and blushed. "Mam is grand for teachin'—though 'twas Clarissa who made the cobbler after I told her it was your favorite."

I managed to meet Quinn's gaze with nonchalance. "A good hostess must do her duty."

The Lieutenant chuckled and looked pleased, as well he might have with two women smiling back. Then he glanced at the window where the pale light of evening was fast coming on. "I need to be going."

"So soon?" Shamus asked.

"You can stay the night," Bridget put in.

Quinn gave me a quick glance and shook his head. "Perhaps another time."

All too soon he was gone, taking the wolfhounds and my happiness with him. *But he'll be back*, I told myself. *Surely he'll be back.*

* * *

The winter rains continued to stay away. Those days of late November and early December were like a prolonged Indian summer—the days mostly sunny, the nights crisp and clear. It was on such a day that Sven and Flora came. Quinn was also there to help Shamus chop one of the trees they'd dragged in. Hans and Little Sarah were in the back of the wagon, but when they saw the wolfhounds, they were reluctant to get out.

"They won't hurt you," Quinn said as he called off the dogs and walked to the wagon. Reassured by his words, Hans scrambled out of the wagon. The dogs were as big as he was, but he held his ground as they sniffed him and Quinn told him their names. After the dogs had been introduced and Little Sarah made to feel safe, Quinn extended his hand to Sven. "It's good to see you again, Mr. Larsen."

The big Swede stuck out his hand. "Sven it is. Just call me Sven."

"And I'd be pleased if you'd call me Quinn." A smile broke the contours of his face. "Though I'm aware of the name that's usually used."

Sven looked a little disconcerted, especially when Hans asked, "What's that?"

"The Odd Brit," Quinn chuckled. "It's true that I'm a Brit, but I like to think I'm not so odd." A pause and his engaging smile. "Just different interests than most of the other settlers."

"What's a Brit?" Hans asked.

While Quinn explained, I took Flora's arm. "You're not going to believe how much Ellen has grown."

Bridget followed Flora and me into the house. After Ellen had been wakened and admired, Flora turned to me. "It's obvious that motherhood agrees with you. There's an absolute glow about you."

"I enjoy every minute of it," I said. "I never knew it could be so wonderful."

"It certainly shows." Her blue eyes looked me over, her generous mouth smiling. "No one would believe you just had a baby."

Flora and I pulled out chairs and sat down. In between playing with the baby, Flora filled me in on the latest news from across the river, while Bridget kept Sarah amused on the floor.

Flora paused and glanced toward the door. "You seem to have plenty of help with your outside chores. Does Mr. Reynolds come here often?"

"Occasionally." I tried to keep my expression as vague as my answer. "He and Mick O'Connor have both been good to come when Shamus needs help with the heavier work." I saw that Bridget had stopped playing with Sarah to listen. "The O'Connors have all been treasures."

It was then that Flora broached the other reason for their visit. "We came to invite you to a party. It's Grandma Sarah's sixtieth birthday on Saturday. She hasn't been feeling well, so we thought a party might cheer her up. Everyone in the settlement has been invited, and she especially wants you to come."

"I'd love to." I paused and looked across the table at Flora. "How long would I be gone?"

"We'll have you home by Monday."

Bridget got to her feet, her face bright with excitement. "Please say yes." Before I could answer she went on in a wistful tone, "I haven't been to a real party since we came to Oregon. Well, there were

Liam's and Fiona's weddings, of course. But that was in Oregon City, not here . . ." Her voice trailed away as she looked at Flora.

Flora gave me a quick glance, but before either of us could say anything, Quinn and the others came in, the look on their faces saying they'd like something to eat. It wasn't until we were sitting at the table over biscuits and tea that the subject of Grandma's party was broached again.

Sven looked at Shamus, who was sitting with Bridget on the side of his bed. "Would the two of you be able to look after things while Clarissa is away?"

The excitement I'd glimpsed in Bridget's face died as Shamus nodded. "But I was hopin'—" Bridget began.

I broke in before she could finish. "I need you and Shamus to go out and gather the eggs and feed the chickens."

Shamus looked as if he wanted to say it was too early, but I read hope in Bridget's eyes. When the door closed behind them, I turned to Quinn.

"Do you think Mick and Maggie would let Bridget and Shamus come with me?" I paused. "And if they do, would one of you be able to care for the animals while we're gone?"

Quinn didn't say anything for a moment, his hazel eyes on my face while his long fingers absently played with his spoon.

"I know this is a big imposition, but . . ." Flora and Sven watched me as closely as Quinn did, their faces hesitant and wary. "Bridget and Shamus are so isolated. Other than family, Shamus has no one except the dogs to count as friends, and Bridget has only me." I paused briefly before hurrying on. "I know extra company can be a strain, but they're both good to help and—"

"They're more than welcome to come if it's all right with their parents," Flora interrupted. The wariness had left her face. "You could bring ten extra people, and I'd say yes if it meant I could have you with me for a few days."

"You're a dear." I looked at Sven. "How about you?"

"If it's all right with Flora, it's all right with me."

"Lieutenant?"

Quinn nodded. "I'll be happy to help in any way I can." His eyes were on his spoon instead of me. "Mick and Maggie will be the ones who will need convincing. Being staunch Catholics, they may be reluctant to let Bridget and Shamus socialize overmuch with Protestants."

"The McKinneys are Catholic too," Sven pointed out.

Quinn pushed back his chair and got to his feet. "That will be a point in our favor, but I still may have to use my best powers of persuasion." He paused and touched Ellen's tiny hand, his expression pensive and a little hesitant. I wondered what he was thinking and if he was reluctant to see me go.

"I'll ride up to the lodge and see what I can arrange." Another pause and that lopsided grin. "You'll probably need to rescue your chickens from Bridget and Shamus. They're not going to know how to act with all that extra attention."

CHAPTER 11

We left for the settlement as soon as Quinn returned from the lodge with permission for Bridget and Shamus to go to the party. Bridget and I sat on a box seat the men had improvised, and Shamus and Hans rode on the floor of the wagon. Little Sarah, who had taken an immediate liking for Bridget, insisted on sitting on Bridget's lap, and Ellen, snuggled down inside the cradleboard, was on mine. Flora's eyes widened when she saw the cradleboard.

"Bright Star, Hawkeye's wife and the woman who nursed Ellie, gave it to me. It keeps her warm while we travel and it will make a good bed for her when we're at your house."

The muscles tightened at the corners of Flora's mouth. A small thing really, but one significant enough for me to know my friend found it difficult to understand how I could put my precious baby into something that had been made by an Indian. Although I was disappointed by her prejudice, we had been friends too long to let it alter our relationship. We'd bonded like sisters over the long miles on the trail; experience had taught me that sisters could be vastly different and still love each other.

The distance from my home to the river crossing was over a mile. Although I was excited to be going, I kept turning to look back at Quinn, his tall frame looking smaller each time I did. Sadness warred with excitement and joined the sense of loss that came whenever Quinn wasn't around. I tried not to think of Deirdre and the time they would be spending together while he taught her to read.

We traveled over thick meadow grass, passing thickets of salal and berries. Blackbirds called from an isolated stand of spruce trees growing in the meadow, and two crows quarreled from the top of a solitary alder.

I thought of the last time I'd come that way, Jacob and I riding in our wagon on the way to worship meeting. I remembered Jacob's complaints and critical remarks about the other settlers, his rudeness when I'd tried to defend them.

Flora looked up at the blue sky where the sun was beginning its swift descent to the west. "Can you believe how warm it is? More like October than December."

Four tall poles had been set into the bank of the Tillamook River to mark the place of the crossing—two on the west bank, two more on the east bank. When I saw them, my hold tightened on Ellen's cradle. I'd seen a wagon swept away with a screaming mother and her baby still inside when we'd crossed the Platte River. Luckily the Tillamook was neither as wide nor as swift as the Platte.

Even so, my breathing quickened when Sven turned the team between the two poles, quickened again when the front wheels of the wagon entered the murky gray water.

As if he'd sensed my fear, Sven looked back and smiled. "The water isn't deep. No more than a couple of feet here. We'll be through before you know it."

I saw Bridget's arms tighten around Sarah, heard the ripple of water as it flowed between the spokes of the wheels.

"Stay right where you are," Sven called to Hans, who was peering over the side of the wagon. I was glad Shamus had a firm grip on the waist of the little boy's britches.

My hold on the baby relaxed when we reached the other side, the water sloshing off the wheels as the wagon climbed the steep bank, Hans holding on tightly and laughing.

It was another four or five miles to Sven's farm, the way winding past plowed fields and fenced pastures where placid cows grazed, their udders almost touching the lush grass. "Cow heaven," Sven had called it when we'd first arrived. I thought back to those first months in Oregon, a time when Jacob had seemed more contented, when I'd dared to hope and dream that things would get better, and perhaps Jacob would find love in his heart. But his blindness and selfishness had conquered even this touch of God's hand.

"See the new house and barn through the trees?" Flora asked. "That's the Watson family. They moved here last spring after waiting the winter out in Astoria."

While we covered the final miles to their farm, Flora and Sven told me about their new neighbors. "We had a barn raising for them, and the men all helped so they could get their house up before winter. They're good people . . . good neighbors."

"Do they have children?"

Flora nodded. "Five. The oldest is a girl about Bridget's age, and they have a boy that's twelve."

Bridget smiled at the news, the prospect of making new friends putting an added glow of excitement on her pretty face.

The sun was slipping behind the shadowed headland of the bay when we reached the Larsens'. The house wasn't much bigger than my own, but the barn was twice as large.

"Home just in time to do the milking," Sven said. "Eight cows we have now. And did I tell you we have help? Joe Sidaway's son comes night and morning to give me a hand with the milking."

"I can help while I'm here," Shamus offered. Like Bridget, he'd been busy taking in the new sights, his boyish face bright with interest.

A spotted black-and-white dog came out to meet us, his tail wagging a welcome. He was followed by a boy bordering on manhood—tall and lanky with a pleasant face and a thick head of black hair. He stopped when he saw us, a bucket of milk in each hand, his mouth slightly agape when he saw Bridget.

Sven pulled the team and wagon to a halt in front of the house and jumped down. After lowering the back so Shamus and Hans could get out, he reached to help Flora. When he turned to do the same for me, I heard a deep voice on the other side of the wagon speak to Bridget.

"Here, let me help you." It was a man's voice, the lanky, boyish body more muscular than I'd first supposed. The buckets of milk had been left in the dooryard, his eager face smiling up at her. "My name's Nathan Sidaway. What's yours?"

"Bridget." Her voice sounded a little breathless.

"And mine's Shamus. Shamus O'Connor. I'm her brother," Shamus put in.

"Nathan, the milk!" Sven cried.

A black cat had her front paws on the lip of one of the buckets, ready to lap the milk. Nathan rushed at her and clapped his hands. "Scat! Scat you old biddy." The cat streaked toward the barn. "Sorry." Nathan's voice was contrite as he picked up the buckets of milk.

"You need to take those into the house. Then come back out and help me finish milking." Sven's voice was stern.

"Yes, sir." Nathan shot Bridget a quick smile before he headed for the kitchen, a smile that said, *Don't worry* and *I'll see you later.*

Shamus hurried ahead to help Nathan with the door and earned a smile for his efforts. As the rest of us crowded into the kitchen, Nathan excused himself and left for the barn.

"What a nice young man," I said.

"A good worker too," Flora responded. "Sven is pleased with him."

Grandma Sarah was waiting in the kitchen. She was tall and straight for so old a woman, her once blond hair now more white than yellow, all of it braided and wound into a coil on top of her head. Her wrinkled face broke into a smile when she saw me. "I'm so glad you could come." Her arms went around the baby and me.

"So am I. I've missed you."

She released us to look at Ellen, whose little face and blue eyes were all that was visible from the swaddling of her cradle.

"And now you have dis baby. What a dear." A misshapen rheumatic finger touched Ellen's cheek. "She is part ours, you know." She paused and nodded. "Ja. Grandma Sarah I will be to her. After so many prayers from us, she is like one of de family."

"I felt your prayers. Thank you."

"God has been good to you, dough not without giving you trials first." Her thin mouth tightened along with her voice. "Dat Jacob I never liked. All talk and no work. I'm tinking you and da babe are better off witout him." She paused and her blue eyes looked deeply into mine. "Dat is how God works, you know . . . gives us da bitter so we can appreciate da sweetness of da good when it comes."

"Lately I've been enjoying the sweetness."

She patted my arm. "Good, good."

Bridget and Shamus were then introduced. If she was surprised or concerned by the extra people, she gave no sign. "What beautiful friends you have. Ja, you, too," she said when Shamus colored. "Sven and Flora have told me about Clarissa's good friends."

Shamus eased toward the door as I lifted Ellen out of her cradle-board to be admired and cuddled. She had slept most of the way and was not bashful about letting us know it was time to be fed.

"In here." Flora beckoned. She led me into the sitting room that doubled as Grandma Sarah's bedroom. "We thought you could sleep with Grandma," she went on after I was settled into a chair with the baby. "I hope Bridget won't mind sleeping on the floor."

"She's so excited to be here that I'm sure she won't mind." I helped Ellie settle to eat, then went on. "Thank you for letting them come. They've been so good to help me. Never a word of complaint."

Flora laughed. "I truly don't mind, and I can see that Bridget all but worships you. Not that I'm surprised." She put her hand on my shoulder. "This is going to be fun."

Flora's words proved to be true. Although the house was crowded, there was ample talk and laughter to counteract the crowding. Shamus was content to sleep in the loft with Hans and Little Sarah, and Bridget acted as if a place on the floor was no trouble at all. Grandma Sarah and I managed to make do with the two of us in her bed, though my sleep was interrupted by her snoring and hers by Ellen waking up to be fed during the night.

Friday proved to be a busy day with the extra baking and cooking for the party. Since Bridget and I were there to help, we insisted that Grandma take the day off. We brought her rocking chair into the kitchen so she could take part in the gossip and laughter of which there was plenty, for Flora and I had much to catch up on—Hannah Mayfield's run-in with a skunk and Mr. Petty's disastrous venture at building a boat. While we talked, Flora rolled out dough for piecrusts and I peeled apples.

"Does the supply boat still come once a month?" I asked.

"During the summer. Not at all in the winter. Sven sent ten pounds of butter and seven cheeses on the last boat that went out. Hopefully it will mean extra cash for us when the captain comes back next spring."

"Was the letter I sent to my sister in time for the boat?"

Flora nodded. "Sven made sure it was put on with the butter. We sent your extra cheese too, but I doubt it will bring you very much."

She paused and looked up from the piecrust. "How are you making out, Clarrie? Do you have enough food?"

"I do." I thought of the flour and beans and sugar and tea that seemed to magically fill my larder. Strange how I'd been so fiercely independent when there was just me. Ellen's coming had changed all that. Ellen and the Lieutenant.

Flora frowned. "How? Where does it come from?"

"My friends," I answered, glad that Bridget had taken Little Sarah outside to look for bugs and that Grandma had retired to her room for a nap.

Flora's eyes filed with sudden tears. "Why them? Why not us? You know we want to help."

"I know, and I love you for it." I put down my knife and went to her side. "Lieutenant Reynolds is a rich man—at least by our standards. He can afford to help me. And so can the O'Connors. But you—" My arm went around her waist. "You and Sven need all you have to buy more cows and take care of your two children."

Flora sniffed at her tears. "Three," she corrected.

"Three?"

She smiled and nodded. "I've been wanting to tell you since yesterday, but I couldn't seem to find the right time."

"Oh, Flora." I pulled her close and felt the dampness of her tears on my face. "When?"

"Not until summer."

"Is Sven excited?"

"He is." Flora paused to brush pieces of dough from her hands. "In fact, he's ordered twins—another boy like Hans and a little girl like Sarah."

* * *

Saturday was upon us before we knew it, the overcast sky failing to cast a pall on our anticipation.

"Everyone has been invited," Sven told me. "Did you know there are fifteen families living around the bay now? Whether they will all come remains to be seen, but we should have a good crowd."

The first of the guests began to arrive around midmorning. "We need to leave early to get home in time to do the chores before dark,"

Naomi Tomkins explained as she set a pan of rolls onto a table set under the trees. "I hope the rain holds off until tonight."

"My rheumatism says it will," Grandma predicted. She smiled wryly. "Ja, this rheumatism's got to be good for someting, even if it's only for predicting a storm."

By noon ten families had come, the yard teeming with people and chatter and rollicking children. The men set up a trestle table in the yard with Grandma ensconced in her rocking chair as the guest of honor. Another eating table had been set up under the trees to augment the smaller one covered with dishes of food and pies and cakes furnished by the guests and Flora. Even so, I wondered how everyone would find a place to eat, and Sven had said there would even be dancing.

I'd deemed it wise to hide Ellen's cradleboard behind a chair in the bedroom. It wasn't that I was ashamed of Bright Star's gift, but I felt there were some who might be offended, and I didn't want anything to spoil Grandma's party.

I was surprised to discover that the baby and I were as sought out as Grandma. My friends from worship meeting were eager to talk to me and admire Ellen, who was considered a miracle and a direct answer to their prayers.

"She is," I agreed. "I thank God for her every day."

"Seven-month babies seldom thrive, but she . . ." Mrs. Petty seemed at a loss for words. "Why, she looks as bright and normal as any baby I've seen."

"Thank you. And thank you for the clothes and diapers you sent."

"Think nothing of it. The Lord willing, I'm past the stage to need them anymore." She paused and leaned her large body closer. "Have you heard anything from that no-good husband of yours?"

"No, and I don't expect to."

"Good." Although the news seemed to please her, I was afraid she was going to launch into another list of Jacob's shortcomings. Instead, she squinted her eyes and looked across the yard. "Who's that redheaded girl flirting with the Sidaway boy?" I'd been watching Bridget, too, seeing her smile and blush when Nathan sought her out, noting her excitement and happy giggle when he said something amusing. Nathan wasn't the only one who had discovered Bridget. The Haycock boy was vying for her attention along with the Petty's oldest son. Oliver, he was called, a bachelor well into his twenties with long arms and legs he didn't seem to have grown accustomed to.

"It's Bridget O'Connor. She and her brother live with me to help and keep me company."

"Live with you?" And in the same breath, "Are they Irish?"

"They are. Catholic too." I made a point of meeting her gaze.

"Oh, my." She took a deep breath, then let it out. "Where on earth did you run onto them? They aren't the ones that belong to that Odd Brit are they?"

"They are, though he doesn't own them. They only work for Mr. Reynolds, who, by the way isn't odd at all, but a very nice man."

"How—" I knew she was about to ask how I knew. Instead she said, "You know, don't you, that he keeps a squaw?"

"That's a lie—one started by my runaway husband."

Her fleshy brow wrinkled. "Lie?"

"Have your husband talk to Sven Larsen, or better yet, why don't you ask Flora." Afraid of saying something I'd regret, I got to my feet. "There's Lucy Haycock. She wanted to have a look at the baby."

There was other talk that afternoon, the most pressing and electrifying news being that some of the southern states were talking of seceding.

After everyone had finished eating, Sven asked the men to help take down the trestle tables so they could start the dance. Just as they were finishing, I felt a hand on my arm.

"Nathan asked me for the first dance," Bridget whispered. "So have Eli Haycock and Oliver Petty. What should I do?"

I laughed and whispered back. "Dance the first dance with the one who asked you first, the second with the one who asked you second, and the third—"

"But Oliver asked me first."

"Then you must dance with him first."

"But he's all arms and legs, and besides, he smells."

I had difficulty keeping a straight face. "The first dance won't last forever. Treat them fairly. It's the best way."

"All right," she sighed, but there was wonder and excitement in her voice too. "Three boys. Can you believe so many? And they all want to dance with me."

* * *

My feelings were mixed as I watched the dancers twirl through the reels. The faces of the settlers who were usually serious in worship service were flushed from excitement and exertion. Their excitement was contagious as I sat on a chair next to Grandma Sarah, my toes tapping as I held Ellen on my lap. How could it be otherwise with the cry of the fiddle and the stomping of happy feet, especially when I saw Bridget's happiness as she danced every dance? But through it all, I was filled with a longing for Quinn. How I wished he could be with me, that it could be me smiling encouragement to a pair of hazel eyes, me feeling the steady pressure of his hand on my waist. My longing was as intense as a physical ache and cut through the music to diminish my pleasure. Strange that I had to wait until I was twenty-two to fall in love. *Quinn, Quinn, why aren't you here?*

Although Quinn was not there to dance with me, others were. Several of the men asked me—Sven, Ben Tomkins, even Mr. Petty. Sven was the first to ask me. When I hesitated, Flora gave me a little shove. "Go on," she said. "I saw your toes tapping. Don't let the happy music go to waste."

So it was that I was able to enjoy myself at dancing. I found pleasure in watching Bridget and Shamus too, seeing them laugh and talk with new friends—young people as starved for new faces as they were. Although the Catholic McKinneys had come with a lively brood of five children, we had discovered that the oldest was not yet twelve. But for the moment, Nathan's hovering attention made me think that the matter of religion was far from Bridget's thoughts.

By late afternoon, most of the guests had gone, distance and the press of chores prohibiting them from staying longer. The Watsons were the exception. Since they lived less than an hour away, they insisted on staying to help put the house and yard back to rights.

The couple, although probably ten years older than Sven and Flora, were pleasant company. Gilbert was of medium build and had a bearded face that contrasted with his balding head. Amanda—Mandy she told me to call her—was a tiny woman with shining black eyes and a ready smile. A ready tongue, too, for she seemed always to be talking. Their oldest daughter, Charlotte, was a younger version of her mother—pretty, vivacious, and not seeming to mind that Bridget had been such a success, since she'd her share of admirers too. I watched the two of them, heads close as they whispered and giggled while they washed and dried the dishes, russet curls next to thick, straight black hair.

Shamus had found a friend too—Charlotte's brother Conrad, who was only six months older than Shamus, but towered over him by a good three inches. Where his height came from, no one knew, but it was a source of great pride to his parents. Their other three children ranged in age from fourteen to six—Cecil, Caroline, and Carl. "All of our children's names begin with 'C'," Mandy told me. "My mother did the same with us—Alice, Arnold, Alexander, Althea, and me." She counted the names on her fingers. "We had a baby brother named Alonzo, but he died before he was three."

I didn't know whether I should commiserate, and before I could decide, Mandy had launched into the horrors of the past winter when they'd been stranded in Astoria waiting to sail south. She was helping me make up Grandma Sarah's bed, her hands working as quickly as her tongue. I had no opportunity to more than smile, nod my head, and think that Flora would never lack for conversation with her new neighbors around.

That night after Ellen had been fed and put to bed with Grandma Sarah curled on her side and softly snoring, I looked up at the faint light that came through the room's only window.

"Thank you, Father," I whispered into the darkness. "Thank you for my sweet baby and good friends, and for helping Shamus and Bridget find people of their own age." I paused and my throat tightened. "And thank you for Quinn. He's such a good man . . . such a good friend." Afraid that God might not deem it proper for me to say more about Quinn, I added, "You must know about Jacob, the kind of man he is and how he's abandoned me." I went on after a moment. "I'm not asking you to pity me, because I know you made me strong, and marrying Jacob was my choice . . . but I guess what I'm saying,

God, is that I don't intend to do anything wrong with Quinn . . . that you can depend upon me doing what's right. Just the same, I've come to love him. So if it's all right to ask, I would appreciate your help in getting freed from Jacob so I can follow my heart." Then, not knowing what more to say, I whispered a soft "amen" and rolled onto my side. But I continued to think of Quinn, hoping he was missing me, and trying not to worry about him and Deirdre.

CHAPTER 12

Heavy rain set in during the night, drumming on the roof and against the panes of the window. I snuggled deep into the covers, thankful I was inside and warm and dry. It was still raining when we got up the next morning. Grandma Sarah scowled as she eased herself up on the bed and looked at the water that ran down and dripped from the eaves in a steady cadence.

"Dat storm outfoxed my rheumatism. It wasn't supposed to start until tomorrow." Her tone was more jocular than displeased, and I thought that despite being tired, she was in better spirits because of the company.

"I'm glad it waited at least until today so everyone could come for your party."

"It was a good turn-out." Satisfaction sounded in her voice, satisfaction that was echoed by Bridget when she joined Flora and me in the kitchen a few minutes later.

Flora had started breakfast, and Shamus had gone to help Sven with the milking. "Here, let me finish fixing the mush," I said when I noted the shadows of gray under Flora's eyes.

"I am a little queasy." She let me take her place at the stove. "I guess you know all about that."

"I do."

"And what a beautiful daughter you have as your reward." Her gaze met mine from the chair she'd taken, and her voice when it came was fierce. "I hope Jacob has the goodness to never come back."

"He won't. I told you, he's too much of a coward to ever come back."

Bridget watched as she made a pretense of setting the table, the clatter of bowls and spoons melding with the crackle of the fire.

"As much as I dislike Jacob, I do like the hair he passed on to Ellen," Flora went on. "But she has your face."

"Aye, she does," Bridget agreed. "The very image of her mother, she is."

"The Lieutenant says she's a scrapper like me," I put in, remembering the love on Quinn's face the last time he'd looked down at Ellen.

Flora frowned. "Why do you always call him the Lieutenant?"

"He used to be in the British army."

"He was wounded in the war," Bridget added. "That's why he has to be using a walking stick."

"I see." Flora's gaze remained on me, her eyes filled with questions. Before she could ask them, Shamus and Nathan came in from the barn, each carrying a bucket of milk. "Just put them on the bench," Flora said absently.

Shamus was quick to comply, but Nathan was so busy looking at Bridget, it took him a second to respond. Water dripped from his hat and the pungent smell of cows and the barn clung to him. Bridget blushed and lowered her eyes, but raised them a second later to give him a bright smile.

I helped Flora pour the warm milk through cheesecloth into a pan where it would be left until the cream had risen, while Bridget finished setting the table. She sang as she worked, a song about the mountains of Mourne.

"What a lovely voice," Flora said.

"Her brother's is just as nice. And they both play instruments."

"So the O'Connors are a musical family." She paused and took a clean cloth to wipe out the empty milk pail. "What about Mr. Reynolds? Does he sing and play too?"

"No . . . at least not that I've heard."

"You seem to have gotten to know him quite well." Her eyes were on me as I tightened the cheese press. "How long were you up at his house?"

"A little over two months." I tried to keep my voice nonchalant, even as a part of me wanted to tell her how Quinn's strength had kept me breathing, of his tenderness with Ellen. *Could I? Should I?* The questions followed me throughout the day, as incessant as the rain.

"A real frog strangler," Sven called the endless downfall. Seeing my concern, he added, "Hopefully it will clear up by tomorrow. It wouldn't be wise for you to travel in the rain with your baby."

I agreed, but it didn't keep me from wishing we were back in our own little house and familiar bed, with Quinn less than an hour up the mountain instead of half a day away. I hadn't realized how much I could miss him.

The rain continued throughout the night, and by morning there was still no sign of letup.

"I guess this is God's way of paying us back for so many days of sun," Flora sighed. "As much as I love this country, I do tire of all the rain in the winter." Her features lifted as she smiled at me. "But I won't complain when it means I get to keep you and Ellen for an extra day."

I glanced out the window. The thick gray clouds seemed to have planted themselves firmly over the bay and showed no sign of moving on. Tuesday came and went, and then Wednesday and Thursday, the constant patter of rain on the shingle roof like a steady heartbeat.

I tried not to show my growing frustration, for Flora and Sven and Grandma Sarah were all graciousness, but inside I was filled with longing for Quinn and I worried about my animals—worried about Deirdre and her charms too. The rain would keep Quinn and the O'Connors inside to talk and sing and generally enjoy each other. I pushed aside a picture of Quinn and Deirdre sitting together in the drawing room while he helped her with her reading—Deirdre smiling over at him and Quinn responding.

"It will be hard for the O'Connors to get up and down the mountain in all this rain," I said to Flora on Friday. We were sitting with Grandma, sewing scraps of cloth into strips for a braided rug for Flora's bedroom. Although it was midmorning, the lamp was lit so we could see to stitch the pieces.

"Maybe one of them will stay at your place so they don't have to go back and forth so often."

"Of course." I knew Flora was right. "It will probably be the Lieutenant."

Flora looked up from her sewing. "Why would he leave his big house to do that? Besides, I doubt he even knows how to milk a cow."

"He does." My answer was emphatic. "He's always doing things for people. He's really a very nice man."

"He seems nice enough," Flora conceded, but her face remained skeptical.

"He read to me every day while I was sick." My lips curved into a smile at the memory. "We went through all of *Sense and Sensibility* together, some of Shakespeare's sonnets too. He wears a pair of gold spectacles when he reads, and his voice is . . ."

I stopped when I realized Flora was watching me instead of sewing. "What? Is something wrong?"

"No. At least I hope not." Flora's eyes were serious, not teasing.

After that, we talked of other things, the importance of using cream instead of milk for a tastier clam chowder, and how Mandy Watson claimed honey was good for curing the croup. As we talked, Grandma's rocker slowed and her breathing changed to a soft snore. We continued our conversation in low voices, our only interruption an occasional guffaw or protest from the kitchen where Bridget and Shamus played cards with Sven and Hans.

"What was it you were saying about Mr. Reynolds's voice?" Flora prompted.

"Only that I like his accent. Don't you find British accents intriguing?"

"I hadn't thought about it."

"I have. And I thoroughly enjoy the O'Connors' Irish brogue." Then, like a floodgate unable to hold back a rising river, I told Flora about the pianoforte and of Quinn's love for music, of his sitting room with its shelves of books, of his many kindnesses to me and little Ellie.

I don't know how long I talked—maybe an hour, perhaps longer, my need to recall everything Quinn had done like a hunger only satisfied by saying more.

Flora was a patient audience, never once looking or acting bored, though her eyebrows raised several times, especially when I slipped and called him Quinn. It was while I was telling her about Quinn and Ellen that she stopped me. "You love him, don't you?" Her voice when she spoke held sympathy, not censure.

"Yes." My throat closed around my admission, one I'd been longing to speak aloud for weeks. "Yes . . . so very much." Tears filled my eyes and ran down my cheeks, the weeks of pent-up longing and emotion loosed by the words, the gate of my heart swinging open.

Flora dropped to her knees by my chair, her hands clasping mine. "Clarrie . . . I'm so sorry."

"Don't be." I strove for control, my mouth quivering as the tears dripped from my chin. "It's wonderful. I . . . I've never been so happy."

"Anyone with two eyes can see that." Flora laughed. "When we came to get you, I thought it was Ellie that had brought the glow to your face. You were like a flower that had just discovered the sun . . . open with your arms spread wide." She seemed embarrassed by her eloquence. "It's true. Love was written all over you. I know motherhood can do wonders, but that . . ."

She handed me a strip of cloth to dry my tears. "Then when I saw how your eyes kept seeking the Lieutenant . . . and he yours." Another pause and her round face turned solemn. "Has he told you how he feels?"

"No . . . how can he when I'm married? But I think he cares . . . at least I hope he does."

A sad smile crossed her face. "You know he does, Clarrie," she whispered.

Neither of us spoke for a moment, the crackle of the fire and the sound of Grandma's soft snoring filling the room.

"What are you going to do?" Flora finally asked.

"I don't know." Seeing the concern on her face, I went on. "Just being in the same room with him fills me with pleasure, as does his voice." I sniffed and giggled. "I'm terrible, I know, and not a bit different than Bridget when she sees Nathan." I paused and held her gaze. "For now that's enough."

"And later?"

"I don't let myself think of later. How can I when I don't know for sure if he loves me? And since I'm married . . ." My voice trailed away, and I was suddenly overwhelmed by the impossibility of it all. "Besides, now there's Deirdre."

"Who's Deirdre?"

It took me several minutes to tell her about Deirdre, of her oveliness and animation, not to mention her availability. "I can't see how he can help but be attracted to her. Even I am. She has a talent for making you feel as if you're her special friend. What man can resist that?"

"Any man who knows you," Flora replied. "Don't you know how lovely you are? How men's eyes follow you wherever you go? Yes," she insisted, when she saw me frown, "you're like a beautiful flower, and I know your Lieutenant has seen it too."

"He's not my Lieutenant. Although . . ."

I met her gaze. Hoping she wouldn't think less of me by what I was going to say. "I'm thinking of getting a divorce." There was a tiny silence, and I saw something flicker through Flora's eyes. "It's not just because of Quinn. This is something that's been building for years. But now that Jacob has gone . . . after the note he left me . . ."

Flora's hand closed around mine. "You don't have to justify yourself to me, Clarrie. I've wondered for years how you could stand being married to Jacob."

"But divorce," I paused and wiped at a tear. "I'm not even certain where to begin. And isolated like we are, where will I find a lawyer?"

"Sven will know. Ever since he heard about the note Jacob left you, he's been wanting to help." Flora nodded and her hand tightened on mine. "I have a good feeling about this. With God's help it will work out."

We smiled at each other through tears—bonded like sisters in every way except blood.

* * *

On Saturday there was a brief letup to the rain. Sven and Shamus rode two of the horses to the river to see if it might be safe for us to cross.

"Don't get your hopes up, though," Sven cautioned. "After so much rain, the river will probably be flooding." A look of satisfaction crossed the broad features of his face. "That's why we built our house on this little knoll and why I told Jake to do the same with yours." He nodded his head. "For once your husband listened to me." Sven looked at me hard when he said that, and I didn't know if he was criticizing Jacob or me.

"Have you told Sven about Quinn?" I asked Flora when we were bathing Ellen. We'd stoked the stove with wood so the kitchen was warm, and clean clothes and Ellie and a towel were spread on the kitchen table next to a basin of warm water.

"Yes." There was an apologetic pause. "We don't keep secrets."

I nodded, thinking that was how I wanted it if Quinn and I should ever be able to marry. "How does Sven feel about it?"

"Worried." She watched while I slipped the baby's arms out of the flannel gown and removed the pins from her diaper. Her chubby arms and legs kicked in a celebration of freedom.

I lathered soap into the creases on the baby's body and put her into the basin of water, her legs and arms splashing as I washed off the soap.

"She's like a little frog," Flora laughed, watching the baby smile her happiness. "An adorable little frog. I'm so happy for you—to have one so beautiful and perfect after your disappointments."

Flora didn't resume our conversation until I'd finished drying Ellie's hair and had formed a golden curl on the top of her head. "Sven is going to ask the captain of the boat that takes our cheese for the name of a lawyer in Astoria. Then you can write to him." There was a tiny pause. "But Sven is worried that Jacob might come back."

"Why would he come back? He's already taken everything there is and told me he was leaving for good." I heard the anger in my voice, heard it again when I added, "It's something I don't want to think about." But inside I was suddenly desperate and scared. *He can't come home. He can't.*

Neither of us spoke for a minute. "I don't think he will," I finally went on. "He knows there's no quick money here, and I never told him about the baby."

"But he might miss you, Clarissa. Surely he must have had some feelings for you."

"I doubt it." I looked past Flora to the shelf where she kept her rose-patterned crockery, my thoughts going back to the early days of our marriage. "I think to Jacob I was little more than a prize . . . the prettiest girl in Mickelboro. I truly don't believe Jacob is capable of love."

Flora looked at me in sadness. "What a terrible waste of his life."

* * *

Sven and Shamus weren't the only ones to venture out during the respite from rain. Shortly after noon, Charlotte and Conrad rode double into the yard on the broad back of one of their father's horses.

"We hoped you'd still be here," Charlotte said as she slid from the horse onto the wet grass. "Pa said you'd be crazy to try to get back across the river after all this rain."

"We're not that crazy," Bridget said. Although the day was still overcast, everyone except Grandma and Ellen had gone outside. It was good to breathe in the cool dampness of the air instead of the smell of yesterday's cooking and too many bodies closed up in a small house.

"I think I'll ride out and meet them," Conrad said when he learned that Sven and Shamus had gone to the river.

Bridget and Charlotte—Lottie, as she liked to be called—were soon engaged in whispered, animated conversation at the far end of the porch. Flora and I smiled, knowing that Nathan's name would appear in at least every other sentence. And I was no better. Since I'd told Flora about Quinn, I had to watch myself to keep from talking about him all the time. The luxury of having someone to share my thoughts and feelings with was a wonderful release, especially when there had been no condemnation from Flora.

Bridget and Shamus were probably the only ones not frustrated by so much rain. Although they might experience brief twinges of guilt for being away from responsibility and home, the guilt was quickly snuffed out by their enjoyment of new experiences, not the least of which was Nathan.

Shamus was as enthusiastic about the young man as Bridget, looking up to him like an older brother. Twice a day Nathan rode through the rain to help with the milking, water streaming off his hat and slicker, both he and the horse with heads bent against the drizzle. It was amusing to see how often Bridget invented excuses to run out to the barn at milking time and how Nathan lingered in the kitchen after they were through, hoping to be invited to stay for breakfast or supper so he and Bridget could talk or exchange longing glances.

"You're going to be eaten out of house and home," I'd told Flora the second time he stayed for a meal.

"God will provide," she'd answered. "When you give away, it always comes back twice blessed."

I knew Flora truly believed this and that her life had been richly filled because of it. *Look at Sven and Hans and Little Sarah. Look at all her friends,* I thought.

Shortly after Conrad left, the three of them returned.

"Too high. It's still too high," Sven called.

I fought disappointment, for I'd clung to the hope that by the end of the day I would be back with Quinn.

After the horses had been unsaddled and put out to pasture, Sven and the two boys came into the house.

"You'll never be believing who we saw," Shamus said.

I looked up from the corn bread I was mixing. "Who?"

"The Lieutenant."

I stopped stirring the batter. "Quinn?"

Shamus grinned, pleased at having gotten my attention.

"How? Where?"

"Waiting on the other side of the river."

My gaze flew to Sven who nodded. "Mr. Reynolds was sitting on his horse at the crossing. He'd come to see if it was safe to cross."

Conflicting emotions rushed through me—disappointment that I hadn't gone to the river, happiness at knowing Quinn had been thinking about me.

"Mr. Reynolds called to tell me not to try to bring you and the baby home until the water went down . . . that it wasn't safe." Sven grimaced. " 'Course I knew that as soon as I saw it, but I must say the man seemed uncommonly worried."

"That's 'cause he's a good man," Shamus said. "The Lieutenant is always trying to help people."

"'Tis true," Bridget agreed. "My mam said he's the best thing that ever happened to us." Before anyone could say anything else, she invited the two boys to join her and Lottie in a game of cards.

While the young people enjoyed themselves, Sven followed Flora and me into the cool room to check the cheeses aging on the shelves.

"How long do you think it will be before the river's safe to cross?"

Sven shrugged and lifted a piece of cheesecloth to get a better look at a cheese. "Hard to say. A week if it doesn't rain . . . longer if it does. The river's flooded in several places." He straightened and gave a half-smile. "Could be you'll have to spend the rest of the winter with us."

"No." My protest slipped out before I could stop it.

Sven threw back his head and laughed. "I must say you're in an all-fired hurry to get back to that place of yours."

"Of course I am. I have a cow and her calf to worry about. Chickens too. And the O'Connors will have fits if Bridget and Shamus are gone that long."

"Then we'll have to start praying that the river goes down soon," he said as he tweaked a tendril of loose hair and walked past me to tighten the cheese press. "By the way, Quinn told me to tell you not to worry about your animals. He said he was staying at your place until you get back."

"He did?"

Sven nodded. "At least that's what I thought he said. Swift as the water was running, it was hard to tell." Though I could tell he was pleased at what a good man Quinn was, concern showed on his face, as if he worried about what the future held for me. "Even with all the noise, I'd say Quinn Reynolds was anxious to have you back."

I held to his words during the rest of the day, words made even sweeter by the knowledge that Quinn wasn't up at the lodge with Deirdre.

CHAPTER 13

Intermittent rain continued during the next week, but it came without its earlier intensity. Sven rode to the river almost every day.

"I'm beginning to feel like Noah when he had to keep sending out the dove," Sven grumbled good-naturedly. The third time he returned, he added, "By the way I saw our British friend again today. He said things were going well on the other side of the river and asked how you and the baby were."

My heart quickened. "What did you tell him?"

"That everyone was well."

Just like a man, I thought. "Is that all you told him?"

"It is." Sven lifted his big shoulders, the light coming in the kitchen window outlining his muscular build. "It's not easy hollering across the noisy water, though it is quieting some." He walked over and planted a kiss on Flora's cheek. "I think that man checks on the river as often as I do."

While I prayed for the river to go down, I suspected that Nathan and Bridget were praying for it to keep raining. The young man kept finding excuses for staying longer, and Bridget wasn't above helping him.

Two nights later something jerked me out of slumber when I should have been sleeping. Only half awake, I waited, expecting to hear Ellen's cry or Grandma's snore. Neither came.

I listened more carefully, but the only sound that came was Grandma's soft breathing. Turning over I burrowed my face into the pillow. Little niggles of unease wouldn't let sleep come. It was as if something wasn't right, or that someone needed my attention.

Mother's instinct moved me to the edge of the bed to feel for Ellen in the cradleboard. My fingers found her warm head and felt the gentle rise and fall of her breathing. *Thank heaven!*

Thoroughly awake now, my eyes sought the shadowy outline of objects in the room—the rocker and the darker square of the table. Rising up onto my elbow I looked on the floor for Bridget's sleeping form. Unease grabbed at my heart when I failed to see her.

I was out of bed before I could think, my feet shrinking from the cold floor. I felt my way to the pallet, then reached with my hands for her curled form on the floor, praying to find her among the quilts.

My heart plunged when I found only the bedding, plunged even further when I realized the quilts held no warmth. Part of me knew where she was. How long had she been gone?

I stumbled on a chair on my way to the kitchen. Although the stove had been banked for the night, enough light came from the slits around the oven door to tell me no one was in there. Shivering, I pulled back the curtain and looked out the window. Heavy clouds half obscured a full moon. Even so, I was able to make out the silhouette of the barn and woodshed, the outline of the trees that bordered the dooryard.

In my heart I knew that Bridget and Nathan were outside somewhere together. *Please, don't let them get carried away.* Indecision kept me by the window as I recalled myself at Bridget's age, remembered the heady feeling of knowing boys thought me more than comely, my high spirits and impetuousness. But I'd never slipped out at night to meet someone.

Unease pushed me out the door and onto the porch. I heard a gasp, saw two figures spring apart, the taller one slipping into the shadows. I knew who it was—knew, too, that Nathan's horse was tethered in the trees. I opened my mouth to call him back, but fear of waking Sven and having him vent his anger on the couple stopped the words before they found substance.

"Bridget!" Her name came in a whisper.

Bridget acted as if she hadn't heard me, and for a moment I feared she would ignore me. Silence settled around us, one unbroken except for the plaintive cry of a night creature followed by the sound of Nathan riding away. Only then did Bridget move, her body stiff with embarrassment. I was grateful to see that she was fully dressed, although her unbound hair hung in shadowy waves around her face and shoulders.

Neither of us spoke as we took measure of each other on the shadowy porch—Bridget's head high and defiant, me upset and not knowing what to say.

My voice came in a whisper when I finally spoke. "I don't want to wake Sven and Flora, so we'll talk about this in the morning." There was a pause while I opened the door. "What were you thinking? Do you have any idea how easily young men can get carried away?"

"It's not what you think," Bridget said. Although her head was high, her lips trembled. Our eyes locked and held, faces but gray shadows as friendship's fragile strands stretched taut with emotion.

Some of the tension left when we entered the house. Bridget hurried ahead, no more than a silhouette as she slipped into our bedroom, her bare feet like whispers on the wood floor.

I heard rather than saw Bridget crawl beneath the quilts of her pallet. Taking care not to stumble, I felt my way to the bed, welcoming its warmth as I struggled not to shiver.

I struggled against emotion too, feeling concern and not liking the uncomfortable position that Bridget had put me in. Sleep did not come and the restless movements from Bridget's pallet told me she was having trouble sleeping too. *What am I going to say to her? What should I do?*

The questions chased around inside my mind and were still with me the next morning, following me into the kitchen and standing like an uncomfortable wedge between the two of us as we cooked breakfast. Bridget made no attempt to speak, nor would she meet my eyes when I looked at her. Instead, she worked in quick movements, her head aloof and a barrier as thick as berry brambles wrapped around her.

By the time the cornmeal was cooked, I was ready to talk, the words seeming to have magically arranged themselves in my mind. But how, when Bridget was stiff with rebellion? When and where in a house overflowing with people?

I looked up when Nathan came into the kitchen with the milk, meeting his uneasy glance before it slid to Bridget. She paused with plate in hand, gave a barely perceptible shake of her head before she set the plate on the table, and turned to busy herself at the stove.

"Did you see the three crows out by the barn?" Shamus asked as he followed Nathan into the kitchen. "If Da was here, he'd be sayin' we should be for takin' care."

"Why is that?" I asked, my mind but half on the question.

"'Tis bad luck to be seein' three crows all sittin' together . . . especially first thing in the mornin'."

A quick look passed between Bridget and Nathan. A second later she picked up the salt shaker and shook it over her shoulder in an imitation of her mother's superstitious hope for good luck.

The morning was half gone before I found opportunity to be alone with Bridget. Seeing Flora and Sven go to the cool room, I touched her arm. "Come," I said.

For a second there was resistance, her pretty mouth as sullen as her green eyes. But she came, the two of us leaving the house and stepping out into the gray, overcast morning. Thankfully there was no rain, but the chill in the air made me glad I'd thought to take shawls from the peg by the door.

We walked in silence across the dooryard to the barn, its height and breadth noticeable as we went inside. Pulling the big door closed, I turned to face Bridget in the shadowy half-light. "Would you like to tell me about last night?" I held my breath as I watched the play of emotion on her face—pride and rebellion warring with the need for a friend.

"Yes." Her answer was so soft I almost didn't hear it. Then with a lift of her head she met my gaze. "'Tis not as you're thinkin'. Nothing happened . . . at least hardly anything."

Her lovely eyes filled with tears, the two of us standing just inside the door with the smell of cows and manure and dampness all around us. "Nathan only wanted for us to be alone so we could be talkin' without everyone listenin'." She sniffed and let out an exaggerated sigh. "Shamus is forever hangin' around and talkin'. Like a burr he is, one that won't let go. Nathan said there were things he needed to be talkin' to me about. And I . . ."

Bridget's lips started to tremble. Seeing them, I took her arm and led her to the wooden milking bench that stretched along one wall, the damp imprints from the buckets still visible.

"You what?' I asked, though instinct told me it was not as bad as I'd feared.

Bridget sat with head bent, her hands nervously gripping each other in the lap of her green dress. Then her head came up, and I saw the rebellion again. "I was hopin' to be havin' myself a kiss. There . . . 'tis said, and if I'm goin' to hell for wantin' one, then 'twill just have to be."

I wanted to laugh and pull her into my arms. Instead, I reached and took one of her hands. "Did you get your kiss?" I asked.

"No." Her lips were trembling in earnest now. "But I would have if you'd but waited a minute before comin' outside."

It was on the tip of my tongue to say I was sorry, for I remembered my own longing for that first kiss. By the same token I didn't want to encourage any more nighttime rendezvous. While I searched for the words that would let her know I understood, Bridget got to her feet and turned to face me.

"Most likely you're shocked from hearin' what a terrible girl I am . . . but it seemed my only chance, what with me livin' so far from everyone. Mam won't hear of me going to live with Liam or Fiona." The look of rebellion came back. "She says I'm too young to be thinkin' of boys. But I'm not. I'll soon be seventeen, and before I know it I'll be too old and no one will look at me and think me pretty."

"Never that," I said as Bridget began to cry, her pretty face twisting up like that of a child. Answering tears came to my own eyes as I rose and pulled her into my arms, felt the shudder of her sobs as I held her close and patted her shoulder. "Shhh . . . it's all right," I whispered. "And I don't think you're a terrible person."

When her sobs had quieted enough to speak, she lifted her tear-stained face. "Will for sure I be goin' to hell?"

"No . . . how can you think such a thing?"

"That's what Father Murphy said . . . that girls who filled their heads with thoughts of kissin' boys were joinin' hands with the devil and headin' straight to hell."

The urge to smile returned. "If that's the case, then hell will be overflowing with females. I doubt there's a girl alive who hasn't longed to be kissed."

Bridget watched me closely as she wiped a wet cheek with the edge of her shawl. "But I was for doin' the kissin', not just dreamin'."

"That's why you need to think before you do something rash." I paused to choose my words. "I'm sorry if I seemed angry last night, but I feel responsible for you, especially to your parents. Although I think Nathan is a nice young man, you need to realize that men are different from young ladies. They . . ." I paused again. "Like I said last night, it's easy for them to get carried away."

"I know. At least, I think I know."

"Although I don't approve of you sneaking out of the house to meet Nathan, I understand why you did it."

"Truly?"

"Truly. It hasn't been that many years since I was seventeen and wanting to be kissed."

Something flickered in her eyes. "Is that why you married Jacob? So you could be kissed?"

"Heavens no!" Again I searched for the words to explain, even as the image of Amos Mickelson's face crawled into my mind. "I married Jacob to escape from a man even worse than he is."

"Oh." Bridget's voice came soft. "I'm sorry."

"So am I." Feeling the need to say more, I went on. "You're so much like I was—impetuous and headstrong. You've got to be careful, Bridget. Think before you act so you won't be sorry."

Neither of us spoke for a moment, the cluck of the chickens scratching in the moist dirt outside the barn door the only sound to break the silence.

"Are . . . are you goin' to be tellin' Mam and Da what I did?" Bridget finally asked.

"Do you think I should?"

I sensed her surprise at my question, watched the play of emotions as they crossed her face. "Could you be keepin' it a secret if I promise not to sneak out ever again?"

"If you'll give me your word."

Bridget reached into her pocket and took out her rosary beads. "You have my promise. The Holy Virgin too. I won't be sneakin' out to meet Nathan again." She paused and nervously licked her pretty lips. "How about the Larsens? Will you tell them?"

"No." My answer came quick, for I wasn't any more anxious to let Sven and Flora know what had happened than Bridget was. "But I do need to speak to Nathan."

Bridget nodded. "Most likely he's wantin' to talk to you too."

Feeling as if my burden could finally be set down, I squeezed her hand. Even so, I felt I should add a note of caution. "Don't forget, Nathan isn't a Catholic."

"Aye, I know. But his grandfather was."

"Oh?"

Bridget nodded. "He has some cousins that are Catholic, too, but they live back east someplace."

"It sounds like you and Nathan have done a lot of talking."

"That's why I wasn't gettin' my kiss," she said and had the grace to blush.

"How old is Nathan?"

"He turned eighteen in October."

"That's still too young."

"Aye, we know." She leaned close and gave me a quick hug. "Please don't be worryin' yourself. I did a great deal of thinkin' and prayin' last night. I'll not be doing anything foolish again. You have my word. Besides, I'm not wantin' to settle on just one boy yet. I'm wantin' to choose from many."

I had to be content with that, though I took extra care after that not to give Bridget and Nathan time alone.

* * *

A week later I looked outside and saw nothing but blue sky— finally blue instead of gray. "See the sun, Ellie?" I held her up to the window where she promptly sneezed as the sun touched her face. I laughed, recalling that Mother used to do the same. "You're just like your grandma," I crooned. "Just like your namesake."

"What's dat you say about a grandma?" Grandma Sarah asked. In addition to her rheumatism, I'd noticed she was getting hard of hearing.

While I explained, Shamus burst through the door. "The Lieutenant's coming! Can you believe? All the way across the river he's come and . . ."

I handed Ellie to Grandma and rushed out the door, shading my eyes against the brilliance of the sun, my heart beating a happy rhythm when I saw Quinn riding Midnight up the muddy lane. He waved when he saw me and urged the horse to a trot. Although his hat shaded his face, I knew he was grinning. Just like I was.

Bridget and Flora joined us on the porch while Shamus ran up the lane to greet him, the sound of the boy's voice indistinct, but happy.

"Sure and Shamus doesn't have a lick of sense. Doesn't he know the Lieutenant didn't come to see just him?" Bridget asked.

"He's come to see all of us," I said, though I could feel Quinn's eyes on me.

He reined in the black gelding a few feet from the porch. Shamus was close behind and panting from the exertion to keep up. "Good morning, ladies." As he spoke, his hazel eyes were busy taking me in, me in my faded pink dress with one of Flora's old brown aprons tied over the top. "You're looking well."

"Thank you." I wanted to say I thought the same of him and that it was much nicer to see him in person than having to rely on a heart-printed memory. "How did you get across the river?"

He patted the horse's neck. "Midnight brought me across. Better than I thought he would . . . didn't even have to swim."

"Sounds like the river's dropped a bit." This came from Sven as he sauntered out from the barn.

"It has. Not as much as I'd hoped, but passable on horses." Quinn swung down from the saddle and took his walking stick out of the scabbard. "I measured the water at the deepest place at the ford. It came up to this knob on my stick." He pointed to a place close to the handle. "From this we should be able to tell how far the water will come on your wagon."

We followed Sven and Quinn to the wagon. When Quinn held his stick against it, Sven shook his head and frowned.

"Too high. You take a wagon in there, and it'll start to float."

"I was afraid it would." Instead of frowning, Quinn turned to me. "How would you feel about riding Midnight across the river?"

"All right," I answered, remembering the gelding's easy gait. "But you're not thinking of leading him, are you?"

Quinn shook his head. "If Sven will loan me one of his horses, I'll be riding just ahead of you."

"What about Ellen?" Flora asked.

"She'll be on my back in the cradleboard, snug and dry until we can get her home again."

Sven and Flora exchanged concerned glances. "I think you should wait until the river drops enough to take them home in the wagon," Sven said.

Quinn fixed his gaze on the big Swede. "That could be weeks . . . maybe not until spring. No." He shook his head and his tone was emphatic. "We don't want to risk Clarissa and the baby getting wet or chilled. This may be our only sunny day for a while, and we need to take advantage of it."

Over a quick meal of fried potatoes and biscuits, the rest of the plan was solidified. Not only would we need the loan of horses to get the four of us across the river, but an extra person from the Larsens' side to help bring the horses back home.

"We can use my two horses, and I'm sure Gil Watson will let us borrow his," Sven said between bites of potato. "He only has one saddle though."

"I can ride bareback," Shamus said. His enthusiasm for Quinn's plan was obvious, but I could tell Bridget didn't like the thought of leaving Nathan. More than that, she lacked experience at riding horseback. Mine wasn't that extensive, either, but with me on Midnight and Quinn just ahead, I was confident I'd do well.

We packed our clothes into our shawls and slipped them over our shoulders—mine red, Bridget's green, the colors bright against the darker hues of our cloaks. We were ready and waiting by the time Sven arrived with the borrowed horses. I turned to give everyone a hug— Hans and Little Sarah, clinging for a moment to Grandma. Flora looked me full in the face before her arms went around me. "God has answered my prayers by sending you Ellen. Now I will be praying for something more." She glanced at Quinn before we embraced. "I know he'll take good care of you and the baby," she whispered.

I smiled and looked at Quinn, who had Ellen strapped across his broad shoulders, her round face peeking out of the cradleboard, eyes wide as she took in the world around her.

Quinn and I led the way when we left, with Bridget and Shamus following and Sven bringing up the rear. I turned for one last wave and saw the sadness on Bridget's face, the sadness of leaving made even more poignant because she'd been unable to tell Nathan good-bye.

"You can visit them again in the spring," Quinn promised when he saw me wave to Flora, "though I doubt Mick and Maggie will be anxious to let Bridget and Shamus stay away so long." He paused and his gaze held mine. "I was beginning to wonder if I'd ever see you again."

"Never that," I said, our eyes meeting and holding, saying all the things that were in our hearts. Then I told him about all that had happened, of Grandma Sarah's party and that Bridget had found herself a beau. My tongue ran on, rather like it had with Hawkeye when he'd been convalescing in the barn. This time, instead of lone-liness, the catalyst for speech was pure happiness. While I talked I kept glancing at Quinn, my eyes needing the sight of him as much as my tongue needed talking. The brown hair that showed below his hat had been freshly cut and his lips were curved in an ongoing smile, the light in his eyes seeming to reflect a happiness that matched mine.

We stopped at the Watsons' for Conrad, who would help Sven bring the borrowed horses home after we crossed the river.

The day, though mostly sunny, was brisk, making me glad for the warmth of my cloak and the woolen socks that went to my knees. For like it or not, Bridget and I both had to ride with our skirts hitched up around our legs.

It was afternoon by the time we reached the river. The Tillamook was more wide than deep and wound through wooded meadows and grassland until it reached the distant bay.

"Hello," Quinn called, lifting an arm and waving. I saw an answering wave from the other side and realized that Mick and Patrick were waiting there for us.

"I told them to look for us this afternoon and to bring rope from the lodge in case we needed to tie the horses together while we crossed," Quinn explained. "I don't expect trouble, but I like to be prepared."

Although I knew Quinn intended his words to be reassuring, I felt a prick of fear when I looked at the blue-gray water. "Had you already decided to bring us home?"

"I had." The look he gave me was also direct. "Sometimes a man has to do what he thinks is best. All of us will rest easier with everyone safely back at home."

By then the others had caught up with us. Quinn and Sven agreed that it would be best if there were only two horses in the water at the same time. Quinn and I would go first and when we were safely across, Sven would lead the way with Bridget. Shamus, who was riding bareback on the Watsons' horse, would come last.

"The water's deep enough to wet your feet," Quinn went on, "so you'll need to take your shoes off and loop them around your neck or tie them to the pommel of the saddle."

After we'd complied, I checked on Ellie. Fearing that a squirming, crying baby would distract both us and the horses, I was glad to see that the horse's steady rhythm had lulled her to sleep.

Quinn turned and looked questioningly at me. "Are you ready?" When he saw me nod, he smiled encouragement. "Good girl. I'll go first. Let me get a horse's length ahead before you follow. Take it slow. Midnight is a good horse. He'll know what to do."

"I'll be fine."

Quinn eased Sven's chestnut horse into the swift-moving water, talking softly to the mare as they moved out into the river. I followed when I deemed it safe. The black gelding's sure feet went down the steep incline and into the water. I kept Midnight squarely between the two poles that marked the crossing. The river was already up to Quinn's horse's belly and Quinn's feet were covered by the cold rippling water. The river came up fast on Midnight. I held my feet firmly in the stirrup to give me leverage against the current, feeling the chill as the rushing water swirled over them.

No one spoke while we crossed. I kept my eyes on Ellen in her cradleboard as she and Quinn rode easily in the saddle. The two people I loved most were just ahead of me, their steady progress a beacon of hope each time I glanced down at the swift, murky water.

I felt relief when Quinn's feet broke out of the water and his horse started up the other side where Mick and Patrick waited. I was close behind, but the cold had set my teeth to chattering by the time Quinn rode the mare onto the grassy bank. Then my own feet were out of the water. I took hold of the pommel of the saddle as we started up the bank behind Quinn. We'd made it safely, just like he'd said.

"'Tis grand to be seein' you and the wee one again," Mick said, but his eyes were on his daughter who was entering the water a few paces behind Sven.

Quinn and I turned to watch, Sven riding one of the Watsons' horses and Bridget on the more dependable twin to Quinn's borrowed chestnut mare. They came at a steady pace, the water swirling and eddying around them. The hem of Bridget's dark cloak trailed in the river, but she paid it no heed. All of her attention was on keeping her place in the saddle and making sure her horse followed in Sven's wake.

"Steady, girl, steady," Mick breathed, and I thought I heard Patrick whisper an ave.

My pulse quickened when Sven's horse almost lost its footing, Sven calling words of encouragement to the horse. Then he and his wet mount were coming up the incline with Bridget just behind him, rivulets of water dripping from their stirrups.

"May the saints be praised," Mick said and crossed himself.

Bridget shot her father and cousin a quick smile, and Sven's face showed a pleased expression.

"Now there's just the boy," Sven said.

"Bring the mare over slow and easy," Quinn called. "There's no need to hurry." As he spoke, he dismounted and eased the cradle-board off his shoulders. "Take the baby and Bridget up with you on Midnight and ride home before you get chilled."

"Aye," Mick said. "Maggie's waiting there with a fire and hot stew to warm you through."

Ellen stirred and opened her eyes when Quinn handed her up to me. I held her close for a moment before I slipped my arms through the straps. Bridget and I were both shivering.

Quinn had turned to watch Shamus. "You're going too fast, Shamus. Slow down!" he shouted.

As the words left his mouth the horse lost its footing and scrambled wildly against the current which quickly swept them into deeper water.

"Shamus!" Bridget screamed. She was off her horse and running along the bank of the river.

I watched in horror as Shamus lost his grip on the horse's mane. He and the gelding separated, both thrashing in panic, the boy's head bobbing as the horse settled into a rhythmic pattern and began to swim toward the bank.

"Da!" Shamus's panicked scream was cut off as his head disappeared under the water.

"Grab the horse's tail!" Mick shouted, but the horse was already moving away.

Shamus's head broke the surface of the water, and he struggled to keep himself afloat, his scrawny arms and legs no match for the fast-moving current.

With Ellen strapped to my back, I was helpless to do anything except watch in horror and pray. "Help him. Please, help him."

Mick shrugged out of his coat as he rushed along the bank, throwing it aside just before he launched himself into the river, Bridget and Patrick but a few steps behind.

Sensing the panic, Midnight snorted and shied. It took all of my skill to control him as I watched Shamus's awkward attempt to counter the current, his head seeming to stay under the water longer each time he went down. "Hurry . . . oh, hurry," I whispered, watching the strong strokes of Mick's arms take him closer to his frantic son.

Shamus continued the wild thrashing, unaware that his father was almost there.

Then Shamus disappeared under the murky water. Seeing him, Mick dove after Shamus, the two of them lost from sight, my own breath held until I saw two heads break out of the muddy water. Mick was trying to hold onto his son and calm him—muscles, prayers, and will were all that kept heads above water.

It was clear that fear had clogged Shamus's mind until finally he realized his father was with him. Then Shamus's struggles ceased enough for Mick to keep him afloat and begin to tow him toward the bank.

"Here, grab hold!" Quinn shouted. He and Patrick had kept pace along the bank with the swimmers.

The end of the rope left Quinn's hand and snaked out over the water. My tightly held breath escaped in a rush of relief when Mick caught hold and the rope pulled taut.

Bridget was there with Sven to help Quinn bring in the rope. As Patrick waded into the water to help Mick and Shamus, Bridget took off her black cloak and held it and her father's jacket out to the bedraggled pair.

Mick grabbed Bridget's cloak and wrapped it around Shamus. "How many times have I told you to use your head?" he cried. Then, overcome with emotion, Mick pulled the boy close, his thin, wet body shivering under the cloak. "Sweet Mother of God, I thought I'd lost you."

I rode my horse along the bank to Mick and Shamus and dismounted. "Take Midnight and get up to the house before you catch cold."

Shamus tried to protest, but his teeth were chattering so hard he couldn't speak.

"Go," Patrick said. He put Shamus barefoot into the stirrup, then boosted Mick, who'd retrieved his jacket, up behind the boy. "Stop your yammering and go." A slap to the gelding's rump sent them on their way.

Meanwhile, Sven had succeeded in catching the runaway horse. It looked as wet and bedraggled as Mick and Shamus did. "I should have made him ride the horse with the saddle," Sven said.

"Don't be worrying about it," Patrick replied. "That it ended with no one worse than wet is all that's important."

Quinn turned to me. "You and Bridget need to get home where it's warm too." He stooped and picked up my shoes that I'd dropped in my haste to help. "Here, put these on."

I didn't have to be told twice, for my feet felt like icicles and my toes had turned numb. I sat down and stripped off my wet stockings. After drying my feet on the hem of my cloak, I thrust them gratefully into the dry stockings I had packed inside my shawl. Bridget dismounted and quickly followed my example. Then I offered Quinn my other pair of dry socks.

His brows rose when he looked at them. "Do you expect my feet to fit into those?" he asked with a grin.

I looked down at his long, slender feet encased in wet, muddy socks and shook my head.

"I'd give you a ride home, but from the looks of the clouds rolling in, I need to get the horses back across the river," Sven apologized.

"A little walking won't hurt us." I paused and extended my hand. "Thank you again, Sven. You and Flora are the best of friends."

His large hand closed around mine. "The feeling is mutual." In a softer voice he added, "I'll talk to the captain about finding a lawyer the first chance I have." He turned and looked at Quinn. "I'll rest easier knowing Clarissa has friends looking after her on this side of the river too."

"She does. She and the baby both."

Sven nodded and held Quinn's gaze, as if they were making a pact. Then he turned and started his horse across the river, a rope looped around the neck of the horse Bridget had ridden.

Patrick stayed to help Sven while the rest of us walked home. It was cold, for a wind had come up, and dark clouds had rolled in to cover the sun. Quinn insisted on carrying Ellie, who had decided she was tired of the cradleboard, and hungry. Bridget and I tried in vain to amuse her, but it was all for naught as her little face screwed up and her mouth opened to proclaim her unhappiness.

"Grand pipes she has along with a bit of a temper," Bridget quipped.

I smiled and wished I could take her out of the cradleboard and feed her. "Poor Ellie," I crooned. "We'll be home soon. Hold on, my sweet."

Quinn was strangely quiet. I thought at first it was because the uneven surface of the meadow required his concentration. But when he frowned instead of smiled at Bridget's banter, I felt concerned.

"Is something wrong?"

Quinn shot me a quick glance, a lock of brown hair falling across his forehead. "Just giving myself a dressing-down for letting my self-ishness put others in danger. I should have listened to Sven instead of insisting it was safe to cross the river when it was still high."

I wanted to tell Quinn he wasn't responsible for Shamus's inexperience, but Ellie's crying was so loud it made conversation impossible. As an added distraction, Sam and the wolfhounds had come to meet us, tails wagging and held high.

My home had never seemed more welcoming. My eyes took it in as I petted Sam—the rail fence running along the lines of the pasture, smoke coming from the chimney, the green-cloaked mountain as a background against the lowering sky.

Hearing the dogs, Deirdre hurried out to meet us.

"How's Shamus?" Quinn asked.

"Just this minute gettin' out of a hot tub of water and into dry clothes." Her blue eyes sparkled with mischief. "I thought 'twould be a kindness to his modesty if I was for steppin' outside to warn you."

"He's all right, then?" Relief threaded through Quinn's voice.

"He is now, though his lips were blue when he first came."

I'd hoped that memory had exaggerated Deirdre's beauty. It hadn't. Her porcelain cheeks were tinged with color from the wind and excitement, and she dimpled prettily as she covered her ears and stepped closer to Quinn and the baby. "Glory, but she's crackin' up a storm."

"Oh, aye. Hungry she thinks she is and her mother bent on ignoring her," Bridget teased.

"As soon as Shamus is dressed you can be for feedin' her." Deirdre joined her steps with Quinn, the white ties of her apron fluttering against the russet color of her skirt. "Just so you'll be knowin', I put your horse in the barn, but I couldn't manage the saddle."

"Thank you." Quinn's expression had turned pleasant again. I couldn't tell whether the change was wrought by Deirdre's presence or the good news about Shamus. Even so, I took heart when he smiled down at the baby as he eased the cradleboard from his shoulders. Then motherhood wouldn't let me think of anything except comforting Ellen and snuggling her against me. Her little mouth searched hungrily along my neck, and for a minute her cries quieted.

Everyone looked up in relief when Maggie opened the door. "They're done. You can be comin' in now."

The kitchen felt as warm as a summer's day, and Shamus sat at the table in a dry shirt and britches, spooning hot stew into his mouth, while Mick sat in a chair wrapped in a blanket. I hurried into the bedroom, the baby's hungry cries seeming even louder in the close confines of the house. The noise stopped abruptly when we settled on the side of the bed. Quiet at last. "Oh, Ellie, I'm so sorry." I whispered.

After the baby was satisfied and freshly diapered, I joined the O'Connors in the kitchen. "I'm sorry about what happened to Shamus. You probably wish I'd never taken them with me."

"Not now that I have them back, but there were a few times I was wonderin' when I would be seein' all of you again."

"We were wonderin' the same," Bridget said.

"Not so you could be noticin' it," Shamus put in. "You were so taken up with—"

The arrival of Quinn and Patrick prevented him from saying more. The news that Sven had gotten all the horses back across the river diverted the conversation away from Bridget and into safer channels where it remained while we enjoyed Maggie's hot stew.

The meal was hurried, for Mick and Patrick were anxious to get the women home before more rain set in.

"I'll come along after I finish milking," Quinn said when they prepared to go. "After Shamus's wetting, I don't think it's wise for him to go out again."

I saw disappointment in Deirdre's eyes, though she made a show of telling me how good it was to have me and the baby back again. After we'd sent them on their way, Quinn took the milk bucket and went out to the barn.

No one spoke while I helped Bridget clear the table. After taking a minute to gather my thoughts, I looked pointedly at Shamus and spoke. "Did you have a good time when you were at the Larsens'?"

"Aye," Shamus answered. "Sven told me all sorts of interesting things about cows, and it was fun finding myself some friends."

"Good. That's what I hoped you'd find. Speaking of friends . . ." I paused until Shamus met my gaze. "Don't you think it would be better for you to tell your parents about your friends and let Bridget tell them about hers?"

Shamus frowned and his tone was tentative. "I suppose so."

"Think about it, Shamus," Bridget put in.

"Oh, aye, I'll likely be thinkin' about lots of things now that I'm back." He shivered and looked down at his feet. "That water was like ice and for a second I thought I'd be joinin' the angels." Another hard shiver shook his slender frame.

Bridget dropped to her knees and took his hand. "I was prayin' for you the whole time you was in the water . . . prayin' and pleadin' with the Holy Father."

I used their preoccupation with each other to slip out of the kitchen and into the barn. It was dim and cold and damp inside the wooden structure. Quinn had brought Brownie inside and tied her to the milking post. I stood in the doorway and watched him, his long legs crouched on either side of the stool and his hand moving rhythmically on the cow's full udder. "Please don't blame yourself for what happened today."

Quinn lifted his head to look at me. "How can I not when it was me who insisted on bringing you home?" He paused and his face turned fierce. "What if it had been you that had been swept away?"

"But it wasn't."

"No, but almost losing Shamus was just as bad. If anything had happened to that boy . . ." His voice turned as fierce as his expression. "A good officer never takes action that will unnecessarily endanger his men."

"It wasn't your fault." I crossed the width of the barn and placed a comforting hand on his shoulder. "It wasn't your fault," I repeated.

At my touch, Quinn stopped milking, his hands growing still, the air charged with suppressed emotion. There was a long moment of silence, neither of us moving or speaking. I slowly took my hand away and said the first thing that entered my head, indicating the cow. "You probably thought once you got us home you wouldn't have to do this anymore."

I heard the release of Quinn's caught breath and watched as a slow smile creased his face. "I don't consider anything I do for you as work. It's all pleasure."

The quiet sound of the cow chewing her cud was the only sound for a minute. Then the trill of a blackbird came, followed by the scurry of tiny feet in the grass.

"Thank you." Such simple words, but ones that came from the depth of my soul. "Thank you for all you do for me."

Quinn nodded, his eyes never leaving my face. "As I told you, I count it as a pleasure."

Not knowing what to say, I smiled and turned back to the house, his words and the sound of his voice wrapped like a warm shawl around me. Deirdre's presence at the lodge no longer seemed so threatening, and I entered the kitchen with a smile on my face.

CHAPTER 14

Although Shamus suffered no ill effects from the river, Ellen came down with a cold that made her fretful. Bridget and I hovered over her, afraid the cold might develop into something serious. On the second day when Quinn arrived, Bridget hurried out to tell him that Ellie wasn't feeling well. Quinn entered the kitchen without speaking, his face showing concern as he crossed the room to look at her. Ellie's eyes were red and watery, and instead of giving him a smile, she started to cry.

He reached and took her from me, bouncing and trying to calm her. "Her temper's not suffered, that's for sure." He paused and gave me a searching look. "What do you think? Do you want me to ride back to the lodge for Maggie?"

Part of me wanted to say yes, for I knew Maggie was more experienced with sick babies than I. But the other part, the part that wanted to be independent, bade me shake my head. "I'm hoping it's just a cold. Little Sarah is always cranky when she has one. I remember Flora had to spend most of a day holding and rocking her." I paused and added, "If Ellen's not doing better by tomorrow, I'll send Shamus up to get Maggie."

Quinn nodded, his rocking having quieted the baby.

"If she should start with a cough, we can be giving her a spoonful of honey. 'Tis what Mam always gave to us." A giggle escaped Bridget's lips as she went on. "I remember once when Shamus had a cough and I saw Mam give him some honey, I pretended to cough so I wouldn't be left out."

"And you weren't the only one pretendin'," Shamus put in. "Long after I was better, I kept coughin' so I could be having the extra honey."

The O'Connors' light banter was just what I'd needed. Quinn, too, for he relaxed and acted like his old self. He was soon sitting in a chair with Ellie and telling her about the squirrel he'd seen that morning. "It scolded me royal, just like you did when I came in."

The rest of the morning passed pleasantly as we talked and tended Ellen. Through it all I was aware of how often Quinn's gaze rested on me. *Everything I do for you is a pleasure,* it seemed to say.

It was over tea that Quinn brought up the subject of Christmas. "I'd like all of you to spend it up at the lodge."

Bridget and Shamus both smiled and nodded, but it was on me that Quinn's eyes paused. Concern for Ellen warred with my desire to be at the lodge with Quinn, especially when I knew Deirdre would be there looking her prettiest. "I think we'd better stay here. With her cold, I don't think it would be a good idea to take Ellen out in the cold and damp." I saw Bridget's smile fade into disappointment. "But there's no need for Shamus and Bridget to miss their Christmas."

The two of them looked at Quinn.

"How would you feel if we brought Christmas down to you?" Quinn asked after a moment, but the look on his face was determined. He wasn't letting me spend Christmas by myself.

"What a grand idea," Bridget said. "Shamus and I can go up in the morning and in the afternoon we'll bring Mam's Christmas pudding down here. Most likely the others will want to come too."

I thought of my kitchen bursting with that many people and my table that did good to seat only four, not to mention a shortage of chairs.

When I voiced my concerns, she brushed them aside. "When have elbows jostling with arms ever stopped an O'Connor from having a party? 'Twill be fine, Clarissa."

So it was decided. Shamus and Bridget would go to the lodge for Christmas dinner that afternoon. Later, everyone would come to my place for raisin pudding and singing.

"I'll see you on Wednesday," Quinn said as he opened the door. He turned and gave me a long look. "Remember, if Ellie gets worse, send for me and Maggie."

"I will." But my mind was on Wednesday. The word danced through the remaining three days as I tended Ellie and tried to think of something to give to my friends. In the end I decided to make candy, one of the few things Mother had taught me to make, something she called Boston Cream.

Each day the baby improved, and by Christmas morning she was full of smiles, with only an occasional cough as a reminder of her cold.

"Thank you, dear Lord," I said as Shamus and Bridget joined me in saying grace. It was something Sven and Flora did at their meals, something I wanted Ellen to have in her life. Hadn't Mother told me to put my life in God's hands?

Bridget and Shamus left as soon as we finished breakfast. After they'd gone, I sat down to nurse the baby. As I thought of the significance of the day I told Ellie about the babe that had been born so long ago while shepherds watched and angels sang.

Five months of being around people made the silence after Ellen fell asleep a little unnerving. Looking for something to do, I put a fresh cloth on the table and went just outside the door in search of pine boughs and cones to decorate the table. When all was trimmed to my liking, I passed the rest of the morning darning stockings.

Ellie had awakened from her nap and was lying on a quilt by the fire examining her dimpled hands when Sam set up a bark.

"He's here, Ellie. Our Lieutenant is here." Although the O'Connors would be with him, my heart's center was Quinn.

My friends entered the house, bringing the smell of fresh air and the damp woods with them. I looked for Quinn, but saw only the women and Shamus, followed by Mick and Patrick carrying Maggie's rocking chair. I shot her a quick look and wondered why she'd had the men carry the chair down the steep mountain.

"'Tis for you," Maggie said as she hugged me. "From all of us to you. Merry Christmas."

For a second Quinn was forgotten. "But it's yours."

"Rocking chairs are meant for mothers with babes or old women," Maggie replied. "Since I'm neither, I thought I should be givin' it to one who has more need of it than I."

I felt the prick of tears as I returned her hug. "Thank you." I turned to include them all. "Thank you." I ran my fingers over the wood of the chair's high-rail back, felt the softness of the padded seat.

"Where would you like us to put it?" Mick asked.

"Why, close to the fire," Maggie answered.

As soon as the men put it down, Bridget told me to try it out while Mick lifted Ellen from the floor and placed her on my lap.

"There." His expression was pleased.

I wrapped my arms around the baby and began to rock. Even though it was pleasant, disappointment bit into my enjoyment. Where was Quinn? Why hadn't he come? And where was Deirdre?

I voiced the question to Maggie. "Where's the Lieutenant?"

Maggie glanced at her husband. "Sad to say, he was draggin' his feet about comin'. Maybe I should have a look and see if he's here yet."

"Mam . . ." Unable to stop himself, Shamus bent over and whispered in my ear. "They're waitin' outside to surprise you."

"What?"

My question was covered by Mick's voice as he called out the door. "Would you like to be comin' inside, Lieutenant?"

Concern ate at my happiness. What surprise did Quinn and Deirdre have? Then I saw his tall frame fill the doorway, watched as he turned sideways so the cradle he carried would fit through the door. A smile lifted the corners of his mouth, and his eyes sought mine, bringing happiness back to dance through the room.

"Merry Christmas," Quinn said.

"Oh!" Emotion made it impossible to speak. I buried my face in the fluff of Ellen's russet curls, while laughter fought with happy tears. I wanted to run to Quinn and throw my arms around him, thank him, and tell him of my love. Instead, I had to be content with heartfelt words. "It's beautiful," I finally managed to get out. "Thank you. Ellie thanks you too." As I spoke, I was vaguely aware that Deirdre had followed Quinn into the kitchen.

"You're very welcome . . . but I didn't mean to make you cry." He quirked his brow, and his voice turned teasing as he set the cradle on the floor. "If I didn't know better, I'd think you were disappointed with your present."

I smiled through my tears. "How could you think that? It's something I'll always treasure—Ellie too." I glanced at Maggie and saw that her eyes held tears as well. "We women are strange that way," I added laughingly as Quinn turned to glance her way.

"Oh, aye," Mick put in. "Always cryin' when they should be laughin' and mixin' up a poor man so he doesn't know what end is up."

While I tried to hide my emotions, I studied the cradle. The bed, which was large enough for Ellen to use for some time yet, was fastened to a stand that allowed it to swing back and forth. "Where did you get it?" Then remembering how Quinn had brought the pianoforte and books with him with the future in mind, I added, "Surely you didn't buy this at the same time you bought the pianoforte?"

Quinn gave a soft laugh. "No. My thoughts weren't anchored that hard in the future."

"He made it for you," Shamus blurted. "He's been working on it for weeks."

"Made it?"

"I like to work with wood. It's something I've done since I was a boy."

I looked at the cradle with new eyes, noting the rounded poles and spindles and the polished sheen of the wood. I pictured Quinn as he'd carved the wood, his forehead furrowed in concentration as he etched the design across each end, his gold spectacles settled on the bridge of his nose. "It's lovely," I whispered, thinking of the hours it must have taken him. "How can I ever thank you?"

"You already have." The warmth in his hazel eyes told me my reaction had been all he'd hoped for.

"Eileen and Deirdre made the ticking," Patrick said, as Deirdre placed the ticking into the cradle. "They've been saving feathers for weeks."

I smiled my appreciation and laid Ellen in her new bed. She kicked and smiled, her arms and legs expressing her happiness. "She loves it." I gave both Eileen and Deirdre an affectionate hug, then turned and threw my arms around Quinn. "Thank you," I said. "Thank you a hundred times."

There was a startled moment after his arms tightened around me, my head resting against his chest. Realizing what I had done, I pulled away, saw the stricken look on Deirdre's face, and Bridget's eyes and mouth rounded in surprise. To cover my embarrassment, I gave Mick and Patrick hugs as well and placed an affectionate arm on Shamus's shoulder. "Ellen thanks you. I thank you. God gave me the wish of my heart when he sent me friends like you."

Only then did I dare to look at Quinn. Seeking his eyes, I hoped he knew something of my heart, a heart that seemed to open wider each time he came near.

* * *

After raisin pudding and candy had been enjoyed and we were relaxing and talking, Patrick brought out his fiddle and began to play. A moment later Mick joined in with the pipe, the two instruments rising in a lilting rhythm. Voices joined them, Shamus and Bridget harmonizing, Eileen and Maggie and Deirdre adding theirs. They sang an Irish Christmas carol, one I'd never heard before.

Ellen didn't know what to make of the music, one minute looking ready to cry, then smiling the next. I rocked her and hummed along, for I loved to sing and my voice was considered sweet. When Patrick led us into "I Saw Three Ships Come Sailing In," I was able to sing in earnest.

Through it all I was conscious of Quinn who stood on the other side of the room. Just how it had happened, I didn't know, but the fact the Deirdre stood next to him I laid to her contrivance.

Such did not speak well of me, for there was no reason why she shouldn't flirt with him, no reason at all. I watched a smile light her lovely face as she looked up at Quinn, her voice sounding sweet as an angel.

Jealousy knifed through me when Quinn returned her smile, his brows quirking up in the way I had come to know and love, a way I'd thought he reserved just for me.

Striving to cover my feelings, I looked the other way, letting my eyes settle on Ellie. I couldn't help but smile at the awestruck expression on her face. Even so, my heart that had brimmed with happiness now felt strangely empty. I managed to get through the song, my voice sounding soft and unsure, my eyes on Patrick and Mick instead of those exchanging smiles.

"Is not Patrick a wizard with the fiddle?" Deirdre exclaimed when the song ended. "He has only to scrape his bow across the strings to set everyone singin' or dancin'. Like magic it is."

"Aye, 'tis," Eileen agreed, the look she fastened on her husband flowing with pride. "Many's the long evening he helped pass on the ship. A grand favorite he was on the way over."

Patrick shrugged and tried to pass it off. "Don't be forgettin' your sister. She was the real favorite."

Eyes turned from Patrick to Deirdre, who had taken a chair and sat with her hands folded demurely in her lap, soft color rising to her cheeks. " 'Twas naught but the singin' of some of the old tunes. Everyone was feelin' a little homesick."

"Give us one of your songs," Mick said. "Shamus and Bridget have never heard you sing. Clarissa either."

Deirdre looked around the room, her manner both hesitant and excited. "If you're sure?"

Everyone nodded, myself included, as Patrick lifted the fiddle to his chin, and his bow took up a soft introduction to a song I'd never heard before, but will long remember. "Greensleeves," Maggie called it when I asked her later, but that night it was sung as a lullaby to the Christ child with Deirdre looking like his sacred mother.

Deirdre and the song were all beauty, in words and pure notes and the look of soft wonder on her face. She was plainly clothed in a black dress unrelieved except for a white lace collar, attire that would have made me look drained and wan. On her it turned milk-white skin ethereal and her hair took on an ebony sheen. No one moved or spoke, every eye on her beauty.

All of my life I had been made much of, my blond curls setting me apart from the dark heads of my sisters, my quick tongue and lively nature a direct contrast to their more somber natures. Being the youngest, I'd been pampered, taking the extra attention as my due and coming to expect it from all. I'd not been disappointed. Nor had I ever met anyone with whom I felt I must compete.

That afternoon I felt it, my same blue dress and pale hair seeming to fade to nothing, black and white the stronger colors. I read admiration in Quinn's eyes, saw it in his stance as his body leaned toward her, this Irish woman with a voice like an angel and a face like the Madonna.

For the first time I felt drab and dowdy, a squirming baby on my lap, a woman still married, and Deirdre available and so very lovely.

Dullness and despair curled around my heart. *Is this how Tamsin had felt all those times when I was the center of attention?*

A lump rose in my throat, and I fastened my eyes on Ellen instead of Deirdre. After a moment something bade me look up—look and encounter hazel eyes gazing at me and Ellie from across the room. Softness filled Quinn's eyes—longing too, unless I'd lost my ability to gauge a man. The Clarissa of old would have tilted her head in challenge and accepted the longing as her due. Instead I dropped my gaze, not knowing what to think. One moment I was certain of Quinn's admiration, the next moment I was envious of Deirdre.

Such was the case that Christmas afternoon while the fiddle and Deirdre's voice filled my home with loveliness, all of us crowded into the kitchen, the table pushed against the wall, the chairs and Shamus's bed forming a circle for me and my friends.

Friends. Unlike my uncertainty about Quinn's feelings, I did not doubt my friends' love. Didn't I sit in a chair from Maggie, have daily help from Bridget and Shamus, and sustenance from the Lieutenant? How blessed I was. Twice blessed when I looked down at my baby who cooed and grabbed at a lock of my hair.

I lifted my head and smiled, saw Mick's hand on Maggie's shoulder, Eileen looking adoringly at her husband, Bridget and Shamus with heads tipped toward Deirdre. Then my eyes rested on Quinn, the one I held most dear, his gaze back on Deirdre, his broad shoulders outlined by the white fabric of his shirt. What I wanted could not be, but it did not keep me from longing.

CHAPTER 15

January was a month of heavy gray clouds and rain, rain that pounded in a steady cadence on the roof and formed big puddles in the grassy dooryard. The storms were so unrelenting they kept Quinn away. A week passed, then two. I tried not to think of what might be going on up at the lodge, of Deirdre's close proximity, of her beauty and ability to entertain with song and talk and smile.

I thanked God every day for the company of Bridget and Shamus through those long, dreary days. Even though Ellie was the most sweet and enchanting of babies, she was nonetheless not adult company.

She could roll over now, and I had to be careful not to leave her unattended on the bed or table. She was also entranced with the sound of her own voice and her babyish babble filled the kitchen.

"What a talker you are," Quinn said on a day near the end of January. The rain had let up enough for him to ride Midnight down from the lodge, his saddlebags filled with more flour and beans and tins of beef. Welcome as the food was, we welcomed the books he brought even more—two of Jane Austen's and *Robinson Crusoe* for Shamus. And I, more than a little in love, welcomed the sight of the man who filled my thoughts and dreams. Even so, I watched for telltale signs that his interest in me had wandered, that someone other than myself might have taken a place in his heart.

Bridget took Quinn's hat and slicker and hung them over a chair near the fire while Quinn talked to Ellen. Ever the proud mother, I stood close and watched as she cooed and tried to grab at the shiny buttons on his jacket.

"Strong too," Quinn went on when he tried to loosen her grip on the button. "Who would think there could be so much strength in that little hand?"

He raised it to his lips and kissed it, his eyes on Ellie for a second, then rising to include Bridget and me. "How have you been?" he asked.

I was quick to note that his eyes had not lingered on me, quick to remind myself that it had been over two weeks since he'd come. "Good, though I think we all have a touch of cabin fever," I managed to get out.

Quinn straightened from the cradle. "I was afraid that might be the case. Even at the lodge Mick does a fair amount of pacing. So I brought you something." He reached into his pocket and took out a deck of cards. "These should help you while away the hours."

Shamus's face brightened and so did Bridget's. "What a grand idea," the boy said. He reached for the cards, which Quinn slipped back into his pocket.

"No cards until we check on the cows."

Shamus frowned in puzzlement.

"One of our cows started limping, and Patrick found fungus growing under one of her hooves." His eyes sought mine. "We need to clean out their hooves so it doesn't get started on yours."

A short time later the four of us sat at the kitchen table with cups of hot tea and the plate of scones Maggie had sent. Quinn's fears about the cows were unfounded, though Shamus was advised to clean and check them periodically. Our conversation took other paths as we buttered the scones, the most important that Patrick had confided to Quinn that they would be welcoming an addition to their family in early summer. I tried to be happy that Ellie would have someone to play with when she got older, but the distance that Quinn wore like a shirt ate at my enjoyment.

"You must take the rocking chair back up to the lodge when the baby gets here," I said.

"Would you hurt Maggie by returning her gift?" Quinn asked.

"No, but—"

"I'll write my brother and ask him to include two rocking chairs on the next ship. One for Maggie and one for Eileen."

"Mam won't like that you're thinkin' she's gettin' old," Bridget said.

"I'm not thinking of her age, just her comfort."

Then Bridget remembered the deck of cards and asked if she could see them.

"You may," Quinn said. Seeing Shamus eyeing them, he added, "Would you like a game?"

Shamus nodded and hitched his chair closer to the table.

We passed a pleasant hour at cards while Ellie napped and a pot of beans simmered on the back of the stove. I don't recall who won or lost, but I remember my awareness of Quinn as he sat at my side, the deftness of his long fingers as he shuffled and dealt the cards, the sweet contentment I felt in just having him there. If only he didn't have to go back to the lodge and Deirdre.

All too soon it was time for Quinn to go. I handed him his still-damp hat and stood with Bridget at the door to bid him good-bye. I envied Shamus who followed him out to the barn where Midnight was stabled, envied Sam, who received a pat as he and the wolfhounds milled around his long legs. A wave of melancholy washed over me as Quinn and the horse and dogs faded into the grayness of the January afternoon.

"I'm thinkin' Deirdre has set her cap for the Lieutenant," Shamus said as soon as he came back into the house.

I lifted my head, and Bridget stopped stirring the beans.

"Whatever makes you think that?" she asked.

Shamus shrugged. "I saw how she was smilin' at him on Christmas and today he was tellin' me Deirdre's wantin' him to teach her to play the pianoforte."

My heart plummeted at the thought of the two of them sitting side by side at the pianoforte. "The Lieutenant doesn't know how to play it," I said, my voice more sharp than I intended.

"He doesn't," Shamus agreed. "But he says she's always pestering him to teach her."

"Too bad if the cover to the piano fell on her hands," I muttered to myself.

Bridget heard and gave me a quick look.

Shamus went on just as if nothing had been said. "He was wonderin' if the next time I came to the lodge, I'd be offerin' to teach her to play the pipe."

I took a small measure of satisfaction when I heard this, but it was not large enough to dispel my chagrin. If Shamus had noticed the way Deirdre was looking at Quinn, then Quinn must be aware of it too. What man could resist such beauty and open attention? Certainly not Mr. Quinton Reynolds. Look how he was pulling back from me. I could already see the writing on the wall.

* * *

We blessed Quinn for the books and deck of cards many times over the next two weeks as the rain continued and a cold wind kept us close to the kitchen stove.

We read Jane Austen's *Pride and Prejudice* aloud together, each of us taking a turn as we followed the story of Elizabeth and her sister Jane and the rest of the Bennett family. Despite himself, Shamus got caught up in the story, though he thought Mr. Darcy's pride and stiffness a dead bore. But it helped to pass the long hours while water dripped from the eaves, the clock on the cupboard shelf ticked, and Ellie alternately slept and played on the floor or in her new cradle.

I would not let myself think overlong on Quinn and Deirdre. The gray days were gloomy enough without such disquieting pictures.

The next time there was a break in the weather, Shamus hurried into the house to tell us that Quinn and the wolfhounds had arrived. Bridget and Shamus made much of him, but my own welcome was less than warm. Each time I was tempted to look at him and smile, I reminded myself that Deirdre had asked Quinn to teach her to play the pianoforte and of the distance he'd exhibited the last time he came.

I held myself aloof, making a play of stirring the soup while he played with Ellen, pretending I didn't hear when he said something to me.

After tea, Bridget asked Quinn if he would like to play a game of cards. The four of us sat around the table, the cards passing between us as laughter and banter flowed from Quinn and Bridget and Shamus. I was a little island of quiet, speaking only when spoken to, my mind on my chagrin instead of the game.

"Sure and I'm thinkin' we have an iceberg sitting at the table," Quinn quipped in imitation of Mick's brogue. "One that's forgotten how to smile." A pause as he leaned his head toward me. "All this way I rode, my head bent against the wind, snow and hail and sleet biting my poor face, and my only thought and hope was to soon have myself warmed by Clarissa's smile. Instead . . ."

Shamus's brows lifted. "Are you daft, Lieutenant? There's been no snow or sleet on the mountain in all the years we've been here."

"Ah, but there has. Five feet or more, and me and my poor horse but barely able to make our way through. Close to freezin' we came. All that kept me goin' was the thought of Clarissa's smile. Just a wee one is all I'm askin'. Can you not be for helpin' a poor frozen man?"

My effort not to smile failed, as did my determination not to laugh. "Some of Mick's blarney has definitely rubbed off on you."

Quinn gave an answering laugh. "Oh, aye. 'Tis the curse of livin' with the O'Connors." But mingling through the teasing in his eyes, I saw concern. Worry too.

When there was a break in the game, Quinn gave me a long steady look. "You're not yourself today. Are you not well?"

"I'm fine," I answered, warning myself not to let my feelings show so readily. "I think it's just that I'm tired of the rain."

"As we all are. That's another reason I came, to invite you to join us at the lodge on Saturday. It's Mick's birthday and Maggie and the women are planning a celebration. They said to tell you there will be plenty of food—singing too, maybe even dancing."

Bridget clapped her hands at the mention of dancing. "It's been an age since we had dancing. Well, there was Grandma Sarah's party, of course." For a moment she looked sad, as if she were remembering Nathan. Then giving a shrug, she turned to me. "Please, can we go?"

Despite thoughts of Deirdre, I felt my heart lift. "I wouldn't think of us missing it."

"Good." The corners of Quinn's mouth stretched wide as he went on. "I thought to come for you Saturday morning right after the cows are milked. Plan to spend the night, for the Irish know how to party, and we'll likely be up late." He paused and glanced at the late afternoon light streaming in the window. "Speaking of being late, I need to be going."

"So soon?" This came from Shamus, who sat with elbows on the table.

"If I want to be home before dark."

"You can stay the night," Bridget said.

Quinn's eyes flicked to me as he rose from the table. "Not today."

After putting on his jacket, Quinn walked over to Ellen's bed. He looked down at her, his face tender as one finger gently touched her cheek. "No wonder Maggie calls the baby her little angel."

"That's when she's sleeping," Bridget said. "Betimes when she's awake she shows us a mite of temper."

Quinn looked pointedly at Bridget's bright hair. "You know what they say about redheads." Then before she could think of a rejoinder he added, "I'll come for you on Saturday."

* * *

Saturday was a word often spoken over the next three days. "Should I wear my green dress on Saturday?" or "Could you be helpin' me fix my hair for the party on Saturday?" And "I'm thinkin' the Lieutenant and Da would not be objecting if I was to bring some fresh-caught fish on Saturday."

So it was that Bridget's green dress was freshly washed and ironed and that Shamus set out for the river, fishing pole over his shoulder, on Friday afternoon. As for me, I tried to appear nonchalant, but inside I was as excited as Bridget. I told myself it was only the prospect of the party that quickened my pulse, but deep down I knew it was more. I'd never experienced such a heady sweetness of anticipation before. *Will Quinn sit by me at supper? What if later he asks me to dance?*

I tried to think of other things—what Maggie would serve for supper, if Hawkeye and Bright Star would come. But my thoughts were hard to school and more times than not they reverted to Quinn. Such were the patterns over the next three days, patterns that made me realize that although I could harness my actions, it was well nigh impossible to harness my emotions.

Quinn arrived on Saturday. Shamus, who'd been watching for him all morning, hurried out to greet him with Bridget not many steps behind. Only stern control kept me inside, for I didn't want to appear too eager.

My flimsy reasoning scattered the minute Quinn stepped into the house. My eyes lifted from the flannel square I'd been folding and fastened on his tall frame filling the doorway. There was a tiny moment of silence as our gazes met, a space no longer than a heartbeat. *You're beautiful,* he seemed to say.

I'm so glad you came, I replied in my heart.

I watched his face break into a smile, saw him nod before he crossed the kitchen to stand by Ellen's bed.

"I never knew babies slept so much."

"That's because they're growing. At least that's what Maggie told me."

"She should know." His hazel eyes lifted to mine. "I want you to know I ordered a day without rain so you and Ellie won't get wet on your way to the party." A pause while he looked out the door. "There hasn't been a day this sunny in over a month."

"And you're taking credit for it?"

"I am."

"'Tis me that should be takin' credit for it," Bridget put in. She'd come back into the house to retrieve her cloak. "I've been prayin' to the saints for good weather since Wednesday." A sheepish look crossed her face, and she glanced down at her freshly blackened shoes. "I didn't want my shoes to get muddy before the party."

"What a silly thing to be prayin' about," Shamus scoffed. "You hadn't ought to be takin' up the saints' time with such things."

"Tisn't a silly reason," Bridget retorted. "They and the Holy Mother are interested in all the things we're for doing."

"That they are, and God too," Quinn agreed. Then quickly before the argument could escalate, "Is Ellen ready to be put in her cradleboard?"

At my nod he gently picked up the baby, snuggling her little head against his cheek before taking her over to her cradleboard. In no time, she and the board were strapped to my back and the two of us were helped up onto Midnight.

The trip up to the lodge was filled with conversation as Shamus told Quinn about the three fish he'd caught on Friday and Bridget asked questions about the party. I listened with half a mind. The rest was taken up with watching Quinn's purposeful climb up the mountain, one hand on Midnight's reins, the other seeking balance with his walking stick. Instead of noticing his limp, my eyes saw only the breadth of his jacket-clad shoulders, the dashing tilt to his dark leather hat.

As if he could hear my thoughts, Quinn glanced back, his eyes meeting and holding mine for a moment. I watched the corners of his mouth lift in acknowledgment, felt heat flood my cheeks. After that I strove to keep my eyes on other things, noting how the moss clung in gossamer strands to the naked branches of the alders, watching a squirrel scurry into the cavelike cavity of a giant uprooted tree trunk. But Quinn only had to speak or chuckle and my gaze and thoughts rushed headlong back to him.

Take care, a voice inside my head whispered. *And remember Deirdre will be there.* Even so, the anticipation of music and dancing was enough to give a happy lift to my heart.

* * *

The evening of Mick's party has been pressed into the pages of my heart like the petals of a beautiful rose. It wasn't just the music and laughter, though they were there aplenty—along with talk, tall tales, and easy banter. Nor was it the love and camaraderie that permeated the air. It was being with Quinn Reynolds—encountering the warmth of his gaze, hearing the rich timbre of his voice, feeling his touch as we danced—which brought acknowledgment of love and the first glimmer of hope for a future that included him.

Everyone was dressed in their best—Maggie and Eileen and Deirdre in dark Sunday best with lovely white lace collars, Mick and Patrick and Shamus in dark-colored clothes that were likely kept nice for church too. Bridget and I were the only spots of color, she in her green dress with tiny tucks across the bodice, and me in the least worn of my blue dresses now trimmed with a lace collar Bridget had loaned me. But it was to Quinn that my gaze kept flying. He went to change as soon as we arrived at the lodge, and when he reentered the kitchen he looked as if he had just stepped from an English drawing room. Like the others, he was dressed primarily in black, his waistcoat and trousers finely tailored and set off by a starched white shirt and snowy cravat. I think I stared, and I know the others did, Deirdre's eyes lingering longer than I liked.

"Well, if it's not a regular gentleman we're seein'," Mick quipped.

"I thought you deserved my best since it's your birthday we celebrate. After all, you're the man who saved my life."

"As to that I'm not rememberin', though I think 'tis exaggerated. I only did what I do best—lift and carry."

"I remember," Quinn said. He placed an affectionate hand on Mick's muscular shoulders. "It's something I never forget."

For once Mick couldn't think of anything to say, so Maggie said it for him, inviting us all to sit down before the food got cold.

The women had prepared the best of dinners—roast beef and potatoes, or "taties" the O'Connors called them, covered with rich drippings from the roast. Shamus's fresh, fried fish was also savored along with carrots swimming in butter, not to mention Maggie's delicious scones. When our plates were empty, Maggie brought out servings of oatmeal cake, moist with raisins and topped with dollops of whipped cream.

"You've not been for losing your touch, Maggie, my love," Mick declared after the first bite. He turned to me and added, "Maggie baked this same kind of cake for me on the day I asked her to marry me, though I'll not be for tellin' you whether 'twas the cake or her sweet self that prompted me to pop the question." He smiled and winked at his wife.

"And I'll not be for sayin' whether 'twas Mick's looks or the shiny new shilling in his pocket that prompted my answer," Maggie retorted.

"Now, Maggie, is that any way for a wife to be speakin' to her dear husband? You know 'twas your cravin' for the handsomest man in county Cork that caused you to say aye."

"You've been drinkin' too deep in your cup, Michael O'Connor."

"Even if I was talkin' cold sober, I'd be sayin' the same." Mick's hand reached across the white cloth on the table to cover Maggie's fingers with his. "But I'd have to be addin' that you're the world's grandest cook along with bein' the world's grandest woman, sweet Margaret O'Connor. And the day you first baked me this cake was the start of my happiest years."

Maggie's eyes filled with tears. "Ah, Mick."

"'Tis the truth, Maggie darlin'." Seeing his wife's emotion, Mick pushed back his chair and got to his feet. "This day marks my forty-fifth year, twenty-five of them spent with the love of my life." He paused and refilled his cup with ale. "Instead of a toast to meself, I'm proposing a toast to the woman who's made these last twenty-five years worth the living. Sweet Maggie O'Connor."

Quinn quickly moved around the table to help me from my chair. He remained by my side as we raised our cups to Mick and Maggie. The two of them stood together, Mick's arm around his wife's no-longer-slender waist, his expression as he gazed into her face filled with love.

"To Aunt Maggie," Patrick said, lifting his cup.

"To Maggie," and "To Mam," the rest of us responded.

One sip was all I took of the ale, wrinkling my face at the sourness. Although my eyes were on Mick and Maggie, my mind was on the man standing tall and dignified at my side. For a second I allowed myself to dream, to wish it could be Quinn and me toasting to twenty-five years of marriage. Just as quickly, I pushed the thought away. Until I obtained a divorce, I had to find happiness in things as they were instead of longing for what couldn't be. Even so, I was aware of Quinn's hand on my waist as he helped me back into my chair, and I savored it as my brief moment of happiness. Savored also, the fact that it had been me he stood by, not Deirdre.

While the women cleared the table and washed the dishes, the men retired to the O'Connor sitting room. By then Ellen had roused from her nap and was making noises from her bed by the stove.

"Let me take her while you help Maggie," Quinn offered. Not waiting for a response, he scooped her up from her bed to coax a smile from her puckered face. "That's better. Smiles are always better than crying."

Quinn managed to keep the baby from crying until we'd finished the dishes, though he was required to do some walking.

"I'm sorry," I apologized. "She's probably hungry."

I could tell he was relieved to relinquish the squirming bundle. After excusing myself, I started for Bridget's vacant bedroom.

Maggie reached to stop me. "Use the kitchen. It's warm." Seeing me hesitate, she added, "I'll close the door so you won't be disturbed."

I was in the kitchen when the music started. I heard the tuning of a fiddle, then the sound of a pipe, both tentative at first, but gaining in volume and confidence as the song progressed. The second time through, Shamus's clear tenor joined them, then Deirdre's soprano, the words and melody both beautiful and haunting: "The harp that once thro' Tara's hills, the soul of music shed, now hangs as mute as Tara's walls as if the soul had fled . . ."

I closed my eyes to savor the beauty, my head resting against the back of the chair, Ellen snuggled close. I could hear the longing in their voices, the wish to be back where life was dear and familiar. The fiddle and pipe echoed the longing, Mick and Patrick missing Ireland too.

By the time I returned to the sitting room, the rug had been rolled up for dancing, and the music had lost its somber air. What replaced it was spirited and soul lifting, a tune to set toes tapping.

Bridget's were doing more than that. Her black shoes made a happy rhythm on the polished pine floor, and the skirt of her green dress fanned above them as Shamus, after a quick bow, joined her. Then Deirdre was dancing too.

Their twirling figures became a joyful extension of the music, the heels and toes of their shoes like happy drums on the floor, their faces alight and Bridget's red curls like rippling flames in the lamplight, Deirdre's like liquid ebony. The expression on Shamus's face showed his happiness, his manner intent as he tried to match the women's steps, his head not quite coming to Bridget's shoulder.

As they danced, Maggie and Eileen clapped their hands, the bow of Patrick's fiddle dancing over the strings while Mick piped accompaniment. All were smiling, and even Quinn, sitting by Maggie, was clapping and his toes tapping, his eyes following the dancers— dancers who could not help but entrance their small audience.

Ellen's body stiffened, calling my attention back to her as her frightened eyes flicked around the room.

"It's all right, Ellie," I crooned. "It's happy noise. Can you feel it? Isn't it grand?" I smiled at my slip into the O'Connors' manner of speech and turned her so she could see my face. Like my toes, my arms responded to the lilting rhythm, and my body swayed. Watching me, the baby's unhappy face lost its fear, and her frown changed to smiles.

"See," I said as her smile grew in size. "When you're bigger and learn to walk, you can dance too."

Watching Bridget, I found myself picturing Ellie in her place, her lovely face lifted and alive with happiness, her hair like coils of amber around slender shoulders. For the first time I was able to view the color of my daughter's hair as an asset, a part of her own unique loveliness instead of a reminder of Jacob. I bent my head to kiss her soft russet hair.

"Sweet Ellie," I whispered as the music and clapping and dancing swirled around us to capture us in its heady beat. My feet wanted to join the dancing, to rap and drum on the white pine floor. All too soon, the music rose to a raucous crescendo and stopped.

"Bravo!" Quinn called.

"Wonderful," I added.

"It was that," Mick agreed. "Our Bridget is almost as light on her feet as her mam, and Shamus is proving himself a true O'Connor." His face beamed as he looked at his two children—Shamus's cheeks flushed from hearing his father's praise as he self-consciously tucked the tail of his shirt back into his dark trousers, Bridget breathing hard and her russet curls loosened from their pins and falling about her flushed face. Deirdre's cheeks were colored too, her quick feet having earned her more than one look of admiration.

In the lull that followed their dancing, Quinn carried a chair over to where I was standing. "The evening is still young, so you'd be wise to sit down." After I did, he added, "What does Ellie think of the music?"

"She likes it, though she was a little frightened when we first came in."

Quinn left me to fetch another chair and placed it next to mine. "You looked a little lonely over here by yourself."

How could I be lonely with you in the room? I wanted to ask and give him a thousand Irish blessings for choosing to sit by me, not Deirdre. Instead, I smiled and offered him a soft, "Thank you."

Mick shot a wry look at his nephew. "How about you, Patrick? Are you ready to show us what the other half of the O'Connors can do?"

"Aye." Patrick set down his fiddle and reached out his hand for Eileen. "My wife is a right lively dancer herself."

Mick nodded and raised the pipe to his lips, his broad shoulders lifting as he took a deep breath. He had only played a few bars of the cheerful tune before Bridget picked up the fiddle and scraped the bow across the strings. Although she wasn't as practiced as Patrick, she managed to keep up with her father. As before, the music sang through the room while Patrick and Eileen twirled.

Now that Ellen knew the music wasn't a menace, she watched the moving dancers with fascinated eyes. From my place in my chair, I was equally taken by the intricate steps and toeing. Although Quinn clapped and smiled, I felt his eyes on me as often as they were on Patrick and Eileen. What were his thoughts? Was he regretting the loss of agility in his injured leg?

When the music ended, Patrick pulled Eileen close and planted a kiss on her upturned cheek, the dark blue of her dress like a banner against the dull black of his trousers.

"You've the feet of my brother Jackie," Mick quipped.

"Sure and I have the right to them since he's my da."

"He is that, lad. He is that."

"When are you going to be takin' your turn, Da?" Shamus asked.

Mick took a long swallow from his cup of ale and looked over at his wife. "As soon your mam tells me she's ready."

A wide smile stretched Maggie's generous mouth. "I've been but waiting for your invitation."

After he'd wiped his mouth with the back of his hand, Mick handed his pipe to Shamus. Giving Maggie a low bow, he reached for her hand. "We'll be needin' you to play our song," he said to Patrick, who'd retrieved his fiddle from Bridget.

Patrick frowned and looked puzzled.

"'Tis called 'Maggie'," Shamus whispered.

I suffered a twinge of disappointment when the music began, for I'd looked forward to another display of the Irish jig. Instead of being bright and stimulating, the tune was soft and plaintive—a love song I realized as Mick placed both of his hands on Maggie's waist and she put hers on his shoulders. They glided instead of twirled, swayed in rhythm instead of tapping, the two moving as one, Mick's head but an inch taller than Maggie's. One did not need to wonder if he loved her or she him. It was written in the lines of their bodies, each leaning into the other. Eyes and smiling lips told all.

For a fleeting moment an image of my parents took Mick and Maggie's place—my father tall, and broad shouldered, looking down at my mother in exactly the same way. Emotion tightened my throat and my eyes clouded with unshed tears. The one I longed to look at me with love was at my side, the dark fabric of his trousers but inches from the soft blue of my dress. I wanted to reach for his hand, his fingers long and tapered on his knees, even as I sensed in the deepest layers of my heart that it was only his tightest control that kept his hand from covering mine.

How I knew it I couldn't say, but the joy of knowing melted the ache in my throat and dried my unshed tears. It was fortunate it did, for as soon as Maggie and Mick finished their dance Bridget declared it was my turn.

"But I'm not Irish," I protested.

"'Tis no matter. Just dance what you feel." She looked at me expectantly and so did Shamus.

Maggie came over and reached for the baby. "I'll take the wee mite."

"But . . ." I got to my feet, having no notion of how to begin. More than that, after watching Deirdre's quick feet, I felt myself at a distinct disadvantage. I looked at Maggie, then at Quinn.

When I did, he rose from his chair. "I would count it an honor if you would share this dance with me."

My heart jerked and I must have nodded, for the next thing I knew, Quinn's hand cupped my elbow and led me to the middle of the floor. The silence that followed his invitation told me others were surprised that Quinn would attempt to dance as well.

"How . . . ?" The jab of Bridget's elbow in Shamus's ribs cut off the rest of his question.

"What a grand idea," Maggie exclaimed.

"Oh, aye, for sure." This came from Mick, who looked as if he'd just seen one of the cows fly over the lodge. Recovering himself, he added, "And what would you like us to be playin'?"

"I believe it's called 'The Love I Bare for Thee.' I've heard you play it several times over the years. I'd be pleased if Shamus sang the words."

"Words?" Shamus's question earned him another jab. "Oh, aye." But the look he directed at Quinn remained astonished.

I saw Patrick lift the fiddle to his chin, watched as Mick fingered his pipe. They and the rest of the O'Connors disappeared when Quinn's long fingers spanned my narrow waist. His other hand took mine while my hand reached up to linger on his shoulders. In that moment I felt as if I were a queen, my drab calico dress changed to rustling satin, the pins holding up my blond curls turned to diamonds and pearls. That's how Quinn made me feel as we swayed to the music—him tall and handsome in his black tailored waistcoat and trousers, me looking up with my head coming only to his shoulders. I have no memory of how well we danced. If Quinn limped, I did not notice. If I missed a step, it was swallowed by the music that pulsed and sang of unrequited love.

I have never heard a voice more sweet and clear than Shamus's was that night as his boyish lips formed the words I knew Quinn wished he could be speaking.

At midnight hour when all alone
I often sit and think of thee
And wish the angels then would speak
To tell the love I bare for thee
The love I bare for thee.

I saw love in the depths of Quinn's hazel eyes, tenderness in the pull of his mouth when he smiled down at me. I answered as best I could—in an answering smile and in the steadiness of my gaze. I knew of his love. He knew of mine. And we both knew our honor.

When the final strains of the song ebbed into the lamp-lit room, we stood for a moment, still holding each other until we became aware of our friends. Tears glistened on Maggie's cheeks, and Bridget looked as if she had just read a wonderful love story. Even Deirdre looked touched.

An uneasy silence settled over the room. I felt the color come to my cheeks, sensed Quinn's discomfort. *What have we done? Dear heaven, what has happened?*

Then Ellie chortled and held out her arms for me. I reached to take her, blessing her for the distraction as she grasped one of Quinn's long fingers in her dimpled hand. As if in a dream, I heard Maggie ask if anyone would like another piece of oatmeal cake and Patrick tell Bridget to take over the fiddle so he could have another dance with his wife. Just like that, the awkward moment passed, swallowed up by the consideration of our friends.

Only then did I dare to look at Quinn and saw the high color that also stained his cheekbones. His gaze met mine for a long steady moment, one that told me that all I'd felt had been felt by him, and that even though love hadn't been spoken aloud, it was nonetheless there. I smiled, my heart sang, and for that moment it was enough.

CHAPTER 16

Throughout the days that followed, the music and words to the song Quinn and I danced to were never far from my thoughts. I had only to hum the tune and I was back in Maggie's sitting room, Quinn and I slowly moving to the rhythm, his eyes filled with love as he smiled down at me. Halfway through churning the butter, I'd catch myself staring off into nowhere with a half-smile on my face. With a shake, I'd go back to the churning, aware that Bridget watched me with an amused expression on her face.

"What are you going to do?" she asked one morning after I'd let the pot of porridge boil over.

"Enjoy it."

"Oh, aye. You've already been doing that." There was an uneasy pause while she searched for words. "I mean later on. What are you and the Lieutenant going to do later?"

I shrugged and met her worried gaze. "I don't know, Bridget. But we both know the Lieutenant is an honorable man. For now, just knowing that he loves me is enough."

And it was. Knowing beyond any doubt brought a peace and happiness I'd never experienced before—peace when I looked down at Ellen's sweet little face, happiness as I sang and tightened the cheese press. I seemed to be singing all the time, my walk almost a skip as I went to gather the eggs. In the midst of a song, I'd break off and look up at the mountain, hoping to see the familiar sight of Quinn on Midnight emerging from the trees.

He waited two days before he came. I knew he'd wanted to come sooner, although he didn't say so. But it was there in his eyes and in the way he said my name. I hurried out to meet him, not minding that Bridget and Shamus watched as Quinn dismounted and the dogs yipped and milled around our legs.

"How are you?" he asked

"Fine . . . wonderful." I was smiling and so was Quinn. "And you?"

"The same."

Neither of us spoke for a moment, our eyes saying it all—of love and of the missing.

The day, though cool, was fair, and a soft breeze blew tendrils of unruly curls against my cheeks. Quinn reached out as if to brush them away, his fingers but inches from my face when he stopped, his mouth firming as his hand dropped back to his side. "Come," he said, reaching for his saddlebags. "I've brought some new books for you and Bridget, and Maggie sent fresh-baked scones."

We walked side by side to the house where Bridget and Shamus waited. Not once did Quinn touch me or speak of his feelings, but they were there for me to read in his eyes, in little gestures and in his concern for me and Ellen.

After that, Quinn came whenever the weather permitted, and sometimes even when it did not with his head bent low against the rain, no more able to stay away from me than I was to stop thinking of him.

By now we were into February, the days starting to lengthen and the grass taking on a greener hue. On an afternoon when Shamus had gone to the river to fish, Quinn rode into the yard with the dogs. While Sam made much of the wolfhounds, I walked out to meet Quinn, my eyes never seeming to get enough of him. Watching the quirk of his brows when he spoke made me happy; seeing his lopsided grin did strange things to my heart.

After he'd admired Ellen, who was napping, and had peeked into the kettle to see what Bridget was cooking for supper, he asked if there was anything that needed to be done.

"No, Shamus is good to look after things. Although . . ." My eyes fastened on the length of rope Shamus had stretched across one end of the kitchen so I could dry Ellen's diapers and clothes on rainy days. "Since you're taller than Shamus, could you raise the rope so we don't have to dodge wet clothes?"

Quinn looked from the rope to me. "I can manage that." His deft fingers quickly untied the awkward knots Shamus had fashioned, and wooden pegs were removed and fitted into the wall a foot higher. As he reached up to refasten one end of the rope, his bad leg gave way, throwing him awkwardly to one side so that he crashed into the table, sending a bowl onto the floor where it shattered into pieces.

"Blast this bloody leg!" His angry voice filled the room. "Why do I think I can do things?"

The crash and Quinn's angry voice woke Ellen. Her frightened cry filled the startled silence. Throwing Bridget a quick glance, I hurried to pick up the baby, snuggling her close and trying to quiet her with kisses and whispers.

Instead of quieting, Ellen cried even louder, as if she knew my sympathy was as much with the noisemaker as it was with her. *It's all right. It's all right,* I wanted to say to Quinn. But all I could do was watch him as he struggled to fasten the rope, his leg trembling from the effort, his face in a taut grimace while Ellen's shrill cries filled the kitchen.

When the rope was finally stretched and in place, Quinn grabbed his walking stick, his limp more pronounced as he left the house, the door closing with a slam behind him.

"Here," I said, handing Ellen to Bridget and starting for the door. "I've never seen him like this."

"I have, though 'twas only once when his poor leg gave out and sent him fallin' . . . the same as today."

When I went outside, there was no sign of Quinn. My first thought was that he'd left, too shamed and angry with himself to stay. Then I heard a small sound from the barn. It was there that I found him, sitting on the milking stool and inspecting one of Midnight's hooves.

I stood in the doorway and watched him, the light such that it left his face in shadows. For a moment neither of us spoke, me in my pink dress watching his long fingers pick at something under the hoof, his eyes intent on what he was doing. Then, as if he'd only just become aware of my presence, he lifted his head and looked at me.

Again there was silence, neither of us knowing what to say. Uncomfortable in the stillness, I said what first came to my mind, something probably unwise, but heartfelt just the same. "Thank you for rehanging the rope." My voice was soft and a little unsteady. "You're always helping . . . and saying kind things."

"Like 'blast this leg'?" There was a bite to his words along with derision. "Sometimes I let myself give in to self-pity."

The light was dim, and I moved closer so I could see his face. Quinn watched my approach, the derision I'd glimpsed on his face slowly evaporating.

"A damaged leg doesn't make you less than other men," I said. "In my eyes you stand head and shoulders above them all." I placed my hand on Quinn's shoulder. "Head and shoulders," I repeated.

At my touch, Quinn's hands stilled and after only the slightest hesitation, one moved up to cover my fingers, the feel of his long fingers caressing mine, speaking of his love.

I forgot to breathe and neither of us moved, the moment spinning out through the fragile silence. *Don't let it end,* my heart begged.

Finally Quinn sighed and spoke. "Staying away from you—not touching you—is the hardest thing I've ever done," he rasped. "Please, don't make it harder."

I withdrew my hand and my voice when it came was no more than a whisper. "I'm sorry."

Biting my lip, I stepped away. Although Jacob had left me, he was still holding me hostage to our marriage—a marriage that wasn't a marriage at all, but couldn't be ended without legal sanction. *Soon, soon,* my heart whispered. Surely a ship would be coming soon, one that would allow Sven to ask the captain for the name of a lawyer.

* * *

Halfway through February the weather broke. Instead of clouds and rain, there was sun and softness in the air that spoke of spring.

"'Tis the false spring," Shamus said as the three of us stood in the yard to enjoy the sunshine. "At least that's what Da calls it. False, so we'd best be for enjoyin' it while we can."

I put a bonnet on Ellie and bundled her in the yellow shawl so I could show her my outside treasures—the rhododendrons with swelling buds, the chickens scratching in the damp earth, the cow and calf grazing in the fenced meadow. The calf was nearly grown now, a heifer Sven said would soon be old enough to put in with his bull. Then I'd have two cows to milk and twice as much cheese and butter, enough perhaps to buy my own flour and sugar and tea. While I showed the outside world to the baby, I kept an eye on the mountain. Surely on such a fine day Quinn would come.

Later that afternoon, after Shamus had taken off for the river to fish, Sam set up a bark. I looked up, hoping it was Quinn even as something in the bark disturbed me. Instead of excitement, its deep tones spoke of unease. Putting Ellen in her cradle, I went to the window, Bridget a step ahead.

"Is someone here?" I asked.

Bridget shook her head. "I can't see anyone."

We peered out at the dog, brindled head and tail lifted, his bark deep and menacing as he looked toward the river.

I opened the door and as we stepped outside and saw two men on horseback riding across the meadow—men and horses I didn't recognize.

Bridget's fingers closed around my arm. "Do you know them?"

I shook my head and raised my hand as a shield from the sun. "No one I know from worship service, but they could be new settlers."

As the men rode closer I could make out the dingy white of their shirts beneath dark jackets, but their hats shadowed their faces so I couldn't see their features.

"Call off your dog," one of the men said.

Instead of complying, I watched the men pull in their horses, saw Sam crouch low, ready to spring.

"We mean you no harm, ma'am."

"We're looking for Mrs. Mueller," the second rider put in. "Mrs. Jacob Mueller."

My heart bumped against my ribs. "Who are you? What do you want?"

"We're friends of Jake's," the heavier man said.

Sam's steady barking made it difficult to hear.

"Quiet, Sam!"

As if the dog sensed my mistrust of the men, he was slow to stop, even slower to back away.

"Sam!"

With wariness in his stance, Sam reluctantly trotted back to me. The two men followed him. I could see their faces now, the heavier one with an unkempt beard, the thinner one not recently shaven.

"I don't like the way they're lookin'," Bridget whispered.

I nodded and noted the rifles nested in the scabbards, the bedrolls slung over the back of each saddle.

"My name's Dewey Clawson," the heavier man said. "This is my cousin, Bert."

"Bert Richins," the younger man said. "We was friends and partners with your husband. Met up with him last summer in Sacramento."

My stomach tightened. "Was . . . ? Is something wrong?"

The men halted their horses and Dewey took off his hat. "I'm afraid we got bad news for you, ma'am."

Bert removed his hat too, revealing a profusion of greasy blond hair. "Jake got hisself shot. Back in July it was."

I closed my eyes and Bridget's fingers tightened on my arm. "Clarissa . . ."

"I'm all right." My voice was shaking and so were my legs. "He's dead?"

Both men nodded, their expressions solemn.

Six months I've been a widow. Six months . . . "How?" I paused and licked my lips. "How did it happen?"

"Gunfight," Dewey said. "Jake was in a card game, and one of the men claimed he was cheating. One thing led to another and . . ."

I welcomed the silence and used it to pull my mind away from the terrible picture of Jacob sprawled on the floor of a saloon, his eyes staring, and blood covering his white shirt—a shirt I'd washed and ironed countless times. Dead. Jacob was dead.

I felt Bridget's arm go around my waist at the same instant I saw Shamus coming at a run from the river. As yet the men weren't aware of him, but they were aware of Bridget. I didn't like the way they were looking at her—Bridget with her delicate features and thick waves of russet hair. I didn't like the way they were looking at me either, the quick furtive glances they shot at each other as they sat on their horses, the breeze blowing their unkempt hair. I'd seen such a look before, filled with excitement and hunger. Such looks had sent me into a loveless marriage and years of pain. I suddenly wanted them gone. "Thank you for coming," I said, hoping they would take the hint and leave.

"We felt it was our duty," Bert said.

Shamus had reached the barn and sauntered out with the pitchfork in his hand, acting as if he'd been there all along.

"Jake was our special friend. Our partner," Dewey added. "As such we could stay on here and help you out. A woman such as you . . . and one but recently widowed . . . shouldn't ought to be doin' man chores and heavy work."

"I have friends to help me. Shamus here and his father and cousin."

They turned and looked at Shamus before dismissing him with a shrug. "Seems a good-enough-sized boy," Dewey said. Though his words were polite, his eyes were calculating as they returned to Bridget and me.

Under my hand I felt Sam's hackles rise, and similar fear pricked the nerves at the base of my neck. On our way to Oregon, I'd seen men like Dewey and Bert hanging around Fort Bridger—men without character and up to no good. Shamus moved closer and Bridget's hand tightened around my waist.

"Mrs. Mueller is needin' some time to herself, so 'tis best that you be leavin'," she said in a crisp voice.

This time the men took the hint. As they turned their horses, Dewey looked back. "We're thinkin' of stayin' on in these parts for a while, so you might be seein' us again." With that, he touched his hat, and he and Bert rode away.

Only then did the full impact of what the men had told me sink in. Jacob was dead. Conflicting emotions ran through me as shock warred with guilt-laden gladness. No longer trapped in a loveless marriage, I was free to follow my heart.

Shamus's voice jerked my thoughts back to them. "I don't like the looks of those men. Don't like the way they was lookin' at you and Bridget either."

"At least they're gone." Bridget's voice held relief as her arm tight-

ened on my waist. "Much as I didn't like them, the news they brought
was . . ." She stopped and hastily crossed herself. "'Tis wrong I know
to be speakin' ill of the dead, but after the mean things your husband
did to you, I'm not for feelin' sadness." She paused and looked at me
more closely. "Are you sure you're feeling all right?"

"Yes." Although I smiled, I was still shaken and disbelieving.

"I'd better be for tellin' the Lieutenant," Shamus said. "Mam will
want to know too." His speech slowed and he looked a little uncertain. "That is, if you want me to be takin' them the news?"

"Yes." I nodded and smiled. "Yes, please. And hurry."

Shamus leaned the pitchfork against the house and started for the
hill at a trot. When Sam saw him, he started to follow.

"Stay, Sam." My eyes were on the two men as they made their
way to the river crossing. Fear tightened my stomach. What if they
changed their minds and came back? "Hurry!" I called to Shamus.

My heart was poised and ready to soar as I started back into the
house. Each time it tried, I'd remember that Jacob was dead, shot in a
saloon. Swimming through my conflicting emotions was the realization that Jacob had died near the time I had been fighting for my
own life, Ellie's world just beginning as Jacob's life ended. I felt the
sting of tears for a man I'd never loved, but could now pity, a man
who'd thrown away all that was precious in his restless search for
nothing.

* * *

The time between Shamus's leaving and Quinn's arrival was short,
but it seemed like hours—days—with me pacing and too distracted
for rational thought or conversation. I looked out the window a
dozen times, my disappointment when I failed to see him quickly
swallowed by hope that sent me back to look again.

Then he was there, Midnight coming at a lope across the
meadow, Quinn riding easy in the saddle. But his face didn't look easy
when I walked out to meet him. It looked as distracted as I felt—
hope and gladness dampened down by disbelief and hard-won
control.

"I met Shamus on my way down," Quinn began.

"He's dead," I said. "Jacob's dead." I started to cry, happy tears, mournful tears, my face screwing up as my fingers tried to still my trembling lips.

In one fluid movement, Quinn was off the horse, his hat swept off his brown hair, a look of concern on his face. "Clarissa . . ."

"He's dead."

Quinn's arm went around my shoulder as if he feared I might faint, his fingers both hard and gentle as they cupped my shoulder, hard and gentle like his voice when he spoke to Bridget. "Will you please see to Ellie while Clarissa and I talk?"

I didn't look to see Bridget's response. My concern was centered on stilling my tears, which seemed to have a mind of their own. What was wrong with me? What must Quinn be thinking?

Quinn led me away from the house, past the fenced pasture and toward a clump of alder and hemlock trees, his arm steady around my shoulder, as one of my hands wiped my tears with the corner of my apron.

When we reached the trees where distance and thick-branched hemlock shielded us from others, Quinn gently turned me to face him. "Did you love him then?" I'll never forget the look on his face—concern mingled with pain, and love overriding them both.

"No. Not ever."

I heard the release of caught breath, saw his relief and gladness.

"Not ever," I repeated.

Quinn's warm fingers closed around my hand and raised it, hazel eyes looking steadily into mine, his lips soft on my wrist, then my palm, my fingers held against his cheek. I'd never had a man kiss my hand like that, the simplest of kisses, yet one that sent coils of warmth around my heart and through my body.

"You had me scared for a minute. I thought—" Quinn broke off, his voice both a groan and a laugh. "I thought maybe I'd been dreaming these last months . . . that it was just me, not you."

"No, oh, no."

He laughed, the groan eaten by gladness, a laugh that brought happy glints to his eyes and set my head to swimming. He brushed a tendril of hair away from my cheek, his fingers soft as moth wings and warm like his lips when they found mine—love, warm and tender.

"I love you," he said when the kiss ended.

"And I you," I whispered.

Then he was kissing me again and again as if he were making up for all the days and weeks of pent-up longing, and I was doing the same.

"Ah, my sweet," he whispered when he could speak. He held me close, the wild pounding of his heart like an echo to my own. Though five-years married, this was the first time love had warmed my kisses, the first time I'd felt love given and spoken in return. I closed my eyes, the two of us standing close, the afternoon sun and the soft breeze like good friends looking on.

"I didn't plan to fall in love with you." Quinn's voice came like a low rumble with my head against his chest. "That first day I saw you playing in the waves, I turned my back on you, guessing who you were—a woman married. That's how I listened when Nastachee told us how you'd helped him . . . told us what your life was like."

Quinn paused and chuckled, his fingers moving through my hair. "By the time Nastachee finished, I was more than half in love with you already, and it only took one meeting to push me all the way."

"How can that be?" I asked, remembering Quinn's interest and open appraisal on that first day at the lodge. But surely not love.

"I asked myself the same question numerous times . . . and reminded myself just as often that I wasn't some lovesick lad, but a man grown and old enough to know better. None of it made a particle of difference. One look at you and I was gone. You were so alive and real, the very opposite of all the English women I'd known, with no airs or pretense about you."

"But what of your wife?" I asked, my thoughts in a tangle between love and amazement.

Quinn's face lost its gladness, and his voice when he spoke was harsh. "The marriage . . . all of it was a terrible mistake. We were doomed before we walked down the aisle, two people thrown together by ambitious parents. We were completely ill suited for each other." He paused and laughed, a laugh as harsh as his voice, the two of us standing but inches apart, the sun painting glints of light in Quinn's tousled brown hair.

"No one was more pleased than I when my brigade was posted to Ireland . . . no one more relieved when Louise said that since she was with child she preferred to remain in England. Relief followed me across the channel and sat with me each day until I learned she and the baby were dead. Instead of sorrow, there was regret and the wish to have tried harder to make love happen."

Now it was me taking Quinn's hand, me bringing it to my lips to kiss and hold against my cheek. He pulled me close, kissing my lips, my eyes, my hair.

"I was afraid you would fall in love with Deirdre," I said when our kisses quieted. "She's so lovely and—"

Another kiss stilled my lips. "Lovely, yes," he said after a minute, "but with a tongue that never stops and a manner about her that grows tiring. Besides, my heart was already yours. Everything else paled next to you." A pause as he lifted my face to meet his gaze. "Will you do me the honor of being my wife?"

"Yes," I said and kissed him. "Yes and yes."

What we talked of after that I don't recall, only our feelings— light and fragile as tendrils of mist moving over the mountain, deep as love when it courses to the center of the soul.

* * *

Love was the word most frequently heard and spoken that afternoon, but there was talk of our future too. In time, Quinn and I started back to the house, his arm around my shoulder and the breeze fluttering the ties of my white apron.

"Since there's no clergy here, we'll have to go by boat to Astoria to get married," Quinn said. He laughed and shook his head. "Married's a word I thought I'd never be able to say to you, but I dreamed of it plenty of times." He stopped and tilted my chin up with one of his long fingers, his eyes looking quietly into mine. "I still feel like I'm dreaming. To be able to touch you like this and . . ."

Then his lips were on mine, gentle and demanding, and mine answering in kind, my arms circled around his neck to hold him closer.

"Lieutenant!" The sound of Shamus's voice clamored into love's stillness. We broke apart, guilt and reluctance warring as we turned to look.

The O'Connors were coming down the last hill from the lodge, Shamus out in front and waving. I knew without hearing that Maggie was scolding him for his lack of manners and Shamus was wondering why.

"It looks as if we have company," Quinn said, for Bridget, upon hearing Shamus, had come out of the house with Ellen.

There was subtle constraint when we met in the dooryard. I think the O'Connors were unsure as to whether they should be looking solemn or happy.

"'Tis true, then?" Maggie asked. "Jacob is dead?"

"Yes." Like them, I was unsure of what expression to use, but my heart was so filled with joy that a smile won out.

Seeing it, Maggie's face broke into an answering one. "May the saints be praised! I won't be tellin' you how many nights I lost sleep worryin' about you and prayin' it would turn out."

Then everyone began talking at once, gladness and laughter interspersed with hugs. Instead of feeling like a widow, I felt free. In the midst of the gladness with friends and voices milling around me, I found myself thinking of Tamsin and wishing that she could be there. Then I felt Quinn's arm go back around me, a place where I wanted it to stay.

"So, 'tis a wedding then you'll be plannin'?" Patrick asked.

I reached for the baby, who'd been clamoring for me.

"We are," Quinn said. "In fact we were just talking of it when you came."

Bridget's eyes were bright with interest. "When? And where will you be finding someone to be marryin' you?"

"We'll have to wait until spring when a boat can get in and out of the bay to take us to Astoria," Quinn told her.

Deirdre, who'd been quieter than usual, moved closer. Her face held a closed expression, and I'd noticed that she'd had a hard time smiling. "When was it the men said your husband died?" she asked.

"July."

Deirdre frowned. "Then shouldn't you be waiting till summer? I mean . . . a year of mourning and all?"

Her words brought an uncomfortable silence.

Mick's voice came into the quiet. "After what that man did to Clarissa, I doubt there's much for her to be mournin' about."

Quinn looked down at me and saw my nod. "We'll be married as soon as I can make arrangements for a boat to take us to Astoria." His voice held authority—gladness, too, as he added, "And all of you are invited to make the trip with us. We'll make a regular celebration of it."

* * *

It was late afternoon before we began to run out of things to say about the wedding. During a lull in the conversation, Mick reminded Maggie of the time. "As grand as the day has been, night will be comin' on before we know it." He glanced at Quinn.

"I'll come along later on the horse. Probably catch up with you before you get home," Quinn said.

We walked across the meadow with them, Quinn carrying Ellie, his arm around my waist, and Shamus walking ahead with his father. Snatches of what he said drifted back to us.

" . . . men said stayin' . . . didn't like their looks. Didn't like how . . . lookin' at Bridget . . ."

I felt Quinn's fingers tighten on my waist, but when I looked at him he acted as if he hadn't heard.

"Do you have plenty of flour?" he asked, just as if Shamus had been telling his father about a big fish he'd caught. "If not, I'll bring some down with me tomorrow." He pulled me close. "I mean to come as often as I can. Rain or shine, you'll have a hard time getting rid of me."

"As if I wanted to." I leaned my head against his shoulder, matching my steps with his as we walked. Even so, Shamus's words put a damper on my happiness, flicking at the edges with tremors of unease. I'd forgotten about Jacob's partners, forgotten their unsavory appearance and leering eyes.

When I broke away to hug Maggie and Eileen, I noticed Quinn talking quietly with the men, their faces serious and Shamus nodding as if he agreed with what they said.

After we'd waved the O'Connors on their way, we turned and walked back to the house. It was my favorite time of day, the sun having slipped down behind the cape, the light slanted and soft like the air and gilding the tops of the mountains with prisms of gold.

"Have you ever seen anything more lovely?" Bridget asked. Like me, she couldn't seem to get enough of the golden day. There was hardly a cloud in sight. Surely spring wasn't far away.

I held to this thought as I took the baby from Quinn so he could help Shamus with the chores. Perhaps spring would come early this year. Maybe Quinn would be able to find a boat to take us to Astoria in just weeks instead of months.

It was almost dark before Quinn led Midnight from the barn. Twice, when I'd looked outside, I'd seen him and Shamus talking intently by the woodshed. Later when Quinn carried the milk into the kitchen, I saw him check the hasp on the lock.

I pretended not to see, knowing that in some small way it would add to his peace of mind if he thought me unaware of his unease. But when Quinn pulled me against him to kiss me goodnight, I wanted to cling to him and tell him to stay.

"Clarissa." I loved the way he said my name, loved the tender way he had of touching my cheek as he kissed me, like I was the most precious thing in the world. He lifted my face to look at him, smiling as he spoke. "You're beautiful. I've wanted to tell you that almost as many times as I've wanted to say I love you. Your eyes . . . your hair and how it's always curling around your face." He laughed and pulled me close again. "What a glorious life we're going to have together . . . you and me and Ellie."

I held his words close to my heart as I lay in bed that night, the sound of Bridget's soft breathing coming from the other side of the bed. The night was clear and moonlight shone through the square of my window, painting silvery shadows onto the wall. I kept my mind focused on love, not danger, and fell asleep with the memory of Quinn's lips on mine.

CHAPTER 17

The next morning when Shamus came in from milking, Quinn followed him into the house. Surprise sent me across the kitchen, my hands outstretched, my lips smiling. I stopped before I reached him when my brain registered the pockets of fatigue under his eyes and the rumpled appearance of his dark coat.

"Quinn." Then quickly, "Is something wrong?"

He smiled and shook his head, the act dissolving the stab of unease that had settled in my stomach.

"The Lieutenant spent the night keepin' watch. He was worried those men might come back," Shamus put in.

Unease jumped back. "Why?" I asked, even as I remembered Quinn, Mick, and Patrick talking when I'd been telling Maggie good-bye.

"I knew I'd never be able to fall asleep up at the lodge, so I figured I'd come down here and keep an eye on things." He wrapped an arm around me and pulled me close. "Do you have any idea how precious you and Ellie are to me?" His voice was low, his hands a caress on my waist.

"But it's cold, and Sam—" I stopped and looked at the dog who was sitting by the door, his tail wagging. "What kind of watchdog are you?"

"A good one," Quinn replied. "That's why I kept my distance. I didn't want him to disturb your sleep."

Aware of the cold and damp on Quinn's coat, I pulled him to the stove where Bridget was cooking breakfast. While he warmed himself, we plied him with questions, learning that he'd kept watch with the horse in the clump of trees between the house and the river. Yes, he had gotten a little cold, but he insisted he was used to such things as a former soldier.

I don't recall what we had for breakfast, only that it was hot and that it felt so right to have Quinn sitting beside me while we ate.

"Do Mick and Maggie know where you are?" I asked.

"They do. We talked about it after I got home last night . . . after I got my gun."

"Gun?" Bridget's eyes grew large.

"Aye. How else do you think he was keepin' watch?" Shamus asked. "And he's for teachin' me how to shoot it. Clarissa too."

I looked at Quinn, who met my eyes and nodded. "I brought two revolvers with me from England. One I'll keep, but the other . . ." He paused and reached for my hand. "The other one I want you to keep here." His hazel eyes continued to hold mine. "I don't want to alarm you, but until I know those men are well away from here, I'll rest easier knowing you have a gun."

"And know how to use it," Shamus added.

"That too."

So it was that after Ellen was down for her morning nap, Quinn took the three of us out to the meadow to teach us how to shoot his revolver. It was another sunny day with a slight breeze blowing inland from the bay, the blackbirds singing from winter-bare trees.

Jacob had owned a rifle, one he kept to himself. I had been glad he did. But until that day I'd never seen Quinn with a gun. He wore the two revolvers strapped around his waist, their presence hidden by his coat. As we walked across the meadow, I couldn't help but contrast how Jacob had left me defenseless while Quinn was concerned for my safety.

When we reached a place well away from the pasture, Quinn took off his coat and laid it on a stump. I looked at the long barrel of the revolver with misgiving when he held it out, saw the sun glint off the blue metal while he explained its workings and loading. What would it feel like to hold such a deadly thing? Could I do it?

I found that I could, and that instead of aversion there was a grim satisfaction in knowing how to defend my baby and myself. The next hour passed in a blur of apprehension and loud explosions as Shamus and I took turns loading the gun and firing it at the twisted trunk of an aged spruce. I gave Quinn an impish grin the first time I hit the target, felt satisfaction when I saw fingers that had been trained to sew tiny stitches or execute difficult scales on the pianoforte curl around the handle, take aim, and squeeze the trigger.

Shamus, of course, was all excitement, but Bridget wanted nothing to do with the gun and quickly went back to be near the baby. My independent nature, however, liked learning a new skill. While the woman in me cringed at the thought of killing and maiming, I had only to think of protecting Ellie, and I was thankful for my competence.

My red shawl had joined Quinn's coat on the stump. With my left hand steadying my right wrist, I took careful aim at the tree. Once, twice, three times a bullet sank deep into the tree, the acrid smoke and noise reflected in the grim pull of my lips.

"Who would have thought?" Quinn asked when another shot hit true. There was pride in his voice, but in his eyes there was regret, as if he wished for a better world.

When he was satisfied that Shamus and I could handle the revolver, and we'd found a place to keep it and the extra bullets in a drawer in the cupboard, he brought Midnight around to the door.

"Are you leaving?" I asked. Disappointment edged my voice, for I thought he was spending the day.

"I want to ride across the river and see if Jacob's partners have actually left. Someone is sure to have seen them. I'll rest easier when I know they're well away from here."

"We'll all rest easier."

His mouth tightened, and I knew he regretted the need to tell me of his concern. "It may take me awhile. If I'm not back soon, you'll know it's taken me longer than I expected and that I'm spending the night with Sven."

My fingers closed around his arm. "Be careful."

"I will. Don't forget, this is an army man you're talking to." There was a flash of recklessness in his eyes, one that gave me a glimpse of the brash young man in a red uniform. Then it was gone and his eyes turned soft. "I love you."

He tipped my chin and his lips found mine, their softness a contrast to the bristle of yesterday's beard.

The three of us stood in the dooryard to see him off, Quinn's black-coated figure erect as Midnight broke into an easy lope toward the river.

I heard Bridget whisper an Ave Maria and joined my prayer with hers. "Keep him safe, dear Lord," I whispered, and peace enfolded me.

* * *

When Quinn wasn't back by dark, I wasn't unduly worried. But when there was no sign of him by the second evening, I began to feel genuine concern.

"I wonder what can be keepin' the Lieutenant?" Shamus asked as he carried in a load of wood.

Bridget frowned and shot him a quick look.

"Well, he was sayin' he'd be back by now," he said defensively.

"Which he will." She gave me a bright smile and dried a plate. "Now don't you be worryin', Clarissa."

We all made excuses to go outside the next morning, our eyes on the distant outline of the river instead of on the task we had chosen. The day was overcast, and dark clouds hovered over the cape.

It was Shamus who saw Quinn first, the boy having gone toward the river on the pretext of finding the fishhook he claimed he'd lost the day before. "He's comin'!" he shouted, hands cupped to his mouth, his slight body framed against the gray sky. "I can see him crossin' the river." I'd taken Ellen outside to watch the chickens. Hearing Shamus, I turned my steps toward the river. Bridget, after setting down a bucket, hurried to catch up with me as Shamus pointed to a horse and rider coming up the bank of the river.

"I told you he'd be comin'," he said, as if concern for the Lieutenant had never crossed his mind.

Seeing us, Quinn waved and set the gelding to a lope, his military bearing evident in the way he sat his horse—erect, yet at ease, with a generous measure of confidence. In no time he was with us, slowing the horse, a grin on his unshaven face as Shamus called out questions.

"What took you so long? Clarissa and Bridget were startin' to worry." Then quickly. "Did you see the men? Are they gone?"

"They are." Though his words were directed to Shamus, his eyes were on me and Ellen—as soft and glad and smiling as mine were. "I'll tell you all about it when we get to the house."

It was over ham and oatcakes that Quinn told us what had happened. "I went to Sven's place first to find out if he'd seen the men." A pause and a quick smile. "By the way, he and Flora were happy to learn that we're getting married."

I returned his smile, aware of his tact in saying they were happy to hear our news, not that they were happy to learn that Jacob was dead.

"Had the Larsens seen Jacob's partners?" Shamus asked, anxious to bring him back to the story.

Quinn shook his head. "Sven went with me to several of his neighbors where we learned the men had been asking about you. Sven was put out that anyone would tell them . . . you a woman alone and two men looking for you."

"They probably weren't thinking," I said, comforted though that soon I wouldn't be alone.

"Did you find the men?" Shamus prompted between bites of oatcake.

"I did, though it took me awhile." He paused and speared a piece of ham with his fork. "They asked Mr. Petty the best way to get to Neahkahnie Mountain."

I handed Ellen my spoon to play with. "Neahkahnie?"

Quinn nodded. "Mr. Petty said there's a story about a shipwreck and gold that the Indians found on the beach and buried there. He thinks the men have heard about it and are on their way to Neahkahnie to try and find it."

I remembered Jacob coming home from worship meeting full of talk about the treasure. There'd been excitement in his voice when he'd spoken of the gold. "They won't be the first to try—the last ones either."

Finished with his ham, Quinn reached to take Ellie, who favored him with a smile. "Do you think it was Jacob who told them about the treasure?" he asked.

"It wouldn't surprise me. He was always talking. Bragging too. Anything to get attention."

"Whatever the case, the men are definitely on their way to Neahkahnie. I picked up their trail and followed them for most of a day." Another pause and his mouth tightened. "Jacob's partners aren't men I'd like to meet up with alone." His eyes shifted to Shamus, who sat with elbows resting on the table. "You were right to be leery of them."

Shamus sat taller at the words of praise.

"When your da finds out, he'll be proud of you too," I added.

Quinn left a short time later, saying he needed a bath and shave and a change of clothes. As I followed him into the yard, I felt a stirring of deep peace and contentment. The man I loved was safely home. Jacob's partners were miles away. Only good things awaited me—the coming of spring and the boat to take us to Astoria. Marriage and happy, shared years with Quinton Reynolds.

* * *

The month of March slipped by, the passing scarcely noted. My mind was too taken up with happiness and Quinn's visits to give thought to such mundane things as the passing of hours and days and weeks. I met life with new eyes and excitement, the mornings greeted with anticipation, evenings spent savoring the goodness of the day.

Quinn came several times a week, often staying for meals. Just seeing him ride into the yard sent me to the mirror to fuss with my hair or pinch color into my cheeks, my greeting letting him know how glad I was to see him. When it came time to leave, Quinn steadfastly refused Bridget's entreaty to stay the night. He smiled at me when he did, his eyes saying what he couldn't speak, that he was counting the days and that in the meantime it was better if he didn't stay. I understood, but it didn't keep me from yearning to be in his arms, the two of us and love.

On days when the weather permitted, Quinn and I went for walks. This was our only time of privacy, since Shamus and Bridget were so gregarious they considered every conversation but an extension of their own.

It was on such a day, with the March wind blowing and gray clouds playing tag with the sun, that Quinn brought up the subject of our future.

"Tomorrow, weather permitting, I'd like to take you and Ellie up to the lodge. There are some things I'd like to show you, and Maggie's been after me to have you look at the bolts of material the ship brought last fall. She and Eileen and Deirdre are of the opinion that every woman about to marry would like something new to wear . . . a special gown for the occasion." He drew me to him.

"I fear I've spent far more years at soldiering than I did in the drawing room, so I have little notion of what it is women need and like. To me, you're lovely just as you are—all I could ever want and more than I dared to dream of."

He kissed me then, his lips warm and lingering, his arms holding me as if he never wanted to let me go. "You are free to fashion yourself as many new gowns as you deem necessary," he said when his lips were free to speak. "I have only one request."

"What's that?"

"That at least one of the new dresses is blue. You were wearing blue the first time I saw you playing in the waves . . . blue when you came to the lodge and I lost my heart to you." The lopsided grin lifted the corners of his mouth. "When I lie in bed thinking of you, you're always wearing blue."

Heat rushed to my cheeks while happiness curled around my heart. Where had I found this wonderful man? Of course I agreed to it. How could I not? A man who could think a worn and faded dress beautiful?

Quinn came for the four of us the next day. He'd left Belle at home, for her first litter of pups was due in a few weeks, but Finn and Balor bounded into the yard with him, as happy to see Sam as he was to see them. As before, I rode on the gelding with Ellen strapped to my back in her cradleboard. She was almost eight months old now, sitting up and trying to crawl. Spring was evident even on the mountain, leaf buds swelling on the alders and tiny trilliums poking dainty heads through the carpet of last year's leaves.

Bridget and Shamus, when not talking, broke into snatches of song, as excited by a change in routine as I was. When we reached the lodge, I looked at it with new eyes—tall, gray-stone chimneys and gabled roof, the two wings sprawled across the meadow in beautiful symmetry. I paused to take it in, finding it hard to think that I would soon be living there—Clarissa Yeager, soon to be Reynolds. It was as if I'd never been a Mueller. Although I would be perfectly happy if

Quinn came to live in my little house, I could not fail to appreciate the advantages the lodge had to offer.

As if he could read my thoughts, Quinn paused after he helped me down from his horse. "Will you mind living here after we're married?"

I shook my head. "How could you think that?"

"I know of your deep attachment for your own place."

"That was before. Now . . ." I smiled as he pulled me close. "Now I want only to be where you are." I remembered my fierce resolve to keep the claim so my child and I would have a place of our own. So much had changed in the year since Jacob had left and I had discovered he'd sold the horse and taken the money. Small wonder there were times when I felt as if I were dreaming.

Bridget and Shamus were already in the kitchen. Maggie's greeting was warm when Quinn and I arrived a few minutes later. After the women had each had a turn holding Ellen, Quinn excused himself.

"When you're through deciding about your wardrobe, I'll be in my study."

Eileen and Deirdre were as eager as Maggie to look at the bolts of cloth. This surprised me on Deirdre's part, for I'd been unsure of how she would react to the subject of my wedding dress. On the way to the storage room she pulled me aside.

"I want you to know I'm sorry for my pettiness the other day. 'Twas a bit of a blow to find out that you and the Lieutenant would so soon be marryin'." She paused and reached for my hand, her blue eyes direct and holding. "I'd be tellin' a lie if I was to say I hadn't had thoughts of the Lieutenant myself. Such a man is hard to ignore . . . rich and handsome and good as he is. But I could tell early on there was no spark on his part toward me. Such didn't keep my from tryin', of course, but . . ." She smiled and a touch of mischief sparkled in her eyes. "As my mother says, there's more than one fish to be caught . . . so that is my intent. To look for another fish. That being said, I'm hopin' we can still be friends."

"It's my intent, as well. You and the O'Connors are counted like family."

I felt the pressure of her fingers as she squeezed my hand. "Thank you."

The five of us spent a pleasant hour holding up material and discussing design. Remembering what Quinn had said about blue, I was pleased to discover a bolt of soft blue chintz sprinkled with tiny dark blue flowers. I chose it for my wedding dress, a fabric of apricot hue for a dress to wear to Astoria, and yards of white for new nightgowns and petticoats. I felt as if I were a queen as we pored over a book of fashion plates Deirdre had brought from Ireland. Having worked as a seamstress, she had a knack for design and fashion. Not once in the six years I'd been married had I had a new dress. Now, as soon as busy fingers could sew them, I would have two.

After the dresses had been decided and Ellen had fallen asleep in the kitchen, I knocked on the door of Quinn's study. I found him sitting at a desk, writing in a ledger. I'd never been in his study before. It was a room conveying both masculinity and warmth with rust-colored drapery hanging at the two windows, shelves of books and military bric-a-brac on either side of the gray-stone fireplace. Quinn removed his spectacles and came around the desk to greet me, his arm on my waist as he helped me into a brown leather chair.

"All finished?"

I nodded as my eyes took in a large painting that hung on the wall above his desk, one that looked to be of the English countryside. "Is this like it is at your home?"

"Somewhat. It conveys much of what I like to remember about it." His expression was contemplative as he sat in a matching leather chair next to mine. "I'd like to take you there for a visit sometime. You and Ellie. Let you meet my sister. You'll like her, I know, and she you. The baby can meet some of her cousins too. My sister has three boys, so Ellen's sure to be a hit."

"But Ellen isn't—" I'd been about to say she wasn't a Reynolds, but something in Quinn's expression stopped me.

"She is." His voice was firm. "That's something about which I want to talk to you. I've written to my lawyer for advice on what recourse I must take to make her legally mine, though in my heart Ellen's been mine all along. "

Unbidden tears came to my eyes. "Do you know how many times I've watched the two of you together and wished that she was?"

His hand reached and took mine. "No more often than I've wished the same, I'm sure. Several of us played a part in getting and keeping Ellen here—a far bigger part than Jacob Mueller did."

I thought back to those fragmented days when my life and Ellen's had hung by a thread, kept on earth's side by sheer will and the love and prayers of my friends—Quinn, Maggie, Bridget, not to mention Bright Star. And Mother.

That afternoon I told Quinn how Mother had come to me, and how she'd said she must go to the baby too. "That's why I named her Ellen," I finished.

Quinn looked at me for a long moment, his hazel eyes liquid and warm with love. "I had something similar happen to me when I was left for dead on the battlefield. It was a man that came, I think my grandfather." He raised my hand to his lips and kissed it. "When I was younger I sometimes doubted the existence of God, but since I was wounded . . ." He paused and cleared his throat. "Since then I no longer doubt."

A knock on the study door ended our conversation. "Mam said to tell you tea is ready," Bridget said. "Would you be likin' to join us in the kitchen or have me bring it to you here?"

"We'll join you."

Tea was a merry affair, for Mick and Patrick were there—a bright time of happy banter, Maggie's scones, and cups of tea liberally laced with sugar and cream. An hour later we were on our way back home.

"You do this so often you and Midnight ought to be able to be travelin' it with your eyes closed," Shamus quipped on our way down the mountain.

"We have," Quinn agreed. "That's why I'm praying for an early summer so we can sail to Astoria and get married." He smiled up at me, his look letting me know there were reasons other than convenience that prompted the wish.

He was not alone in that. I looked through the trees at the sun slanting from the west. In a few weeks we would be on our way to being a family.

* * *

In April the weather turned sunny again—days of blue sky and warmth and a lift to the heart. On one such a day when I was outside gathering kindling, I looked up and saw two men on horseback riding toward us from the river. My heart jerked at the memory of Jacob's partners just as Sam ran out of the barn, his bark one of greeting instead of warning.

Quinn and Shamus followed Sam out of the barn. "Who is it?" Quinn asked.

I shaded my eyes with my hand. "I can't tell for sure. Maybe Sven Larsen."

"It is," Shamus stated. "It's Mr. Larsen and Nathan." He set off at a run, waving and calling a welcome.

"I wonder what brings him?" Quinn asked.

I wondered the same, for Sven always came in his wagon. Was something wrong? I took heart when Sven waved and urged his horse into a lope.

Bridget, who'd heard Sam's bark, came out of the house. When she saw who it was, she squealed and ran after Shamus to greet Nathan.

I smiled as I watched her, then turned to greet Sven. "Where's Flora?" I asked.

"Home resting."

"Is she all right?"

Sven nodded and dismounted. "Just tired. You know how women are when a baby is on the way."

Quinn extended his hand to Sven. "It's good to see you." He glanced at Bridget and Nathan who were talking excitedly. "It's easy to see why Nathan came," a pause and a grin —"but what brings you?"

Sven reached inside his vest. "The captain of the *Skylark* made a quick trip from Astoria with supplies and mail."

My heart quickened. "Is there mail for me?"

Sven smiled. "There is. Flora said I was to bring the letter to you today and not wait for her."

All I heard was "letter." Maybe something from Tamsin. I held out my hand, heard the rustle of paper as Sven pulled it from his vest pocket. In my eagerness, I snatched it from his hand, my eyes scanning the return address. Disappointment stabbed at me when I failed to see Tamsin's name. *Mrs. Caleb Tremayne,* it read. Who was that? And why no letter from Tamsin?

I slowly walked into the kitchen, the men's low voices and Bridget's giggle scarcely noted. My breathing quickened when I looked at the letter more closely. The handwriting was familiar. It *was* from Tamsin. I sat down at the kitchen table and pulled out the letter with excited hands.

> *February 16, 1861*
> *Dearest Sister,*
>
> *I do not know how to explain or where to begin. Suffice it to say that Deacon Mickelson intercepted your letters to Mama and me, and I did not learn of your whereabouts until much later. Your letters were retrieved from his home by Betsy—bless her—and my dear husband. Yes, Clarrie, I am now married to a wonderful man, and like you I am also a mother, a little boy born just two months after your sweet little Ellen. All of this I will tell you about later, but first I must impart the sad news that Mother has died. She passed away in the summer of 1858. Her last words were to call for Father. I take comfort in knowing they are together again in heaven.*

I paused in my reading to look over at my baby asleep in her cradle. Although my heart had known since Ellen's birth that Mama had died, reading the sad, confirming words in Tamsin's letter still brought sorrow. Gone, her lovely face never to smile again, the soft cadence of her voice forever stilled. But I knew her spirit lived. I had felt her angel presence when she came to me and Ellen that night. I had to write Tamsin and tell her of the sweet experience I'd shared with our mother, let her know I had no doubt that she still lived, only in a different state.

> *I didn't receive the letter you left for me—the one explaining your reason for marrying Jacob and asking for my forgiveness—until after Mama's death. Let your mind*

*be at rest, dear sister. You are forgiven and are as beloved
to me as you ever were. As for Amos Mickelson, I too
know of his lewdness, for I was forced to flee from him
just as you did. Sad to say, our dear mother knew of his
evil character as well. Can you believe the deacon made
improper advances even toward her?*

Sickness gathered in my heart. Sweet Tamsin and Mama both? I
stared at the shelf of crockery without seeing it, heard the voices of
my friends outside as if they weren't there. For a dreadful moment I
was back in the cottage with Amos Mickelson, felt the bite of his
hands on my arm, his fleshy face coming closer.

No! I jerked my mind from the ugly memory.

*After leaving Mickelboro, I was able to find employ-
ment as a housekeeper to a man by the name of Caleb
Tremayne. I was drawn to him at once, for in addition
to possessing good looks, he is also kind and intelligent
and good. I could fill pages in praise of him and still fail
to tell you all. Suffice it to say that I am much in love
with him and he with me. How I wish you could meet
him and see for yourself. Even better, if we could be
together to enjoy each other's company instead of being
separated by the miles and forced to rely on letters.*

*Although I was sorry to hear that Jacob has left you, I
do not have the feeling that you are unhappy at his
absence. Even so, I can't fail to worry about you out in all
that wilderness. God has indeed been gracious to you by
sending good friends like the O'Connors and Lieutenant
Reynolds to help you.*

*Your little Ellen sounds like an angel. As lovely as you
are, I'm certain she is every bit as beautiful as you say.
How I wish I could hold her and see her red curls. Like
you, I am enamored with motherhood. Little Jonathan is
almost five months old and has just cut his first tooth.
Mary and Sally, dear friends and servants, help me spoil
him, as does his father. Like Caleb, Jonathan has thick*

*black hair and the deepest of blue eyes. Tremayne eyes, I
like to call them.*

*What I tell you next, I must charge you never to
divulge to anyone else. It concerns the manner of Amos
Mickelson's death. His body was found washed up on the
beach, and it was given out that he died as the result of
an accident. Truth be told, he was killed while trying to
prevent me from helping a runaway slave get to a boat
and freedom. Though I had no part in the killing, I was
there and witnessed his death. Horrible as it was, I
cannot mourn his passing. I also sleep better knowing he
can no longer thwart unfortunate slaves or pose a threat
to any Yeagers.*

I stared down at my sister's neat handwriting. Could this be my
timid Tamsin, helping runaway slaves? My mind grappled with this
new image of my sister, one who was now capable and confident and
not afraid to take risks. I shook my head and smiled, realizing I was
not the only one changed by the passing of years. How I wished I
could see her and ply her with questions. Instead I had to content
myself with reading the rest of her letter.

*It was Susannah Partridge who forwarded your
letter to me. She got it from Lucy Ogelthorpe. After
Mother's death, when I was in need of friendship and
advice, I visited Susannah. We have kept in touch since
then.*

*Caleb and I live in a big farmhouse near the hamlet
of Glen Oaks, which is half a day's journey from
Bayberry. If you send letters to me there, I will get them.*

*I have also received letters from Harriet and Mary
Ellen. As you know they are living in the Great Salt Lake
Valley with a shared husband, one Edson Tipple. Though
I could have no liking for such an arrangement, they
both sound happy. Harriet has three children and Mary
Ellen has two. Catherine and her husband William are
living in Utah Territory too. Although I haven't yet heard*

from her, Harriet says they are well and that William is
working as a printer in the valley.

I do not know how much news of our country you
have received in Oregon. Things do not look promising.
After Abraham Lincoln's election as president in
November, South Carolina seceded from the Union. In
January, five more states followed. My heart trembles at
the thought of what might lie in the future. There is open
talk of war, especially now that the southern states have
formed their own confederacy. Slavery is at the bottom of
it, the practice of which my husband and I both find
abhorrent. Even so, I cannot like the thoughts of war,
especially when my dear husband might well be asked to
take up arms.

The final paragraph of the letter was taken up with expressions of happiness at hearing from me and a plea for me to write again as soon as I could. I smiled, thinking of all I would have to tell her—how Jacob's death had freed me to marry a man just as wonderful as her Caleb.

Almost as if Quinn had heard my thoughts, he knocked on the side of the open doorway. "I thought I'd give you some time alone to read your letter." Then in a quieter voice, "Is everything all right?"

"Yes, though Mother is dead."

Concern softened Quinn's features as he stepped into the kitchen. "Something you knew, though hearing of it in writing must cause you pain." He put his hand on my shoulder. "What of your sister Tamsin? Was there anything from her?"

"A long letter, one filled with much news I will share with you later." I got up and set the letter on the cupboard shelf and looped my arm through Quinn's. "Poor Sven hasn't been properly thanked, and Nathan will probably welcome something to eat."

A short time later everyone was gathered in the kitchen. Over cups of tea and slices of bread, Nathan kept Bridget and Shamus entertained with a tale of his adventure in a homemade boat while Quinn and Sven discussed their concern about civil war. The captain of the *Skylark* had brought several newspapers from the East. Like

Tamsin's letter, they were filled with news of the southern states seceding and threats of war.

"It can't be good," Quinn said. "Although I don't hold with slavery, I've seen firsthand the horrors of war. I'd hate to see it come to the people in this country."

Sven's face was solemn. "Even though it's thousands of miles away, I don't want war either."

No one said anything for a moment, the young people's spirits dampened by the news too. It wasn't until they were leaving that the conversation turned cheerful again.

"Has Quinn told you yet that I spoke to Captain Bergman about taking you to Astoria?"

I shook my head and gave Quinn a questioning look.

"You were up to your ears in your letter," Quinn protested.

"The captain said he'd be back sometime next month, and he promised to arrange his cargo so there'll be room for passengers." Sven put his foot into the stirrup and mounted his horse. "How many were you planning to take with you?"

"There'll be nine—ten counting the baby." Quinn put his arm around my shoulder. "If Captain Bergman can accommodate more, we'd like for you and Flora to go with us too."

Sven gave a slow smile. "Let me talk to Flora about it. Now that I have Nathan to do the milking, I might be able to arrange it."

The four of us stayed in the yard to wave them on their way, Quinn holding the baby and my red shawl wrapped around my shoulders to ward off the afternoon breeze. Although Bridget looked a little dejected as she waved to Nathan, I knew that like me, she was looking forward to May and the excitement of a boat trip to Astoria.

CHAPTER 18

Now that arrangements had been made with the captain of the *Skylark* to take us to Astoria, the need to sew new clothes loomed large in my mind. Bridget and I spent another day at the lodge where, after measuring and adjusting, the bolts of fabric were cut in preparation for sewing. Bridget and I brought the cut fabric for my blue dress and a petticoat back to the house to sew. Although Bridget's experience at sewing was limited, her stitches were accomplished enough to make the petticoat. The blue wedding dress would be mine to sew.

Thus it was that whenever we weren't cooking or cleaning or caring for the baby, the two of us gathered near the stove to work on the sewing. It was a pleasant time, the lamp lit for light on overcast days, Ellie playing on the floor. She had four teeth now and could crawl, her little face determined as she tried to reach the cloth ball I'd made for her out of scraps. I shared parts of Tamsin's letter with Bridget while we sewed.

"'Tis glad I am that we live so far that fightin' won't be comin' here," Bridget said after I read of Tamsin's fears concerning war. "I'll be saying a prayer for your sister and her husband. She'll be wantin' him kept safe, her just wed and lovin' him like she does."

I thought of this as we stitched, picturing Tamsin clasped in the arms of her dark-haired husband before she sent him off to war. Bridget wouldn't be the only one saying prayers on their behalf.

It was while we sewed that our conversation turned to Bridget and Nathan.

"You haven't said very much about him since he left," I observed.

Bridget's answer was to shrug and plunge her needle into the white fabric she was sewing.

"Didn't you enjoy seeing Nathan again?" I persisted.

"Yes . . . at least at first. But later . . ." She looked up from her sewing and frowned. "Somehow Nathan didn't seem as wonderful as I remembered him bein'. It was like he had changed . . . or maybe 'twas me." Her frown deepened. "'Tis just that since he left I find myself thinkin' more about all the new boys I'll be meetin' when we go for your wedding . . . wondering who they might be and if they'll be likin' me . . ."

"And you liking them?" I finished for her.

"Aye." She brightened and giggled. "Is it so terrible of me?"

"No. It's quite normal, in fact, and goes with being sixteen."

A pleased expression traveled over her pretty features. "Fiona was sayin' in her last letter that there's ever so many young men comin' to the Willamette Valley and that more than one has asked if she has a sister." She paused to study her stitches. "I'm thinkin' that for now I might just want to be friends with Nathan."

"I see."

Bridget smiled and gave me a mischievous glance. "Course that doesn't mean I've given up on someday havin' a kiss."

* * *

The following week Shamus asked if he could go fishing. Instead of the river, Shamus wanted to try his hand at one of the mountain streams. I wrapped slices of bread and cheese in a cloth for him, and he and Sam set off for the mountain.

The day was warm and sunny. After putting Ellen down for her nap, we took our sewing outside where the light was better. I'd finished the bodice and was working on one of the sleeves—long to the wrist and gathered at the shoulder—and Bridget was making progress on the petticoat. Unused to sewing, she often pricked her finger.

"I'm makin' an awful botch of this," she complained, sucking the tip of a freshly pricked finger. "'Tis the third time I've left blood on your new petticoat. I'm fearin' it won't be fit for wearin' by the time I get through."

"No one besides you and me will know about it," I assured her. "And every time I see it, I'll think of your love . . . little prints of your love."

Bridget threw me a grateful look, strands of red hair curling over her forehead as she concentrated on her next stitch.

Though still close enough to hear Ellen and reach her in just a few steps, we had taken our chairs to the sunny side of the yard, the side that faced the mountain instead of the river. The alders had leafed out, their leaves a tender spring green, and the rhododendrons would soon be blooming. The air was balmy, and black-crowned sparrows chirped merrily as they hopped from branch to branch.

The clink of a bridle jerked my head away from my sewing. My heart jerked too when I saw two men on horseback. Recognition collided with fear at the sight of Jacob's partners.

"Looks like we've found ourselves a sewing bee," the heavyset one said. Dewey, I thought his name was.

I got to my feet and set down my sewing, aware that my hands were suddenly moist and that my heart still jumped unnaturally. I tried to keep my voice steady. "Is there something I can do for you?"

"Did you hear that, Dewey?" the thinner one said. "The little lady wants to know if there's something she can do for us." There was a leer in his eyes, a brute hunger in his voice, one that made me want to turn and run. I edged closer to the house and the door that would take me to Quinn's revolver.

"Actually we were hoping you could help us." This came from Dewey, who shot his cousin a reproving glance. "Your husband gave me and Bert a map to a buried treasure . . . said that years ago a Spanish ship sunk up this way. Some of the sailors got ashore with part of the gold they was carrying." He paused and gave me a calculating look. "Did your husband ever tell you about it . . . that Indians killed the sailors and moved the gold to a secret place on Neahkahnie Mountain?"

"I've heard of it," I said evenly, "but I've never seen the map. I'm afraid I can't help you."

"Jake said some old geezer what used to live with the Indians gave him the map," Bert put in. He raised a jug to his mouth and took a deep swallow.

I knew that Jacob had lied. He'd heard the story from Sven at worship meeting, and there hadn't been a map, unless Jacob had drawn a fake one. "I'm afraid I can't help you," I repeated.

Dewey went on just as if he hadn't heard me. "Jake and us made a deal—the map for a gold nugget we found when we was pannin' gold on the Yuba River. Trouble is, we've looked all over Neahkahnie Mountain, and we ain't found no treasure. We're startin' to think maybe your husband tricked us. Are you sure you don't know nothing about a map?" Dewey's features had tightened and his brown eyes had turned cold.

"I'm sure." As I spoke I moved a step closer to the house, my mind on Ellen asleep in her cradle, on the gun hidden behind the coffee tin.

Bridget had gotten to her feet and was looking at me for reassurance. I sensed she was remembering that Quinn had said he wouldn't like to meet up with these men alone. And we were alone. So very alone.

"Since you ain't never seen the map, would you like to have a look at it?" Bert drawled. This earned him a sharp look from Dewey, but he ignored it, his voice smooth as lard, his narrow gray eyes traveling over Bridget, then flitting back to me. "That's a right pretty friend you got there . . . and you're right nice on the eyes too." He nodded and grinned, showing tobacco-stained teeth. "What do you think, Dewey? If'n these pretty ladies was to be nice and friendly, might'en we let them have a look at our map?"

Dewey's bearded lips pulled into a smirk. "I think maybe that could be arranged." He shifted his weight as if to dismount.

"Stop right there." The force of my voice surprised me. I was further surprised when Dewey stopped. "We're expecting company. I don't think they'll like it if they thought you'd stayed long enough to get off your horses."

Breath held, I waited, aware of the pounding of my heart.

A sneer replaced Bert's grin. "You talk mighty big for a woman who lives alone. Besides, we saw the boy take off fishin'. As for helpful neighbors, we ain't seen no sign of such in the two days we've been watchin' your place. No one's come near except for a crippled fellow."

Watching. They'd been watching and spying. I'd edged closer to the house, but was still several steps from the door. I threw a quick glance at Bridget, saw her white face and her eyes darting around like a scared kitten not knowing which way to run.

Dewey and Bert dismounted from their horses. There was an ugly look on their faces, one of men bent on doing evil—mean and unkempt and dirty. Dewey was closer to the door than Bert, who was busy looking at Bridget, the jug of liquor in his hand.

"Run!" I screamed and launched myself toward the door, my feet churning over the grass, head bent on purpose. *If I can outrun Dewey . . .* My feet found the step and my hand grasped for the doorknob. I heard Dewey's heavy steps behind me followed by Bridget's scream. Not daring to look, my fingers clawed for the knob and turned it. I stumbled through the door, knew Dewey was but a step behind, felt the thud of his body hit the door after I threw it shut. Heart pounding, I slid the bolt through the hasp, my fingers shaking in an uneven rhythm like my heart. I felt the thud as he threw his weight against the door the second time. *Help! Oh, help!*

I was glad Jacob had insisted on a sturdy door, even more glad Quinn had reinforced the bolt. But would it hold?

A terrified cry from Bridget sent me to the cupboard. I felt along the shelf behind the coffee tin for the revolver, pulled opened the drawer for the bullets, not wanting to think what Bert might be trying to do to her. Dewey, too, for he'd ceased to pound on the door.

A tiny sound from Ellen's cradle reminded me of my sweet baby. I glanced at her, letting out caught breath when I saw she had only stirred.

I quickly loaded the revolver, putting the five bullets into the chamber and closing the breech. While I did, I glanced out the window. Bert had hold of Bridget and was kissing her, Dewey waiting his turn. Although Bridget struggled and fought, she was no match for the bigger man. She was crying, and one of the sleeves of her russet dress had been torn to reveal the milky whiteness of a shoulder. As I was putting the last cartridge into the chamber, I saw Bridget bite Bert's hand, heard him cry out, then slap her and throw her to the ground. Bridget, who'd longed for her first kiss. *But not like this. Never like this.*

Anger and cold determination sent me to the door. The gun and I were all that stood between Bridget and the men. This was why Quinn had taught me to use it. I pulled open the door with the gun pointed at the men. Bert and Bridget were struggling on the grass, the skirt of her dress pushed up above her knees while Dewey stood over them with a ribald grin on his unshaven face.

"Stop it!" I yelled. "Let her go or I'll shoot!"

Startled silence followed my words.

"I mean it," I yelled.

Bert laughed and got to his feet, pulling Bridget up with him. "Look at that, Dewey. The little lady thinks she's going to shoot me." He gave another laugh, one that was mean and ugly. "Bet she's never held a gun and knows even less about shooting it."

Bert's hat had fallen off and lay on the grass a few feet from Dewey. I took aim and fired. The force of the bullet sent the hat skipping over the ground, and its loud report spooked their two horses.

"Be glad you weren't wearing your hat," I said.

Bert threw a quick look at Dewey, his expression less sure. Dewey's face had lost its ribald grin and he was scowling like he thought this wasn't the way the game was supposed to end.

"Let her go," I repeated. The knowledge that Ellie and Bridget were depending on me put firmness to my voice and kept my hands steady.

Dewey cast a quick look at the mountain as if he feared someone had heard the gunshot. "Let her go," he said to Bert.

Cursing, Bert shoved Bridget away from him. "You ain't seen the last of us," he growled. He bent and picked up his hat, the look he gave me malevolent. "Your husband cheated us out of our gold nugget. We mean to get satisfaction one way or the other." When he stuck his finger through the bullet hole in the crown of his hat, he gave me another hateful glance. "We'll be back," he promised.

The vehemence in his eyes made my mouth go dry, their grayness narrowing as his lips pulled back into an ugly sneer.

Sheer will kept the gun aimed at the men. The sight of Bridget lying in a heap where Bert had shoved her strengthened my resolve— that and the frightened cries of my baby.

I wouldn't let myself think of Bridget and Ellie—couldn't if I wanted to keep the gun pointed at the retreating men. What if they changed their minds and tried to rush at me? *Steady, steady,* a voice seemed to whisper.

The horses were well on their way to the river. Dewey went at a walk after them, but Bert kept looking back, like if he could have his way, he'd still be enjoying himself with Bridget.

Out of the corner of my eye I saw her get to her feet and run toward me, almost tripping in her haste to reach the door. I motioned her behind me, my ears hearing her sob-torn breathing while my eyes kept the two men clearly in my sight—Dewey's dirty tan jacket an easier target than Bert's dark one.

We backed through the door and into the safety of the kitchen. "It's all right," I whispered to Bridget. "We're going to be all right." I started to push the door closed, but changed my mind. I didn't want to be trapped inside if the men decided to come back. Hurriedly putting the gun on the table, I ran to Ellen's cradle. Her piercing screech filled the room as I snatched her up and cradled her head into my shoulder. "It's all right, baby. Mommy's here." Her little arms wrapped themselves tight around my neck, her cry still shrill and high. My slender hold on control was all that kept me from sinking onto the padded seat of the rocking chair. Instead, I comforted Ellen and turned to Bridget. She was close to hysterics, trembling and gasping hard. My heart ached at the sight of the reddened, swelling of the eye Bert had slapped, at the trickle of blood coming from a cut on her lip. "We're going to be all right. Do you hear me, Bridget? We'll be fine."

For a second she acted as if she hadn't heard, her eyes fear-glazed and frantic, her breathing coming in shuddering gasps. "What to do . . . the men . . ." She wiped at her lips with her hand. When she pulled it away and saw blood, she let out a whimpering cry.

"The men are gone." Still quieting the baby I pulled Bridget close. I could feel the rapid beat of her heart, heard the rasp of choked tears. "You've got to be strong, Bridget. I need your help while I quiet Ellie."

My words and the baby's cries pushed through the panic. I felt her take a deep breath, saw a trembling nod.

"Good. Try to be calm. You can do it." I turned my efforts to quieting Ellie, rocking her and snuggling her close. "Shhh, Mommy's here. No one will hurt you," I crooned.

It took a bit before Ellen quieted, even longer before I could get her to loosen her grip around my neck. "That's better. See, sweetheart. Mommy's here."

I meant the words for Bridget too and held her gaze over the baby's tear-damp curls. "Are you able to walk to the lodge?"

She sniffed and nodded, the corner of her apron serving as a handkerchief.

"Good. Let's go."

I snatched Ellie's yellow shawl and an extra diaper from the cradle and hurried toward the door. Bridget came like a silent shadow behind me, her breathing still gasping and uneven. When I saw the revolver lying on the table, I hesitated. Caution bade me pick it up and take it with me, but mother's instinct worried about carrying a loaded gun and Ellen too. *Leave it*, something whispered. I obeyed without thought and thrust it back in its hiding place in the cupboard.

I feared Bert and Dewey might have given up chasing their horses and would come back. But when we got outside I saw that they were still slogging after them, the horses ahead and almost to the ford. Seeing that their attention was firmly focused on the horses, I grabbed Bridget's hand and hurried around the house to the path leading to the lodge.

I remember little about our climb up the mountain, only the need to hurry—me carrying Ellen, both of us needing the closeness, and Bridget crying softly and following.

Halfway up the mountain we met Shamus and Sam coming at a run down the trail, feet and paws slipping on the uneven surface, Shamus's fishing pole clutched in one hand.

"I heard a gun," he panted. "What happened?"

"Jacob's partners came back."

Shamus's gaze moved past me to his sister. His eyes widened at the sight of her torn dress and swollen face. "What—?"

I shot him a quick look and shook my head

Comprehension settled over his freckled features. "Right," he whispered. With his eyes still on Bridget, he edged past me and offered her his skinny arm. " 'Twill make the walkin' easier," I heard him say.

The rush of the nearby stream and an occasional birdsong replaced conversation as we climbed the trail. Although Ellen no longer cried aloud, little shudders still came from time to time. "See the birdie? See the pretty flowers?" I asked. In time her hold on me loosened. "Sweet Ellie," I whispered. "Mama loves you."

The sound of hurrying hooves on the trail above made me stop.

"I'm bettin' 'tis the Lieutenant who heard the gunshot same as me," Shamus said.

His words proved correct, though two horses emerged from the trees instead of one, Mick riding just behind Quinn.

"Clarissa . . ." Fear clung to Quinn's voice. "Are you all right?" He was off the horse before he stopped speaking, his eyes looking searchingly at me and Ellie as his arms went around us both.

"Jacob's partners came back. They . . ." Emotion closed my throat and I leaned my head into his shoulder, telling myself to be strong. For Quinn's sake. For Ellen's.

"Da!" Bridget's voice was shrill and edged with hysteria as she threw herself into her father's arms. "The man kept kissing me. I tried to get away. Oh, Da." Loud sobs contorted her slender body.

"Easy, girl. Easy," Mick soothed. While he rocked and held her, he took in the damage to her face and dress. "What did he do?" Mick's clipped words were directed at me, not Bridget.

"Kissed her and roughed her up. Then—"

"He . . . he threw me down," Bridget's shaking voice cut in, "and was tryin' to get on top of me, but Clarissa got the gun—"

"Did he?"

"No." Both of us answered, me aloud and Bridget shaking her head.

Mick cursed and scowled over his daughter's shoulder. "Where is he? Where'd the bloody scoundrel go?"

"They're chasing their horses."

Mick loosened himself from Bridget's grasp. "Go to your mam. You'll be safe with her." Then his gaze was back on me. "Where?" he repeated. "Which way did their horses go?"

"The river."

Three quick steps took Mick to his horse. Before anyone could speak, he was mounted and urging it down the trail. "I'll see that he pays for this," he snarled. His eyes were hard like his voice. "He'll be wishin' he was dead by the time I get through."

Quinn's face was grim as he lifted my face and kissed me. "I'd better go with Mick," he said. "When Mick explodes, there's no stopping him." He pulled me to him. "Are you sure you'll be all right?"

Seeing me nod, he laid a gentle finger on the baby's tear-stained cheek. "I'll be back, Ellie. Daddy will be right back."

I saw the rifle in the scabbard when he mounted Midnight, remembered the revolvers strapped to Mick's waist. *Don't kill them,* I wanted to say, but had no chance as Quinn gave Shamus the charge to see us safely up to the lodge.

"Patrick and Maggie are there. They'll look after you," he called over his shoulder.

A glance at Bridget's pinched face told me she needed a big dose of mothering right now. If the truth be told, so did I.

Patrick was coming out of the woodshed when we entered the clearing. He dropped the wood and came to meet us as Maggie hurried out of the lodge.

Bridget brushed past me and ran to her mother. "Oh Mam, the men tried . . . it was terrible." Tears choked off the words before she could finish.

As I watched Maggie's arms enfold her daughter, I wished Quinn were still with me and Ellen. Wished, too, that the morning had been a dream—a terrible nightmare of uncouth, evil men that would vanish when I opened my eyes.

* * *

After explanations were given, Maggie hurried Bridget into the house. The rest of us lingered in the yard where hemlocks cast long shadows onto the grass. Deirdre, who'd been strangely quiet since we arrived, moved to stand by me, tucking a strand of dark hair back into its pin as she looked at me with concern.

"Are you goin' to be all right?" At my nod she crossed herself and went on. "'Tis what every woman fears—men turnin' cruel and wantin' what isn't theirs to take." Her voice held a tone I'd never heard her use before, one both fierce and angry. "'Tis glad I am you had a gun and wasn't afraid to be usin' it. Glad, too, that Bridget suffered no more than she did."

"I worry about her," I sighed.

"Aye. The poor dear will be needin' to stay close to her mam for a few days."

I thought about this as Deirdre and I turned to go back into the house, remembering the degradation I'd felt after Amos Mickelson's unwanted kisses. Along with her mother's reassurance, Bridget would need reassurance from the rest of us too.

Eileen joined us by the door. Although her pregnancy was now evident, she moved with a quick step. "'Tis the waitin' that will be hard," She said, referring to her absent protectors. She paused and crossed herself. "Patrick says Mick has the devil's own temper. What do you think they'll be doin' to those men when they find them?"

I shook my head, my mind too caught up in the present to have given thought to this. "I don't think Quinn will let things get out of hand." Despite my confidence, there was concern. I'd seen the meanness in Bert's face, the flat coldness reflected in Dewey's murky brown eyes.

Maggie's thoughts must have been traveling along similar trails, for when we entered the kitchen, she looked at me and spoke. "Mick and the Lieutenant know how to take care of themselves." She paused and crossed herself. "Still and all, an extra prayer or two wouldn't be hurtin'." She pulled me close, patting me and kissing me on the cheek. Her look when she finished was long and searching, one that asked if Ellie and I were all right and that she was sorrier than words could say about what had happened.

Exhausted from crying, Ellen had fallen asleep in my arms, her long lashes soft against her cheeks, her face peaceful despite the tearstains.

"Poor mite," Maggie whispered and kissed her. She looked at Deirdre. "Would you ask Shamus to bring the big washtub into the kitchen? I'm thinking Bridget will feel better if she can have a warm bath and wash her hair."

"I'll get it myself," Deirdre said.

While Maggie and Deirdre heated kettles of water and prepared a bath for Bridget, Eileen helped me settle the baby onto a quilt in the corner of the sitting room.

"I'm thinkin' to put you and Bridget in her room for the night," Maggie went on, nodding at me. She gave me a significant look too, one that said she didn't want Bridget to be left alone for the next few hours.

Conscious of Bridget's need for privacy, the rest of us found things to do in other rooms—the sitting room straightened, Ellen, who'd wakened, changed and fed. Eileen and Deirdre made much of her, the baby's smiles and happy prattle like a breath of fresh air blown into worry-dampened minds.

After Bridget had finished her bath, she and Maggie joined us in the sitting room. Eileen had made a fresh fire in the gray-stone fireplace, and the baby was playing on a quilt on the floor. It was a scene that should have prompted warmth, the pale afternoon sun slanting in the window, the fire making a merry crackle, five women sitting close and talking. Instead, an underlying tension and concern for Bridget ate at the warmth, and none of us knew quite what to say.

There were snippets of small talk—remarks about Ellen's unique form of crawling, hope for more sunny weather—but the bulk of our attention was taken up with Maggie and Bridget. It was as if Bridget had turned into a little girl again and Maggie her doting mother. I watched Maggie dry Bridget's hair and gently untangle the long tresses with her fingers, followed by the comb.

Bridget sat on the floor at Maggie's knees, the firelight painting roses onto her pale cheeks, her lips unsmiling and her eyes almost closed. I wondered what she was thinking. Was her mind still trapped in those awful moments when Bert had forced tobacco-stained lips onto hers, bruising and cutting while his fingers tore at the bodice of her dress? Or had she let her mind travel back to a safer time when she'd sat, like today, at her mother's knees?

Maggie's voice broke into my thoughts. "I don't like it that you're not talkin'," she said to Bridget. " 'Tisn't good for a body to close in on itself like you're doin'."

Bridget's only answer was a slight shake of her head.

Maggie's sad eyes met mine, and for a moment it was as if she sought my help, though what she wanted, I didn't know. She continued to comb Bridget's long hair, the room silent except for Ellie's soft prattle. There was a pensive look on Maggie's face.

"Do you remember the time you got that big sliver in your finger, how it was for painin' you and makin' you cry?"

Bridget nodded.

"And do you recall the fight you put up when I told you I must take a needle to get it out so it wouldn't fester?"

Bridget nodded again.

"What happened to you today is like gettin' another sliver." Maggie paused as if she sought a higher power, and when she went on, her voice was stronger. "I'm thinkin' that unless you talk about this, 'twill turn putrid inside you, just like a sliver—throbbin' and angry . . . perhaps makin' you sick."

There was another pause, the comb stilling and Maggie's fingers stroking her daughter's damp hair. "'Tis better to say what you're seein' and thinkin' instead of lettin' it stay trapped inside your poor mind. There's just women here, women who love you, whose hearts are hurtin' too."

This last brought tears to my eyes. "Bert and the sliver were dirty, but you're still clean, Bridget." I swallowed and went on in a stronger voice. "Just the same, I wish it had been me, not you the men caught."

"No, oh no," she whispered. "Not your pretty lips . . ."

Then it came pouring out, Bridget's voice so low I had to strain to hear it, her body trembling as she described Bert's meanness, the stench of his breath, how he'd tried to touch her where he shouldn't, his bawdy laugh when she'd tried to fend him off.

My tears joined hers as she spoke, her pretty face in pain and distorted, staring into the fire as if the flames were conjuring up more hateful pictures.

Her words drew me back to the cabin where my own fear had coiled like a snake and sent me to load the revolver. Thank heaven I'd gotten the gun before worse things had happened.

Quiet replaced Bridget's torn words when she finished. Love mingled through the room as all of us silently cried, Deirdre wiping her damp cheek with her fingers and Maggie shaking her head and looking lost.

"The same thing happened to me when I was your age." I couldn't believe it was me speaking, my voice low like Bridget's—

trembling too. "Remember when I told you I married Jacob to escape from a terrible man?"

Bridget nodded and lifted her head.

"The same thing happened," I repeated. The years of suppressed shame rose like a putrid sore drawn out by a warm poultice, words when they were strung together describing Amos Mickelson's fleshy body, his strength as he'd crushed me to him, the bruising of his lips as he'd torn at my bodice. "I know what it's like," I finished, my voice as low as when I'd begun.

All the women were crying again, especially Deirdre. She was the first to move or speak, dropping to her knees beside Bridget and taking her hands in hers.

"Like Clarissa said, sometimes things with men happen. But don't you be blamin' your sweet self or keepin' the shame inside to grow into something uglier." Deirdre shot a quick look at me. "Instead, be thankin' God Clarissa had a gun and wasn't afraid to be usin' it." She paused and swallowed. "Some women aren't so lucky."

"At least you left your teeth marks on the dirty skunk." Maggie's voice held laughter, but her eyes were fierce. "I'm glad you bit him."

"Aye." Eileen's laughter bespoke a grim satisfaction, one echoed in Deirdre's giggle.

A peaceful silence settled over the room to replace the terrible word pictures, our bodies and hearts united by a bond so strong it made us one.

* * *

By suppertime things were almost normal. Although there was a more subdued tone to the banter, Bridget spoke and smiled in a semblance of her old self, and Patrick was quick with his stories. Seeing that I was slower than usual to smile, he added, "Now don't you be troubling yourself about the Lieutenant. If there's a man that knows how to take care of himself, 'tis he."

I knew this was true, but worry about what would happen when Quinn and Mick caught up with the men still occupied my thoughts.

Everyone made a play at pretending that things were normal. Shamus and Deirdre both sang and Patrick treated us to a lively tune on the fiddle. Even so, I noted that he made a careful check of the doors before he and Eileen and Deirdre left for their home, and I heard him call for the wolfhounds as they crossed the yard.

When Bridget and I were getting ready for bed, a knock sounded on the bedroom door. I opened it a crack and saw Shamus standing outside with his hand resting on Sam's head.

"Just so you'll be knowin', me and Sam will be keepin' watch from the kitchen tonight. That way you can sleep without worryin'."

I wanted to tell him to go to bed, that nothing was going to happen, but something in the boy's expression—eagerness and the need to protect and be important—stopped me. "Thank you, Shamus." I pushed at the dog trying to ease his way into the bedroom. "We'll sleep better knowing you and Sam are keeping watch."

Shamus nodded and gave a cheeky grin, one very much like his father's. "There's ways to protect without havin' a gun."

I smiled as I watched Shamus and Sam make their way to the kitchen, his walk almost a swagger, the dog padding softly at his side. I was still smiling when I closed the door.

"It sounds like there's those that are plannin' to keep us safe," Bridget giggled. Although her laugh was low and indulgent, I knew Shamus's words had touched her.

Ellen had fallen asleep again, and I'd put her to bed on a mattress of quilts on the floor. As I bent to blow out the lamp, I saw Bridget kneel in front of an icon of the Virgin Mary that hung on the wall. Seeing her, I knelt by the bed and said a prayer of my own, one of thanksgiving that we'd come through the day without serious harm—a petition, too, to watch over Quinn and Mick.

Bridget was in bed by the time I finished, her body a shadowy outline under the quilt, moonlight coming through the window. I doubted she was asleep, doubted even more that her rest that night would be easy. Even with the peace that had come from talking, there would still be unpleasant thoughts and pictures. Ones I might not be immune to myself.

I tried to set my mind on pleasant things, but worry scraped at the corners of my thoughts. Had Quinn and Mick caught up with Jacob's partners or had they bivouacked in a grove of trees somewhere? "Please, keep them safe," I prayed. "And don't let them do anything rash."

Bridget's soft voice interrupted my thoughts. "Did that man truly force you to kiss him, or did you make it up so I wouldn't be feelin' so bad?"

"It happened just like I told you, though I no more kissed the deacon than you kissed Bert." I paused, knowing she was listening closely. "What happened today doesn't count as a first kiss, Bridget. And when that first kiss finally comes from someone you love, I promise it will be every bit as nice as you imagined it. Even nicer."

"Truly?"

"Truly."

"Was that how it was with you and the Lieutenant? Like a first kiss?"

I smiled into the darkness, remembering how it had felt, the wonder and softness, a first kiss and so much more. "What do you think, you cheeky girl?"

"I think it was." Although I couldn't see Bridget, I knew that she was smiling, and that part of her had turned from Bert and Dewey and was looking straight ahead at hope.

Remembering Quinn's kiss helped me too, setting my mind on love-brightened paths—how he looked when he smiled, his gentle touch. Did I love him? All that the word implied and more, and just as fiercely and completely as I loved Ellen.

"You're very right," I whispered. I turned onto my side and positioned my head on the pillow so I could look down at my baby as she slept by the bed, moonlight casting a pale sheen on her little face. My gaze took in her soft curls, curls she would likely complain about when she was older, but ones I loved, just as I loved her tiny upturned nose, perfect ears, and the pattern of dark lashes above rounded cheeks.

The sight of her made my heart tighten with love, then expand to fill me with warmth and peace. I held the warmth close until I was able to relax enough to fall asleep.

CHAPTER 19

After a restless night I arose early, my mind consumed with Quinn and Mick. Had they caught up with Jacob's partners and put the fear of God into them? How soon would they be back?

When I'd finished breakfast, I told Maggie I was going down to the cabin. "Just long enough to get a few things," I said when Maggie's mouth opened to protest. "Diapers for Ellie. A change of clothes for the rest of us."

Maggie nodded. "I suppose it won't be hurtin' anything. Shamus left a while ago to see to the cows and chickens. He can help you carry things back."

I took Ellen with me. After the fright of the day before, she was still clingy and didn't want me out of her sight. I planned to put her in her cradleboard for the trip back so my arms would be free for carrying.

It was another bright day, one of sunshine and warmth and the song of birds. Halfway down to the cabin, we met Shamus bringing the cow and her heifer up to the lodge. Sam followed, nipping at the cows' heels.

"I'm thinkin' the Lieutenant will be wantin' you to live at the lodge until you marry. Leastwise, that's what I'd be doin' if I was in charge."

I agreed, though I was hard-pressed not to smile, thanking him instead for taking the responsibility of seeing to the cows and telling him I'd be back as soon as I got a few clothes.

A rueful look crossed his freckled face. "I should have been thinkin' to do that."

"You've done enough just by getting the cows. I only need a few clothes. We can go for the rest later."

Hoping Quinn and Mick were on their way home by now, I kept my eyes open for them. Ellen was more her old self, cooing at the moving leaves and squealing a response to a scolding jay. By the time we reached the cabin, she had fallen asleep.

The cabin showed signs of the haste with which we'd left it, the door not closed tight, and the sheet in the cradle rumpled from where Ellen had cried. But the rocking chair looked just as if it waited for me. Tired from the long walk I sat down and relaxed to the chair's soothing rhythm. Nostalgia washed over me as I looked at the familiar arrangement of plates and crockery in the cupboard. I remembered the pride I'd felt in my new home, my excitement when Jacob had returned from Oregon City with the stove and oak cupboard. This was probably the last time I'd sit in the kitchen and rock Ellen. The last time I would consider it my home.

I smiled down at my baby, my heart gathering warmth as I took in her beauty—the flawless white skin and pink parted lips, her dimpled hand resting next to her cheek. I gently brushed a damp curl away from her face. Who would have thought Jacob's hair color and my natural curls would combine into something so perfect?

"I love you, Ellie." Her little mouth twitched at the sound of my whisper, but she didn't rouse when I wrapped her in my red shawl and laid her in her cradle, her beauty and innocence like a balm to soothe away the fear of the day before.

I caught a glimpse of my partially completed blue dress and the white petticoat lying like grim reminders in the yard. I went to get them, pleased to see that except for a stain on the petticoat, they didn't seem to have suffered any harm.

I laid them on the table, humming softly and thinking about Quinn. A sudden unease made me stop. It was no more than a twinge, a quick need to look over my shoulder. I brushed it aside, telling myself I was being silly. Even so, I threw a glance at the cupboard to assure myself the revolver was where I'd left it. A stealthy noise from the bedroom made my heart jerk.

"Hello, Clarrie."

I whirled around and my breath caught in my throat at the sight of the lank auburn hair and unshaven face, a dirty hat held in one hand. My mind screamed out *Jacob!* while my heart fought against the thought. *No . . . please! Jacob is dead!*

"Aren't you going to say hello?" Jacob asked, for it was Jacob, not a ghost—my husband alive instead of dead.

I felt the breath leave my lungs, heard my cry of dismay. My mind couldn't think right and inside my heart was still screaming, *No . . . No!* while it urged me to run where there was no Jacob—just me and Quinn and my baby.

"You weren't here when I came, so I tried to catch a few winks." A pause and that irritating smile. "What's the matter? Cat got your tongue?"

I nodded, my shock such that I could only stare at the gaunt-faced man with scruffy clothes and eyes that looked at me in a mean fashion. "Jacob?" My question came out low and trembling.

"The same." He gave a mirthless laugh and rubbed his unshaven jaw.

We took measure of each other, me in my pink dress and white apron, my lungs breathing quick—Jacob staring and with a tightness to his unshaven face. I could feel myself starting to shake deep inside, but I wouldn't let it surface.

"They told me you . . . you were dead," I managed to get out.

"Well, they were wrong, weren't they?" There was meanness in his voice, in his eyes too—a meanness that hadn't been there when he'd left for California. "The dirty louts left me for dead and ran off with my map." He paused, his eyes narrow and mean. "I heard all about it from Eli Haycock from across the river, how my cheatin' partners was good enough to come and tell you I was dead." Another pause as his mouth pulled into a grimace. "He told me too how you was fixin' to marry the Brit and move up to his fancy house." He gave another mirthless chuckle. " 'Course none of that's going to happen now, is it, Clarissa . . . cause you already have yourself a husband . . . don't you?"

I wouldn't give him the satisfaction of an answer, indeed, it was all I could do just to keep my mouth from trembling.

Although Jacob was shorter and of a smaller build than Quinn, he still took up most of the bedroom doorway. He moved into the kitchen, his booted feet clunking so hard on the pine floor they made Ellen start and cry out.

I hurried to the cradle and soothed her with my hand. "Mama's here, Ellie." Hearing me, she quieted and rolled onto her tummy, her eyes slowly closing.

"Eli told me about the baby." Jacob crossed to the cradle. "Will you look at that?" he said in a softer voice. "Red hair just like her papa."

"Please don't wake her."

Jacob gave me a look that said he'd do what he darn well pleased. "Too bad she ain't a boy. Girls are more trouble than they're worth and no help a'tall to a man . . . except for cooking and such. Speaking of which, you need to get busy and fix me something to eat. I'm starving."

I wanted to tell him to fix it himself, but thought better of it with him standing so close. The stench of his unwashed body made me glad to step away. How could I go back to being Jacob's wife? Dear heaven, how could I bear it? Just as quickly, I knew I couldn't. Wouldn't!

I moved to the cupboard, my mind on Quinn's loaded revolver behind the coffee tin instead of on cooking. "Let me see what there is."

"Just make sure it's good. I haven't had a decent meal since I left Oregon City." There was an edge to his voice, one that matched his restless brown eyes that were busy taking stock of the room's furnishings.

Turning so my skirt hid the coffee tin, I quickly slipped the revolver into the pocket of my apron. The gun's weight dragged at the apron and its size was such that the handle protruded several inches above the pocket. Not daring to turn, I took a plate down from the shelf. "It will take a few minutes to fix it."

"I'm in no hurry."

His sudden change made me turn my head to look. What I saw made my heart jump, then plunge. I knew that look . . . recognized his hunger.

"Havin' a baby didn't hurt your looks none." Jacob smiled as his eyes made a lazy survey of my person. "No indeed." His smile widened in appreciation. "I'd almost forgotten how pretty you are . . . pretty enough to make a man forget all about eatin'." He stepped toward me and his voice came low. "I haven't had a woman in weeks."

Heart pounding, my fingers closed around the handle of the revolver, pulled it free of the pocket, and aimed it at Jacob. "Don't come any closer."

Jacob's eyes widened and his smile turned stale. "What's this?" he asked, attempting a laugh.

"A gun. The same one I used on your partners when they tried the same thing you're thinking."

"Come on, Clarrie. I'm your husband."

"How can you call yourself a husband?" Bitterness climbed into my voice and made it hard. "Deserting me and leaving me to fend for myself, taking all the money, selling the horse and wagon." Anger kept my arm steady and my finger curled around the trigger of the gun. "For all you cared, I could have starved."

"Naw, you wouldn't. I knew Sven and Flora would look after you." He attempted another smile. "Now put that thing away before you hurt someone."

I shook my head. "I'm not taking you back, so you'd just as well get on your horse and try to find that treasure." I lifted the revolver an inch. "Quinn Reynolds taught me how to shoot, and I'm not afraid to use it if I have to."

His smile changed to a sneer. "We'll see what the law has to say about this. Remember my name's on the deed to this homestead the same as yours is."

"Is that why you came back? So you could get your hands on the homestead?"

Jacob shrugged. "It seemed as good as stayin' in California. Besides there might be somethin' to that story about the treasure."

I motioned to the door with the gun. "Get out, Jacob." My voice was as cold as his eyes.

Jacob shot me a hateful look, then turned and snatched Ellen out of her cradle. "I got me a better idea, one that says I ain't leavin' alone."

"No . . . Jacob."

"Yes . . ." Triumph sounded in his voice.

My eyes took in Ellen wrapped in my red shawl, saw her sweet little face screwed up and about to cry as Jacob clutched her in front of him. "Put her down," I ordered. It took all I had to hold the gun steady and keep the panic out of my voice.

"Don't believe I will, Clarissa. Leastwise not unless you're willing to make it worth my while." He paused and his voice changed to a chortle. "How much is she worth to you? Fifty gold eagles? A hundred?"

Ellen was into a full cry, her arms reaching out for me, one leg hanging out of the shawl, her eyes asking why I didn't take her. "You know I don't have any money."

"But the crazy Brit does. Since you're so all-fired fond of him, he ought to be willin' to pay a right good price to get her back." Jacob eased toward the door. "On second thought, let's make that two hundred. Two hundred eagles in exchange for the baby."

"Jacob!" I stepped toward him, the gun still at the ready.

"You try shootin' at me, and I'll guarantee you'll hit the baby," Jacob said, still easing toward the door.

My mind went frantic. "Please Jacob, don't take her."

His answer was a hollow laugh as he slowly backed through the door.

"You can have anything you want. Me. The farm. Just give me Ellen."

"Ellen? Is that what you named her? After your sick, crazy mother?" He paused for breath. "Two hundred gold eagles is what I'm askin'. That'll buy me all the women I want—women more willin' than you."

By now Jacob was crossing the yard to the barn where he'd left his horse, me but a few steps behind him, Ellen's cry turning shrill when I failed to take her.

"Please, Jacob."

Jacob's unshaven face stretched into a grin above Ellen's auburn curls. "Sorry, Clarissa. You can't have her unless you come up with the money."

When he mounted his horse, I dropped the gun into my pocket and grabbed his leg, pulling in a frantic effort to stop him. "Don't take her," I cried, my voice as frantic as my hands.

Jacob's booted foot caught me in the stomach and sent me hard to the ground. For a second I couldn't breathe, my mouth agape and struggling for air as I took in the red shawl hanging against his filthy clothes, Ellen's arms and legs kicking and flailing, her cries so wild they drowned out Jacob's taunting laugh.

"Shut up!" The words were directed at Ellen, his distaste for her piercing cries and writhing body tightening his face into an ugly scowl.

I scrambled to my feet and lunged for the stirrup as he wheeled the horse and urged it away from me.

"Stop, please, stop!" I screamed. Then I was running after them, my feet churning at the grass, the gun retrieved from my pocket, and me, no matter how hard I ran, unable to keep up. "Ellie . . . Ellie!"

Her name came out in a gasping sob, and then my mouth tightened in grim determination. Twice my pink skirt tangled around my legs so that I tripped and almost fell. Each time I looked ahead, Jacob and the horse and the red shawl were smaller. *Stop . . . please stop.*

My mind was a jumble of erratic thoughts, gasping for purpose just as my lungs gasped for air and my legs for balance. "Please, God. Help me."

As the prayer formed, I pitched onto the grass with such force the gun went off. I flinched as the explosion of sound jarred my senses and made me cry out in a grated sob of surprise. For a second, I could only lay there—stunned, hurting and utterly exhausted—until thoughts of Ellen jumped into my mind. What if I'd shot her? Dear heaven, had I hurt my baby?

I pushed up onto my knees and saw that Jacob had reined in the sorrel gelding, he and the red shawl but a distant outline against the dark green of the mountain. When he saw me move, he lifted a hand in a taunting salute and set the horse into a canter that took him farther away.

I stayed on my knees, pulling air into starved lungs, conscious of my heart's hard thud against my ribs and the trembling of my arms and legs.

"Ellie . . ." With the whisper of her name, I picked up the gun. Cocking it, I pointed it at the sky and pulled the trigger. The gun went off like a clap of thunder, slapping at my hand and filling my nostrils with the smell of sulfur. Surely Patrick and Maggie would hear it and come. Shamus too, the three of them running to see what was wrong.

Then I was running again, the gun cast aside so I could pick up my skirt and move faster. By now Jacob and the horse looked no bigger than a dog, and the shawl was no longer visible. But I could still hear Ellie crying. *Hang on, honey. Mama's coming.*

Love pulled me on, my breathing a tortured sob as Jacob disappeared from view, he and the horse swallowed by the trees, my baby gone.

Still I continued, one step following another, tears making it difficult to breathe, no thought or emotion left except my need to have my baby in my arms again. Then a missed step pitched me forward. I felt the ground's hard jar and the prickle of grass on my face. I struggled to bring air into my tortured lungs and knew that in a minute I would be on my feet again, running after Ellie. I had to find her . . . bring her back.

CHAPTER 20

"Clarissa!"

I lifted my head and the voice came again, its urgency mingling with the sound of pounding hooves. I pushed up into a sitting position and saw two men riding toward me. "Quinn," I breathed, recognizing him and Mick with the wolfhounds stretched long and running hard. Then he was off the horse and hurrying toward me, his face anxious as I got to my feet.

"Clarissa!"

I took heart at the sound of the familiar voice, felt strength return as I was caught tight in muscled arms.

"Jacob's alive. He came back . . . and took Ellie."

A stunned expression crossed Quinn's tired face.

"Jacob's ridden off with the baby. We've got to go after them."

"How did he get her?"

My explanation came in a hodgepodge of half-formed phrases and sentences—ones that when put together told of a man who'd returned from the dead and snatched his child from her cradle. As I spoke, Quinn's face looked heartsick. Stunned, too, like a man who'd been kicked hard in the stomach.

I was crying by the time I got to the part about the money, crying for me and Quinn and Ellie—Ellie who'd been carried off by a stranger who had no feeling for her auburn curls and dimpled smile. "Go after them, Quinn." I grabbed his vest, my voice frantic. "We've got to get Ellen back."

Quinn's mouth had turned hard. "How much of a start does he have?"

"Not much. I fell just after he rode into the trees."

"Good." He turned and looked at Mick who'd dismounted and was standing next to us with the dogs. "I want you to take Clarissa up to the lodge."

"No, Quinn. I'm coming too," I insisted

"Clarissa!" Quinn's voice was firm. "Please get on the horse and let Mick take you home. I promise I'll get Ellen back."

Determination stiffened my back. Quinn threw me a quick glance when I made no reply, gave me another searching look as he helped me fit my foot into the stirrup.

"I'll find Jacob and bring her back," he repeated.

Instead of answering, I dug my heels into the mare's sides. She responded with a lunge and took off at a gallop. While I sought balance in the saddle, I grabbed the reins and set the mare in the direction Jacob had entered the forest.

Help me find her, I prayed. I was dimly aware of Quinn calling my name and galloping Midnight after me, but my main focus was on Ellie. I had to find her and make Jacob give her back. As I neared the trees, I glanced back and saw the gelding coming at a full gallop, the horse's legs stretched long and Quinn bent low, the wolfhounds on either side. A second later he caught up with me. I expected him to try to catch the reins and slow me. Instead, he set the gelding to a pace that matched the mare's, throwing me a look of understanding.

"Show me where he went in," he called.

I pointed to a boulder that had tumbled down from the mountain. "On the other side of that rock."

We slowed our horses, Quinn's right hand resting on the stock of his rifle, my ears listening for Ellen's cry.

"What were Jacob and Ellen wearing?"

"Jacob had on a brown hat and a dark jacket. Ellen . . ." My throat closed around her name. "A white dress and my red shawl wrapped around her."

Quinn slowly rode his horse along the edge of the trees, looking for where Jacob's horse had pushed into the undergrowth of ferns and salal. "Here," he said after a moment.

I followed Quinn into the shade of thick hemlocks and firs, the horses moving in single file, our ears tuned for the sound of Ellie's cries. The noise of dogs pushing through underbrush was all that came.

I wanted to call to Ellen and let her know I was coming, but something in the way Quinn sat his horse told me to bide my time. To ride in such a cautious manner went against the grain, especially when my motherly instincts bade me hurry.

"Can you see any sign of them?" I asked in a low tone.

Quinn's only answer was to shake his head.

I bit my lip and willed myself to be patient as I looked around the forest. Beauty met my gaze in trailing patterns of moss and thick-crowned firs, their delicacy scarcely noted when they failed to yield a horse and rider. *Ellie where are you?*

We were now well into the rainforest, the path we followed a game trail that skirted the thickest undergrowth and wound upward into the mountains. Where was Jacob taking her? If he wanted money, why go so far?

"If I'm correct, I think there's an old lean-to up this way," Quinn said. "He's probably taking her there."

Before I could voice a reply, my horse stopped, black ears pricked, prancing sideways instead of forward. I grabbed the pommel and urged her on with a kick, aware that Midnight had turned skittish too.

"Easy, boy." Quinn's soothing voice was almost lost in the horse's frightened snort, the wolfhounds alert and milling around.

My horse plunged and shied, fighting to turn and run. My hold on the pommel was all that kept me in the saddle as fear and caught breath collided with the horse's whinny and rose to join the raucous cry of a jay.

I struggled to keep the horse from bolting, aware that Quinn and his horse were experiencing the same thing, Midnight under taut control, his sides quivering. *What is wrong? Dear heaven, what is wrong?*

"Easy boy." Quinn's voice came again as he urged the horse on, skittish hooves trampling the needle-carpeted path, my horse following with a frightened toss of the head.

A dozen prancing steps took us deeper into the forest, the trees and a fallen log scarcely noted as I struggled to keep the mare from turning. I sensed her fear and she mine, both of us reaching out for the calmer influence of Quinn and the gelding.

Another few steps and the quiet of the forest was shattered by a growling roar. Panic shot to my heart as hands and feet clawed and scrabbled to stay in the saddle, the mare rearing and plunging in terror.

"Bear!" Quinn cried.

The mare's terror meshed with mine as she turned and bolted. Her panicked rush broke my hold on the saddle and sent me tumbling through the air. I felt a heart-stopping moment of flight before needles and fern stopped me. For a second I couldn't breathe, couldn't think as instinct fought for air, but dimly aware of pain in my jarred ribs and hands.

"Clarissa!" Quinn's voice was drowned out by another roar.

"Yes . . ." As I drew ragged breath back into my lungs, I heard panicked movement from the trail above us. A second later, Jacob's sorrel gelding crashed through the trees and undergrowth and rushed past us, the saddle empty.

I scrambled to my feet, pain and fear forgotten. "That's Jacob's horse," I screamed.

Quinn's tight control was all that kept Midnight from following the gelding, the wolfhounds growling and cautious as Quinn urged Midnight up the trail. "Stay where you are," he called.

Fear for Ellen shut my ears to his words and sent me toward the ear-shattering growl that quavered through the trees and trembled the air with terror. *Ellen . . . Ellen!* Nightmare images of the bear coming toward my baby tumbled through my mind.

The nightmare turned to reality when the trail curved past an outcropping of stone and tumbled logs, and I saw a black bear cuff Jacob to the ground with a blow from its massive paw. Before Jacob could get to his feet, the bear was on him, claws and teeth tearing at flesh, a scream that will long remain in my mind torn from his throat.

I frantically looked for Ellen. Were we too late? A tiny cry and the movement of something red in the bushes caught my gaze. Keeping frightened eyes on the bear, I slipped into the bushes. Ellie's piercing cry was unmistakable now. It led me like a beacon to where she lay in a nest of broken branches and bracken. Scratches and blood streaked her arms and legs as they kicked and flailed, and the air echoed with her terrified cry. But she was alive. *Thank you, God. Thank you.*

She stopped crying for a second when she saw me, but quickly resumed to pour out her pain and fear. Kneeling, I gathered her to me, my voice a croon. "It's all right, Ellie. Mama's here, Mama's here."

Her little arms went tight around my neck as she burrowed her head into my shoulder while my arms pulled her closer. I felt the smear of blood when I laid my face against her russet curls, blood that oozed instead of pulsed and told me the cut wasn't serious.

"You're fine, sweetheart. Shh . . . shh. Mama's here."

We both jerked at a crack from Quinn's rifle. From my hiding place in thick-brushed salal I saw the bear flinch and turn from Jacob's torn, inert body. The wolfhounds flew at the bear, snarling and biting its furred legs while Quinn took aim the second time with his rifle.

With a rumbling bellow, the bear reared onto its hind legs, blood glistening on shaggy black fur. One mighty forearm caught Balor and sent him crashing into the undergrowth while another roar echoed like a challenge to horse and rider.

The sound of Quinn's rifle burst through the snarl and growl of dog and bear. The bear staggered, then dropped to all fours and charged at Quinn, Finn darting like a gray shadow between shaggy legs.

I watched in horror, my mouth opened in a silent scream as the terrified horse reared and the rifle resounded, Quinn barely keeping his seat. *Please, God, help him!*

The rifle exploded again, the bear but steps from the horse. Its lumbering gait slowed, red-rimmed mouth opened and snarling, but impetus lacking. My scream and Ellen's cry melded with whinny and growl as the bear faltered and Midnight plunged and reared again.

Another scream left my lips when Quinn was thrown from the saddle, his body striking the ground and rolling toward the bear. "No!" Fear tore the word from my throat and sent me scrambling out of the undergrowth, Ellen clutched in my arms. I was close enough to hear the expelled breath of the bear when it collapsed, its gargantuan form splayed on the forest floor next to Quinn's.

Before I could reach them Quinn was on his feet, his revolver pulled from the holster and pointed at the bear while Finn and Balor growled and attacked the motionless beast.

"Get back," he gasped, his voice and breathing uneven.

I halted, my heart beating like a frantic bird while my hand strove to quiet Ellen whose little head was tucked tight against me.

"Stay!" Quinn commanded when he saw that the bear no longer moved. "Stay, Finn."

The dogs obeyed, just as I did. Finn's square muzzle was red instead of gray, and blood oozed from a cut on Balor's side.

Quinn kicked the bear with a booted foot. When there was no response, he slowly returned the revolver to its holster and walked over to Jacob.

I closed my eyes, not wanting to see his mangled remains.

"Dead," Quinn said after a moment. Then he was walking toward me, his eyes holding mine. "Are you all right?" he asked in an unsteady voice. When he saw me nod, he asked, "Ellen?"

"Yes."

I don't know which of us moved first, only that I was caught hard in Quinn's embrace, his arms pulling us tight, Ellie and I crying and Quinn repeating our names over and over like a man who couldn't believe those he held most precious were back in his arms.

"I thought I'd lost you," he whispered into my ear. "Thought Jacob had won and would have you both." He lifted my face and wiped my tears with the palm of his hand, his touch gentle. The scene was a curious one to say the least—me in my grass-stained pink dress, Quinn with a two-days' growth of whiskers covering his chin, little Ellie sandwiched between us.

A look of terrible longing crossed his face. He pulled me to him, his hands across my back and his mouth on my lips. I did not think about Jacob, or the bear, or the runaway horse. In the quiet of the rainforest, it was enough to know I was back in the strong arms of the man I loved.

* * *

Quinn managed to find Midnight, but there was no sign of the runaway mare. So the three of us rode the black gelding—Ellen fast asleep in my arms and Quinn riding double behind me.

Sunlight filtering through thick-branched trees and a chorus of birds enfolded me in beauty and peace, one augmented by the quiet rhythm of Midnight's hooves and the comforting weight of Quinn's arms as they encircled me to hold the reins. The nightmare scenes in the forest had become no more than wispy shadows along the edge of thought. Bone-weary, my mind and body needed peace and somehow they found it.

Midnight plodded along, his pace slow and even. I gave no heed to my hair that had come loose from its pins and hung in waves around my shoulders, or the pain in my shoulder from my fall from the horse. It was enough to know that we were safe and back together again.

We were nearing the end of the forest when Quinn spoke. "Who would have thought?" His voice was low and filled with wonder. "You know, you're quite a lady."

I snuggled my head into the curve of his neck. "And you're some man."

I felt the movement of his lips on my hair as he smiled, the tightening of his arms as he pulled me closer.

The numbing peace still enveloped me when we met Mick and Patrick with the runaway mare and sent them back for Jacob's body. It stayed with me on the ride up to the lodge, muting sight and sound and emotion and gathering them into a soft coating before they entered my mind. *Thank you. Thank you.* Over and over the words came, to God and the angels who had kept watch over us in the rainforest—for my baby snuggled close and Quinn's arms enfolding us both.

Kind words and gentle hands welcomed us into the kitchen where a chair was pulled out for me and Ellen. I read the shock and concern in Maggie's eyes, saw it mirrored on Bridget's pretty face.

"Sweet Mary," Maggie whispered when she saw the congealed blood matted in Ellen's curls. "Here, let me take her."

I was reluctant to relinquish her, for Ellie's soft warm body was a vital part of my peace. When Maggie tried to take her, Ellen's eyes flew open, and her arms tightened around my neck as she puckered to cry.

"Poor mite," Bridget crooned as she held out her arms. But she was no more successful than her mother at getting Ellen to come.

"Let her be," I said. Ellen stayed on my lap while her face and arms were sponged with warm water. The cut on her head had stopped bleeding, as had the scratches.

How the baby ended up in the bushes instead of on the ground beside Jacob will always be a mystery. Mick thought that Jacob lost his hold on her when the horse panicked and reared, and that Jacob, who managed to stay on, was thrown off at a different place.

"'Tis a likely enough explanation," Maggie agreed. "But you know there are such things as fairies and angels who watch over these precious little ones." She paused and gently touched Ellie's cheek. "I'm thinkin' one of God's angels played a part in it."

This was my belief too, though the angel had a name, that of my baby's grandmother.

Quinn stayed in the kitchen until he was certain Ellie was going to be all right. Only then did he leave to check on Midnight and the wolfhounds. His limp was more pronounced when he left to go outside, and I knew that like me, he was feeling the effects of the fall from his horse.

I went to bed early, not long after Maggie had lit the lamps. It was all I could do to force food into my mouth, all of it tasting like sawdust instead of Maggie's fresh-baked shepherd's pie.

Quinn did not eat much either, his eyes more often on me and Ellie than on his food. After the baby and I were in bed, he came to check on us, leaving the bedroom door open as he crossed the room to stand by the bed. His eyes were soft in the lamplight and matched his voice. "I love you." Simple words, but ones I knew he meant as he bent to kiss my cheek and rest his fingers on Ellen's head.

"What about Jacob's partners? Did you find them?"

Quinn nodded and a satisfied look crossed his face. "After Mick got through with the younger one, he won't be showing his face around here again." He paused and rubbed the knuckles of his right hand. "The older one either."

Ellen slept fitfully, jarring awake every few minutes, her eyes flying open until she felt me near her.

"It's all right, Ellie." These words were repeated many times during the night as her little body snuggled next to mine in the bed. Strange to say, I do not remember dreaming of death or the bear or Jacob—I did not dream of anything though I cried out from time to time, the same as Ellen did, my fingers clutched tight around her little body, my heart jumping and pounding. Sometime toward morning, the tension receded, and I slipped into exhausted sleep—one where there was only warmth and softness and love.

* * *

We buried Jacob the following afternoon. I did not see his pitiful remains before they were laid in the coffin Quinn and Mick made, along with a wooden marker with *Jacob Mueller* and the date etched into the wood.

Bridget and Shamus sang a hymn, and Quinn read a verse from the Bible and commended the body into God's care. No tears were shed, but neither were there any words of criticism. The grayness of the sky was a reflection of the mood as we stood around the dark hole and the wooden box with the lid nailed down tight. Ellen had fallen asleep in my arms, her little head against my shoulder. A blustery wind ruffled our skirts and bent the branches of the alder that marked his grave on one corner of the homestead.

After the short service, Quinn stepped away to give me a moment alone at the grave. The O'Connors followed him. As they walked away, I saw Mick's arm go around Shamus's bony shoulder, and heard him say, "Your mam told me all you did while I was away . . . how you looked after your sister on the way to the lodge, then went down on your own to get Clarissa's animals." Mick's arm tightened around his son. "Looks to me like you're well on your way to being a man."

My lips lifted in a smile as I witnessed Shamus's pleasure. Then I returned my attention to the fresh-dug grave. That I was now truly a widow did not make me feel anything new, for I'd thought myself a widow since February and had done my bit of mourning then.

Good-bye, Jacob, my mind whispered as I looked down at the rich brown earth that now filled the hole. Instead of sorrow, there was pity for a man who'd done so little with his life. He hadn't known how to be a proper husband and had known even less about being a father. The previous day's anger had fled and left me feeling nothing for the man who had been my husband. Poor Jacob.

I turned then and made my way to Quinn. His arm went around my shoulder, giving of his solid goodness and strength. Ellen stirred and her blue eyes opened. For a second there was panic, then as her eyes locked on us, her face broke into an impish smile and she reached out for Quinn. Jacob and the past were behind us while Quinn and happiness lay ahead.

* * *

Three weeks later Quinn and I stood under an arbor covered by red climbing roses as Parson Uriah Thompson read the holy words that joined us in matrimony. The small garden in back of the rectory served as a chapel, green grass the floor, thick leafy branches the roof—all so the O'Connors could be present to witness the Protestant moment when Quinn and I were pronounced one.

Parson Thompson had proved to be a forward-looking minister, one used to the nonconformity of the frontier and who placed our desire to have our Catholic friends present ahead of religious propriety.

My heart was full as I looked at my circle of friends. All were dressed in Sunday best, the men looking a little uncomfortable and standing straight behind the chairs of their wives, Flora and Eileen rounded with child.

The others stood next to them, Bridget and Deirdre both wearing new dresses—Bridget's a soft green and Deirdre's a stunning shade of plum—Shamus with the marks of the comb still fresh in his slicked-back sandy hair.

A happy crow from Ellen drew my eyes to my daughter who sat on Maggie's lap, her white dress contrasting with the dignified black of Maggie's, her curls shining bright as copper coins as she smiled and waved her arms. The fear of that day in May was all but forgotten, washed away by warm hands, gentle voices, and the security of love.

As happy as the moment was, there was regret that none of my family was present. *Tamsin,* my heart whispered. In my mind I pictured her standing with the O'Connors, her dark hair glistening in the sun as she smiled up at her husband. *If only she could be here to share in this wonderful day.*

My answer to the parson's question came clear and joyful, as did Quinn's. "Do you take this man?" and "Do you take this woman?" resonated in my heart along with their answers. Hands joined, we faced each other under the arbor of roses, the reverend's words like the accompaniment of the happy song my heart was singing. Soft sunlight filtered through the tree, and a pair of juncos chattered from the branches.

Quinn was dressed in the same tailored black waistcoat and trousers he'd worn at Mick's party, the snowy linen of his shirt freshly starched and ironed, his cravat looking as if it had been tied by the skilled hands of an English valet. His hazel eyes were warm and filled with love, his lips lifted in the lopsided smile that never failed to give me pleasure.

I gave him an answering smile, one that set my eyes dancing while tendrils of blond hair brushed around my face. Deirdre's deft fingers had fashioned another blue dress for my wedding, one unstained by fear and tailored to fit as flatteringly as any I'd seen in Massachusetts.

Quinn needed no prompting from Parson Thompson to kiss the bride, needed no prompting after dinner with our friends in Astoria's finest hotel to kiss me a second time, then a third.

After posing with Ellie for a wedding picture taken at Astoria's newest daguerreotype studio, we saw our friends off as they set sail upriver for Oregon City and a reunion with the rest of the O'Connors. Sven and Flora left shortly after the ceremony to return to Tillamook Bay. I felt a twinge of loneliness as I watched Maggie carry Ellen onto the boat.

With his uncanny way of reading my thoughts, Quinn's arm tightened around my waist.

After waving good-bye, we returned to the hotel where we would stay until we went to retrieve Ellen in Oregon City. Our steps slowed as we climbed the wide, carpeted stairs to our room.

"Happy?" Quinn asked after he'd unlocked the door.

I smiled my answer, my hands going up to twine around his neck and finger through the softness of his freshly trimmed brown hair. I wanted his closeness. His love.

I heard the soft click of the door as it closed behind us, felt Quinn's arms go around me, the press of his lips, and knew as he held me that I'd found the fulfillment of all of my dreams.

EPILOGUE

Tillamook, Oregon—2003

As she read the last words on the page, Jessica Taylor leaned back against the pillows on the motel bed and wiped happy tears from her eyes. What a life Clarissa had lived, one turned from sadness to joy when she'd found and married Quinton Reynolds.

Bob Whiting had insisted that Jessica take the trunk with her to the motel room and had generously told her that the trunk was hers to keep—Clarissa's mementos hers to treasure and pass on to her children.

Stretching tired muscles, Jessica walked over to the trunk and looked down at Clarissa's keepsakes. She picked up the daguerreotype and studied it with new eyes, wishing Quinn had smiled so she could see his lopsided grin. She'd been right about the couple's happiness though, but wrong about the identity of the baby sitting on Clarissa's lap—little Ellie, whose precarious hold on life had been won by love and help from the other side. No wonder Quinn and Clarissa had loved her.

Dropping to her knees, she reached for the leather dog collar, then the spectacles. All had meaning now that she'd read Clarissa's story. There were still holes, of course, the largest being the years following their marriage. Why hadn't Clarissa finished the journal? Had Quinn and Clarissa had children? Had they traveled to England and stopped off to see Tamsin and Caleb on the way? And what about Bridget and Nathan?

The black-bound family Bible was the only thing she hadn't examined. She picked it up, hoping it contained some of the answers.

She thumbed through the pages until she came to the center of the Bible. With caught breath she looked down at the names of Quinton Reynolds and Clarissa Yeager entered in the same flowing script as the journal. Next to it was their marriage date—May 30, 1861, followed by the name of Ellen (Mueller) Reynolds—born July 28, 1860. Directly after, she read the names of four other children—Edward, Tamsin, Frederick, and Robert—brothers and a sister for Ellie, more children to complete the family circle.

Tears filled her eyes as she looked at the names. If only she could see them and let them know of her feelings—the love she felt streaming down through the years, the gratitude she felt for her heritage.

It had taken three years to find them. Long hours of research and perseverance. But what treasures the trunk had revealed! Not only Clarissa's keepsakes, but even more importantly, her story. Now the story would be complete, with husband and wife and children sealed together in the temple, their love welded in a golden, eternal chain.

ABOUT THE AUTHOR

Carol Warburton has always enjoyed writing and reading. Her love of reading led her to work for the Salt Lake County Library for thirteen years, while her love of writing has led to the publication of several books; this, her fourth published novel, is a sequel to *Edge of Night.*

Carol's other hobbies are gardening and genealogy. She has served in many ward and stake Church callings, both as a teacher and leader. At the present, she and her husband, Roy, are serving a mission in Adelaide, Australia. They are the parents of six children and eleven grandchildren who contribute greatly to their happiness.